"One of the steamiest romances of the year . . . a downright revolutionary story about modern women owning their desire."   —Popsugar

"With vividly drawn characters, steamy sexy times, and a fast-paced plot, this is a fun read."   —NPR

"Rosie Danan's *The Roommate* is seriously sexy, seriously smart."
—Helen Hoang, *USA Today* bestselling author of *The Bride Test*

"Genuinely swoonily romantic."
—Rachel Hawkins, *New York Times* bestselling
author of *Her Royal Highness*

"Fresh and different, a special, superbly written slow-burn."
—Sarah Hogle, author of *You Deserve Each Other*

"A deliciously fresh romance with strong characters and feminist themes."   —*Kirkus* (starred review)

"Red hot and fiercely feminist."   —*Publishers Weekly* (starred review)

"Newcomer Danan is definitely an author to keep tabs on."   —*Booklist*

THE

Intimacy

EXPERIMENT

ROSIE DANAN

JOVE
NEW YORK

A JOVE BOOK
Published by Berkley
An imprint of Penguin Random House LLC
penguinrandomhouse.com

Library of Congress Cataloging-in-Publication Data

Names: Danan, Rosie, author.
Title: The intimacy experiment / Rosie Danan.
Description: First edition. | New York : Jove, 2021.
Identifiers: LCCN 2020035563 (print) | LCCN 2020035564 (ebook) |
ISBN 9780593101629 (trade paperback) | ISBN 9780593101636 (ebook)
Subjects: GSAFD: Love stories.
Classification: LCC PS3604.A4745 I58 2021 (print) |
LCC PS3604.A4745 (ebook) | DDC 813/.6—dc23
LC record available at https://lccn.loc.gov/2020035563
LC ebook record available at https://lccn.loc.gov/2020035564

First Edition: April 2021

Printed in the United States of America

1st Printing

Cover art by Vasya Kotolusha / H Plus Creative
Cover design by Colleen Reinhart
Book design by Alison Cnockaert

For generations of Danan women who have been told they were "too much" and still refused to dim their light

Chapter One

NAOMI GRANT KNEW that every superhero worth their salt had a secret identity. An alter ego that represented their humanity and kept them tethered to "the real world," usually by virtue of being unassuming—Bruce Wayne notwithstanding.

Naomi could relate, though her given name was dusty from disuse. Hannah Sturm, with her easy smiles and trusting eyes, hadn't made a public appearance in over a decade. And why would she? Naomi Grant was the one people wanted.

The one musicians invited to launch parties. The woman paparazzi followed to the drugstore. The shiny sexpot that tech moguls attempted to fuck when they wanted to feel edgy.

Of course, Naomi Grant wasn't a superhero.

She was a porn star. Well, former porn star turned co-CEO of an inclusive sex education start-up. Try fitting that on a business card.

Her superpowers, at least most of the marketable ones, were of the distinctly bedroom variety.

There wasn't much use for her lauded talents here at the Los Angeles Convention Center, for a national teaching conference full of harried, unappreciated, and underpaid people in sensible shoes.

At the registration desk this morning, bent over her blank name tag, a strange urge to write *Hannah* had flitted across her brain. The impulse so strong, she had to stop her hand from moving, from clumsily following the long-dormant instinct to re-create a signature that no longer belonged to her. It would have been nice to slip on anonymity for a few hours. Hannah could blend in with a crowd, while Naomi, in unforgiving contrast, had been born—or rather made—to stand out.

Ever since her thirtieth birthday had come and gone last year, she had spent an inordinate amount of time thinking about the seams of her identity. Making sure no one found out that the line separating where Naomi Grant ended and Hannah Sturm began had grown wan and thin. Some days the current pulling her toward her past was an undertow that threatened to take her out at the knees.

It didn't help that her best friends and business partners, the people she spent the most time with, were normal-adjacent. Engaged. Homeowners.

Sure, Clara and Josh fucked more than average, but that hadn't stopped them from sending out a saccharine Christmas card this year. It was still hanging on her fridge in March. Yesterday, she'd caught herself smiling at it when she'd gone to get cream for her coffee. Gross.

Hannah would have known better than to show up to an all-day teaching convention wearing vegan leather pants and a bra that left her trussed up like a Thanksgiving turkey. But at least Naomi wasn't the only one uncomfortable in this lecture hall. Behind his lectern at the front, the poor workshop instructor was sweating bullets.

"Thank you all for joining me today." A crack of piercing static cut through the room as he brought his mouth too close to the microphone.

Naomi winced.

"Let's kick off today's inclusive design workshop with some brief introductions. I'd like to get a sense of what and where you teach so I can tailor my materials to your collective use cases. Let's stand, shall we?"

Everyone got to their feet in the slow, grumbly way that stank of collective reluctance. This conference on the future of education had seemed like a good idea last month when Naomi had received yet another rejection on an application for an adjunct professorial position at the local community college. She figured the broad appeal of the programming would provide opportunities for her to network in expanded education circles, as well as the chance to learn new techniques for Shameless, the subscription web platform she ran. It was a stretch that adding conference attendance as a credentials line on her résumé would convince higher ed to take her accomplishments in the analysis of human sexuality and relationship dynamics seriously, but she'd run out of better ideas.

To her left, a man in his midfifties introduced himself as a medieval literature professor from Green Bay. This wasn't exactly her usual crowd. She had a feeling her fellow educators weren't going to warm to her subject matter expertise in quite the same way they did to more benign departments. She braced herself for the impending impact of leers and jeers, but the shift in her normally fluid posture felt like overkill. Hadn't she faced worse crowds than this?

Back in her waitressing days, she'd once hosed down a pack of drunk frat boys on the Venice boardwalk.

The workshop attendees moved through the rows of participants at a rapid clip. Classics. Communications. Molecular biology. Naomi pressed her tongue against the back of her bottom teeth, an old habit from when she'd had it pierced and the sound of stainless steel meeting bone warded off strangers.

She liked to pretend she found average people boring, with their sitcoms and their mortgage payments and their shame over what made them hot. But the truth was, she knew better than anyone how quickly they could turn hostile, especially in groups as large as this one. Naomi swept her hair off her damp neck, snuffing her flight response before it could flicker fully to life.

She'd paid good money to be here and had just as much right to stand in this sweaty auditorium as anyone else.

Ever since she'd finished getting her master's in social psych last year, she'd missed classrooms. Not just the physical environment, but the energy. The exchange of knowledge. She loved testing hypotheses, which made sense when you considered the fact that her entire adult life was built on the principle of proving other people wrong.

Finally, every pair of inquisitive eyes in the room turned her way. Her throat went tight. She wished she'd bought a soda on her way in. Something cool and fizzy enough that the bubbles stung her nose. She knew soda was a nutritionist's nightmare, but that was half of the appeal on the rare occasion she indulged. It was like the way a drag on a cigarette made her feel like she'd been cast in a film noir for a moment, before she remembered she was taking years off her own life with each inhale. There was something about flirting, just a little—the tiniest sip—with her own destruction that appealed to the darkness in her.

"Hi there." Naomi's stage voice came out unbidden, husky and inviting. She shook it off. These people wouldn't appreciate her Jessica Rabbit impression. "I'm Naomi Grant, and I'm a sex educator." A few participants bristled at the word *sex*. One woman's eyes popped wide like umbrellas. How predictably pedestrian.

The familiar pleasure of shocking sensibilities rushed over her, and she cocked her hip. "I run a website, Shameless, focused on promoting healthy and satisfying emotional and physical intimacy through instructive videos, essays, and interactive tutorials."

Green Bay coughed hard enough to make an angry vein throb in his forehead.

"Our online platform features content that blends education and entertainment and has a monthly paid subscriber base of about five million global users." She recited the practiced sales pitch with as much bravado as she could muster in the face of so many furrowed brows. "I'm hoping to extend my classroom into face-to-face learning environments."

The instructor nodded, making a valiant attempt to look nonplussed. "And have you found success in that endeavor?"

She gave him a rueful smile. "I haven't"—she read off his name tag—"Howard." Poor guy, he never could have imagined when he woke up this morning that he'd accidentally trip the wire on her bruised pride. "I've reached out to a few colleges and community organizers, have even made it to final-round interviews for a few positions, but as it turns out, some people," she said with a pointed look around the room, "are resistant to hiring a lauded sex worker to join their faculty."

A low hum of conversation broke across the room as her words landed. Everyone else had just given their name and the subject they taught, but Naomi wasn't satisfied with the mixture of skepticism and confusion her introduction had received. A ridiculous urge to make these strangers understand her experience kept her talking, even when she knew they'd wave away her qualifications like everyone else.

"Look, I think we can all agree that pompousness and privilege rule academia. It's bullshit."

"Umm." A man raised his hand to interject.

Naomi ignored him.

"I've got an advanced degree from Cal State. My website collects over a billion data points about relationship dynamics and sex annually, and I have the unique lived experience of navigating intimacy as not only an adult performer but a public figure to boot. You'd think that would qualify me to teach people how to establish intimate connections, but apparently"—she threw her arms up—"you'd be wrong."

Enough people had told her no at this point that her mind had turned earning acceptance from a stuffy institution into a dare. She wanted the gravitas of an employer with an established name. Besides, she'd already built Shameless from scratch, and while a start-up was rewarding, it was also exhausting.

"Don't you think, Howard, that the world would be a better place if we opened a dialogue that made people feel comfortable advocating for themselves in their relationships?"

"I suppose . . ." Howard had started to turn puce.

"Do you ever ask yourself why people are so afraid of sex?"

Naomi winked at the woman staring at her in open horror, in an effort to fight a sinking feeling of disappointment in her gut. For all her grand speeches, she'd finally hit a wall she couldn't swim under.

"I do. All the time. I've got theories. And maybe they could actually help people. But no one wants to hear it."

Outside of her ego, Naomi believed sex ed and relationship discourse had a place in accessible, mainstream education. Her experience and theories would have the greatest impact if she could establish a wider audience. As much as she loved society's rebels, she didn't believe healthy resources for establishing intimacy should be restricted to them.

"And it's not like I didn't know that going in." Naomi huffed out a dramatic exhale. "But I guess—call it the naivete of youth, but I thought the world might get a little more open-minded by the time I retired from performing. But I was wrong. And you know why?" She pointed an accusatory finger at her startled audience.

"Because if anyone let me teach, they would have to address the toxic environments and toxic people they continue to uphold. And that would be really uncomfortable, wouldn't it? That would be really fucking inconvenient."

"Miss Grant," Howard tried to cut in, "perhaps we might move on to the next—"

"Don't you ever get mad, Howard?" She walked up and placed her hands on either side of the lectern. "The numbers are bleak. We're facing a dating epidemic, not to mention an orgasm deficit. The sooner we stop pretending the digital age hasn't changed the way we interact, the better we make our chance that entire generations don't die horny and alone."

"Right." The instructor tugged at his collar and raised his voice, trying to rein in the room. "Anyone else want to jump in here?"

Naomi sighed and returned to the circle, letting the new tension in the room roll off her back. Her shame sensor had run out of batteries a long time ago. She'd made her career out of being an outlier, and a safety net out of being an outcast. It was easy enough to tune out the rest of the intros. At least until they got to a man who was way too hot to be a teacher.

He looked like a Calvin Klein model, and she observed that with the authority of someone who had fucked more than her fair share of Calvin Klein models. The shadow cast by his bearded jawline was ridiculous. She could wait out a summer storm underneath that thing.

"Hey everyone. My name's Ethan Cohen," the model said, "and I used to teach high school physics."

Naomi immediately wanted a follow-up on that *used to*. Had he been cast as an extra? Those cheekbones deserved at least a hundred thousand followers on Instagram. Her eyes traced his profile as he kept talking. On closer inspection, he was too short and lean to be a model. In heels, she'd have the advantage. The chiseled sculpture of his face had distracted her inspection. That and the way he carried himself. His legs were spread wide enough that . . . damn. She couldn't tell with him in those khakis.

Still, she smiled, target acquired. He was the perfect distraction from her occupational woes.

It had been a while since she'd wanted to jump someone the way she wanted to slither all over this guy. She loved her job, but running a start-up meant regularly working eighty-hour weeks. The combination of stress and exhaustion was hell on her libido. How ironic that satisfying sex was her life's work and yet her last few months had been decidedly sexless. She smirked. Unless you counted solo sessions. Those were still A+.

What kind of underwear had she put on this morning? Certainly, if she'd known the day would present such delectable opportunities, she would have pulled out something set to stun.

Introductions wrapped, and Howard released them back to their seats with a wave. As the familiar scratch of multiple pens moving over paper lulled her into a daze, she sifted through approach tactics. Usually when she wanted to get someone into bed, she just took off her top to save time. One cursory scan of the room confirmed that plan wouldn't fly in this environment. Oh well. She'd wing it.

But, as it turned out, she didn't have to. While she packed her bag at the end of the lecture, a pair of khakis stopped next to her desk.

"Excuse me. I'm sorry to bother you, but I wondered if I could make you a proposition."

Naomi raised her eyes slowly. Above his leather belt, he wore a perfectly pressed white button-down, open at the collar, though not enough to pay off the shadowed promise of chest hair. Once again, she lingered over his jawline. It was even better up close. She couldn't wait to feel that beard against the inside of her thighs.

"Sure," Naomi said, putting a little purr into the *r*. "Give me your best."

When he smiled, his whole face went to work. Damn, this guy was trouble. It was a good thing she'd shown up as Naomi. Hannah Sturm wouldn't have stood a chance.

Hannah would have shown off to get his attention, dropped her pen so he'd have no choice but to bend down and find himself face to face with her legs, for example—but Naomi knew that moves like that were for rookies. The key to seduction was to make the other person think falling for you was their idea.

"You mentioned you've had trouble finding an institution that will hire you?"

At least she knew one person had listened to her spirited diatribe. Naomi nodded.

"Are you still interested in securing a live lecture role?" His voice treated the matter with an appropriate amount of concern. Naomi appreciated that. She had found a new respect for serious people in her thirties.

"I am." She paused her hand where it had been decadently skimming a path across her collarbone in casual invitation.

"In that case, I'd love to offer you a position to consider."

Now they were talking. Luckily, she could forgive a slow start.

"Just one?" Naomi smirked.

He blinked at the shift in her tone but gave no other sign of awareness that he was receiving an opening other people would kill for. This guy was either immune to innuendo or so earnest it bounced right off him.

"Would you be interested in conducting a seminar on modern intimacy for my synagogue?"

That was—did he say—had she really been out of the game so long that she couldn't tell flirting from . . . this? The reason for the goose bumps on her arms transformed. She hadn't thought about synagogues in a long time.

When she spoke next, her carefully constructed walls were back in place.

"I can't imagine a religious organization would offer me a more welcome reception than higher education, but thanks anyway." She started walking out of the classroom, leaving him to lap at her heels.

"I can assure you that you'd be very welcome at Beth Elohim."

"How's that?" She threw the words over her shoulder.

Ethan managed to jog in front of her, shoving his hands into his pockets and offering her a weak smile. "Well, for starters, I'm the rabbi."

"I'm sorry." She stopped walking to gape at him. "You're the what now?"

"The rabbi?" He tilted his head, like he was trying to figure out if she didn't understand the meaning of the word or simply that he'd used it to describe himself. "I'm a religious leader at the synagogue."

She brushed aside the unnecessary definition. "Aren't you a little . . ."

"Young?" He ducked his chin, as if he got that comment a lot.

"Hot."

He laughed, the sound strangled at first and then a bit more relaxed. "There aren't any rules dictating the appropriate level of attractiveness for religious leaders. At least not in Reform Judaism."

Well, he hadn't tried to deny it.

"Unbelievable." And to think she'd had so many wicked plans for him.

"Is that a no?"

Naomi smiled at him with her mouth closed and resumed walking. She checked the schedule in her hand. "That's a no, pal."

"Can I ask why you won't consider it?" He jogged a little to catch up with her long-legged strides. "I'm told given the opportunity, I can be very convincing."

She huffed low in her throat. Now, that she could believe. "I'm surprised you have to ask."

"Are you an atheist? Even though the course would be affiliated with the synagogue, as the instructor, you'd be under no obligation to practice." Ethan's words tumbled over themselves as he rushed to reassure her. "We offer quite a few secular meetings. Knitting, for example, and water aerobics at the JCC."

Naomi's eyes narrowed, and her feet came to a halt. She could smell a stunt a mile away. "I'm not into being used in some kind of publicity farce." If her name made headlines, she'd dictate what they said.

He stopped dead in his tracks so that the two of them were now creating a blatant traffic jam in the stifling hallway. "Of course not. I would never—"

"Or a charity case." Naomi had no interest in "rehabilitating her image." No desire to let her life become the *before* in some motivational recruitment video. The last thing she needed was saving.

"Naomi . . . erm . . . Ms. Grant . . . You'd be doing me the favor. If anyone's a charity case, I am. Me and my crumbling synagogue. Seriously, our attendance numbers are so low we can barely fill the first ten rows."

"Trust me, I'm not the answer to your prayers." He obviously didn't understand who she was or what she did. "Look me up, you'll see what I mean." Naomi didn't regret any of her actions, but she also wasn't naive about their consequences.

"With all due respect, I know who you are," he said, and to his credit, he didn't smirk. "My sister was an early adopter of your company's subscription platform." He did lower his eyes at that, but only for a moment. "She's a big advocate of the work you're doing to build an inclusive online community. She went so far as to send me your profile in *Forbes*."

And there, finally, was a blush. A poppy shade, high and bright on his cheeks.

"I believe they called you 'Alfred Kinsey in stilettos.'"

Naomi wrinkled her nose. "I'm sure they meant well."

"I think you're very impressive," he said, his voice deliciously deep.

"*You're* not a Shameless subscriber, are you?"

Reform Judaism might be relatively chill, but it wasn't that chill. At least, not the last time she'd checked.

"No. I mean, not yet. If that's important to you, I'll certainly look further into it."

Naomi's heart stuttered, and she had to remind herself again that he was persona non grata. It had been a long time since she'd received a proposition that wasn't carnal.

"Ms. Grant." He opened the door for her as they got to the end of the hallway. "I'm offering you a classroom because I believe in your capabilities as an educator. I'm trying to rebuild a community of my own. To appeal to younger people. To show them that Judaism and their lifestyles are complementary rather than at odds. If I can't make Judaism relevant, if its practice can't accommodate what intimacy looks like today, what's left of my congregation is going to get rid of me well before I show them what I'm capable of."

Naomi was shocked that the hallway full of conference attendees hadn't stopped to clap at that little speech. She had to get out of there before she did something reckless.

"I'm not the person you're looking for. It was nice meeting you." Sort of. "Good luck saving your synagogue."

"Wait. Just one more moment. I promise to stop bothering you after this." He had no idea how much he was *bothering* her. "But is there any chance you could recommend someone else from your company who might consider the opportunity?"

Naomi slowed her stride. "Are you married?"

The question landed like a piano between them. "Uh . . . no."

"Engaged or otherwise romantically attached?"

"I'm not." He shook his head for good measure.

"Then I've got nothing to offer you."

"Kol hat'chalot kashot," Ethan said under his breath.

"Excuse me?"

"Sorry," he said, offering her a smile. "It's an old Hebrew adage. It means 'All beginnings are difficult.' I have to confess. I've lost the thread of this conversation. Are you still rejecting my job offer?"

"I haven't stepped foot in a synagogue since my bat mitzvah," Naomi said, which wasn't exactly an answer, but he'd leaned toward her and she'd caught a whiff of spicy aftershave, and now she didn't remember where she was supposed to be walking.

"Oh." Ethan's breath caught on the word. His pupils went wide. "You're Jewish."

"I wouldn't say that." She'd imagined this entire interaction going a lot differently a few minutes ago.

"Right. Okay. Sorry. I'm not trying to hassle you. If you change your mind, I'm at Beth Elohim in Pasadena almost every day of the week." He passed her a card.

Naomi opened the door to a new classroom but didn't enter. Instead she moved to stop his progress with an extended arm. "You're sure you're a rabbi?"

He gave her a last smile, probably relieved he knew how to answer this question.

"Very sure."

"Just my luck," Naomi muttered under her breath, crumpling the business card in her fist as she walked out of his life forever.

Chapter Two

··

SOMEHOW, NAOMI GRANT, renowned rebel of the status quo, had found herself with a nine-to-five job and a corner office. Two years in, Shameless, once little more than a defiant idea to revolutionize and democratize sex education, now brought in enough paid subscribers to fund an official headquarters in West Hollywood, in addition to studio space in Burbank. Despite her best efforts to resist routine, Naomi could now reliably be found at an established location on weekdays.

What was worse, when her company responsibilities had naturally evolved from taking her clothes off to organizing vendors and spear-heading meetings, she'd had to surrender large swaths of her strategically vampy wardrobe in favor of slightly more boardroom-friendly workwear. Naomi's one consolation was that most of her new blazers had spikes on the shoulders. No one was getting chummy on her watch.

A few days after the teaching conference, Naomi's co-founder and unlikely best friend, Clara, entered her office presenting a tiny loaf of bread.

"It's banana," she informed Naomi the way one might try to entice a particularly grumpy bulldog to swallow a pill, "your favorite."

"Uh-oh." It was no accident that when Naomi had approved the office floor plan, she'd put Clara on the opposite end.

Not to be dramatic, but if Naomi could carve out the hard-won affection Clara had engendered in her with a steak knife, she'd consider it.

"Oh, come on." Her visitor deflated. "Don't 'uh-oh' like you hate presents. I happened to have extra bananas." Clara bent in front of the bar cart Naomi had purchased to remind herself she used to be fun and opened a drawer to reveal cutlery and tea plates that Naomi definitely didn't recognize.

"Did you hide flatware in my office when I wasn't looking?" Naomi had never imagined herself in a permanent partnership of any kind. This invasion of her space really was a step too far.

"Relax." Clara ignored her friend's indignation. "We spend so much time here, I thought we'd have occasion to break bread eventually. Plastic cutlery is bad for the environment."

No one except Naomi realized how devious Clara could be. Even her fiancé probably didn't fully comprehend how much planning and strategy hid behind those big eyes. There was a reason they worked so well as co-CEOs. They both knew how to get people to do what they wanted. The difference was, people expected Naomi to scheme and seduce to get her way. Really, all she had to do was create enough air cover for Clara to disarm people through a lethal combination of well-bred manners and zealous enthusiasm. As it turned out, "fanatical but also polite and well-spoken" were excellent traits for a founder of a start-up.

"I feel like you're about to ask me to donate a kidney." Naomi accepted the treat anyway.

The choked little laugh Clara gave was unsettling. "I promise it's not that bad."

The bread melted in Naomi's mouth, further arousing suspicion.

Either Clara had significantly outdone herself or, more likely, she'd bought the confection and transferred it to her own Tupperware.

"All right, let's have it." The weight of the impending favor request hung in the air.

Clara closed her eyes and then spoke very quickly. "Will you be my maid of honor?"

Naomi stopped chewing. A piece of walnut stuck in her molar.

She'd known, after Josh—Clara's fiancé—had proposed in the fall, that a wedding was inevitable. She'd just never stopped to consider the scale of the event's consequences. Shameless took up so much of their time and energy, and Josh was booked solid as an expert witness in a new round of court cases defending the rights of sex workers.

Still, Naomi should have seen this coming, and would have if, for whatever reason, she hadn't fallen so far off her game lately.

Her silence seemed to fuel Clara's urgency.

"I know it's a lot to ask, and if you'd rather not do it, I can call my cousin. It's just, no one in my life knows me the way you do. You realize what a complete mess I am and still trust me to run a business with you. You're the most competent person I know, and you always bring me pizza after my mother calls." Clara cleared her throat. "Also, obviously, you know Josh rather intimately."

Naomi wondered how many women who got asked to be maid of honor used to fuck the groom, and on camera no less. She sighed.

"You don't have to wear a dress," Clara said, as if that would be the biggest point of contention. "You can wear one of those jumpsuits that make you look like you're gonna murder everyone and then use their warm blood for your lipstick."

It was useless for Naomi to try to hide her smirk. "I have been meaning to pick out a new signature red."

All humor aside, weddings meant family and toasts and line dancing. Cake cutting and smiling for hours' worth of pictures. Bachelorette, bridal shower, rehearsal dinner. They meant open bars and men who thought they knew her because they'd jerked off to her videos a few times. Naomi felt the commitment closing like a lasso around her, ready to yank.

"Please, just say you'll consider it." Clara shoved her dark hair out of her eyes. She'd gotten bangs in January—despite Naomi's many adamant warnings—and they were finally starting to grow out.

Naomi folded her arms across her chest. "I don't have to consider it."

Clara's face fell like a stack of cards.

"Obviously, I'll be your maid of honor." There had never been a question, really.

"You're serious?" Clara literally clutched her pearls.

"No, this is one of my many hilarious jokes," Naomi said flatly.

"Ahh. Thank you. Thank you." Clara jumped out of her seat to throw herself into Naomi's arms.

Maid of honor was never a title Naomi had expected to earn. She had a lot of friends and various lovers, both past and present tense, but she still kept most of them at arm's length. It was kind of nice, maybe, that she was important enough to someone to be invited to stand up next to her on one of the biggest days of her life.

"Yay!" Clara shouted into her ear.

"Yeah, yeah." Naomi didn't mind the responsibility as much as she minded the tradition. And the guest list. Knowing Clara's family, the Wheaton-Conners nuptials would be no small affair.

She groaned. Love really was a terrible weakness. No other vice made you vulnerable in quite the same way. Naomi wasn't a monster. Despite the consequences, she still loved people. She just tried to keep it to a minimum, firmly believing that you didn't have to be close to love someone, you just had to be committed.

Like her parents, for instance. She loved them fiercely. They had moved from Boston to Arizona last year to retire and were now members of an elder living community that all available evidence suggested was also a nudist colony.

Apparently, getting naked for public consumption ran in the family.

Naomi couldn't remember if the community didn't allow cell phones or if the inhabitants just never had any pockets to carry them in. But either way, the result was she spoke to her mom and dad every few months and saw them once a year or so. Neither party seemed to mind.

"Can we talk about business now that you've gotten what you wanted?" One was Naomi's cap for tender moments in a day.

Clara finally released her and plopped into the chair across from Naomi's, folding her hands neatly in her lap. Her co-founder was practically glowing now that she'd received good news. "Where do you want to start?"

Naomi opened one of the meticulously color-coded spreadsheets Clara had built to organize their daily status. Sometimes obsessive, type A overachievers came in handy. "Partnership strategy?"

She scrolled through the file before reading aloud. "We've got a team of female engineers coming in on Wednesday to pitch sex-tech prototypes."

That should be fun. Expanding the line of merchandise in Shameless's business model was a priority for this year. So far, they'd limited their merchandise to purely aesthetic items: coffee mugs, stickers, pins, the occasional decorative cross-stitch bearing their tagline, "Equal-Opportunity Orgasms." The Shameless brand held weight, and Clara and Naomi subjected any extensions of the company to extensive vetting.

Naomi scanned for the next item. "Casting new performers for the sixties series?" One of their content priorities for the next few months was developing different videos dedicated to enjoying sex in the later decades of life.

Clara flipped through her planner. "Auditions will be held Thursday through Sunday. Cassidy is running the show, but of course if you want to stop by, you're welcome."

Cassidy was their executive producer, and Naomi trusted her completely. They'd worked together before Naomi had left to run Shameless, back when Cass was making queer erotic films out of her garage. Cassidy was essential in helping make their site more inclusive. She was also the elder queer who had helped baby Naomi navigate coming out as bi over a decade ago. It had been a no-brainer to make her one of their early hires.

Naomi marked the dates in her own iCal. "Got it."

Clara absently straightened Naomi's Post-its to ninety-degree angles. "Hey, how was that conference you went to on Monday?"

Naomi ran her nails across a run in her silk skirt. She could hardly confess to Clara that she'd spent the better part of the last few days thinking about a smoke-show rabbi who'd made her an offer she'd had to refuse.

"It was nice. I learned a new approach for how to optimize subtitles for audio-impaired subscribers."

"Oh, great. I'll let production know we need a regroup." Clara looked at her expectantly. "And . . ."

"And what?" The words came out more urgent than she'd meant them.

"Did you network?"

Naomi could tell she was one wrong move away from another lecture on the importance of "expanding" their "business ecosystem."

Naomi wrinkled her nose. "Not really."

Clara leaned forward. "What's that face?"

What face? would hardly fly. "A man tried to pick me up."

"That seems annoying but unfortunately not out of the ordinary." Clara frowned.

"No. Not like that. I mean he offered me a job. A teaching job."

"Oh." Clara's face shifted. "But that's good? You've been looking for an opportunity to educate in person for months now."

"He's a rabbi."

"As in . . ."

"There's only one definition of rabbi."

"Wow." Clara leaned back in her chair. "What did he want you to teach?"

"Modern intimacy." He hadn't even blushed when he'd said it. Every inch of him—the ones she could see anyway—had been sincere.

"Huh." Clara tilted her head. "That's actually kind of perfect, given your experience and areas of interest."

Naomi picked up a pen and flipped it end over end between her fingers. Just because Ethan had offered her a classroom and the chance to reach the types of people she most wanted to help didn't mean it was a viable option.

"It's not perfect. It's organized religion. You know I don't like organized anything, and religion specifically makes me itchy. All those people believing in things larger and more powerful than themselves?" She shivered. "Besides, no matter how liberal he is, Judaism still has a lot of rules, and I always forget them." There was a difference between fun rule-breaking and embarrassing rule-breaking, and she knew from experience that this offer would lead to the latter.

"Wait a second . . . Are you . . . Oh my gosh . . ." Clara squinted like she was putting the pieces of a mental puzzle together. "You're Jewish?"

Naomi crossed her arms. "Not actively."

"Whoa. Okay, but you were raised Jewish?"

"Barely." Her parents had mostly phoned it in. They'd celebrated the High Holidays until after graduation when Naomi left for L.A., and then petered out to just Yom Kippur. Maybe Rosh Hoshana and Passover, if someone invited them over.

L.A. had its fair share of trendy kabbalah enthusiasts, but even on days when a higher power would have been welcome, the idea of "a porn star walks into a synagogue" had always been better suited to a punch line than real life.

"You should absolutely do this." Clara stood up, using her meager height to add gravity to her declaration.

"I'm not. I can't. It's too late." Ethan Cohen had probably secured a less inflammatory instructor by now.

Clara pursed her lips. "You just made three excuses in one breath. There's something you're not telling me here."

"I'm scared," Naomi said, dropping a veil of sarcasm over her voice in an attempt to position the truth as a lie.

No dice. Clara came over to lean her butt against Naomi's side of the desk.

"Don't even try it." Her tone was softer now that they were at a closer range, but still firm. "You want to help people, to educate them. You should do this. Besides," she said, tapping the desk with her fist in emphasis, "I don't believe you're afraid of a rabbi."

"Ugh, fine." Naomi exhaled extravagantly. The chances of that excuse working had been slim anyway. "The truth is, I'm attracted to the stupid, inexplicably sexy rabbi, and I'm worried that if I spend an extended period of time with him, I'm gonna ruin his life."

"Excuse me?" Clara blinked several times in a row.

"He's young and handsome, and if I'm in his general vicinity for too long, I'll lure him away from the path of righteousness, and then I'll wind up a dirty cliché." Naomi had spent her entire career avoiding society's stereotypes about adult performers. The idea that she'd let a man flip her narrative into tawdry territory was unpalatable, to say the least.

Clara was looking at the ceiling with her brow furrowed. "I'm so confused right now. Did this man hit on you?"

Naomi bristled at the idea. "No. Of course not." His beard alone was practically stalwart.

"But he gave you a bad vibe?"

Naomi wiped dust off her keyboard. "The vibe was fine. Wholesome, you might even say."

"Did he in any way indicate that he was attracted to you?"

She shrugged. "Most people are attracted to me."

"That's true." Clara tapped her foot on the floor. "But it's not like with priests, right? Rabbis aren't forbidden from having sex?"

"No, rabbis are definitely free to fuck. But they do have to maintain a certain public reputation, which my particular brand of notoriety goes against."

"Well, that's his problem, then. This man is obviously confident enough in his religious convictions to dedicate himself to a lifetime of study. I think he can resist whatever spontaneous lust you inspire and focus on your professional virtues."

"I don't want him to resist me." She sank her lips into an indulgent pout. "I don't like being resisted."

"You're a grown woman. You can fall into bed with almost anyone you want." Clara's tone shifted into one Naomi recognized from their daily team stand-up meetings: authoritative but kind. "Stop using sex as a shield to keep people at arm's length. This is your dream. No excuses."

When had the universe fallen so out of sync? Naomi was supposed to be the aggressive one in this pair. She'd empowered Clara too much over the last few years. The old Clara, fresh off the plane from Greenwich, Connecticut, would never have told Naomi what to do.

"All right. Fine." A diluted sense of dignity kept her from pouting. Her business partner grinned.

"Not because you told me to, but because I'm getting old and boring, and if I don't create some new controversy to hold public interest, I'll fade into the shadows of infamy."

"Don't be so hard on yourself," Clara said. "Infamy is beneath you. Your collective exploits are worth at least a hardcover memoir on the *New York Times* Best Seller list."

Naomi pretended to adjust the seat of her chair so Clara wouldn't see her smile. "You know, you really came in hot this morning."

"Yeah, well"—Clara tucked her hair behind her ear—"this intimidating redhead at work keeps telling me I'm a badass business bitch and I better act like it."

"I've created a monster." Naomi shooed Clara off her desk by spanking her hip with a file folder.

In no hurry at all, Clara made her way toward the door. "So, you'll call him and tell him you accept?"

Naomi clicked her mouse a little harder than necessary. "I don't have his number." She'd fully destroyed the business card.

"Hello, he's a rabbi in L.A. You know his name. Google him."

"Oh yeah." Naomi rolled her eyes. "Because Googling a hot stranger worked out so well for you."

Clara looked wistfully down at her engagement ring. "Man, it really did."

Chapter Three

....

ON WEDNESDAY NIGHTS, Ethan ran a meeting for mourners. It was outside the purview of Beth Elohim's historical programming, but since the majority of the congregants he'd inherited had been born during the Second World War, death quickly became their common denominator. The gathering, held in one of the synagogue's smaller side rooms, had ended forty minutes ago. But Morey, seventy-eight and a regular, liked to linger and malign Ethan's shuffleboard skills over paper cups of juice.

In the middle of a groan protesting one of Morey's more colorful claims, Ethan's gaze landed on the doorway.

He blinked twice.

If the frown on her face was anything to go by, Naomi Grant was wondering if she was in the right place.

Unfortunately, Ethan couldn't blame her. The outdated wallpaper and scuffed floors didn't exactly show the synagogue, originally built in the 1920s and updated for the last time somewhere shortly after, to its best advantage. Budgets were tight. They kept things clean and running, but they didn't have any of the glamour of some of the other Hollywood shuls. Ethan himself had been up on a ladder that afternoon cleaning air ducts. He still had stubborn smudges of dust up and down both forearms to prove it.

If Naomi took one look at their sorry state—his and the facility's both—and didn't like it, well, there wasn't much he could do.

He gave her a little wave that had no effect on the downward curve of her lips.

"Excuse me a moment," he said into Morey's good ear, getting to his feet from the folding chair he'd been occupying.

Gesturing for Naomi to join him in the hallway, Ethan shut the door behind him.

Sometime earlier this week, he'd convinced himself that the way her beauty had hooked him behind the navel and yanked was a fluke. A trick of the conference center lighting. Or a consequence of an empty stomach.

No such luck.

She frowned at him now, brows drawn together over her nose. Her obvious displeasure did nothing to dampen the fact that there was something brilliant about her. Like she was painted in brighter colors than everyone else. He found himself a little breathless, drinking in the sight of her in the dim corridor like oxygen.

The word "Wow" escaped his lips. He shook his head immediately, heat rushing up his neck. "I mean, hi."

A ripple of something passed across the surface of her scowl, and for the first time since he'd met her, Ethan could imagine how devastating it must be when she smiled.

"I think I prefer 'wow,'" she said, studying him without apology.

A wave of self-consciousness rushed over him. Last time she'd seen him, the time she'd called him hot, he hadn't been wearing his kippah. The ritual head covering should hardly make a difference, but maybe it did. Maybe when she looked at him now, she saw baggage and responsibility.

It was probably for the best. He wasn't sure he'd be able to concentrate if she looked at him now the way she had at the convention center. Like he was something to be devoured.

"I wasn't expecting to see you again." If ever there was a woman who had better things to do than speak to him, it was Naomi Grant.

"Am I interrupting?" She gave a nod toward the room behind him.

Morey was now blatantly watching them through the interior window.

"Don't mind me," he shouted through the plexiglass, straightening to his full five feet, five inches. "I was just on my way out." He exited the room and escaped down the hall as quickly as Ethan had ever seen him move.

Once he was gone, Naomi pinned Ethan in her gaze. "Do you still want to hire me?"

"Uh," he said, thrown. "I mean, yeah. Yes." Just having her in the building seemed to make the faded space come to life. "I do."

"Okay." She nodded. "Then pitch me."

"I'm sorry?" Maybe if he looked at her from an angle instead of straight on, it would be easier to concentrate.

"This is a business proposition, right?" She folded her arms. "You outlined the basics at the convention, and now I'm willing to consider your offer, but in order for me to come to a decision, we need to go over the details."

While Naomi seemed slightly less hostile tonight than she had at the convention center, the hallway's dim bulbs couldn't hide the way her flame-colored hair flashed, threatening to send their immediate vicinity up in smoke.

Ethan said the first thing that came to mind. "I'm not trying to trick you."

Her eyes lingered on the exit behind him. "That's what they all say."

Right. It was on him to show her that she was safe here, that she was welcome.

"Why don't we go outside? There's a bench out back we can use."

She might feel less caged outside the synagogue walls.

"I'm not usually skittish," Naomi said as she followed him to the door, as if worried he'd bring up the way everything in her body language threatened to run.

They got to the old bench Sal Stein had dedicated to his departed wife. Ethan said a quick prayer as he touched the plaque, his thumb brushing absently over the inscription, lingering for a moment in borrowed memory.

As they took their seats at opposite ends, silence and the early-spring evening stretched out between them, everything fragile and new.

She'd asked for a pitch, he reminded himself, and cleared his throat.

"So, the synagogue supports a variety of cultural and educational programming—"

"I don't get it," Naomi interrupted him.

"Don't get what?" He didn't mind the immediate interjection. Lots of people got defensive when they were uncomfortable.

"You said you were a physics teacher. Back at the conference center."

Ethan sat up straighter, surprised she remembered.

"I was. At Greenbrier in Santa Monica." The fancy prep school catered to the offspring of the rich and famous.

"But now you're a rabbi?" The set of her shoulders was intensely defiant. "Isn't there inherent contradiction between science and religion?"

Ethan exhaled. His call to become a rabbi had occurred as a messy combination of grief and yearning. It was easier to distill the origin of his belief system to a single book, though it wasn't any book people expected.

He lifted a shoulder. "Blame Einstein."

"Really? That's what you're going with?" Her words were flinty, testing his speed to spark.

He let them smolder and die.

"Einstein wrote, in 1930, 'To know what is impenetrable to us really exists, manifesting itself as the highest wisdom and the most radiant beauty, which our dull faculties can comprehend only in their most primitive forms—this knowledge, this feeling is at the center of true religiousness.'"

Naomi shook her head. "You memorized that?"

"Those words made sense to me when nothing else did," he said, thinking of standing in the rain at his father's funeral. "The idea that there was so much in the universe I would never understand, never unravel, no matter how much I studied. The knowledge that my life wasn't a problem I could ever solve let me focus my energy elsewhere. Those words felt like freedom."

She stared out at the dark courtyard. Probably cataloging all the overgrown weeds.

"So," Naomi said, as if choosing her words carefully. "You're saying Einstein helped you discover that ignorance is bliss?"

"More like faith," he corrected, his voice light.

"Tomayto, tomahto." The hint of teasing in her tone shot pleasantly up his spine.

Well, that was inconvenient.

"I've always wanted answers." He used to make himself sick over the lack of them, actually. "Both my study of physics and my study of the Torah started in pursuit of understanding the infinite mysteries of an interconnected universe. Both are continuous study. Man's search for meaning. Judaism offers a ladder to being a better person that I never have to stop climbing." Ethan rubbed the back of his neck. "I just realized how idealistic it sounds when I say it out loud."

Naomi let out a gentle scoff. "If idealism is the worst of your traits, you're the best man I've ever met."

He was grateful that the twilight provided some cover for the way that half of a compliment went straight to his head.

"I bet you're a big hit at services," she said, throwing her arm across the back of the bench and shifting a few inches closer to him. "Young, handsome, smart." She wrinkled her nose, alarmingly mischievous all of a sudden. "Good with your mouth."

Ethan swallowed hard, shifting to survey the door of the synagogue even though he knew they were alone.

She laughed gently. "I meant this whole scientist-meets-man-of-God spiel you've got going on. It works. Or I mean, I assume it works on people who are interested in that kind of thing. You don't need me here to act as bait."

"I'm not looking for bait," he said, frustration bleeding into all the ways he found her charming. "Look, if I can convince you to do this seminar series, and that makes Judaism accessible to new people, maybe I can appeal to a wider base. Keep the religion of my ancestors from fading into oblivion. Faith and science, at least in my definition, are fluid. They flex and adapt, bend and evolve, just like people, to survive. It's a thoroughly logical proposition."

"That," she said, slowly, "is a very fancy and complicated justification for attempting to hire a former porn performer to bring young people to your synagogue."

Ethan ran his fingers through his hair. He knew he needed a haircut. The overlong strands brushed the back of his neck, but he didn't feel particularly inclined to give up anything that he could hold on to at the moment.

"You don't have as good a read on me as you think you do."

She turned to look at him more directly. "How do you know?"

"Because you keep trying to catch me in a lie."

She shrugged, the movement too fluid by half. "I've met a lot of liars."

"I want to hire you because you're magnetic." The truth came out too soon, too unguarded. Stark enough to hit them both in the face. For a long moment, no one said anything.

"I mean"—Ethan began to course-correct—"obviously you have unique expertise. Besides," he rushed to add, "you want to teach, and you deserve a classroom."

Her mouth kicked to the side. "Did you memorize that speech too?"

"No." He wiped his thumb across his lips. "But I would have put something together," he said, "if I'd known you were going to show up here tonight."

Ethan hadn't been able to get Naomi Grant out of his head. There was something refreshing about her. *Grit* wasn't the right word. Everything about her outward appearance was polished to a high shine. She just seemed . . . tough.

Naomi was what his synagogue needed. He hadn't exactly planned on offering prospective congregants a lecture series about sex and love before he'd heard that she was an educator without an audience, but in hindsight, the curriculum felt perfect. A modern intimacy seminar to spark Beth Elohim's rebirth.

"It probably won't work, you know," she said, as if she could read his mind. "Your hopeful vision, I mean. People are afraid of porn."

"Yeah. Well, people are afraid of religion too." Life had been easier when he was just Ethan Cohen, absentminded physics teacher.

"Are you suggesting," Naomi said, "that makes us a double negative?"

He mustered a smile in the face of her stoicism. "I can work within the odds of probable failure if you can."

She chewed her bottom lip for a moment. Ethan envied her teeth.

"Those are the only odds I've ever known."

In the beat that passed between them, something absurdly hopeful built in his chest.

As if sensing this, Naomi narrowed her eyes at him. "If you start waxing poetic about divine intervention, I will clobber you."

"I've never been clobbered," he supplied cheerfully.

"It shows." Her eyes gleamed in the darkness.

Ethan could tell he was close to winning her over. At least for tonight.

She crossed her legs, back to being impatient. "Why modern intimacy?"

Ethan wondered if some people found battling her demanding instead of exhilarating. He'd always loved pop quizzes.

"Intimacy is the least common denominator between the popular zeitgeist and the kind of community I want to build here. It's the most accessible entry point I can think of for young single people."

"Because young people are all horny?"

"Because," he said, avoiding that conversation like the plague, "we've left the communal village of our ancestors and migrated to big cities, and now we're suffering."

"Speak for yourself," Naomi muttered under her breath.

"As soon as I met you," Ethan kept going, "I thought, what does today's version of connection, today's love, look like relative to Jewish faith? If we can answer that, if we can even scratch the surface of the answer, it's revolutionary."

"Does the phrase 'too big for his britches' mean anything to you?"

"Yes. Believe it or not, even rabbis understand dick jokes," he deadpanned before breaking into a grin at the flash of surprise that washed across her face.

He had to school himself to stop smiling at her. She was going to think there was something wrong with his mouth that meant he couldn't keep it closed.

"The content of the seminars is relatively flexible." He tried to shift back into business mode. "I trust you to develop the right series of lectures, given the audience and what we're trying to accomplish."

"And what we're trying to accomplish is . . . for young people to find religion?" She said it like his mission was a lost cause.

The statement was true, but it wasn't the whole story. Correcting her was probably a bad idea, but he knew that in order to really get her on board, he'd have to at least try to get Naomi to understand. His job was full of deceptively small words like *faith* that had infinitely complicated definitions. Luckily, Ethan was pragmatic by nature and realistic by virtue of experience.

"It's simpler than that. I want to give people a reason to believe. In themselves, each other, and something more."

She stared at him for a long time. Ethan could feel her trying to peel back the layers of him, to find out whether his center was rotten.

"Come on, Naomi Grant. Don't tell me you're not a little intrigued."

What if he wanted this too much? He never stopped to ask himself what failure would cost.

"Oh, I'm intrigued all right." She brushed her thumb across the bench's inscription, mirroring the way he'd done it earlier. "But for all your grand declarations, you still haven't said anything about logistics."

"I'm bad at details." A flaw for anyone, but especially a rabbi.

"Most people don't claim their weaknesses so easily." Her voice was soft now, thoughtful.

He held her gaze for a long moment. "Maybe they should."

Perhaps when the seminar ended, he'd ask her out. Ethan hadn't asked anyone out in a long time, but then again, he couldn't remember ever wanting to learn about someone as much as he wanted to learn about her.

Naomi broke first, her eyes narrowing. "You're stalling."

"Okay, okay. Here's what I've got. Once a week, we do an hour-long, maybe an hour-and-a-half, seminar at the Jewish Community Center—less intimidating than the synagogue," he answered before she could ask. "Ideally the curriculum stretches across six to eight weeks. That way it falls into the same schedule as the rest of our activities calendar."

Naomi considered her cuticles. "Can I pick the night of the week?"

"Sure. As long as it doesn't fall on Shabbat."

"Tuesdays," she said. "I have Krav Maga on Monday and Wednesday nights."

"Done. You can outline the syllabus. Whatever you think people should know about pursuing modern intimacy."

She arched a brow. "You're giving me carte blanche?"

"You make that sound like a bad thing." Ethan didn't usually review the class materials of the professionals he hired.

Naomi got to her feet. "We should have a trial run. If the first seminar doesn't work out, let's agree to be honest with one another and call it."

"All right." He stood up too. "In terms of compensation—"

She waved him off. "You can't afford my speaking rates. I'll do it as a volunteer."

"No. That's really not necessary." He must have looked serious, because she relented.

"Fine. Sixty bucks a session?"

That was insultingly low and they both knew it. "I want to argue with you, but something tells me I'll lose."

She smiled at him, the false one that he remembered from the convention center. "You should trust those instincts."

"Does it work for you to hold the first session in two weeks? That should be enough time to book the space and spread the word to the congregation. I'm planning to contact the Hillel organizations at USC and UCLA."

"Two weeks." Naomi stuck out her hand.

Ethan took it after a moment. Up close her eyes were almost green.

He had fourteen days to get his act together. He hoped it was enough.

Chapter Four

WHEN ETHAN'S MOTHER called him in the middle of the following week and said she wanted to have dinner on Friday to celebrate his sister coming home, he immediately knew she'd forgotten about Shabbat.

This was a fairly common occurrence. He'd gently reminded her about his weekly observance, assuming they'd make alternative plans. But she'd insisted and, in a few rapid-fire keystrokes that he could hear through the phone, sent him an email calendar invite. In Renee Cohen's book, iCal was legally binding.

Only on rare occasions did his mom pull out one of the family's handwritten recipe cards, passed down across multiple generations— half the words still in German—and decipher them. Especially on short notice.

Ethan prepared himself for an evening of minor disaster.

Sure enough, on Friday night, it was hard to decide who felt worse as his mom's hand shook as she tried to light the candles. Renee's cheeks colored as her tongue tripped over the Hebrew words, rushing to recall them before the match burned her fingers.

His sister, Leah, kept apologizing for not being able to step in. Leah spent the majority of her time filming in remote locations for her job as a reality TV show producer, and by her own admission, it was harder to keep up with the traditions living in a tent on a tiny island off the coast of Maui.

Ethan sweated under his kippah. His mother's dining room was easily seventy-five degrees. Right off the kitchen, it seemed to absorb residual heat from her out-of-shape and consequently overworked oven.

"Why don't you just recite the English translation?" Ethan's stomach twisted. He was a jerk for putting his family in the position of practicing rituals that they didn't fully embrace.

Before he'd become a rabbi, Shabbat dinners at the Cohen household had been few and far between, less religious practice and more an excuse to have friends or family over. The prayers had been hastily muttered in an effort to get to the food sooner. For a moment, Ethan selfishly envied the rabbis who had generations of devout practice in their bloodlines.

It was impossible to deny that on the spectrum of religion, he'd spent the last six years moving further away from his closest kin.

His mom winced. "I didn't think this through, huh?"

"I've seen worse," he said, which was technically true, but not by much.

When Ethan was growing up, the Cohens had worshipped ambition more than the Torah. His mother had made herself in this town, had risen through the ranks of the studio machine against men who wanted nothing more than to prove she didn't belong. By the time Ethan was in high school, she'd become a powerful agent. Everyone had always assumed her children would follow in her footsteps, and maybe if his father hadn't died, Ethan would have.

Renee had worked so hard and accomplished so much, sometimes all of them forgot there was anything she couldn't do. Ethan had been groomed from childhood for a slick role behind a big desk, making and breaking deals and dreams. Renee liked to blame the cherublike curls he'd inherited from his dad for the fact that she thrust him into the arms of various strangers from an early age and then never stopped. "You were born with a face that's good for business." Productive, efficient, and goal oriented. That was his mother in a nutshell.

When the candles were finally lit, Ethan quickly moved to do the blessing over the wine.

To her credit, his mom had shrugged it off when he'd studied physics instead of business in college. She'd built a reputation on rolling with the punches, which was why it was so obvious how uncomfortable she was now, trying to recall prayers that she hadn't said with any regularity in almost a decade.

After a few more awkward stops and starts, they made it through the remainder of the blessings, the hand washing, and the challah. With simultaneous sighs of relief, they finally sat down to eat. The table seemed to stretch a mile long from end to end.

"Do you like the challah?" his mother said, breaking the awkward silence. "I went down to that bakery on Melrose you're always talking about." She leaned forward slightly, obviously eager to pull off at least one part of this evening without a hitch.

"It's great," Ethan said, and it was. Light and mouthwatering, the top a perfect golden-brown braid. "Thanks for going to all this trouble, Mom. I appreciate it."

Renee smiled. "Of course. I want you to feel comfortable here." She stared at the empty seat at the head of the table.

Her meaning was clear. She wanted him to keep coming back, even after his father's death. After Ethan had run away to Brooklyn to live with his cousins. After he'd decided to become a rabbi and built walls between them she didn't know how to climb.

It was his dad who had always cared about maintaining the Jewish traditions, including Shabbat dinner. Ari Cohen had held together a lot of things in this family that they didn't notice until he was gone.

So many of Ethan's interactions, with Leah and his mother both, had pivoted in the wake of his dad's death. In their individual responses to it. They'd all thrown themselves into work. Had let it pull them in different directions until every time they came back together, they bumped into each other like puzzle pieces warped so that they no longer quite fit.

Ethan reached across the table and squeezed his mother's hand, trying to will some of the stress away from her brow.

"This is where I grew up. I always feel comfortable here."

It wasn't until his mom looked away that he realized maybe he'd lied. The truth was, he avoided the house when he could.

He recalled a concept from the Jewish mystics—*rishima*—"the imprint an experience leaves." They believed that if you endured something and let it pass without memory or reflection, if you didn't change after having gone through it, it was as if the event had never happened. But if an experience left an imprint, if it inspired growth or altered the course of your life, then, according to the mystics, even the most painful and challenging experiences become a blessed teacher.

The hollow echo of his dad at this table, the phantom feeling of his hand heavy on Ethan's head as he said the blessing over his children, was rishima, and even as it ached, it was better than living a life that didn't acknowledge what had happened to them all.

His mother went to the kitchen and returned carrying bowls of soup. Ethan jumped up to help her. She pressed a quick kiss to his cheek with her hands full. His mom thought that his commitment to religious study had changed him, turned him into a man she didn't fully recognize, but for all the ways he'd evolved since twenty-six, he still craved the comforts of this house and the people inside it.

"So," Leah said once they'd all tucked into their bowls, her voice like a bridge across the void of uncomfortable silence that had settled between them. "What's new?"

"We closed an acquisition today." His mom passed him the salad. "Brings the agency's employee count up to four hundred."

Leah let out a low whistle. "Damn, Mom."

His mother ducked her head in acknowledgment. "Thank you. Thank you."

Leah turned her gaze toward him. This last work trip had left her with an extra dose of freckles. "What about you, E?"

Ethan turned his fork over a few times, pretending he was checking for water spots. "Umm . . . well . . . I hired someone to run a new seminar series, actually."

Why had he brought that up? Probably because he found himself thinking about Naomi in most of his free time.

"That sounds nice." His mother dipped her spoon into her bowl. "Anyone I've heard of?"

"Maybe?" Ethan couldn't decide whether he wanted his mother to know who Naomi was. "Her name's Naomi Grant."

"Shut up." Leah smacked the dining table with both palms, rattling the glassware and making the butter quiver. "You hired Naomi Grant? Are you kidding me? Is she as badass in person as she seems online?"

Two scalding spoonfuls of soup didn't save him from the dual sets of eyes awaiting his response.

"She's very remarkable, yes," he said finally, his throat on fire.

Leah sat back in her chair and folded her arms. "I can't believe you got someone as cool as Naomi Grant to work for you."

"Are you saying I'm not cool?" His ego was really taking a hit this month.

"That's exactly what I'm saying," Leah said without even an ounce of remorse.

"Aw, honey, I think you're cool." His mom shrugged. "You know, for a rabbi."

Ethan sighed.

"So, who's Naomi Grant?" His mother looked back and forth between them.

Ethan paused, not sure how Naomi preferred to disclose her professional history. "She's a local entertainer and entrepreneur."

Leah helped herself to more bread and grinned. "Ethan's pointedly trying to avoid saying she's a former porn star who now runs the most popular sex education website in the country."

He shot her a glare. "Yes, thanks." Even though they were both now in their thirties, because Leah was still so obviously the rebellious, problem child, she took every opportunity to get Ethan, with his squeaky-clean-since-grade-school reputation, in trouble.

Across the table, his sister beamed.

"I see." Renee's eyebrows had traveled toward her hairline. "And what will this Ms. Grant do at the synagogue? Surely she won't reenact any . . ."

Leah snorted.

Ethan closed his eyes and counted to three.

"I've hired her to teach a seminar on modern intimacy."

"Oh." Renee lowered her spoon carefully. "Well. That's certainly . . . different."

"That's the idea," Ethan said. "I told you I'm trying to bring younger people to the synagogue. These events put Beth Elohim on the radar of people who never would have considered us otherwise. Naomi has a unique résumé that makes her perspective incredibly valuable."

"You should bring her around sometime," Leah said. "Mom and I would love to meet her."

Ethan pressed his foot down hard on hers under the table.

"What?" Renee lowered her spoon and frowned, catching the tension between them. "You think I'd embarrass you? I'll have you know I have seen plenty of pornography in my lifetime."

Ethan and Leah shared a panicked glance.

"Look what you've done," he said, cutting his gaze to where their mother was now placidly helping herself to slices of brisket from a covered dish in the center of the table.

"I regret my actions." Leah dropped her spoon and took a long swallow of wine.

Renee hummed thoughtfully. "What exactly is covered in a modern intimacy seminar?"

"Ooh, good question, Mom." Leah could not have looked more pleased that Ethan was taking the brunt of the uncomfortable dinner conversation. He made a mental note to ask about her ex-boyfriend at the first opportunity.

Ethan helped himself to green beans. "The syllabus Naomi has come up with is built around seven relationship milestones." She'd emailed him a draft earlier in the week. "It starts with how to find someone you want to date, then introduces a first-date framework to help you decide if you actually like that person."

"Ooh, that sounds super useful." Leah pointed her fork at him. "I can never tell if I'm only dating someone because I'm bored."

"That's a thing?" His mother frowned into her glass.

"Definitely a thing," Leah confirmed.

"As I was saying," Ethan continued. "After the first-date module, there's one about communication practices. Then I think it's integrating a new person into your life?" He took a bite of salad and chewed thoughtfully. "That's like introducing them to your friends and that kind of thing."

"Oh. That should be fun for you," his mother said. "All your friends are octogenarians."

"Not all of my friends." Ethan considered. "Just most of the people I spend time with." To be fair, there were younger people in the inter-synagogue softball league he played in. Though not really on his team.

Leah cracked pepper over her vegetables. "What happens after you introduce the women you're dating to your silver-haired pals?"

"The curriculum isn't built for me." Ethan gave her a warning look. "It's built for . . . eligible people."

"Who says you aren't eligible?" his mother said sharply.

He mouthed *Change the subject* at Leah.

She tilted her head and pretended she couldn't understand him.

They both thought it was so simple. That he could just meet someone he liked and date like anyone else. But tonight was a perfect example of how uncomfortable it was to have people he cared about go through the motions of religion for his sake. He didn't want to put any of his romantic prospects in that position.

As for dating someone who wasn't a practicing Jew, was he really ready to test the limits of his faith before he'd firmly secured the synagogue's foundation?

"No, Mom. No one said that, I simply mean . . ."

"Ethan's afraid of dating," Leah announced. "He's worried no one will ever understand him now that he's a rabbi."

It was a shame that he was going to have to shun his sister so soon after she'd come back from filming.

"The next module," he declared before his mother could dig into that proclamation, "covers initiating physical intimacy—or the lack of it, I suppose, depending on your and your partner's preferences."

"That sounds very healthy," his mother said, suitably distracted by allusions to procreation. "I'm sure Ms. Grant will provide valuable perspective given her work."

Ethan nodded, trying not to think too hard about Naomi's professional history because he was certain, though he hadn't personally verified, she'd been naked for at least parts of it.

"What comes after the sex session?"

Leave it to Leah to cut to the chase.

"That's where things get really interesting, in my opinion."

Leah smirked. "You *would* think the parts after sex were the fascinating bits."

Ethan made a mental note to refuse to let her borrow his car when she inevitably came asking.

"Module six is about opening up about your past and discussing your future together."

"There's some lovely symmetry there." His mother nodded happily. Apparently sibling bickering did nothing to dampen her enjoyment of an evening of family time. Either that or she'd had more wine than he'd realized. "More kugel?"

"Yes, thanks." Ethan took a few more slices. Despite being out of practice, his mom was a surprisingly good cook.

Leah counted on her fingers. "What's the last one?"

"How to break up."

"What?" Leah and his mother said in unison.

Ethan lowered the gravy boat. "Naomi says breakups are inevitable, and the kindest thing we can do is give people tools to survive them."

"Well," said his mother as she wiped her mouth with her napkin. "Naomi certainly sounds fun."

"I don't think it's the worst thing in the world," Ethan said carefully. "No one ever teaches us how to let go. How to rebuild. How to move on."

His mom cleared her throat. "No. You're right." She tore her challah into pieces as she stared at the mantelpiece. "Though I'm not sure how much it'll help prepare them."

Ethan knew without turning that she'd zeroed in on the black-and-white snapshot of his dad, laughing over a tiny fish he'd caught on a family trip to the lake, his head thrown back and his skin tan from days in the sun.

"The tricky thing about grief," his mom said, "is that even when we know it's coming, we underestimate our own capacity for suffering."

Guilt ate away at Ethan's insides, as corrosive as lighter fluid. He realized that in his mom's eyes, he'd run to religion the same way Leah had run to adventure. They'd both found places to fill their time that weren't here, with her.

He'd been relieved that providing service to his community meant carving off parts of himself. The more time he spent thinking about God, the less he spent thinking about what he'd lost.

How could he offer anyone his heart, when already there wasn't enough of him to go around?

"Mom?" Leah got up and wrapped her arms around her mother's shoulders.

"Oh, don't worry about me." Renee forced out a laugh as she patted Leah's hands. "I'll just pop into Ethan's seminar. Take a few notes from Naomi Grant."

"Oh no." Ethan groaned. "Please don't."

"Well," Leah scolded, "that's not a very generous attitude. I thought you were trying to appeal to new members."

Minor disaster, as it turned out, may have been an understatement.

Chapter Five

MODERN INTIMACY—LECTURE 1:

Get out of your own way, asshole

NAOMI NORMALLY DEALT with imposter syndrome through stoic teeth-grinding and angry-girl music. But standing behind a shoddy lectern on wheels, with the eyes of her first live educational audience upon her, neither of her go-to coping mechanisms was viable. She fought to control her breathing, to make the rise and fall of her chest less obvious. No small task when her chest was one of the most recognizable in the country.

She hadn't gotten nervous like this in a long time. The buzz of it under her skin, making her a little sick to her stomach, was kind of nice. Like fuel for the weary engine of her heart.

Since she'd visited the synagogue, two weeks had flown by, aided by a packed schedule and a general sense of discomfort over having agreed to this gig. She and Ethan had exchanged a few breezy emails about her proposed syllabus. She'd only found herself lingering over the signature line once before deciding in the end that there really wasn't much difference between *Have a good night* and *Have a good night!* She'd never used a chipper exclamation mark in her life, and she wasn't about to start now.

Based on his leadership position, and—let's be honest—the fact that he was a man, she sort of expected Ethan to have a lot of notes on her outline. But aside from suggesting she incorporate a discussion of values, including but not limited to religious affiliation, into the module about building a future together, he'd given the green light.

He was introducing her now, reciting lines she recognized from her official bio on the Shameless site, her credentials and media awards—she'd made "30 under 30" with only a few days to spare.

Naomi dug her nails into her palms as the crowd gobbled up an embarrassing dad joke. She supposed, scanning the room they'd reserved at the JCC, that *crowd* was a generous term.

The multipurpose room held six rows of twelve folding chairs each, behind long plastic card tables. Only the back few rows had anyone in them. Naomi did some quick mental math. Fourteen people had shown up expecting a meaningful lecture on modern intimacy. At least she could say there was room for improvement.

"You're probably wondering why a synagogue is sponsoring a seminar by a sex educator," Ethan said.

She held her breath. Naomi had wondered if he would address the elephant in the room. These people had come through traditional Jewish channels, and she was far from traditionally Jewish. How long would her tough-girl bravado last if they all decided to get up and walk out?

Naomi's response to moving through the world as a sex worker was to never let down her guard. Not even for a second. She'd learned from experience that she never knew when someone was going to make a joke at her expense. Or issue some casual slander about her past profession. It was better to live always ready for the punch line. Always spoiling for a fight.

"How many of you consider yourselves Jewish?" Ethan asked.

Almost every hand went up.

It made sense, considering he'd recruited primarily from Hillel alumni groups.

"Great. And how many of you have been to shul in the last three months?"

Only a few hands stayed in the air. Apparently Ethan hadn't been wrong about the disconnect between youth and religion.

"Last six months?"

Only one or two more.

"Okay." Ethan nodded, obviously not surprised. "So I'm going to attempt to change that, and I figure in order to do that, just like with any relationship in your life, I need to show you why our synagogue is worth your time."

The crowd, mostly women between the ages of what looked like twenty and thirty, glared back at him with an amusing mixture of either stoic bitch face or nervous apprehension.

"Basically," Ethan tried to explain, "if you're not coming to me, I have to come to you. And since enough of you seem to care about dating, and intimacy is a core value in our faith, here we are. Gathered to learn. To connect. To hopefully, if Naomi does her job"—he gave her a cheerful nod—"enrich our lives. So yeah. I'm playing the long game, and this seminar series, Modern Intimacy, is my starting pitch. If you like what you hear tonight, there's an open invitation to attend Shabbat services with us on Friday. We've got excellent cookies in the social hall afterward."

It was a good speech. Relaxed enough to appear casual. Earnest enough to start to win the trust of those assembled.

". . . and with that, I'll hand things over to Naomi Grant, who I promise will make the rest of your evening more entertaining than I ever could." Ethan gave her a quick smile and then made his way to an empty seat in the second row.

Naomi bit the inside of her cheek. It took a lot to rattle her, usually. Through the combination of years of therapy and sheer force of will, she prided herself on her ability to not engage with negative thoughts. Mind over matter.

Public speaking didn't make her nervous. It was just another kind of performance. But baring her soul had always cost her more than baring her body. She wanted this too badly—to be taken seriously as an authority figure instead of just an object of desire. It was one thing to court lust. Respect was a lot harder to earn.

It didn't help that the walls of their room at the JCC were covered floor to ceiling in children's artwork from the daycare. There was no neutral place to lay her gaze. Everything was glitter and googly eyes. Very disorienting.

The force of attention from the audience was palpable, shot like tequila straight into her veins until her tongue felt dangerously loose in her mouth.

Clara had made her print out notes, just in case. Naomi was supposed to open with a personal anecdote, something to put the audience at ease, to make herself seem relatable, approachable, human. Her notes read, *Open: story about ferryboat.*

The audience seemed to devour her silence, restless and ready for her to fail. From the back of the room, a muscle-bound guy in a baseball cap yelled, "Yo, are you gonna teach us about blow jobs, or what?"

"Of course not," Naomi said without thinking. "You have to enter your credit card number online for that."

The caller, who had been elbowing his buddy a moment ago, fell back into his seat.

She crumpled the paper in her fist. Since when did she start anything slow and easy? Her strategy, the only one she'd ever trusted, was to throw everything she had at a problem. To run so fast and so far that she couldn't remember where she'd been. These people had seen *Naomi Grant* on the door. No one here had signed up for toothless anecdotes.

"How many of you are single?" The question shot naked across the room. No preamble. No polite warm-up. Begin as you mean to go on.

For a moment, no one did anything. Naomi became very aware of her own heartbeat.

Then, almost every hand in the room was raised.

That was something, at least. Common ground for their discussion.

Cassidy had once told her, in her thick Texas drawl, "The audience doesn't get to read the script; as long as you sell it, you can go off book and no one will ever know."

Her notes were already toast. She could hardly smooth out the sheet and start again. Naomi didn't want to talk at these people, she realized. Shameless fulfilled her desire to send a one-way message. The reason she'd pursued a classroom was that she wanted a dialogue. To understand individual experiences, to create connections, to be able to adapt her curriculum based on the needs of her students.

"How many of you are currently dating?"

About half as many hands went up.

"Okay, so why not?"

After a beat of heavy silence and empty air, Ethan raised his hand. "Occupational hazard."

The room tittered, and Naomi rolled her shoulders away from her ears, a little lighter. Even if it was a reminder about why he was off-limits, it was also a reminder she wasn't in this alone.

Naomi locked eyes with a pretty blonde wearing a denim jacket, the collar tagged with an enamel pin that read *Feminist Killjoy.* "How about you?"

The girl looked mildly harassed. "Men are pigs?"

The woman next to her offered a commiserating nod, and afterward the blonde sat a little straighter in her chair.

"Not just men, unfortunately." Naomi had earned her share of disappointment from across the gender spectrum. "What else?"

A hand went up toward the back. "Dating apps suck. Everyone's constantly swiping for upgrades."

"Ah yes, it's easy to gorge yourself at the digital dating buffet. We've gamified our mating rituals." She scanned the room. "Good. Who's next?"

Slowly, and then all at once, more and more people volunteered answers, until the conference room was littered with the woes of modern dating. Los Angeles was vapid. All the good ones were taken. Dating was expensive. Dating was exhausting. Half the people on the market only wanted to hook up. And the sex was terrible. She made a mental note to hand that last woman a Shameless business card. The list went on and on. Together they were exorcising dating demons, and the room was getting looser with each confession.

Naomi had her work cut out for her. Seven weeks of lectures might not be enough. These people were tired of suffering in silence. They were here because they wanted a public pyre for their grievances.

"All right." She called for attention, bringing the room back from the side conversations of commiseration they'd descended into. "Before we go any further, I want you to give yourself permission to fail." As the words left her mouth, they stirred up Naomi's own insecurities and mistakes.

She wasn't a fraud, exactly, acting as an authority on this quicksand-filled subject. She'd worked hard to gain credibility in the space of emotional and physical intimacy. Her entire career was based on understanding the intersections. But writing the syllabus for a healthy relationship was one thing. Following it was another story entirely.

"Love or intimacy, together or separate, I can't guarantee you'll find them as a result of this seminar. I can't even promise you'll ever find someone—or multiple people, if that's your thing—who can tolerate you, even most of the time. Compatibility, trust, sex, none of the stuff we'll talk about in this seminar is scientific."

Naomi's eyes found Ethan. He sat straight in his chair, legs spread, hands linked in his lap. She didn't have time to worry about whether her style of lecture met his approval. The only thing she knew how to trust was her own instincts. An unreliable north star, perhaps, but the one available at the moment. "Maybe that's why intimacy pairs so well with religion. The best we can do is show up and try to be worthy."

A woman with dark braids raised her hand.

"Yeah?" Naomi placed both hands on the lectern, a little dazed.

"So what I'm hearing you say is that the dating equivalent of 'dress for the job you want' is 'dress for the dick of your dreams'?"

Naomi let out a sharp, grateful laugh. And just like that, she knew she could do this. "I mean, if you're fishing for dick, sure. But keep in mind that it's not in short supply." She picked up a whiteboard marker and scrawled out a sentence. *If you don't know what you want, you shouldn't be dating.*

"You can thank my therapist for that one—it's a direct quote."

The room relaxed a few degrees further. Clara had been right. She couldn't effectively discuss vulnerability without showing these strangers her soft underbelly.

"Now, that advice may sound harsh. I'm sure some of you are saying to yourselves, 'Isn't dating how I figure out what I like?' and you're right. It is. But your efforts will go further faster if you first do the work of asking yourself, and being honest about, what you're prepared to give and receive in a relationship with another person."

The familiar sensation of performance settled over her, and suddenly, speaking felt like running downhill.

"We all want and need different things. Despite what the Hallmark Channel might tell you, not everyone's happily-ever-after involves settling down in a small town. We don't all want commitment. We don't all want sex. And we certainly don't always want them in the same serving sizes. That's okay. Good, even. There aren't wrong answers to the question 'What are you looking for?' But there are infinite lies and only one truth."

She lowered her voice from lecture to conversation. She moved out from behind the lectern, stole one of the chairs from the front row, and made herself comfortable in it.

"You have to know your own tendencies. What kind of traps do you tend to fall into, not just romantically, but in any relationship?"

She swallowed once.

"I, for example, consistently fall for people I know I can't have, as a way of avoiding opening myself up to love."

As if on cue, Ethan's head shot up from where he'd been bent over his notes.

Naomi took a deep breath. "Unfortunately," she said, holding his gaze, "knowing your weaknesses doesn't make you immune."

Her saving grace was that she had learned how to throw grenades in her own path.

"We'll discuss as many of the external challenges you named as possible over the course of the seminar, but for tonight, I want you to focus on yourself. I want you to answer two questions. What kind of relationship do you really want? And how are you sabotaging yourself from getting it? There are notecards in front of each of you. Your challenge is to get as specific as possible."

She held up a hand as attendees' eyebrows rose and mouths pursed to protest. "Before you ask, no, I'm not going to collect your answers or make you read them aloud. You can burn them when you get home if you want."

For a tense moment, Naomi waited, half expecting a rebellion, but though it took a few moments, with people looking at their neighbors to make sure they weren't the only ones participating, eventually the room went quiet again as every hand began to write.

After the group completed the silent exercise, Naomi spent the next half hour outlining common dating pitfalls. She knew from experience that nothing broke down barriers and forged camaraderie like bad blind date stories. The anecdotes naturally built off one another, providing their own patterns and making common weaknesses easy to spot.

"Sometimes you don't realize how bad a date was until it's over," Naomi said, wiping away tears of laughter as the young man who'd hollered at her earlier, Craig, recounted an exchange that ended with him dipping his entire hand into a fondue pot.

"I'm just saying, do they really need to make the cheese that hot?"

Ethan had to stand up and tell everyone they were being kicked out of the room when the discussion ran long. The authoritative voice he put on to project across the buzzing classroom made Naomi lick her lips.

"Thanks for showing up tonight," she said as the meager audience packed up. "If you had fun talking about recipes for dating disaster, chances are you'll appreciate the rest of the seven-week series."

She realized belatedly that she should have confirmed with Ethan that he considered this evening a success before committing to more. It had just felt so good. The energy, the hope born out of the weary resignation she'd seen walk in with so many of these people.

"Let me know if you have any questions on your way out."

When Ethan climbed down the stairs with a grin on his face, something traitorous inside her diaphragm purred.

"You were great."

Naomi blamed the adrenaline in her veins for making her loose and giddy. Her body wanted her to do something stupid, something reckless. Something carnal.

"Thanks," she said, turning away from him to remove the temptation. "It was fun." She threw her crumpled notes in the trash can. Naomi wanted to tell him to put his guard up, to hide the surprise and gratitude already coloring his face. Didn't he know that he was making this harder by leaving himself open?

"Wait." Ethan caught her hand, urging her to look at him, oblivious to the danger. "I'm serious. That lecture. The way you got everyone to relax and laugh together. It was more than I was hoping for our first time."

The praise coupled with double entendre sank into her skin until it lit her up from the inside. "Jeez, if you liked that performance, you should watch one of my movies." The comment was out of her mouth before she could stop it, a runaway train—and like a train, she watched as it plowed right through him. Shit.

He shook his head, but he didn't glower or faint, the way she half expected him to. No, after a moment, Rabbi Ethan Cohen laughed. And it wasn't one of those tarted-up laughs full of awkwardness and tension. It was a real laugh, from his belly, like she'd pleased him almost as much by mentioning her unmentionable past as she had by leading the lecture.

She wanted to ask him what he thought he was doing, acting like he wasn't afraid of her, but she didn't get the chance before one of the participants stole his attention to ask a question.

Naomi went to push in the empty chairs.

She wanted to set a good example for these people. And if that meant showing a little restraint for once in her life? Well, surely she could hold out longer than Josh and Clara.

Chapter Six

NAOMI DROPPED BY the synagogue on her way home from work and found Ethan bleeding blue ink. She held herself in the doorway while he stood behind his desk glaring at his assailant, a ballpoint that seemed to have exploded in the pocket of his oxford shirt.

She rapped her knuckles against the inside of the wooden door frame to draw his attention.

"Did I catch you at a bad time?"

He threw the leaking pen away from him, uttering a little yip, and they both watched as it skidded across several stacks of important-looking documents.

Ethan closed his eyes for a long moment before giving his head a shake and gesturing for her to come in.

"No, I'm good. I've just been dealing with some unexpected appointments, and then there was a . . ." His eyes dropped forlornly to the Rorschach test on his front. ". . . pen situation."

"Looks dire." She pinned her lips together to stifle her amusement. Her life would be a lot easier if Ethan Cohen could find a way to be less endearing.

He wiped at the ink uselessly with a handful of tissues, spreading the stain around. The button-down was nice: crisp and white and soft-looking, like he was one of those rare men who actually use fabric softener. It didn't deserve this extended abuse.

"Don't move." She walked over and removed his hand from where it had paused, midswipe, on his chest. "Were you trying to make it worse?"

The corner of his mouth ticked up, revealing a flash of full upper lip, normally hidden by his beard.

Naomi forced her eyes away and grabbed her purse, hunting for the promotional flask she'd gotten that morning from some cheesy vendor trying to get her to sell ad space on Shameless. Once it was uncapped, she tipped the flask's contents carefully onto the handful of tissues, having commandeered them from his fist.

Ethan nodded his chin at the flask, his frozen body still obeying her earlier command.

"Is that vodka?"

As if she'd settle for clear liquor.

"It's water." Naomi didn't know shit about skin care, but she'd determined that if she hydrated until she pretty much constantly had to pee, her face remained a viable tool for negotiation and influence.

She paused for a moment, the damp material dripping in her palm, weighing her next move. There was a way to attack the blooming ink that minimized the potential embarrassment of both parties, and then there was the way that might actually work.

"Do you mind if I . . ." Naomi brought her empty hand to the hem of his shirt and pulled the fabric slightly away from the T-shirt he wore underneath. She didn't even let herself enjoy the fact that her fingers were now inches from the button of his pants.

"It'll work better if I can press on the fabric from both sides."

Ethan swallowed hard enough that his whole jaw flexed. "Oh. Sure."

Naomi ignored the flare of heat in her body at the way his voice seemed to have dropped an octave.

She made an effort not to make eye contact. Minimizing her charm, which she supposed was a demure way of saying *sex appeal*, went against every instinct, but she had no choice.

Flirting with Ethan was bad enough, but now, standing so close she could see the thin white scar that rested just above his brow, she was flirting with his boundaries.

It was . . . bad. Naomi had made a habit of testing how much she could get away with. Proximity to Ethan was one big game of chicken, and she wasn't sure if she wanted to win or lose—only that she didn't know how to stop playing, even if it was in the best interests of both of them.

Fueling and fulfilling desire was her domain. Her signature. She was comfortable when everyone else was shocked and stuttering. The real danger came when she surprised herself.

Naomi took extra care not to let her knuckles brush against his stomach as she worked her hand up to the stain just below his left pectoral, but the shirt was fitted, and it was a near miss by millimeters. She'd bet good money that he was holding his breath.

"Maybe you should unbutton it," she offered, a little breathy.

"Right. Of course." His fingers worked the buttons quickly. Naomi's mouth watered at the sight of his wrists flexing. The fabric fell open. "Is that better?"

"Yes," she said, lying.

Even without touching, Naomi could feel the warmth of Ethan's body through the thin layer of cotton separating their skin. She brought the wet tissues back to the stain and tried to work quickly.

When she moved to adjust her grip, bending her knees and lowering her head so she could examine the stain, Ethan winced.

Uh-oh. None of this should hurt. "Wait, did the pen actually puncture you?"

"No. Sorry," he said, sheepish. "The water's cold."

Naomi swore under her breath before she could stop herself. The entire time she'd been pressing, water had sluiced off the tissue to drip down his belly. Imagining the trajectory of the droplets was alarmingly carnal.

She took a step back. Then another. It wasn't enough.

"I think this might be a lost cause," she said.

"That's okay." Ethan frowned down at the slightly faded but still prominent stain. "Maybe I can figure out a way to cover it with my tallis."

"Ah yes. I've heard prayer shawls are not just a sign of communal solidarity and devotion to God, but also a pragmatic fashion choice for spring." She slipped back into the comfort of sarcasm like a warm bath.

This time Ethan's smile was indulgent. "So, what can I do for you? You didn't come here to rescue my wardrobe."

Oh. Right.

"I actually came to talk to you about the lecture series, but if this is a bad time"—she looked meaningfully at his shirt—"I can come back later."

"No." He waved her off. "Please sit."

Naomi let herself sink into the chair across from his desk. Easily convinced. "Okay."

He waited expectantly with his hands folded in front of him.

She forced herself to gather the reluctant words she'd come to deliver. "I'm not sure I can keep doing the seminars."

"Oh." Ethan lowered his gaze, picked up the broken pen, and fiddled with the cap. "I see. Has else something come up?"

"Not exactly." More like spending time with him made her want things she shouldn't crave.

Not just sex. Though—she eyed the hard sweep of his jaw—definitely sex. The lecture earlier in the week had filled her with this false sense of community, and she knew she couldn't let herself get used to the artificial high of acceptance. There were too many variables in the Modern Intimacy series that Naomi couldn't control. If she kept going back to the JCC week after week, sooner or later she'd forget that there was no place for her in Judaism, or, more specifically, in this synagogue.

"I'm just really busy with my company right now," she said tightly. "I'm sure you could find someone else who can step in—"

A knock on the door made them both start.

An older man with a white beard nodded at her before turning to Ethan.

"Rabbi Cohen, I'm sorry to interrupt, but I need a private word, please."

Ethan shifted the scowl he'd been wearing a moment before and nodded. "Of course. Give me a minute."

The man ducked his head in acknowledgment and then returned to the hallway to wait.

Ethan stood, glaring at the ink stain on his shirt. "I'm sorry. That's Jonathan Weiss, head of the synagogue's executive board," he said, keeping his voice low. "He cuts my paycheck, so it's ill-advised for me to make him wait. Do you mind sitting tight for a few? I'll make it quick."

While slinking away would be a relief, Naomi was at least made of tougher stuff than that. "Don't worry about it. Go ahead. I'm very adept at keeping myself occupied."

"I'll be right back," he said, neglecting to shut the door behind him in his haste.

Naomi pulled out her phone, flipping through text messages and emails. If she ordered Chinese food on her way home, she could probably beat the delivery driver to her door. Assuming the traffic on the freeway wasn't worse than usual.

"Listen, Ethan, I know you're a good kid."

Wow. That Jonathan guy's voice held a lot more condescension in the hallway than it had a moment ago in Ethan's office. Shouldn't he show the rabbi a little more respect?

"Kid? Come on, Jonathan. Even Morey doesn't call me *kid*, and he's got about twenty more years on me than you do."

Okay, so eavesdropping was rude, but also, Naomi couldn't help herself. She leaned her chair onto its back legs to get her ear closer to the open door.

"The board hired you with the assumption that you'd go about recruitment in new ways, but we're advising you to tread carefully," Jonathan was saying, the words coming out terse. "We're concerned about potential breaches in propriety in regard to recent programming decisions."

"I can assure you that all programming, new and otherwise, remains appropriate and professional," Ethan said, with traces of warning in his tone.

"I hope that's true. The board can't afford to take any chances. Beth Elohim is already struggling with an image issue. The last thing we need is complaints from the community. I'll be keeping an eye on things, just to be safe. As I'm sure you'd agree, where there's smoke, there's usually fire."

Naomi tightened her grip around the arms of her chair.

"Jonathan." Ethan's voice was infinitely patient. "As you know, our interests are aligned. We both want to save this synagogue. In order to do that, something's gotta give. These Modern Intimacy events can work to bring in younger members, I know it. But you've got to give me the benefit of the doubt here."

"I know that, Ethan, and I'm trying, but do you really think it's appropriate to entertain behind closed doors?" Jonathan had lowered his voice, but Naomi's hearing was perfect.

Her stomach clenched.

When Ethan spoke next, his voice was hard in a way Naomi never would have thought possible. "Jonathan. You're riding dangerously close to insulting one of our overqualified volunteers, not to mention threatening my honor."

She'd never gotten the hype before, but damn if having someone defend her good name didn't make something foreign flutter in her chest.

"We bit our tongues when you hired Naomi Grant because frankly you didn't tell us until after the first lecture. But now you're spending more time with her. It's all a little . . . unseemly. You must understand that people are uncomfortable with her background."

"Have we not set out to build an inclusive community? Does the Torah not teach us to welcome all who wish to enter our shul?"

Okay, so maybe she wasn't special. Ethan would have stood up for anyone being maligned unfairly in his presence, but still, being part of the rule instead of the exception had never felt so nice.

An edge of pleading had entered Jonathan's voice. "I'm sure she's a lovely person, but the optics are bad, Ethan. Surely you can recognize that."

"I've already given you a few chances now to save yourself in this conversation." The steel was back behind Ethan's words. "You've ignored all of them, so let me make myself clear. Naomi Grant is providing a valuable service to this congregation, and any unflattering optics you're accusing her of creating are a direct result of your own prejudice and insecurity. I stand completely by my decision to hire her, and if anyone else on the board has a problem with that, I'm happy to tell them the same thing."

Ethan's footsteps moved back toward his office, and Naomi righted her chair with a jolt.

"Don't forget, Rabbi Cohen," Jonathan called, "that you serve at the board's discretion."

"Have a good night, Jonathan."

When Ethan arrived back at the entrance to his office, Naomi was already turned to meet his tired eyes.

"Well, he certainly seems like a treat." She made sure her face was neutral of any emotion. She did not need Ethan trying to comfort her.

He sagged against the wall. "Please tell me you didn't just hear all of that."

She pressed a finger to her lips. "I could lie?"

"Ugh. Naomi, I'm so sorry. The board is . . . honestly, they're old. And they're scared. They're not used to change."

"And yet change is the only thing that can save them," she said dryly. "How inconvenient."

"If you don't want to continue to work for us, especially after that"—he gestured to the door—"I understand."

It was an easy out. But circumvented defamation couldn't hold a candle to her ego. Ethan really didn't know her at all if he thought a few carefully worded warnings would cause her to back down.

"I don't scare that easily."

Ethan pinched the bridge of his nose. "Jonathan never should have said those things."

"I don't care about what Jonathan said."

He lowered his hand. "Okay."

"I care about what you said." Her mouth was surprisingly dry.

"You heard that too?"

"That's pretty much how sound works," she confirmed, feeling lighter already. "I thought you studied physics?"

"I do." He shook his head. "I mean, I did. I still try to keep up with new theories. As a hobby."

His hair was in disarray and his shirt was a disaster. Worry was written all over his face. What was wrong with her that she found him more desirable when he was frazzled?

"For someone whose job entails a lot of oration, you're often tongue-tied."

"A recent development," he said, clenching his jaw ruefully, "I can assure you."

Well, that was flattering.

"Look, people have disapproved of me for over a decade. You know what the best recourse is?"

He shrugged helplessly. "Ignore them?"

"Make every single person who rejected you want you instead."

Naomi smirked. "We're going to bring in so many members, the board's gonna beg me to stay."

Ethan's brows rose. "You're not worried about the fact that we've had . . . shall we say . . . modest turnout thus far?"

"Nope." Naomi reached into her bag and pulled out a notebook.

"But I thought . . . what about what you were saying a few minutes ago, about being too busy at work?"

"Don't worry about it." Naomi uncapped a pen with her teeth. "Thanks to your pal Jonathan, I've got a renewed sense of motivation." Her desire to make people eat their words had always outweighed her insecurities.

"Oh." Ethan looked slightly dazed. "So, what do we do?"

Naomi crossed her legs. She had an idea. It was either great or terrible.

"I'd like to bring in a PR consultant."

Ethan shuffled through the ink-stained papers on his desk, letting out a triumphant little "aha" when he uncovered a spreadsheet. He frowned at the numbers he found there. "I'm not sure we've got the budget to cover that."

"Don't worry about it," Naomi said. "I know someone who will do it pro bono. She owes me."

"So, we're just going to . . ."

"Prove everyone wrong?" She smiled. "Yeah. That's exactly what we're going to do."

Chapter Seven

....

"OKAY." NAOMI TIGHTENED her hands on the steering wheel of her Prius. "I'm allowing you to grant me this favor, but only under the strict stipulation that you make a conscious effort not to embarrass me."

"Turn right up here." Clara held up her phone to the windshield, as if that would make Google Maps more accurate.

They'd arranged to meet Ethan at a coffee shop downtown, and as the passenger, it was Clara's responsibility to navigate.

"Also"—Clara lowered her phone and fiddled with the A/C, sending a blast of frigid air directly at Naomi's face, making her eyes water—"since when do favors come with qualifiers?"

"Since you're doing one for me, Connecticut." Naomi's favorite and most benign nickname for Clara was the one in reference to her home state. You could take the girl out of Greenwich, but you couldn't stop her from crossing her legs at the ankles and referring to Manhattan as "the city" even though she'd lived in L.A. for almost three years now.

"I've spent my entire life trying to minimize embarrassment," Clara bristled. "I think I can make it through forty-five minutes of coffee without saying anything uncouth."

Naomi grimaced at the reminder of Clara's family—bluebloods

with enough scandals to rival the Kennedys, though with fewer political aspirations.

"He's not a normal rabbi." Sure, Ethan had all of the qualities rabbis were supposed to possess; he was kind and smart, a good listener, thoughtful. But he was also— "You'll have to check that impulse you have to literally run from the room when confronted with an extremely hot person."

Clara tipped up her nose. "I have gotten much better at that in the last three years. As you know, I am, in fact, set to marry an extremely hot person."

"Obviously, after a steady diet of vitamin D"—she shot Clara a knowing look—"you've built up an immunity."

Covering her eyes with her hand, Clara groaned. "Sometimes you are a true nightmare."

Mood considerably brightened by torturing her friend, Naomi adjusted her sunglasses. "But seriously, Ethan is hot in a different way than Josh."

Clara squirmed, adjusting her seat belt where it bit into her neck because she was so short. "Okay. So describe it."

"He's disarming." Naomi never brought the right armor into battle against him.

"Disarming how?" Clara lowered her sunglasses and peered at Naomi over the top of them.

"He's sexy when he shouldn't be."

Sexy was a word Naomi heard thrown around a lot, and like any word used too often, it had started to lose meaning. Because of the nature of her work, she usually heard it describing something orchestrated and deliberate, built with the singular intention to tantalize.

Ethan wasn't like that.

He was like a current. Powerful and fluid in ways that had nothing to do with wanting her but that pulled her in all the same.

"Oh." Clara slid the seat forward and back in tiny increments. "Is that all?"

Naomi should have insisted they take separate cars from the office. She flicked the side of Clara's thigh. "What do you mean, is that all?"

"Ow." Clara reached over to pinch her arm in retaliation, but Naomi warned, "I'm driving," and Clara sat back with a huff.

"You think everyone is sexy," the brunette said simply.

"Not everyone," Naomi protested. She didn't think her current mail carrier was sexy. Now his predecessor, on the other hand . . .

"That's true," Clara said, thoughtful as she wiped the lens of her sunglasses on her skirt. "Lately it's narrowed down to everyone mean."

Well, sure. It was easier to keep mean people at arm's length.

"That's just it, though." Naomi smacked the steering wheel with her palm and accidentally hit the horn. She waved in apology at the car in front of her until he flipped her the bird. Rolling down her window, she yelled, "Well, fuck you too, buddy," before turning back to Clara. "That's the thing about this guy. He's not mean. He's nice, like aggressively nice, and kinda funny, but not really on purpose, and . . . it's confusing."

Obviously, Clara didn't understand why Ethan was so dangerous. How could she explain that he possessed near-lethal levels of persuasive powers? There was something about his shoulder-to-waist ratio. Despite his average height—maybe below average, honestly—he was so broad. Actually, what was a bigger word than *broad*? *Expansive*?

"Wait a second." Clara sat straighter in her seat, which frankly shouldn't have been possible since she had like finishing school posture already.

Naomi pulled up to a stop sign. "What?"

"You really like this guy." An annoying singsong quality permeated Clara's voice.

"On a professional level." With Naomi's résumé, it was reasonable to use *professional* to mean she wanted to fuck him.

"No," Clara chewed her bottom lip. "On a . . . hand-holding, picnic-in-the-park, do-his-whole-astrological-chart-to-see-if-you're-compatible level."

"That's the grossest thing you've ever said to me."

"I never thought I'd see the day." Clara grinned. "You totally have a crush."

It was one thing for Naomi to acknowledge her feelings privately, but another entirely for Clara to be able to see them and give them a name.

"That's it. Get out of my car." Naomi Grant did not have crushes. She crushed other people. No, wait, that wasn't right. Ugh.

"We're barreling down the freeway," Clara said, admirably non-plussed.

"I'll slow down." Naomi hit the button to unlock the doors. She was nothing without her intimidation factor.

"I bet you miss the days when I was actually afraid of you." Clara clapped her hands. "Ahh. This is so exciting. I can't believe I'm about to meet your crush."

"It's not exciting, and he's not my crush. It's a business arrangement. If you imply otherwise again, I will have no choice but to go full Krav Maga on your ass."

Clara pressed a hand to her heart. "I'm honored that you've chosen me to share in this experience."

"Clara, I'm serious. If you so much as think the word *crush* inside that coffee shop, I swear I'll show up to your wedding fully nude." Naomi ground her molars.

"Oh, fine. Maybe *crush* is a little adolescent. We'll call him the apple of your eye. The fodder for your daydreams. The——"

Naomi thrust her arm forward and punched on the stereo.

Unfortunately, she'd forgotten that she'd been listening to an audiobook.

"Deconstructing Reform Judaism. Chapter Six." The serene narrator's voice filled the car.

Shit. For a moment, both women sat very still, but as soon as her wits returned, Naomi leaned forward to turn it off.

Unfortunately, Clara had two arms free to Naomi's one. She was surprisingly strong for being so little.

"Stop fighting me. Your hands should be at ten and two, lady," Clara said, a little breathless from their scuffle.

The audiobook kept playing, the narrator unknowingly continuing a lecture about Purim.

For several uncomfortable minutes, they both sat listening.

"So," Clara said, voice light, "are you, like, religious now?"

"No," Naomi protested, too loudly and too quickly. "I've just been thinking about this stuff more lately. You know, spending time at the synagogue, and I'm writing all these lectures and I can barely remember anything from Hebrew school anymore, and it's annoying me."

Spending time with Ethan was dragging up memories of singing B'yachad at summer camp and the candle lighting at her bat mitzvah and the sweet, crisp taste of apples dipped in honey playing across her tongue. She just wanted to remember—so that she could then promptly go back to forgetting, of course.

She couldn't lay claim to a lot of rituals or traditions, but these bright, precious moments kept flashing in her brain. Naomi had grown up in a predominantly Catholic neighborhood in Boston where Jewishness made her an outlier. She'd never forget the first day of sixth grade, standing at her new locker and hearing Carter Wentworth mutter "dirty Jew" under his breath. Her whole face had gone red, assuming he was calling her a name, but when she looked up, she realized he was talking to his uncooperative backpack. He was using the phrase to name something annoying, something that pissed him off. She'd stared at him, shock freezing her.

"What? Are you Jewish or something?" he'd said when he caught her looking. Naomi would never forget shaking her head and running away, hoping people didn't find out. Even thinking of the memory now made her feel sick.

Sturm was a Jewish last name, but not as obviously as some others. It was easy enough to keep her family's religion under the radar, but even when she was a kid, her cowardice had filled her with shame. She'd make excuses every time she missed school for a holiday they didn't get off because closings were built around the Christian calendar. Would slump down in her chair, just a little, when her history teacher talked about the Holocaust and Elie Wiesel. Her guilt gave her stomachaches.

So yeah, she'd been ashamed, but not enough. The terrible truth was, it had been easier not to be outwardly Jewish. Easier to fit in with the girls on the soccer team who did Secret Santa. Just like it was easier, now, not to have a crush on a rabbi.

"I usually listen to podcasts on my commute anyway," Naomi said, knowing she'd been quiet for too long. "This isn't that different. It's like any other subject. I'm just trying to learn. I have a lot of questions."

"You know," Clara started, "if you have questions about Jewish stuff, I can think of someone you could to ask."

"No," Naomi said, putting extra emphasis on the word.

"I'm sure Rabbi Cohen would be happy to—"

"I don't want Ethan to know about this. Not that this"—she gestured at the speaker—"is even a thing. But he'd get the wrong idea. He'd think I was only doing it to impress him or to somehow fit in."

"Neither of those things is a crime, you know," Clara said gently.

"I don't try to impress anyone, and I certainly don't lobby for membership to groups that don't want me." Her life, her identity was built around a code. She couldn't break it now.

Clara turned off the podcast. "Wanting to belong is normal. There are lots of places, lots of people, that make you work for it."

"You don't understand." Everywhere made Naomi work for it. Every academic institution she wanted to work for wanted her to jump through hoops. Every reporter interviewing her wanted Naomi to fulfill their stereotypes.

Clara reached over and squeezed Naomi's free hand. "Okay, but I want to."

"My mom's a Quaker," Naomi said, barely believing she was going into this whole thing.

"Oh."

"I don't know how much you know about Judaism . . ."

"Not a lot, honestly," Clara said.

"Well, Reform Judaism considers a child of an interfaith couple to be Jewish if one parent is Jewish. So in my case, because my dad's Jewish, and because I was raised Jewish, Reform Judaism allows that I'm a Jew."

"Allows," Clara repeated.

"Exactly. I received a Jewish education and had a bat mitzvah and everything, and it's not like every time you show up at shul someone asks, 'Oh, by the way, is your mom Jewish?' but it still always made me feel like kind of an outsider."

Clara nodded in understanding. "And you already feel like an outsider in a lot of other ways."

"Yeah." There was the understatement of the year. "I grew up uneasy in my faith, knowing that for many Jews, I don't even qualify as a member of my own marginalization. Then you add on the fact that society consistently erases and undermines bisexuality . . ."

How many times had she been told to "pick a lane" or "stop making excuses to be slutty"? That one was always extra charming for its added misogyny.

". . . Then you add in the whole sex worker thing"—people loved that—"and the sum of all my parts, my entire identity, becomes either invalid or unwelcome. It's . . . it just gets exhausting."

Constantly having to justify herself, to fight for who she was. Facing endless rejection or reproach. "I'm tired."

Clara squeezed her hand one more time and then gave it back, as if she knew Naomi wouldn't tolerate any coddling, any apologies or advice.

"I can continue exploring my connection to Judaism without Ethan. He's not the sole source of religious knowledge." If anything, it seemed like his religious interpretation was outside the norm. "You should hear him talk about God and faith, Clara. It's different. Or at least it feels different to me. The reverence in his voice. It's not just about following rules or practicing traditions for him. It's like he's discovering the secrets of the universe or something. He lives and breathes Judaism. And if he found out about my mom, I'm sure it wouldn't change the way he sees me, but . . ."

"But what if it did?" Clara finished. "I get it. The coffee shop is up here on the left. And hey, I promise not to mention your crush or your religious reeducation. But . . . for what it's worth, I think at some point you should."

Naomi sighed. No one had given her advice in ages, and now here she was, getting lessons in bravery from a socialite. Either she'd truly gone soft, or Clara had grown a skin thick enough that Naomi's admittedly empty threats could no longer penetrate it. Both ideas were terrifying.

Naomi pulled into a parking space but kept the doors locked. "Just stick to PR in there. Please."

Clara leaned over and kissed her cheek before opening her door and hopping out.

"You got it. My lips are sealed. Strictly shop talk. All business, all the time."

"Stop issuing platitudes," Naomi commanded as she shut her own door.

Rusty aches inside her stirred, angry at being disturbed. She put the odds of this encounter not ending in disaster at slim to none.

Chapter Eight

···

IT HAD TAKEN Naomi less than forty-eight hours to deploy her plan to subvert the board.

"Sorry for the delay," she'd said when she'd called to arrange a meeting between Ethan and her friend Clara at a Silverlake coffee shop. If this was slow, he was terrified to see what full speed looked like.

The two women, a study in contrasts, were already seated at a small corner table when he arrived. Naomi wore sharp, straight lines and a lipstick that turned her mouth into a stop sign. Clara, on the other hand, had on a white dress and matching smile.

"Ethan, this is Clara, one of my business partners. She used to work in PR, and now she oversees publicity for Shameless," Naomi said in a droll tone. Then, shifting her gaze to Clara, she continued, "She's going to be extremely professional during this meeting and not stray from the lane of her very specific expertise."

"It's nice to meet you," Ethan said, shaking her hand and pretending he hadn't noticed any tension between the two of them. "I really appreciate your help."

"Oh, it's my pleasure." Clara gave Naomi's arm a little squeeze. "It's a treat to meet the man Naomi can't stop talking about."

Ethan's grin froze on his face until Naomi cleared her throat loudly.

"I'm going to grab us all drinks," she announced. "Ethan, what would you like?"

"A green tea, please." Naomi nodded and set off for the counter without asking for Clara's order. Either she knew it already, or her friend wasn't getting a beverage.

"So," Clara said, opening the notebook resting on the table. "Can you run me through the challenges your synagogue is facing?"

"Oh. Sure." Ethan took his seat. "Well, when I became the rabbi a little over a year ago, the congregation was losing members at a steady rate of twenty percent or so every year. Since I've been with Beth Elohim, we've slowed the leak, but I haven't been able to turn things around completely using traditional tactics like promoting our Intro to Judaism course in local ads."

"I see." Clara jotted down some notes. "And I'm guessing you've got aggressive recruitment targets?"

"*Aggressive* is putting it mildly." The synagogue was bleeding money. "The executive board has strongly suggested that if I can't show significant increases in membership in the next six months, they're going to start looking for prospective buyers." Ethan didn't mention that his recent altercation with Jonathan had probably moved that date up considerably.

Clara nodded. "And you figured the biggest opportunity comes from people who are currently unaffiliated versus trying to poach?"

"Yes. One, I wouldn't feel right trying to steal members from another synagogue in the city, but two, I'd lose. We don't have anywhere near the kind of resources Endmore Boulevard can tap into, for example." He'd grown up going to that synagogue. They had incredible facilities and membership in the thousands. If he was lucky and worked his ass off, Beth Elohim might get there in ten to twenty years.

"Going after nonaffiliated Jews is an uphill battle but, I'm pretty sure, our only shot," Ethan continued. "Synagogues all over the country are struggling to appeal to younger members, but ours has an especially tough time because our current congregation skews toward the other end of the spectrum. I figured I'd need to change our offering to appeal to people under the age of sixty, so I went looking for innovative educators and met Naomi."

"Drastic times call for drastic measures." The woman in question set down three drinks—Ethan's tea and two iced coffees—before passing one of the latter to Clara with a very pointed look of warning.

"Well." Clara leaned forward to take a sip. "I must say the two of you make quite the pair. What was it you used to teach, Ethan? Chemistry?"

"Physics," he corrected, while Naomi sat with her arms crossed and her back to the wall, surveying the entire coffee shop like Tony Soprano and refusing to rise to what he suspected was bait from her friend.

"Ah yes. That's right." Clara let out a little hum around her straw. "Well, I certainly think we can do some press outreach. If you don't mind me saying," she told Ethan, "you've got human-interest piece written all over you."

Naomi grunted into her beverage while Ethan covered his embarrassment with his cup.

"You know." Clara tapped her pen against the table while she considered. "I think that's where I'll start. Pitching profiles and interviews. *LA Mag*'s preparing their list of hottest bachelors. You are single, aren't you?"

"Clara," Naomi said sharply.

"What?" Clara raised a shoulder, the picture of innocence. "I'm just asking so I know how to frame the narrative."

Naomi gripped her coffee so hard her knuckles went white. "Focus on the synagogue and the seminar series."

Ethan had spent most of his life surrounded by powerful women, but Naomi and Clara might be the most intimidating pair he'd ever encountered. This was due, largely, to the fact that they seemed to be conducting a silent, private conversation right in front of him. It was like watching a high-stakes tennis match conducted primarily through eyebrow raises and mouth twitches.

He wasn't going to be the one to suggest it, but they'd likely make a killing as a team of con artists.

"Oh, fine." Clara flipped over to a clean page in her notebook. "What type of promotion have you done for the series so far?"

Ethan shifted in his seat. "Well, I sent an email to our synagogue's discussion list and posted the events on our website, as well as reaching out to some local Hillel groups at UCLA and USC." It wasn't much, but between his normal duties and all the new programming he'd added, marketing was so far down on his overflowing to-do list, it was a miracle he'd accomplished that much.

Clara circled something in her notebook. "So, you haven't contacted any members of the media?"

He peeled the cardboard holder off his cup. "No. Not yet. You think we should?"

Naomi bristled. "I might not have the same lurid appeal as I used to—opening an LLC will do that to a girl—but I'm pretty sure the idea of partnership between a sex worker and a rabbi is worth at least page six."

Ethan took a big swallow of his tea. Hearing her lay it all out was . . . a lot. He stood by Naomi and their work completely, but he wasn't naive enough to think the Internet would give them the benefit of the doubt.

"You're nervous about what the board will say if this gains too much attention," Naomi said, trying to read his face.

That wasn't even half of it. Mostly, he didn't want anyone to punish Naomi for teaching for him the way they had at every other institution she'd approached. But he guessed the last thing she'd want to hear was that he wanted to protect her.

"The board is uneasy about our partnership and this new type of programming, but they also recognize how imperative it is that we appeal to a wider community. I've already made the gamble on these events. Promoting them is just doubling down."

Naomi leaned forward, directing the full force of her gaze at him. "You don't sound sure."

He tried to match the intensity of her tone, the fire that made her cheekbones pop as she pursed her lips.

"I'm sure."

Only Naomi would demand complete transparency from everyone else while simultaneously giving nothing away.

Ever since he'd met her, he'd worked to slowly chip away at her armor, only to find it all back in place the second they were in public. This slide back down the hill to friendship was probably an effective deterrent more often than not, but Ethan was a scientist and a rabbi. His life was oriented around asking better questions, not expecting easy answers.

Still, he was sweating in the hot seat. "I'm going to get a glass of water. Anyone need anything?" Ethan stood up abruptly, eager to escape the lingering moment of tension at the table. His foot knocked against the table leg, sending Naomi's iced coffee splashing against her chest.

She jumped back, dripping, a huge stain blossoming along her formerly white top.

He closed his eyes.

It was one thing when his clumsiness ruined his own clothes, but quite another for it to spread to Naomi's wardrobe. "I'm so sorry. Let me get some napkins."

If only his buddies from college who had accused him of womanizing could see him now. He was about as smooth as a cactus. He grabbed handfuls of napkins out of one of those torturous holders specifically designed to keep paper captive.

By the time he made it back to the table, Naomi was nowhere to be found.

"She popped into the bathroom to clean up," Clara said in a gentle voice that told him his embarrassment showed on his face.

Ethan rubbed his temples. He had a headache forming.

"I feel terrible." He was already so far out of his depth with Naomi. This was the last thing he needed.

"Don't." Clara assured him. "It was an accident. Besides, this is L.A. Every woman worth her salt has at least four spare outfits in her car at any given moment. She'll be fine."

Ethan wasn't so sure. There was no reason for Naomi to give him second chances. "I'm already so deep in her debt, and each time I see her the ledger goes down. At this rate, I'll never be able to break even."

Clara grabbed the napkins from him and mopped up the table. "Everyone feels like that with Naomi at some point, which is exactly the way she likes it. She's like a craggy, wounded old war general."

Ethan paused his own cleanup efforts.

Clara's mouth curved. "Okay. Not on the outside, obviously. But emotionally. She's lived in survival mode so long, she doesn't know how to turn it off. It's like she's constantly scanning herself for weakness. Trying to weed it out with her bare hands. Naomi's powers of reason are so strong, they're dangerous. She can justify any action in the name of self-preservation."

Ethan collected her wet napkins and deposited them in a nearby trash can.

"You seem to know a lot about her."

"Yeah. Well. I'm one of the few people she lets love her."

Envy bloomed, unbidden, in Ethan's chest. He shoved a thumb behind his back toward the counter. "I should probably order her another coffee before she gets back. To replace the one I spilled."

He placed his order with the barista only to find Clara standing behind him.

"She's single at the moment, you know."

"Oh. Um. Cool? I mean, good. Or not good, but neutral. Fine." *Stop talking.*

"You should ask her out," Clara said, followed by another bright smile.

"I'm sure she wouldn't be interested in getting involved with someone like me. She knows she's too good by half. I can barely keep up with her professionally. There's no way I could hold her attention romantically." He handed over a few bills to pay for the coffee.

Behind him, Clara crossed her arms. "What makes you think that?"

"Come on." He took the drink off the counter. "We both know the idea of Naomi Grant and me dating is ridiculous." Whether he wanted it to or not, his job would place unwelcome demands on whoever he got involved with. Even after only a few weeks, Ethan could see that no one made Naomi do anything she didn't want to.

"What did I miss?" Ethan turned to find Naomi standing behind him holding her ruined shirt, wearing nothing underneath her blazer. A single button secured at the navel held the sides together. His heart climbed into his throat as he admired the curve of her breast before dragging his gaze away.

Without missing a beat, Clara piped up. "Nothing much. I was just telling Ethan that I'll send out the first press push today."

He hoped, foolishly, that Naomi hadn't overheard his last comment to Clara. Even if she agreed that the idea of romance between the two of them was absurd, he liked it better when they both pretended that all their toothless flirting could lead somewhere.

"Is that for me?" Naomi took the beverage from Ethan's slack grip and slid back into her chair, seemingly oblivious to the fact that no one in the entire shop, Ethan very much included, could take their eyes off her.

If he survived the rest of this seminar, it would be a miracle.

Chapter Nine

....

MODERN INTIMACY—LECTURE 2:
You only get one chance to make a bad first impression

WHATEVER PRESS RELEASES Clara sent out following their coffee date worked, because just four days after bringing her onboard, turnout had more than doubled for their second seminar. Naomi appreciated the broader audience, the peppering of gray hair and crow's feet mixing among the sunburned shoulders of eager-eyed college students filling the chairs in the JCC classroom.

Like Shameless, these discussions of modern intimacy worked better when they included an array of experiences. Being single wasn't reserved for the young and hot.

"Today we're going to talk about first dates," Naomi said. A few people nodded. An eager guy in the second row set the audio recorder on his cell phone. "Specifically, we're going to talk about how you should stop viewing them like job interviews—hiding your weaknesses and overplaying your strengths—and start treating them like games of chicken."

That earned her a few eyebrow raises.

"Look, your time is valuable, and presumably so is the other person's, so just cut to the chase. Tell him you're high maintenance and let him rise to the occasion. Fill her in on your crippling self-loathing, but, and here's the important part"—she held up her index finger—"only if you're taking steps to address it."

A hand went into the air, a guy with a tattooed sleeve full of different kinds of pizza. "What if you're broke?"

"Definitely tell your date that you're broke. They're going to find out sooner or later. Do you have any idea how much time and energy it takes to fake being rich?" Over the last twelve years in L.A., she'd seen plenty of people try it. She shook her head at the image. "Pass."

Another guy, with a delicate jaw and a crop-top with Dolly Parton on it, caught her eye. "What if you're a virgin?"

"You don't have to tell someone your sexual history on a first date, or ever, if you don't want to. That's your business. In my experience, having sex—even lots of sex—doesn't make anyone a better or more qualified partner, and a person who deserves you will know that."

Naomi didn't hide her sexual history from anyone she dated, but she also definitely didn't think they were entitled to the information. Still, she wanted to make sure this guy, and everyone here, knew they could give themselves permission to bring it up on their terms.

She chewed her lip for a moment, considering.

"If it's something you're nervous about, and you want to share it with the person you're seeing, you absolutely can bring it up in a casual, 'hey, let's skip the part where we ask about each other's siblings, and talk about things that might actually affect whether we want to see each other again after tonight' kinda way."

Dolly Parton Shirt nodded gratefully, and Naomi's heart melted. This feeling, tiny liberations and radical transparency, this was why she'd wanted so badly to teach in person. So she could see people's faces when they shed their shame. It was amazing that one look of hesitant confidence could cancel out so many years of disapproval and distrust.

Naomi swallowed an unwelcome swell of emotion. "Okay, who else wants ceremonial permission to air their dirty laundry on a first date?"

Every hand went into the air, including Ethan's. Something suspiciously like butterflies took flight in her stomach when he returned her *Really?* look with a grin.

"Okay," she said, to him and the room both, "let's do this."

After a few more shouted-out confessions, the seminar conversation quickly melded into a blend of commiserations, recommendations, and catharsis.

The more comfortable the audience grew, the more Naomi realized she didn't need her prepared notes to fill an hour-and-a-half session with lecturing. She just needed to present a hard-won but still admittedly imperfect theory or two about the syllabus-dictated dating milestone and then hold space for people to process and respond. No one would ever be a dating expert. It was too variable a subject for that kind of intellectual hierarchy.

But Naomi figured she could be a sort of conductor for discourse. She relished the chance to use techniques she'd learned for her psych degree, teasing out truths from amid the cyclone of hope and insecurity that permeated the room.

Even more, she appreciated the distraction from Ethan and his soft-looking cardigan. The more buttoned-up he dressed, the more she wanted to unravel him. Her attraction was messy and wild and . . . unwelcome. He'd made it perfectly clear to Clara that he didn't want anything unprofessional to do with her. That the very idea was beyond comprehension.

Naomi was handling it about as well as could be expected, which was to say not at all. Her best bet at this point seemed to be avoiding him. That wasn't so hard, really. What was once a week in a classroom full of people? She could get through the next month and a half with minimal non-electronic interaction.

She had basically unlimited access to sex toys and a buffet of hot, sexually experienced friends. Naomi hardly qualified as hard up. And if something deep in her chest protested, well, too fucking bad. She'd taken this job to help *other people* get lucky.

When the alarm on Ethan's phone—changed to sound like an old-fashioned school bell—rang, signaling the end of their time together, she found herself reluctant to end the night.

"Okay, this week we are focusing on putting ourselves out there both emotionally and also literally," she said as a close to the session. "We're doing a little experiment. I want you to arrange for at least one first date before we meet again. Two if you're feeling well-rested." She waved away a few groans.

"Ask out your butcher. He looks great out of that bloody smock. Take him for coffee or a cocktail. Something you can cap at an hour if need be. None of us are sitting out the unofficial lab portion of this course, okay?"

Naomi gathered her things as people started heading for the exit. If she was quick enough, she might get out of there before Ethan and his blue eyes decided to ask her about her day. His consistent, genuine concern for her was hard to shake. A woman could get used to that sort of treatment, if she didn't watch herself.

When they'd arrived in the parking lot at the same time earlier that evening, he'd noticed one of her tires was low and gotten down on his knees, in fucking slacks, to inspect it. The man had zero regard for his clothing.

She shoved her phone into her bag and tried to make a break for the door. If she was lucky, she and her wimpy tire would make it out of there in one piece.

"Ms. Grant?" A blonde Naomi recognized from the first lecture stopped in front of her. She wore a green dress under her jean jacket and the same *Feminist Killjoy* pin. At close range, Naomi noticed she had pale pink streaks running through her highlights. She shivered as goose bumps broke out on her arms. This blond woman reminded her of someone, though she couldn't decide who.

"Hey." Ethan made his way toward them. Shit. "You can call me Naomi. What's your name?"

"Molly." She shifted her purse higher on her shoulder. "Barnett."

"Nice to meet you, Molly." Naomi tried to commit the name to memory. Maybe she could order name tags off Amazon. Actually, she was sure Clara probably had some on hand at the office and was breathlessly waiting for the chance to pull them out.

"What can I do for you?"

"I just wanted to say thanks." Molly tucked her hair behind her ear. "It's refreshing to hear someone talk about dating like you do. Like it's not a nightmare to be endured, but like it could be fun."

"I'm a big advocate of having as much fun as possible," Naomi said as Ethan joined them at the front of the room.

"Hi there." He grinned at them both.

"Oh. Hi, Rabbi Cohen." Molly's cheeks tinted to match her rosy hair.

Naomi could hardly blame her. He had a pleased glow about him at the moment that made Naomi want to suck the goodness right out of him.

"Hey. Molly, right?" He pushed his hair off his face. "You're president of the Hillel association at UCLA?"

"That's right."

"Are you enjoying the course?" Ethan gave Naomi a little nod. "I'm learning a lot myself."

Fuck, she was going to have to rush the door.

"I am," Molly said, apparently less affected by his extremely inconvenient good looks. "But . . . I've got kind of a problem, and I was speaking to a few of the other participants here, and they said the same thing. It's just . . . well, you said to try going out on a first date this week, but . . . where do you meet people? To date, I mean. I basically go from work to the gym to the grocery store. And I have to tell you, there are not as many eligible hotties shopping for produce as romantic comedies led me to believe."

Naomi frowned. She remembered being Molly's age, which she estimated as around twenty-three, but she'd been performing at that point. Even before she moved in with Josh, she'd mostly dated her co-stars. But she probably shouldn't mention looking for eligible partners at work. That kind of pairing had a tendency to implode, one way or another.

"You don't go to parties or anything?"

"Not really," Molly said. "I find the whole loud-music, tons-of-people thing kind of exhausting."

"Well, what about all the apps or whatever?" Naomi didn't have much personal experience with them outside of her friends reporting random people for using her pictures to catfish, but she knew they were pretty ubiquitous.

"I do have some of the apps, but it's rough out there. I'm a Minnesota eight, which makes me like a solid five in L.A."

"No way," Naomi said, protesting in earnest. "You're gorgeous." In a weirdly familiar way.

Molly ducked her head. "All the same, I think I'd do better if I could meet people in person. You know, show off my sparkling personality," she said with a sarcastic hair flip.

Suddenly Naomi knew who Molly reminded her of.

Hannah Sturm. Her younger self. Before she'd tasted betrayal. Before she'd remade herself into something gleaming and sharp. Back when wanting to belong, wanting to be loved, hadn't felt like a capital crime.

Ethan leaned forward. He had the same wide-eyed eagerness he'd worn at the teaching conference. His *I've got an idea* face, Naomi supposed.

"Are you saying you'd like a more intimate environment to meet eligible partners?"

Molly nodded. "Yeah, exactly. Like, should I sign up for woodworking classes or take up bartending or something?"

Ethan rubbed his hand through his beard. "Well, the synagogue could certainly organize some type of singles mixer."

"Would Naomi be in charge?" For the first time, Molly looked unsure. "No offense, Rabbi Cohen. I just feel like she'd make it cool."

Naomi folded her lips together. She really didn't have the extra time to add another synagogue-sponsored event to her social roster. Besides, spending time with Ethan made her goofy and giggly in a way that she didn't trust. It was too much like crushes she'd gotten before she knew what they could cost.

At the same time, she appreciated Molly's vote of confidence. She tried to think of a way to let the girl down gently, but Ethan was already there, smoothing things over, making them easy.

"I'm not sure we could impose any further on Naomi's time. But hey, I promise that I will try to make it cool. Give me a chance?"

Naomi and Molly both looked at the elbow patches on his sweater and frowned.

"Come on," he said. "I've got ideas."

The weak smile he wore made Naomi want to spend hours corrupting him. No. Days.

"Might as well let him try," she told Molly. "It can't be that bad."

Chapter Ten

....

ETHAN COHEN WAS an embarrassment to his people. Matchmakers
had held an honorable position in the Jewish community since the ear-
liest days of their faith. Some of the most illustrious rabbis had once
made their living as shadchonim. Ethan was literally supposed to be
doing "God's work" right now. Instead he was avoiding his imminent
failure by drinking a beer.

Any way you sliced it, his first singles mixer was a spectacular dud.
Unfortunately, he had no one to blame but himself.

The bar he'd selected, a new pseudo-dive (the furniture looked like
something from his grandparents' garage, but cocktails cost twelve dollars), should have provided at least an adequate backdrop for this exercise. Google reviews had labeled the place "trendy, in the sense that they
have tried very hard to look like they're not trying at all."

Despite the ambiance, turnout was . . . less than desirable. Only five
people had shown up. Including Morey, who at least had on a spectacular pair of suspenders. Ethan gave him a blithe smile across the room
and tried not to throw up.

Okay, so he should have asked for Clara's help with recruitment. Or at least asked Naomi to ask Clara for her help. But his pride wouldn't let him accept any more of their generosity.

Lots of synagogues hosted singles meetups. There was no reason his should flop like this. The board had hired him because, in theory, he knew how to attract young people—due to the fact that he was a young person himself.

The few people who'd shown up from the lectures attempted stilted conversation in the corner, drinks sweating in their hands as they waited for the event that he'd told them was running "just a little bit behind."

He swallowed his guilt along with another bitter sip of lager.

After Molly's request at the second lecture, he'd hastily thrown together some plans for Wednesday night. Speed dating had seemed like a brilliant idea. Easy. Structured. Low stakes. But nothing about tonight was going according to plan.

With the current number of participants, he'd have to extend the planned five-minute blocks with each single into half an hour each. Also, he currently had an odd number of people signed up to take part.

The writing was on the wall. He would have to call the whole thing off.

Ethan took a healthy swig for courage and pushed himself off the bar stool he'd chosen as his designated sulking station. Then the last person he expected to see walked into the room. He stood very still as Naomi Grant surveyed the sorry scene in front of her. When her eyes caught on his, he didn't pause to examine whether his face heated out of pleasure, embarrassment, or both.

"I wasn't expecting to see you tonight," he told her when she made her way over. Now that he'd had a few moments to drink in the sight of her, Ethan decided he'd prefer she hadn't arrived to witness his humiliation.

Naomi gestured to the empty bar. "What's going on? Molly sent me an email saying the mixer started at seven."

He experienced a flash of annoyance that Molly had doubted his event-planning skills enough to slip Naomi a warning, but since she'd obviously been right, he let it go almost as quickly as it had come.

"Things are off to a bit of a slow start. This was supposed to be speed dating, but I don't have enough people to make pairs." He spoke without opening his mouth much, trying not to raise the alarm with the few stragglers they had managed to attract.

"Oh. Well . . ." She checked the anxious attendees over her shoulder. "I'll just sit in." Naomi smiled at him in a way that was surely lethal in large doses.

"You'll . . . oh." Ethan fought to control the way his mouth wanted to slip into an O. "You're going to . . ."

The idea of her and Morey making small talk had short-circuited his brain.

"Are you all right?" Naomi's glib expression did nothing to hide her amusement at his mental implosion.

"Yes." He covered his mouth with his hand and cleared his throat. "I didn't realize you might want to participate."

"I hadn't planned on it." She lowered her eyes for a moment, which was fortunate, because he needed to catch his breath, and he wasn't sure he could have managed it still pinned in her gaze.

"I got out of a meeting early and thought I'd check in on things, but it's not exactly a hardship. Besides"—she nodded with her chin—"the one standing closest to the door is kind of cute."

Ethan tracked the direction she indicated. Emma Klein was cute . . . Oh.

"Do you normally . . . with women?" That pause was incriminating. "I mean, is that your preference when it comes to dating?" He'd heard she used to date her male co-star. And obviously he'd been entertaining delusions that she might consider dating him. "Or um . . . do you . . . ?" Wow, he really had no idea how to ask her if she was bisexual or pansexual, and probably—no definitely—it was none of his business. He closed his mouth with a snap.

Naomi tipped her head back to study him.

"Rabbi Cohen, you're blushing."

That was the least of his problems. Her eyes were alarmingly green. Ethan was pretty sure points were falling off his IQ as he stood looking at her.

"I'm sorry. It was rude to inquire like that. I shouldn't have said anything."

"I'm not sure you did say anything." Naomi wrinkled her forehead. "I date people of all genders, if that's what you were trying to suss out."

"Right. Of course. Good for you." He threw up both hands. That hadn't come out right. "Not that it wouldn't be good if you didn't. Any kind of dating you choose to enjoy is fine by me. Though obviously you don't need my permission." Thank goodness there was a fire extinguisher in here, because he was absolutely going to have to set himself ablaze. He let the daydream that they'd actually been flirting die a quick death.

Naomi seemed to be enjoying herself. "Your eye is twitching."

"I'll just go splash some water on my face," he said, already halfway across the room.

"Good idea," she called after him.

He'd never behaved like this around anyone before, tongue-tied and fumble-footed. He forced himself to look back at her.

"Will you be okay on your own for a moment?" He realized it was a stupid question immediately after the words passed his lips. Ethan just really wanted her to only ever have good things happen to her.

"Yes." She practically glowed in her amusement. "Pretty sure I can manage."

At least things couldn't get any worse.

Or so he assumed, until the door swung open and suddenly the mixer had seven participants.

Ethan groaned. *You've gotta be kidding me.*

"Sorry I'm late," Leah said, rushing over and giving him a quick peck on the cheek. "What are you doing?"

"I didn't realize you were coming." He tried to use his eyebrows to convey that he wanted her to leave. Immediately.

"Are you kidding?" She punched him none too gently on the arm. "I wouldn't miss the chance to support my big brother and find true love."

Evidently, Ethan's eyebrows were not as expressive as he'd hoped. Naomi approached.

"Everything okay?" Naomi glanced at the clock over her shoulder. "The group's getting antsy. We should probably get started."

Before Ethan could intercede, Leah was thrusting her hand toward Naomi's. "Hi, I'm Leah. Ethan's sister. It's so nice to meet you. I'm a platinum Shameless subscriber."

"Oh. Wow. Thank you." Naomi glanced between the two of them.

They didn't look that much alike. Though they both took after his dad, short with dark hair, Leah favored their mom's family with more of a heart-shaped face.

"It's my pleasure. Literally." Leah raised her eyebrows lasciviously.

This event was rapidly turning into a nightmare.

"Leah, would you go tell those people clustered in front of the door that we're about to begin, please?" The excuse to get rid of her was flimsy, but he wanted to put as much distance between Naomi and the person who had witnessed his awkward adolescence as possible.

"Sure. I can do that." Leah turned so Naomi couldn't see her and mouthed *Get it!* at him before making her way to the meager refreshments table, where everyone else had congregated.

Ethan longed for an aspirin.

"Well, guess we're back to odd numbers," Naomi said.

"Oh, shoot. Sorry." His shoulders relaxed a little now that Naomi wouldn't have to participate.

"Wait, actually"—she snapped her fingers—"why don't we both try? It'll help round out the small group, and we'll get better data about the attendees and the model firsthand. That way we can see if we need to tweak it for next time."

"I'm not sure that's the best idea," Ethan said, which, he credited himself, was nicer than his initial reaction of *Are you nuts?* He had to admit, though, the scientist in him had perked up at her quick-thinking proposal for collecting data.

"Why not?" Naomi raised a bare shoulder.

Ethan tried not to think about kissing said shoulder.

"You said you're single."

"I'm not dressed for the occasion," he said, blindly groping for an out. The truth was, he didn't date, especially not potential members of his congregation. It wouldn't be appropriate.

To be fair, if he'd known he was going to be roped into participating, he would have changed into something more casual. He was wearing his work clothes. Dress pants and a button-down and leather shoes with tassels.

Not that a T-shirt would have made this situation any less anxiety-inducing, but still. The majority of the participants were under thirty and wearing street clothes. In comparison, he looked like someone's dad.

"I'm sure no one wants to sit across from—"

"From a hot, smart, compassionate, eligible man. Oh, no, you're right. What a burden." She rolled her eyes at him. "Relax. No one's asking you to get married." Naomi reached out and straightened his collar, her fingertips barely brushing the back of his neck. "This is supposed to be fun, remember?"

The interaction lasted only a few seconds, but Ethan still found himself breathless.

"I can't in good conscience speed-date my sister," he said, voice slightly strangled.

Naomi's mouth curled into something dangerous. "Even I'm not that kinky."

Ethan worried she could see his heartbeat through his clothes.

"I'll make sure the Cohens don't end up on opposite sides of the same table, okay? You can issue a broad disclaimer about your lack of eligibility to everyone else. Come on. All you need is something to grease the wheels a bit, you know."

"Right. That's a good idea." He could handle that much.

"What's your go-to question on a first date?"

"My . . . ? I'm not sure I have . . ." Ethan hadn't dated in years. Mostly because he'd been busy with study and service, but also because he wasn't ready to settle down, and the nature of his position made any attempts at dating feel, at least to him, inherently serious.

"Come on. Everyone has a conversational standby. Even rabbis."

He ran his thumb across his forehead. "I suppose I'd ask someone what matters to them. Why they get out of bed in the morning?"

Naomi pursed her lips. "Most people ask about jobs or hometowns."

"Sorry. I don't have to use it if you think it's weird."

"No. I like it." She nodded decisively. "So, why do you get out of bed in the morning?"

Something about the intensity of her voice when she asked pulled the truth out of him.

"There's a moment, when you're speaking to someone, and you're listening to something they said, or actually"—it didn't even require conversation—"maybe not, maybe you're just giving them your attention, holding a door open at the deli, and something shifts behind their eyes and you know that they feel seen."

He lowered his chin, feeling goofy. "Not just seen but acknowledged in some way. They know they matter. That they're not alone. And when that happens, I think about all the times someone has done that for me. The way that interaction saved me, shored me up against a thousand invisible aches I didn't realize I was carrying."

Naomi's face gave nothing away when he met her eyes.

"It's, uh . . . why I always come back to that Einstein quote I told you about. I guess I get out of bed because I think about the connection that we all have, this fragile humanity, each of us insignificant and at the same time precious. A continuation of a species that is recklessly unique. I remember that life is a finite gift, and I'd be an asshole to waste it."

"Holy shit," she finally said, more breath than words.

"Sorry for saying 'asshole.'" His mouth twisted. "Twice."

"Trust me, I'm not offended. Are you always so—"

"Verbose? Yes."

"I was gonna say optimistic."

Ethan could focus on nothing but the fact that her perfume smelled like wood smoke and cinnamon. He couldn't stop his next question. "Why do *you* get out of bed in the morning?"

She blinked. "Easy. Because the world is cruel and unrelenting, full of pain and injustice."

Ethan's brows drew together. "That sounds more like a reason to stay home."

"You didn't let me finish." He hadn't expected her to be so playful when he met her. It was sort of ruinous, how much he liked it when she teased him.

"The world is cruel and unrelenting, full of pain and injustice," she said again, leaning just slightly toward him, "and I am a stick of dynamite."

Ethan's breath caught in his chest, but she wasn't done.

"Sometimes ineffectual, other times unnecessarily destructive, but, on occasion, enough to at least temporarily disrupt the rhythm of the patriarchal abyss threatening to suck down everything I care about and hold it hostage."

"Wow." He meant *wow* in its original sense: in awe, astonishment.

She laughed. "Too much for a first date?"

"Not the *right* one," he said without thinking.

Her lips parted. The sudden urge to run his thumb across the skin there made his next inhale harsh.

"We should go. Leah's gathered everyone. Come on, America's Most Eligible Rabbi."

"I really shouldn't," he said, but followed her reluctantly. "It's too complicated."

"Complicated isn't always a bad thing." She grabbed his hand and dragged him toward the tables he'd had set up in the back with a sign that said *Beth Elohim Singles Mixer.*

"Naomi," he said as she continued to pull him along. "There's a certain level of expectation and attention that would be placed on anyone I went out with."

She glanced back at him, her eyes more serious than they'd been all night. "I know."

Once they got to the tables where their hodgepodge of participants sat wearily, Naomi called for attention.

Everything in Ethan was screaming that giving anyone the slightest illusion he might be looking to mingle was a recipe for disaster.

But she was already in motion, and he knew there was no stopping her.

"Hi, everyone, and welcome to our first speed-dating session. We know this format can be awkward, but I see you've already availed yourselves of the bar. Wise. Feel free to continue to apply social lubricant as necessary."

The nervous cluster of singles laughed mildly. Ethan smothered how much he liked the idea of Naomi referring to herself and him as a *we*. She waved for him to continue the intro.

Oh, right. This had been his idea.

"Tonight's going to be simple," he said. "We'll rotate clockwise from seat to seat at, let's say, fifteen-minute intervals. I know fifteen minutes probably seems like forever right now, but I promise it'll go quickly. I'll give a one-minute warning toward the end of each date, in which you're free to exchange contact info if you mutually agree you'd like to stay in touch. Even if there's no romantic connection, hopefully you'll meet some people tonight who can become potential friends or even business partners."

"Smooth," Leah said.

He glared at her until Naomi gently prodded him to an empty seat.

"Anything I should know about your sister going in?" Great, the only other open spot was across from his traitorous kin.

"She's a pathological liar."

Naomi squeezed his shoulder before walking away. He felt the contact across his whole body.

"In that case," she said, walking backward, "I'll make sure that any childhood anecdotes are backed up with photographic evidence."

So this is what it feels like to swallow a live frog.

Ethan was pretty sure God wasn't cruel enough to let Naomi fall in love with his sister.

Mercifully, the rest of the night went better than he'd imagined. The volume of the conversation rose steadily as people got into the groove of the rotations. Ethan enjoyed getting to know the seminar participants one-on-one. Each time a burst of laughter cut through the room, something inside him lit up like fireworks.

He found himself watching Naomi, how she effortlessly kept them all moving while still managing to make the person sitting across from her bloom.

It was obvious now that the connection he felt with her was one-sided. She made everyone feel special. He'd been grasping at conversational straws trying to turn their professional engagement into something more personal. He supposed years of celibacy would do that to a man.

The last rotation brought the two of them face to face.

"So," he began, "What do you think?"

"Not bad for our first try. Obviously we need to advertise more if we want to increase the turnout, but"—she nodded over his shoulder until he turned to find Molly and a man in a plaid button-down—

"I wouldn't be surprised if we didn't get at least one second date out of this group."

Ethan breathed a sigh of relief that Molly had found someone she liked. "I didn't realize how rusty I was at the whole dating thing."

"This barely qualifies. It's a glorified screening process. All you need is a good opening line."

He tilted his head. "Wait. You never told me your go-to opening."

"I'd tell you, but"—she ducked her head for a moment, almost shy in a way he'd never seen—"I can't risk you falling in love with me."

Her tone was light enough, but Ethan had a feeling she was issuing a friendly warning. Of course she would notice how her presence affected him, how much he obviously liked her.

He cleared his throat and tried to pretend he wasn't stung. "No, we wouldn't want that."

"Although . . ."

Ethan snapped his gaze back to meet hers. When it came to her, his heart was quick to call back hope.

"You might be immune."

Was she kidding? He was the opposite of immune. He was so sick with infatuation, he was probably spreading it to everyone else in the room by sheer proximity.

In that moment, it was hard to reason why he shouldn't just ask her out. They were both adults. There were no rules against it. If she said no, he'd of course back off immediately, but something in her eyes every time she looked at him made him think that maybe she wouldn't say no. Maybe he'd get more than fifteen minutes to impress her. More than fifteen minutes to drink in the way her hair curled against the nape of her neck. Was he really such a coward that he wouldn't even risk going to bat?

"Hey." He heard how low his voice had pitched. "Would you ever—" An incessant chirping started coming from his back pocket. So loud and unexpected that they both jumped.

"Sorry." He took it out to silence it, but when he did, over ten messages flashed angrily from the home screen.

Rabbi Cohen, since you're dating now, I've taken the liberty of calling my daughter Marissa, who lives in San Clemente.

Didn't realize you were on the market again. Call me.

Why are you lying to your mother? Rebecca Feinstein says you've already been out with five women.

What in the world?

Naomi raised an eyebrow. The moment was officially dead. "Everything okay?"

"Uh . . . I don't know. Somehow the whole synagogue is under the impression that I'm dating now . . ." When he thought about the types of PR that could help this cause, this definitely wasn't on the list. His email lit up with badges; his voice mail clogged before his eyes. This wasn't just his congregation. This was every eligible Jewish woman in the greater Los Angeles area, or at least their mothers.

"This is insane." He'd known that the congregation felt entitled to know a certain amount about his private life, but this level of siege at the exact moment it seemed like he might be interested in a relationship was unreal.

Naomi leaned forward to check out his phone.

"Well, the good news is, looks like we might not have to advertise the next mixer that much after all."

....

THOSE WHO CAN'T do, teach, and those who can't date, get other people laid.

By the time Naomi finally bellied up to the bar, Ethan had worked himself into a state. The bartender tried to console him with a plate of mozzarella sticks on the house before moving to bring Naomi another club soda with lime.

While Ethan pulled at the cheese sticks forlornly, Naomi dug out her phone, flipping through texts and emails she'd missed over the last few hours. She hadn't meant to stay so late.

A name in her inbox caught her eye, and she hovered her thumb over it for a few seconds before clicking it open.

"Oh, you've gotta be kidding me." Naomi slid some cash out of her wallet for the bartender.

Ethan lowered his snack. "What's up?"

After handing the bartender a big tip, she turned to him. "The new administration at my old high school has invited me back to speak on the future of sex education."

He blinked at her, his absurdly long lashes working overtime. "Is that bad?"

Yeah. She hated that school and everyone in it. They'd completely abandoned her when she'd needed them. Not that Ethan would understand that. She downed half her soda, wincing at the sourness of the lime.

Before she had time to think of a plausible lie, a man in shorts with lobsters printed on them approached, depositing an empty glass close enough to her elbow that the condensation brushed her arm.

He squinted at her for a long moment. "Hey, I know you."

His breath informed her it was far from his first drink.

"You're that porn star."

Oh great. Just what her night needed: a drunk asshole.

Ethan stiffened beside her.

She raised her shoulder an inch. "Which one?"

Guys like this didn't respond to a firm *Get lost*. That only riled them up. Any sign of politeness was interpreted as invitation. Holding up a mirror was the only thing that ever worked. Smooth and slippery and hard. Giving nothing away. Simply reflecting each of his comments back at him.

"The one who used to get railed by Josh Darling." The guy laughed, his mouth hanging open so she could see the red of his throat. "Damn. You're fine as hell," he slurred. "Where you been all my life, sweetheart?"

Sensing Ethan shifting behind her, Naomi pressed her foot backward until her heel aligned with his instep. It was a subtle cue to stand still, but effective nonetheless.

She really didn't have time for this. Her plans for the rest of the evening involved stewing in old rage and writing a scathing retort to that invitation.

Naomi shook out her hair. Her new drunk admirer followed the shiny locks like a cat following a laser pointer. "Why don't you buy me a drink?"

The guy looked eagerly toward where the bartender was breaking ice.

"At the bar four blocks down," Naomi clarified.

It took a moment for the guy to puzzle out that he was being dismissed, but once he did, he didn't like it.

"I've got a better idea." His entire mouthful of teeth was on display in a slimy smile. "Why don't you show me your tits?"

"Hey," Ethan said, sharp and loud.

This time Naomi had to curl her hand around his wrist to keep him from stepping forward. Lobster Shorts wasn't worth a confrontation. He was just another man in a long line of men who expected her to respond to their degrading come-ons like they were Hallmark Valentines.

The amount of time she spent batting them away was overwhelmingly tedious. Both she and Ethan had better things to do.

Naomi moved her club soda to the other side of her body. With the way this guy was swaying, she didn't want to risk it.

She kept her hand on Ethan and dialed up her charm. No way in hell was she letting this dude ruin her night.

"Well, when you put it that way, I—"

But the guy was tired of waiting. "Come on. Don't be a bitch. Everyone's already seen them." The sound of his voice, the vicious twist of his mouth into a sneer—it all hit, dead center, against a barely scabbed wound.

Naomi hadn't realized until that moment that she'd left herself open. That in order to organize all these conversations about love and intimacy and religion, she'd had to poke holes in the shield of her apathy. She'd had to believe the words she delivered in her lectures. Had to invite hope and all the danger that came with it.

Now, those same holes were expanding without her permission, blasted open by a comment that should have been innocuous, and water was rushing in. Up to her knees, her elbows, her collarbones, her mouth. Each second that he stood there, smirking at her, was a death sentence.

The memory hit her so hard, she staggered against the bar.

Naomi had been propositioned and catcalled and leered at so many times since then. But you never forget your first time.

She was back in the hallways of Jackson High School. It was that stupid fucking email, hitting her like kryptonite when she was already down. The straps of her backpack dug into her shoulders as Clint Marshall from her calc class showed her naked pictures she'd sent to her boyfriend on his cell phone, asking for a glimpse of the real thing. "Come on, Hannah. Everyone's already seen them."

She tried to pull in air, but it wouldn't come. Each breath was a battle. *No. No. No.*

Just like in high school, the urge to cry burned the back of her throat. She forced it down, tasting bile. No matter how hard she tried to slam the door on the memory, she couldn't. Her therapist's voice rang in her ears. "This is trauma," she'd said the first time Naomi had recounted the memory.

He was still talking, this guy in the bar. His eyes vicious and wild with intoxication.

"Come on, slut. How much for a quick peek?"

"That's enough," Ethan said, breaking the hold she had on his wrist and stepping between her and the guy. "You need to leave. Now."

Her arms were cold even though the bar was sweltering. She wanted to sit down or run away. Wanted both, but her legs wouldn't listen. All her clever retorts died on her tongue.

Her harasser looked down his nose at Ethan and broke out in a wild grin. "Is that a challenge?"

"It's a promise," Ethan said, so quiet Naomi wasn't sure she hadn't imagined it.

Then he whistled through his teeth until the bartender scurried over.

Ethan flicked his gaze toward Naomi, whose legs were now threatening full mutiny. The bartender nodded minutely, obviously picking up on the charged air.

"Let's go," Ethan said to Lobster Shorts, walking toward the exit without looking back.

The guy returned his focus to Naomi for a moment, obviously deliberating between targets. But even through an alcoholic stupor, he must have been able to see that the fight had gone out of her. It wasn't as much fun without resistance. He followed Ethan.

As soon as he was out the door, Naomi let herself drop to a bar stool. The bartender pulled out a bowl of pretzels and dropped them in front of her. "I'm sorry," he said. "I have no idea where that guy came from." He poured her a fizzing Coke. "The sugar helps."

Naomi downed most of the drink in a few gulps, her hand shaking around the cold glass. Around her, the mixer kept running, people too preoccupied to notice her meltdown.

Thank God.

Naomi shoved pretzels into her mouth and chewed mechanically.

They tasted like cardboard. She hadn't lost control like that in years. And never so publicly.

How could she have let this happen? A single email? A run-of-the-mill drunk guy?

She shook her head. And in front of Ethan.

Oh shit. Ethan.

She pushed herself to her feet and hustled out the door.

Chapter Eleven

ETHAN HAD NEVER been in a fight. He'd never even thrown a punch. One time when he was in ninth grade, his sister had taken his signed first edition of *The Amazing Adventures of Kavalier & Clay* and buried it in the backyard. A terrible betrayal.

He'd written her a strongly worded letter.

A cocktail of anger and adrenaline ran through his body, making his heartbeat thunderous and his hands ball into fists. He hadn't been planning to fight the guy when he was harassing Naomi in the bar, at least not consciously.

Just imagining the way she had gone pale and started to shake made Ethan almost dizzy with distress. All he'd been able to think about was getting her harasser away from her. Even if it meant literally throwing his body between her and the person causing her pain. Whether dormant alpha instincts or simple stupidity, his actions had led him here.

To a poorly lit, crowded Venice sidewalk with a frat guy bouncing side to side in a bad Rocky impression.

"Come on, pussy. You wanted to defend the honor of your slut girlfriend. Let's go."

It wasn't hard to see that Ethan had made a mistake. Or rather that he'd underestimated the consequences of his actions.

This drunk frat guy with his blond hair sweat-slicked to his forehead knew it. The pedestrians on the sidewalk who gave them a wide berth knew it. The bouncer at the bar a few doors down, sitting on a wooden stool with his arms folded giving Ethan a *Not my problem, buddy* look, knew it too.

Frat guy clearly wanted blood. He was cracking his knuckles and rolling his beefy neck and probably imagining the vibrant red color of Ethan's blood as it poured from his nose.

Out of pure survival instinct, Ethan tried to call up any self-defense techniques he knew.

The only advice that came to mind was a scene from *Miss Congeniality*.

He let out a burst of semihysterical laughter.

If he survived the next fifteen minutes, it might very well be thanks to Sandra Bullock teaching the audience her S-I-N-G self-defense mechanism. Solar plexus. Instep. Nose. Groin.

This guy was a disaster. Not fit to breathe the same air as Naomi. But still, even as anger roiled in his gut, Ethan didn't want to fight. What he wanted to do was recommend counseling and hand the man a pamphlet on drinking responsibly.

Ethan wasn't even sure he was morally allowed to punch this guy. Rabbis were supposed to set an example for their congregations.

On the one hand, Moses had struck down an Egyptian he found beating a Hebrew slave in Exodus. But on the other, Proverbs 16:32. *Slowness to anger is better than a mighty person, and the ruler of his spirit than the conqueror of a city.*

Considering the relative level of injustice at hand, Ethan should probably try to settle this altercation without violence.

"Come on, dude. Throw 'em up," his companion said before spitting on the sidewalk, presumably in some kind of display of machismo. "Let's do this." He seemed reluctant to throw the first punch. Though it seemed a safe bet that Lobster Shorts was not reviewing various religious resources to settle a philosophical debate on whether he could beat the crap out of Ethan.

"What if we didn't?" Ethan said, using the kind of soft, gentle voice he practiced when comforting children. "This whole ritual of aggression is sort of barbaric, right? Surely a man with crustaceans on his clothing can see that?"

Lobster Shorts frowned in the general direction of his fly.

It was possible the phrase *ritual of aggression* had gone over his head.

"Look." Ethan decided to try again. "You're drunk and belligerent. I can't say whether it's because you don't respect women in general, or if it's because you think sex workers opt in to harassment by virtue of their profession. In either case, let me assure you that you're very much mistaken. It would be easiest on both of us if you could acknowledge fault and take a cab home, where you will ideally reflect on your actions and consider methods of penance, but I do realize that's reaching."

"Reach for this, asswipe." The guy cupped his own crotch in vulgar suggestion.

"Seriously?" Ethan shook his head. "How old are you? Even if we assume that you don't regret your actions, which I must stress is extremely disappointing, is laying me out really worth assault charges?"

"What?" For the first time, frat guy lowered his fists. "Are you, like, gonna call the cops or something?"

At last, a translation that had found purchase.

"I imagine I might find it difficult to personally make the call if you remain intent on rearranging my face, but I have to assume that one of those nice people"—he waved at a cluster of rubbernecking diners on the patio across the street—"might do me a favor and alert the appropriate authorities, once they've gotten the show they came for, of course."

Frat guy wiped his brow and grimaced at the onlookers before lowering his voice.

"I don't really want this going on, like, my record or whatever. I'm applying for jobs right now."

"Ah, I see." Ethan smacked his head in an exaggerated pantomime of enlightenment. He figured adding illustrative hand gestures couldn't hurt. "Once those recruiters see *convicted felon* on your résumé, they're hardly going to be able to recommend you. Bet that cab's sounding better and better, huh?"

With furrowed brows, frat guy seemed to be weighing the bodily demands of an abundance of testosterone versus his career aspirations. "I don't know. Maybe."

Ethan could work with *maybe*. "She's an incredible person, by the way, that woman in there."

It might be a stretch to get this guy to recognize Naomi as a human being, but it was worth trying.

"Are you serious, man? That chick? There's videos of her fucking all over the Internet. I don't get why she's acting all high and mighty about keeping covered up now."

Ben Zoma was really testing Ethan at the moment. He groped for a metaphor to get this jerk to see that he'd actually done something wrong.

"Okay, let's say you saw Bruce Willis on the street, would you ask him to walk over broken glass barefoot for your entertainment?"

"No . . ."

"Why not? He did it in *Die Hard*."

"'Cause that would be insane," Lobster Shorts said, crossing his arms petulantly.

"Right. Because what a performer chooses to do on film doesn't commit them to a lifetime of reenactment on demand for strangers."

Frat guy kicked his toe across the pavement. "I guess not."

That was probably the closest Ethan was gonna get.

"I'm going back inside now. Don't forget about the cab."

"Hey, wait a second."

He slowed his footsteps. Was this guy actually grateful to have been shown the error of his ways?

"Just tell me one thing. What's her pussy taste like?"

Ethan dragged his fingers across his face and stared accusingly toward the heavens. Some men really were hopeless.

"Okay. So this is happening, I guess." Ethan cocked his fist. *Thumb on the outside. Weight on your back foot.*

The next thing Ethan knew, he was on the ground, a searing pain across the left side of his face. Through the pulsing agony, he appreciated the bitter irony. Okay, so God didn't want him to throw any punches.

He pushed up to his elbows with difficulty. "Well, you're never gonna get that job in finance now."

His assailant's fists closing around his collar, lifting him into the air, though unwelcome, were not entirely surprising.

"Hey, asshole," someone called from the door of the bar. While he considered turning to look at the person whose sentiment he very much shared, keeping his eyes on the man attacking him seemed more prudent.

Whoever was speaking surprised the guy enough that he lost his grip on Ethan's collar, sending him splaying back against the pavement ass-first with enough force that his teeth rattled. His tailbone screamed in protest, but it was arguably better than getting hit in the face again.

Tilting his chin to survey his savior, Ethan blinked to find Naomi launching an elbow at his assailant's nose. The crunch of bone meeting cartilage announced she'd met her intended target.

"Bitch," the guy yelled through a handful of blood.

Apparently, that was the breaking point for the bouncer across the street. He made his way over slowly.

"Time to go, pal."

"She hit me!"

"No," the bouncer said as he escorted him away, "I'm pretty sure you fell."

Ethan tried to get to his feet and stumbled. His eye throbbed.

"Easy, cowboy." Naomi knelt down and placed both hands gingerly on his jaw, tilting it to inspect the damage to his face. "Oh yeah. You're gonna have a gorgeous shiner in about six hours."

"Did you hit that guy?" It seemed entirely possible that Ethan had imagined the last five minutes.

"Trust me, he needed it." She released his face, and he registered the loss.

"Are you okay?" He'd seen the way her eyes had gone haunted back in the bar. She looked better now, flushed and alert, but the sight of her shattered wasn't one he'd soon forget.

She rolled her shoulders and dropped his gaze.

"Why wouldn't I be?"

He didn't know how to tell her that even now, despite her bravery, her hands were shaking.

"If you want to leave, I'm more than happy to close out with the bar."

Naomi shook her head and fed him a smile, offering him a hand and pulling him to his feet. "What I want to do is buy you a shot of tequila and get some ice on that eye."

"Naomi . . ." He imagined it was hard to look disapproving with only one eye open, but he attempted it.

"Stuff like this happens to me all the time, Ethan," she said, weariness written across her entire body.

He squeezed her hand gently. "Don't pretend it's okay. Not on my account."

For the first time tonight, he noticed there were dark circles under her eyes. Faint, as if she'd tried to cover them with makeup. He had a stupid urge to run his thumb across the thin skin there, try to smooth them away.

"It sucks." Her voice hardened from water to ice. "But I've got a short recovery time."

Aggressive was the last word anyone would use to describe Ethan, but still he'd known a moment when he'd craved nothing more than to knock out that guy's teeth and hand them to her.

"I tried to reason with him," he said, half leaning on her as they made their way to the bar.

She reached up again to press two fingers to the tender skin around his eye. The touch was featherlight and bittersweet with the promise of pain.

"No wonder he hit you."

Ethan wiped his watering eye on the bottom of his T-shirt. "I should have known you didn't need me to defend your honor."

She stopped under the neon sign heralding the bar's name, its pink light dappling her red hair. "I didn't mind as much as you might think."

As they walked in, she looked back at the bar, where earlier the sounds of music and laughter had confirmed their success this evening. It was quiet now.

"If you want to talk about it . . ."

"Tequila first." Naomi bodily deposited him on a bar stool and then whistled for the bartender. "Two double shots of Herradura and a bag of your finest ice, please."

Movies never lingered on the aftermath of getting punched. Turned out that was because it sucked.

When the bartender handed over her requests, she took Ethan's palm in hers and pressed the ice into it. "Keep this on until your face goes numb or the ice melts, whichever comes first."

Ethan followed her instructions and pressed the ice to his cheek. The bag was at once soothing and awkward. She lined up the shot glasses in front of him.

"Both?"

Naomi nodded, her mouth pressed into a grim line. "That eye's really starting to swell."

The smell wafting off the tequila burned the insides of Ethan's nose. "I'm not much of a drinker."

He tipped back the shots one after the other. Alcohol blazed a path from his tongue to his stomach. He tried clearing his throat, but the movement sent a shooting pain across the left side of his face, so the sound died halfway out of his mouth.

"Don't worry," she said. "I'll make sure you get home safe, Rabbi Cohen."

Chapter Twelve

....

"OH NO." ETHAN laid his head back against Naomi's passenger seat. "I think I might be a little drunk."

She waited until they reached a stoplight to look over at him. His eyes were half-lidded, and the smile that stretched his mouth was definitely fueled by tequila. Whoops.

A better woman would have apologized. Apparently that fifth shot had been overkill. Back at the bar, shame and guilt had threatened to choke her. Watching the bruise on his face bloom in real time, she would have done anything to make the pain go away. Since she couldn't mount him in the middle of the bar, liquor was the less volatile option at her disposal.

Besides, Naomi liked this version of Ethan, loose and flushed. She liked time alone with him in the dark privacy of her tiny car, close enough to reach out and touch.

Not that she was going to touch him. Naomi had a strict no-groping policy. But the idea of running her hand down the inner seam of his jeans? The idea that he might want her to? Ooh, that fantasy was as delicious as it was dangerous.

"How are you feeling? Want me to lower the window?" He wasn't the only one at risk of becoming overheated.

"I feel good," Ethan said, his words lilting together slightly. He moaned as a bump caused the injured part of his face to thwack against the headrest. "That's probably bad, huh?"

"Not bad so much as the aspirin doing its job," she corrected, lowering the window just in case.

Ethan closed his eyes against the night air whipping his hair. "I love Los Angeles."

Naomi couldn't imagine why at the moment. This part of the freeway was hardly scenic. Traffic was moving, but the roads were clogged, even though it was past midnight on a weekday. Classic.

"Everyone hates the freeway, but it's sort of magical, isn't it?"

"Define *magical*." All Naomi perceived was smog and impatience as far as the eye could see.

"All those lights"—he pointed unnecessarily—"coming and going, each one a person with a whole world inside their head. People don't think about that enough. How everyone we pass on the street has just as much complexity, just as many aspirations and fear and failures, as we do." He brought his fingers up to his face and winced. "Maybe if they did, I'd get punched less."

"Should I be recording this for your next sermon?" Even three sheets to the wind, he found ways to be poetic. Despicable.

"Sorry," Ethan said, eyes drooping. "I told you I couldn't hold my alcohol."

"You sure did." Naomi batted away another wave of guilt. "Here, drink some more water." She handed him a plastic bottle from her cup holder.

"I usually drink the grape juice on Shabbat." Ethan guzzled the drink.

"Hard to resist grape juice." Especially when it tasted better than most kosher wine anyway.

He'd tilted his head to an almost perpendicular angle on his neck.

"How are you so beautiful?"

Pleasure shot through her spine. She liked the way he said *beautiful*, like it was powerful instead of just aesthetically pleasing.

She took the water back before he managed to drown himself. "I didn't realize you were a chatty drunk."

"Everything about you is . . . more," he continued, obviously not deterred by her attempted deflection. "You're like . . . da Vinci."

"Now that is a new one." Just when she thought she'd heard every line in the book . . .

"No. Listen." He pushed himself up from where he'd gradually slumped down in the seat. "You're exactly the person you were born to be, and you're not even afraid of it. Do you know how hard that is? How rare?"

"I think I've got an idea." Sometimes it felt like it took all her energy just to keep her body from flying in a million directions at once.

Naomi had received a lot of compliments in her life, but never one that acknowledged the work she'd done on herself. How hard she tried to be a good person. The way she strived, even when it was exhausting, which was most of the time. She lowered her own window a crack, out of necessity. It figured that in a lifetime of compliments, the best one she'd ever received came from someone who could never make good on it.

"I'm sorry that man hurt you tonight," Ethan said, his tone stony and quiet.

She knew he wasn't fishing for her story, the reason she'd lost her composure. Her past, especially that past, belonged to Hannah, and she hardly ever gave it up. But . . .

Maybe it was because he was drunk, or because he'd taken a punch for her earlier tonight. Maybe it was because he was a rabbi, and lots of people dropped their problems in his lap. Maybe it was because he'd just compared her to one of the most brilliant artists who'd ever lived. In any case, telling him didn't seem like the worst idea she'd ever had.

"Normally, I can let that stuff roll off my back. Occupational hazard, you know?"

"I hate that." His jaw snapped on the word *hate*, turning the sound into the way the emotion felt.

"I try to anticipate people being terrible," she said. "So I won't be caught unaware again."

Ethan tipped his head back. Naomi could feel his gaze on her, sweet and inquisitive.

"Again?"

She swallowed around her tongue. No matter how much time had passed, it was still hard to let the words out.

"When I was eighteen, my boyfriend shared naked pictures I'd sent him with my entire high school. He was pissed I didn't want to sleep with him." Sleep with him again, actually. He'd convinced her to try it once. Whether it was the guy or the timing or just starting to discover she was queer, she hadn't been ready to continue.

"Naomi, I'm so sorry. What a horrible betrayal of your trust and privacy."

He had a good voice for sympathy, smooth and warm and rich.

She let it wrap around her. Wished she could keep it.

"Yeah. It was awful," she said, the word only a little hollow. "Everyone turned on me. My friends, my teachers, they all looked at me like I'd done the bad thing. Like I'd offended them by making myself vulnerable." The email on her phone had felt like it weighed down her pocket. "That was the first time that I realized my body could be both desirable and disgusting to people at the same time. That those two emotions could twist inside a person, mixed with their own shame, and turn venomous." She couldn't even count the number of times she'd been told she should have known better.

"But in the end, I wouldn't take any of it back. That moment is pretty much the catalyst for my whole career. I wanted to prove that being naked, being sexual, didn't make you less valuable, less worthy of respect. In my quest to redeem Hannah Sturm—that's my given name—I became Naomi Grant. Sex work let me save myself. Let me regain my power."

"Do you ever miss who you were before, miss being Hannah?"

She drove for a while. Long enough that when she did speak, it startled him.

"I didn't know who I was back then. It's hard to miss the potential of a person. I may be a coldhearted bitch now, but I like the life I've built. Maybe if I'd stayed Hannah, stayed in Boston, gone to veterinary school like I planned, my quiet life out of the public eye would be depressing and awful."

"I don't think there's as much difference between the time Before Naomi and After as you think there is."

She shrugged. It didn't matter anyway. There was no going back.

"Being exploited changed my life."

"You can change but still be the same," he said, the words thick on his tongue from the tequila.

She knew what he was trying to say, but where was the breaking point? The threshold where identity fissured? Some experiences must shock the system on a molecular level.

She should ask Ethan. He was a physicist. He would know. But she was tired of talking about herself. Tired of dragging up old wounds. She'd given enough time and energy to the past tonight. To men who had behaved badly. Neither deserved any more of her breath.

"This is my exit," Ethan said, granting her the favor of changing the subject.

Naomi caught another angle of his face when she turned, and sucked in a sharp breath through her teeth. "Fuck. Does that eye feel as bad as it looks?"

Ethan squinted into the side mirror. "No. Not yet."

"Don't worry. The ladies will love it."

"Oh no." He squirmed in his seat, groaning. "Not the ladies, please."

Naomi took a bit of perverse pleasure in his discomfort. "Oh, come on. I heard Rabbi Cohen was finally thinking about finding a Mrs. Rabbi."

"Stop. Ahh." He wrinkled his nose. "You sound like my mother."

Welp. Guess compliment time was over.

"She keeps having her assistant email me write-ups of every eligible Jewish woman in Hollywood. And also some who I'm pretty sure are married."

"Not above adultery?"

"I asked God not to smite her just yet."

Naomi turned her head so he wouldn't see her smile.

"Sometimes I think she forgets that I don't work for her," Ethan said, not mad but not fully joking either.

"She's a boss bitch?" Naomi's dad was a welder and her mom was a nurse. They both worked extremely hard, but neither of them had much appetite for management. Her career was sort of a black box for them. They weren't disapproving, at least not to her face, but they didn't exactly engage with her day-to-day responsibilities.

"Oh," he said. "Yeah." He dropped his eyes to his lap. "Have you heard of Crowne Artists' Agency?"

Naomi let out a huff of laughter. "Uh, yeah."

Everyone in L.A. had heard of Crowne. They were the cream of the crop, repping the town's entire A-list. Models, actors, directors.

"My mother's the president of the agency."

"Your mother is . . . holy shit. Wait a second. Are you loaded?"

Ethan choked on a sip of water. Maybe there was a polite way to ask that question, but she didn't know it.

"My mother has a lot of money."

Such a rich-person response. She shook her head. What the fuck? Naomi fought to keep herself from pulling over on the shoulder of the freeway.

"If your mom is the president of Crowne, why isn't your synagogue full of celebrities? You don't need me and my singles mixers and seminars. All you need is one phone call—hell, I'm sure even an email would—"

"I don't want a community built on nepotism, and I certainly don't want to be the shepherd of an elite institution where people care more about who they're wearing than why they're praying."

Ah. She'd hit a nerve.

"I love my mother, and I'm extremely proud of what she's accomplished, but I chose a different path for a reason."

Well, Naomi had inadvertently found the fastest way to sober Ethan up.

"I respect that." And she did—well, she mostly did. His good intentions didn't change the fact that money and power were always resting at his fingertips. Connections mattered in L.A., arguably more than anywhere else. She felt even more out of sync with him than before. A former performer and a rabbi were an unlikely pair, but a former performer and a rabbi descended from Hollywood royalty were a nonstarter.

She'd been quiet too long, she realized. "Still, one date with Natalie Portman couldn't hurt."

"She's married!"

"Oh shit. Tell God not to smite me either."

He threw back his head and grinned at the roof of the car. "I'll put in a good word."

"Am I anywhere near your house?" She needed to get him and his smile out of here before she did something stupid. They'd been climbing these hills for at least ten minutes. It was gonna be a hell of a ride back down.

"Yes, sorry. Just a little farther," Ethan said, and then, "She's not my type, you know. Natalie."

That shouldn't have sent a pleasant flutter through her belly. And yet . . .

"Oh please. Natalie Portman is everyone's type."

"I'm up here on the left." Naomi slowed the car. The houses on this street were surprisingly normal, given his recent confession about his mom. Neat but small.

"I'd like to find someone who's strong where I'm weak."

Naomi wanted to stop talking about Ethan's dating preferences, but she couldn't stop fishing. Without tequila loosening his tongue, she knew he never would have told her so much about his personal life. Maybe she was a bitch for taking advantage, but there were worse things in the world.

"So, where exactly"—she looked him up and down—"are you weak?"

"How much time do you have?" He rubbed his hands on his thighs. "I take myself too seriously. I'm indecisive. I'm not good at saying no to people. I'm irredeemably clumsy."

I like that about you, she almost said but didn't. She coughed instead. "I think this is your house."

"Yeah." He unbuckled his seat belt but didn't rush to open the door. Naomi's heart took his lingering in all the wrong ways.

"Let me see that battle wound before you go."

She pressed the light above their heads on. The damage made her wince. Before she knew what she was doing, Naomi had leaned across the center console and taken his jaw in her hands, tilting his head slightly so she could survey the depth of the damage. The skin around his eye was red and swollen. His cheekbone held the dark promise of a bruise. Were men allowed to be so lovely?

"Bad?" At some point he'd closed his eyes. He was probably tired. Tired and sore and drunk. At least two-thirds her fault.

"You're going to have to come up with a good story," she confirmed.

"You don't think getting punched in the face by a drunk frat guy is a good story?" He smiled again. No one ever smiled at her this much.

"I don't trust you to tell it right." In actuality, tonight, Ethan stepping in to protect her, seeing him lying on the ground with his hand pressed to his face, still trying to lecture the man who had insulted her about respect, had been one of the most quietly heroic things she'd ever seen.

Oh shit. She was still holding his face, his beard softer than she'd expected against her fingertips. It would be so easy to pull him just a few inches closer. Stop his smiling with her lips.

"I'm good at advocating for others, but I don't always ask for what I want." Ethan didn't seem in a rush to reclaim his chin.

"Maybe you should practice," Naomi said, holding on even though it was stupid and ruinous.

Ethan was looking at her bottom lip. He was looking at her bottom lip and then up into her eyes and holy shit was Rabbi Ethan Cohen going to kiss her? And if he was, should she let him? And if she did, was that considered taking advantage of a drunk person?

He cleared his throat and slipped slowly out of her grip. "Will you help me find someone to date?"

Well. That was . . . not where she'd thought this conversation was going.

She killed the engine. If he wasn't gonna get out anytime soon, she might as well save gas.

"I thought you didn't want to date."

Even with the bright light on between them, she couldn't read his face.

"I think I just changed my mind."

Great. What fun timing.

"You hardly need me to act as matchmaker." Naomi fought hard to keep her voice from growing hostile.

"No, I think I do. I certainly don't want my mom doing it, and I saw you at the mixer tonight, making introductions, pairing people off. I trust your judgment in matters of romance way more than my own."

"It's not a good idea." She imagined shoving him, gently, out of the car so she could get the fuck away from this conversation, but he'd already been injured in the name of her ego once this evening.

Ethan frowned. "Because no one will have me?"

"Oh please." You know what, maybe she should find someone to occupy Ethan's attention. Then they could stop having these long, tension-filled moments where they stared at each other and panted.

Maybe if she saw another woman holding his hand, arranging his tallis, Naomi would remember that he was off-limits.

It was a lot to gamble. But that had never stopped her before. This infatuation with Ethan had gotten out of hand. She'd found herself admiring his collarbones through his shirt earlier.

"Why the sudden urge to date?" His timing was terrible. And she knew a lot about bad timing.

He dragged his hand over his face. He really did look wretched.

"All those people tonight, nervous and excited, dressed to impress. They reminded me that I miss the potential. The dizzy, light-headed feeling of falling for someone. The way you catch yourself thinking about them at all hours of the day and night. Finding excuses to spend time with them."

Naomi bit her tongue. Literally.

"I forgot that love is essential. That even in its absence, you occupy yourself with the lack of it."

Her therapist would tell her not to do this. That she was torturing herself.

"It might not be easy, finding someone," she warned him. Who in the world was good enough for Ethan?

He swallowed, and she watched his Adam's apple bob. "That's why I need your help."

Naomi licked her lips. She wanted to press her nose against his neck so much, she ached.

"I'll see what I can do. But don't get your hopes up."

He finally got out of her car, bending low, leaning in toward her, the open door letting in cold night air that met her heated cheeks. "I've had my hopes up since the day we met," he said, and then shut the door quietly.

Naomi watched him walk through his front door before she let her head drop onto the steering wheel. Apparently, she was the worst sort of fool, and to prove it, she'd find the woman of Ethan Cohen's dreams.

Chapter Thirteen

. . . .

THE MIRROR HANGING above his bathroom sink reported that
Ethan's black eye had taken up residence with relish. He couldn't tell
whether the throbbing in his head had resulted from getting punched
in the face, consuming too many tequila shots on an empty stomach, or
both. While the temptation to spend the morning in bed feeling sorry
for himself had been strong, he'd persuaded Leah to meet him at the
synagogue early to help clean out old boxes from one of the storage
closets, and good help was hard to find. After a hasty shower, a vigorous
teeth brushing, and a couple of aspirin, he was on his way.

"Holy shiner, Batman," Leah said, perched on the hood of her car
in the parking lot when he arrived.

Ethan tugged the baseball hat he'd thrown on lower. "Please tell me
one of those coffees is for me?"

"You're in luck, brother mine." She scooted off the hood, steaming
cups held aloft. "Looks like you need it."

He accepted the coffee and kissed the top of her head. Ethan was
short, but at least Leah would always be shorter.

"Whoa. Someone's extra grateful this morning. What'd you do?

Drop your cell phone on your face while reading in bed again?" Leah tried to grab his hat, but he dodged her.

"I don't wanna talk about it." Every time he thought about last night, he got nauseous, and it wasn't just because his skin was still sweating out Herradura.

"I'll bet. The board's gonna love waking up to the combined news that you're the first Jewish Bachelor and you ruined your face."

"I didn't ruin my—my face is not ru— I said I didn't wanna talk about it." Ethan brushed past her, achy and flustered, trying to cut her off before she could remind him again that he was going to have to explain his appearance to a board that was already on edge.

"Why not?" Leah trailed him as he unlocked the synagogue and led her toward the closet in question. "This is the most interesting you've been in a long time."

"I suppose you think that's a compliment?" He was pretty sure no one had opened this closet in a decade.

"Well, yeah." Leah leaned against the door frame. "First you hire Naomi Grant, then you decide to start speed dating—"

"I wasn't speed dating. I was evaluating the environment for optimization opportunities—" Ethan started hefting down boxes for Leah to sort.

"—then you get into a street brawl—"

"A street brawl?" Ethan whipped around to face her. "What am I, an extra in *West Side Story*?"

"*West Side Story*?! Wow, you are such a nerd."

Ethan shoved a box into her arms. "Let's start with three piles. Keep, donate, and trash."

"Sure thing, Marie Kondo," Leah said, setting down the box and pulling out masking tape and a Sharpie from her backpack.

Despite her abundance of sass, Leah worked harder than almost anyone he knew, and she always came prepared.

It only took five boxes and one giant spider sighting for Ethan to break.

"I did something dumb."

Leah looked up from her position, cross-legged on the ground surrounded by dusty mahzors.

"Shocking."

Ethan pinched the bridge of his nose without thinking, yelping as he aggravated the tender skin around his eye. "I did something because I thought it would make one thing better, but actually it made everything worse."

"Sorry. No information was disclosed in that sentence." Leah tilted her head as she ripped a new piece of tape. "Does this confession have something to do with you getting your ass kicked?"

He reached for his coffee cup only to find it empty. This day felt a thousand years long, and it wasn't even ten yet.

"If I tell you something, do you promise not to be a jerk about it?"

"How very dare you." Leah put a hand to her heart. "I have never been a jerk in my entire life."

At Ethan's eye roll, she relented.

"All right, yes, I promise. Sheesh. So delicate."

"I think I almost kissed someone."

Leah stared at him expectantly.

"Still relying on a lot of qualifiers and ambiguity." She waved for him to continue.

He sighed. "I think I almost kissed Naomi Grant."

"No way." Leah's shout reverberated across Ethan's aching eye socket.

"Why is that so hard to believe?"

"Because she's a five-foot-ten goddess and you're . . . you," Leah said slowly, as if this were very obvious.

"What happened to you not being a jerk?"

"I forgot." She picked up another High Holidays prayer book to label. "Look, I'm both listening and helping. A model sister, I'd say. Tell me about your almost-kiss."

He really needed to find other people to talk to about his romantic misadventures. But at the moment, Leah was his best and only option. If anyone not compelled to secrecy by blood found out about his interest in Naomi, the already rampant rumor mill would get completely out of hand.

Slumping down to join her on the floor, Ethan wiped his hands on his jeans.

"I think we almost kissed. I was kinda drunk, and I could only see out of one eye at the time, but I'm pretty sure."

Leah curled her lips together in a way that he knew meant she was holding back a laugh.

He flattened himself on his back like a pancake and groaned, not caring about all the dust they'd kicked up in the last half hour. "Why are you the worst?"

"I didn't do anything," Leah said, pseudo-innocent.

"You were thinking something uncharitable."

Leah rolled her eyes. "Please describe the circumstances that led up to the almost-kiss."

"You're making me feel so dumb right now." Ethan touched his wound and winced.

"Not sure I can take full credit for that one, bud." Leah tipped the rest of her coffee into his empty cup. A worthy peace offering. "Come on. Keep going."

Ethan sat up to drink. "Okay. So, our faces were really close together."

"Mm-hm."

"And she was looking up at me."

"Oh, wow," Leah said, displaying exaggerated interest.

"I hate you so much." Ethan was already embarrassed enough as it was. He was thirty-two. Way too old to be agonizing over a kiss that hadn't even happened. But somehow even an almost with Naomi was one of the most exciting and subsequently terrifying things that had ever happened to him.

"What? I'm invested."

"Ugh. Fine, whatever." They'd come this far. "Anyway, so yeah, I felt like she wanted me to kiss her, and I really wanted to kiss her, but then I thought, what if she doesn't actually want me to kiss her and then I do kiss her and then she hates it and never wants to see me again? Then I've failed the synagogue and offended the most incredible woman I've ever met."

Leah nodded slowly. "That is a lot of thinking."

Ethan let out a gusty sigh. "I know."

"So if you didn't kiss her, what did you do?"

Ethan closed his eyes, not wanting to risk Leah's reaction to his next confession. "I asked her to find me a girlfriend."

Leah was quiet so long he opened his eyes again to make sure she was still there.

"Wait. You . . ."

"Yeah."

"But that's . . ."

Ethan took off his hat and groaned into it. "I know."

"So now . . ."

"Right."

"Fuck," Leah said.

"What do I do?" Ethan couldn't believe he was asking his little sister for dating advice. The last twenty-four hours had been extremely humbling.

"Well." Leah stood up, shaking out her legs as if her feet had started to fall asleep. "I think to start, you should tell her you're an idiot. And please don't do it by using some story from Exodus. Please, please."

Ethan picked up a vibrant hand-stitched kippah from one of the boxes. Maybe he'd wear it for services. "Oh. You know, there actually is a story from Exodus that would provide a fitting simile."

"Noooooo." Leah flicked him on the arm.

"Okay, fine, I won't use any biblical stories." Unless he could find a subtle way to work one in . . .

Leah narrowed her gaze at him. "Don't use any, like, science equations either."

"Excuse me?"

She waved her hand in a circle. "Don't be like, 'When the mass of my affection encountered the catalyst of alcohol intoxication, the stimuli of our proximity caused a reaction in my—'" She stopped at the look on his face. "Get it, 'cause you love science? Aw, come on, that was funny."

"I'm gonna go talk to Morey about this."

"I forgot how high-strung you are." Leah offered him a hand and helped him to his feet. "This isn't complicated. Just tell her the truth. You got scared because she's extremely hot, and you didn't wanna mess up the relationship you have with her, but if she's open to it, you'd like to take her to dinner sometime."

Ethan stared at the ceiling. "That actually sounds reasonable."

"Ah yes. Well, I *am* the smart one. Everyone says so."

"Wait. Then which one am I?"

"Hmm." Leah tapped a finger against her mouth. "The hairy one?"

"When do you go back to Maui again?" Ethan started on the next row of boxes with a frown.

Leah tossed his cell phone on top of the box he was carrying. "Call her."

"Did you go through my stuff?" He changed his mind. Free labor wasn't worth it.

"Oh, relax, prom king."

He lowered the box carefully so his phone wouldn't slide off the top. "Even if I was going to call her, I'm not doing it now in front of you."

"Oh, okay. Yeah, that makes sense." Leah grabbed his cell while he was still holding the box.

He really needed one of those lock codes. "Don't—"

"Oops. It's ringing." She shoved the phone at his chest.

"Are you kidding me?" Ethan scrambled to check the number on the screen. Sure enough . . .

"Hello?"

"Uh, hi. This is Ethan." Of course Naomi knew that. They'd exchanged numbers. Ugh.

Leah covered her mouth and shook her head.

He mouthed something unbecoming of a rabbi at her.

"Hey there. How's your face?" Naomi's voice on the other end of the line was unusually light.

"It's okay." It definitely didn't hurt as much as his pride right now. *Just go for it. Rip off the Band-Aid.* "I was wondering if I could, um, speak to you after the next seminar."

"Oh." A long pause on the line. "Sure. I mean, do you wanna just talk now?"

"Er . . . no." Ethan scrambled for rationale. "I can't because I'm . . . on a boat."

"On a boat?"

Leah threw her arms in the air like he was a lost cause.

Ethan covered the mouthpiece of the phone. "You caused this. Help me."

To Naomi he said, "Yeah. Sorry. Gotta go, it's—um—blustery—but let's catch up Tuesday."

"Okay . . ." Naomi sounded skeptical. "See you then."

Hopefully she'd blame his odd behavior on his recent head injury. The whole I-have-feelings-for-you thing just didn't feel like it could happen over the phone.

"You're a mess," Leah said when he finally hung up.

Ethan shook his head. "I really am."

Chapter Fourteen

MODERN INTIMACY—LECTURE 3:
Let's talk about text, baby

ETHAN HAD NO idea there was so much subtext involved in texting.

Over the course of the last hour and a half, Naomi and the seminar participants had discussed the timing of messages sent and received—*For better or for worse, anything that comes in between the hours of 11:00 p.m. and 5:59 a.m. is a booty call.* Proper meme etiquette—*No, Jaime, listen, if you send him an objectively hilarious meme and all he says back is "lol nice" he's not trying hard enough.* The perils of screenshotting a message from a woman you'd gone on three dates with for peer analysis and then accidentally sending said screenshots, along with *She's joking, right? I can't tell*, to the aforementioned woman. *There's not much you can do but be honest. Just tell her you're into her and that all of your friends are going to make fun of you for at least a week when they hear about this. The bigger test is how she responds. If she makes you feel weird about it, that's a red flag.*

Ethan found himself both intrigued and slightly terrified by the potential make-or-break impact that texting held in modern courtship. He thumbed open his message thread with Naomi on his phone, but there was nothing flirty or even intriguing. Just stark, professional co-ordination. Ethan told himself he didn't mind.

"Okay, that's it for tonight." Naomi closed her notebook. "Thanks for coming, everyone. See you next week."

Ethan got to his feet but lingered against the back wall until most of the participants headed for the exit, chattering among themselves, a few lingering to exchange what looked like flirty banter.

Luckily, Clara had organized an online sign-up form for the remaining lectures (to collect email addresses for follow-up recruitment efforts). While the lectures did build on one another, each module could stand alone, so newcomers shouldn't have too much trouble joining in midseries. The email replies helped Ethan and Naomi anticipate a head count for the week. Thus, they'd moved to an auditorium instead of a classroom at the JCC when they'd received over seventy submissions for week three.

Naomi rose to the occasion of commanding the larger space, projecting her voice effortlessly and strolling the aisles as she spoke. While she made herself accessible, she retained an aloofness that made the audience crave her approval. In contrast, Ethan tried to create a relationship with his congregants in which they could forget to be formal with him. He tried to come across as someone who could as easily be a friend as a mentor or leader. But maybe that had contributed to the board not taking him as seriously as he'd hoped. Naomi's oratorical style was more fluid than his, flexing from authoritative to empathetic depending on the conversation. Perhaps he ought to take a leaf out of her book.

The impact of the seminars was slowly flowing to the synagogue. Turnout at services had started to pick up. Yesterday Ethan had taken a phone interview with a local reporter. The progress, though obviously welcome, also made him surprisingly nervous. Would he live up to the expectations of his new audiences? Would they accept the middle ground he occupied between traditional teachings and modern adaptation?

To add to his stress, the rumors about his "hunt for a wife" had only grown. He'd started getting calls from as far as the East Coast. Even tonight, a cluster of women lingered at the door, waiting to ambush him. The one in the center kept squinting up at him and then down at a picture clutched in her hand. A flash of the distinct cobalt blue of his favorite tallis told him it was his headshot from the synagogue website. Good grief.

He needed an exit strategy. Maybe if he could somehow signal distress to Naomi, she'd come rescue him?

At the front of the room, she bent her head, deep in conversation with one of a handful of people who'd lined up to speak to her. When she tossed her hair, laughing at something one of the guys said, a stab of envy hit Ethan in the gut.

Finally her line dwindled, and she looked up to find him loitering. She probably wished she could avoid this conversation after he'd made things so awkward on the phone. But Ethan had given himself a pep talk in the parking lot this afternoon, so one way or another, he was going to tell Naomi how he felt.

"Sorry," she said, making her way over to the brave women still waiting for him, "but you're going to have to exit the auditorium. Rabbi Cohen and I need to have an official debrief of tonight's lecture, and it's probably going to take a while." She pushed the door open with her hip and waved them cheerfully through. "I've been known to go all night."

"Get home safely," Ethan offered sheepishly. "Hope to see you next week."

The heavy door shut behind them with a loud slam, leaving him alone with Naomi in a very quiet room.

He joined her where she'd started wiping down the whiteboard, leaning against it for a moment before realizing he had pressed his sweater against the marker, then jumping back.

"So, about the other night," he said, too loudly.

She kept moving the eraser without turning to look at him. "What about it?"

"That thing I said in the car, about looking for a girlfriend?"

"Oh." Naomi stopped wiping for a moment, and he watched her spine go straight as a ruler. "Yeah."

"That was nonsense." Releasing the truth on an exhale, he breathed out relief.

Finally Naomi turned around. "It was?" Her words came out careful, giving him plenty of time to reconsider his excuse, but he didn't want to have this flimsy deception between them. He didn't want anything between them, if he was honest.

"Yeah. I was a little drunk, and perhaps vaguely concussed. I wasn't thinking clearly."

She put the bottle of cleaning spray down on the lectern as if it had suddenly become too heavy to hold. "So, you're not looking to date anyone, then?"

Did she sound relieved? He wished he could wipe the tension from her forehead. He shoved his hands in his pockets instead.

"It's not that I don't want to date, exactly. It's more that I don't want to impose upon you to find someone for me." Why was telling her how he felt so hard? Why couldn't he just say that he liked her?

She reached up and swept her hair off her neck into a knot, securing it with a band from her wrist. "I don't mind."

"You don't?" There was his answer, then.

If she had any romantic interest in him herself, surely she wouldn't volunteer so nonchalantly. He supposed this was for the best, her subtle dismissal. Obviously entering into a deeper relationship with Naomi would make continuing the seminar series more complicated.

Still, disappointment curled his shoulders toward his ears.

"Nope," Naomi repeated. "As you said, chemistry—even other people's—is one of my gifts." Her tone softened for the first time all night. "And besides, you deserve to find love."

Her emphasis on the word *you* caught him off guard.

"Doesn't everyone?" To have something to do with his hands, Ethan walked the aisles and collected stray pens and crumpled-up paper left on or under the seats.

"No," she said simply, resuming her task. "I keep a list."

"Of people who deserve love?" He should like the vicious side of her less, probably.

She shrugged. "Love is precious, right? Something coveted. Why shouldn't people have to earn it?"

He wanted to tell her love was inherent. That it existed in many intangible forms. That she could build love by extending it. But something in the twist of her mouth and the guarded curve of her jaw made him swallow the promises.

"Love is valued at an individual, societal, and evolutionary level, and certainly Judaism tells us to honor marriage, the most commonly held institution in love's name," he conceded instead. "But I think in the simplest terms, love makes surviving easier, and everyone deserves that."

Naomi flattened her mouth into a hard line. "Not everyone."

Her undercurrent of anger warned Ethan to tread carefully. He bent and made a little *Lost and Found* sign out of notebook paper and placed it with the pens on the lectern.

"Anyway," Naomi said after a long moment, picking her supplies back up and resuming cleaning. "Tell me what you're looking for in a partner."

"Now?" Ethan's insides twisted in alarm. He sank down into a seat in the front row.

"Now seems as good a time as any." She finished up her task and joined him.

Ethan racked his brain for adjectives Naomi might not immediately recognize as describing her. He settled for a trait she held but thought she masked.

"I'd like someone kind." He couldn't keep himself from adding, "Who knows themselves and what they want."

Naomi frowned. "*Kind* is too subjective to use as a filter for potential dates."

Ethan turned toward her. "What if we settled on a common definition?"

"You and me?" She gestured between them skeptically.

He nodded. "What if we define *kind* as someone who treats others with respect and tries to think the best of them?" Surely they could find common ground, in language if not in practice.

Naomi granted him a bitter smile. "I think the word you're looking for is *naive*."

A shot of pleasure ran through him. He liked when she was a little mean, could feel the affection underneath it. Sitting so close to her was a privilege, as ridiculous as it might sound. She was so often in motion when he saw her, splitting her attention in ten different directions. Juggling. Performing. Relative stillness made her appear deceptively docile, even as she remained fearsome to behold. Eyes flashing. Mouth too quick by half.

His wanting was so palpable, he could feel it in his throat.

"I've always found that shared values are more important than common interests," she said. "People bond over a love of football or classical music or whatever, but studies show that hobbies are a terrible indicator of long-term compatibility. We covered it my social psych courses."

"Who said anything about long-term?"

Naomi lowered her chin and gave him a look. "You're a rabbi in his thirties."

"So?"

"The rabbi part means you're responsible and you like taking care of people." She reached over absently and straightened his tie. Ethan hoped she couldn't detect the flurry of his heartbeat. "And the thirties part means you understand your biological imperative to breed."

He supposed he had signed up for this kind of analysis when he recruited her, albeit reluctantly, to find him a date. Still, he wished she hadn't said the word *breed*. He shifted in his seat against an inconvenient tightening in his pants.

"You asked for this," Naomi said, reminding him in the face of his discomfort.

"I had a feeling you'd already sized me up anyway," Ethan admitted.

"You're easier than most." Naomi's voice wasn't unkind. "You wear your emotions on your sleeve."

Well, he couldn't argue with that. Ethan had learned long ago that his feelings didn't care whether he found them at all convenient. They made themselves known. He might as well face them headfirst. Better than letting them take him out at the knees.

"Let's start with the basics." Naomi hopped up to write on the recently cleaned whiteboard. "You have to marry someone Jewish." She scrawled the imperative.

"It certainly makes it easier if the person is Jewish," Ethan acknowledged.

"Family-oriented." She kept writing as she spoke. "I saw you with Leah. You want someone who cares about keeping family close."

"I love Leah and my mom," he agreed, "and I spend as much time with them as I can, but *family* has a lot of definitions. I would never disqualify someone because they weren't close to their parents or siblings. Sometimes people don't have a choice."

Naomi pushed her hair out of her eyes. "What do you mean?"

"Well, my dad's dead." He'd said the words before, many times even, but always they felt as wrong in his mouth as they did in his head.

"Shit." Naomi took a step toward him and then, almost immediately, two steps back. "I mean, I'm sorry."

Ethan forced himself to smile, because she looked so worried, so serious, and he wanted her to relax. "It's okay," he said, and found that today it was closer to being true than the last time he'd said it.

She wrung her hands for a moment. "When did he die?"

"Six years ago. Cancer," Ethan said so she didn't have to ask the second question. Normally that was the end of the conversation. He might wear his emotions on his sleeve, but he didn't like to splash around in his grief.

"It was the worst thing that had ever happened to me." At the time, it had been the worst thing he could imagine. "My dad was my compass. The reason anything in the world made sense. And when he was gone, nothing mattered anymore. My teaching job didn't matter. My friends didn't matter."

Since he'd become a rabbi, his work had exposed him to so much suffering. But anguish wasn't something you could build up a tolerance to. Increased exposure didn't stop Ethan from closing his eyes against the memories of his father, sick and suffering. How many times had Ethan wished he could take up the doctor's scalpel and carve out his dad's pain from his own skin? Pound for pound. Flesh for flesh. It was a macabre recollection. Naomi didn't need to hear it.

"There's no right or wrong way to grieve," she said. Her hair was falling out of her hasty bun. He drank in its downfall against her cheeks.

"I tried to run from it." He'd booked a plane ticket as soon as shiva had ended. "I left everything—everyone—here. Went to Brooklyn to stay with my cousins, because it was the farthest place from L.A. with a couch to crash on."

"What did you find in Brooklyn?"

"Well, I ended up teaching Sunday school at my cousin's shul. They needed people, and I had classroom experience and no other job. I didn't tell them that I'd barely practiced in years. It was classic. I'd left L.A. to escape memories from my childhood, memories of my dad, but then I had no choice but to paw through them, searching for scraps of language and memories of rituals I'd forgotten. All of it covered with his fingerprints."

"You had to put yourself back together from the fragmented pieces of your former life." Naomi crossed her arms, and he had the distinct impression she was trying to hold in her emotions, giving his words space.

"Yeah. Exactly."

"It's hard," she said, like she knew.

In an auditorium with forty-foot ceilings, their shared experiences became magnetic, pulling them together.

"They had a rabbi there, her name was Mira, and she'd come visit my classroom occasionally. She'd heard I was new, from out of town. One day, she asked why I never came to services." Ethan couldn't stop the words tumbling from his mouth. If Naomi had given him a sign that she didn't care about his history, a subtle, polite nod, maybe then he could have brought himself to heel, but she didn't.

"I think I'd been there three months before I finally went. I showed up full of anger and fear and pain, and it was different than what I remembered. Saying the Kaddish in shul instead of at home somehow made me feel closer to my dad, so I kept going."

Tension released from his chest. Ethan spent so much time listening, sometimes he forgot how much he missed being heard.

"The more I went to services, half because I didn't have anything else to do, the more I realized that all the things I loved about physics, the questioning and the interconnectivity and the practice of it, the testing and the iterations and the debate, they were magnified when I practiced. The language came back to me, then the rituals, until I wasn't alone in my grief any longer."

"And so you decided to become a rabbi?"

"No, actually," Ethan said. "I just wanted to study. I'm a career academic. The rabbinate was just another excuse to go back to school at first. Besides, I was worried about my mom. So I applied here in L.A. Got in. Substitute taught while I did my course. I never really expected to get my own synagogue. There are more applicants than positions.

But after I graduated, Beth Elohim started interviewing. Most people said it was a lost cause. Attendance has been on a steady decline for over a decade. The location is tricky, with two other, well-funded synagogues within walking distance."

"But you took it anyway." She didn't sound disparaging. If anything, she sounded glad.

"I took it anyway," he said. "I figured my path to becoming a rabbi was nontraditional—why not adopt a nontraditional approach to building a congregation? I'd found my place in an unlikely ecosystem once. Why not again?"

"I get that." Naomi nodded. "I thought I'd never trust anyone after what happened to me in high school, but then I came out here and I found my people. I got to build my own community, and then when Shameless happened, I got to give them a home. Your shul and my start-up, they look drastically different on the outside, but in a funny way they serve a similar purpose. We built the spaces we needed."

"Sounds like a common value to me," he said, bringing the conversation full circle to matchmaking, his whole heart in his throat. The words hung in the air, accompanied only by the hum of the air conditioner.

"I'll make sure to add *community-oriented* to my scouting list." Naomi turned away from him, uncapping the marker again, and he felt the loss all the way to his bones.

"Thank you." Ethan got up and met her at the board, reaching out and wrapping his hand around her wrist, pausing her list making. "For listening. I mean."

"Don't mention it." She stared down at his hand. "You know, I don't think you're as innocent as you'd like me to believe."

"I never claimed innocence." He stepped back and away, guilty.

"You don't have to say it, it's written all over you." She waved a hand in the general direction of his face. "Those long-lashed eyes, the tousled curls, that eager 'can I help you, ma'am?' expression. You're a trap, Ethan Cohen."

"What sort of trap?" That description sounded like a compliment, and he was desperate for her to keep going.

"A good-natured one. I bet women fall in love with you every day," she said, more to herself than to him. "They come to your office and you listen to them, and we all know getting a man to listen is an accomplishment in and of itself. Then you probably share a story, something equal parts relatable and inspirational, and they want to pay attention, but at the same time they can't stop themselves from watching the way your mouth moves."

Her tone was completely matter-of-fact, but her breathing was a little ragged.

"It's so easy to imagine those lips running across their skin. Your teeth against their neck."

Ethan was pretty sure he was choking. He coughed, trying to bring reluctant air into his lungs. "I don't . . . I would never." He'd thought he'd done a better job of hiding his attraction to her—and worse, his longing—but if she thought he was entertaining women in his office like that, she obviously felt he was some kind of indecent seducer.

"Oh, I know. That's the fantasy. Making the good rabbi lose his concentration. His control. Creating a craving so undeniable, propriety is forgotten." She pressed her tongue against her teeth. "But you probably wouldn't want a woman like that anyway."

"I'm not sure that what I want matters that much."

Not anymore. Therein lay the problem. What mattered most was finding someone who didn't see his occupation, his religion, as a burden. He could only hope that one day love and his religion wouldn't be mutually exclusive.

"You've got your work cut out for you. Nothing about my life has followed a plan. I've landed in situations and been surprised off my ass and tried to make the best of them."

"So," Naomi said, "the question at the center of my efforts then becomes, can I find someone who surprises you?"

No, he wanted to say. *The question is, can you find someone I want more than I want you?*

Naomi had a list of people who deserved to find love, but Ethan was too afraid to ask if her name was on it.

Chapter Fifteen

....

ETHAN WAS IN the middle of reassuring a nervous thirteen-year-old that she would not in fact forget her entire Torah portion in the next twelve hours when Ira, one of his favorite members of the board of directors, hurried over to interject.

"We're running out of seltzer," Ira explained, with the kind of gravity one might employ to express a matter of global importance.

"What?" Ethan struggled to hear over the din of conversation in the synagogue's social hall.

"Seltzer," Ira practically shouted. "There's only a few cans left, and they're all vanilla."

"Shira"—Ethan ducked down so they were eye level—"you're going to nail it tomorrow, I promise. I'm so confident in your singing skills that if I'm wrong, I'll watch an episode of that *Below Deck* show you're always telling me about, okay?"

She gave him a watery smile.

Ethan followed Ira toward the refreshments spread.

"We're really running low already?" He checked his watch. Oneg Shabbat had barely started. "We've still got iced tea, right?"

Ira nodded.

"We'll be fine. I'll talk to Cheryl about doubling the seltzer order for next week."

"It's pretty nice, huh?" Ira nodded toward the crowd. "I'll admit, I was a little nervous about having so many young people show up all at once, but it feels good. The synagogue seems . . . perkier."

Ethan smiled at that description. He had a feeling Naomi would appreciate it.

"They came thirsty."

Ethan followed his companion's gaze across the ravaged buffet table in the center of the room to the various card tables set up for people to mingle at during the late Friday evening social hour. Now that he could see them spread out, the crowd was considerable. Definitely more than usual. Several faces from the seminar series jumped out at him.

Craig, holding out a chair for Mrs. Horowitz. Molly, laughing as Morey pantomimed what was either fishing or something decided less PG. A cluster of women who always sat together at the JCC, lingering by the beverages table.

"Hey, come with me for a minute. There's some people I want you to meet." He steered Ira toward Craig.

Turnout at various synagogue events, including services, had risen gradually over the past few weeks since the seminar series started, slowly enough that Ethan almost didn't notice the influx right away. But tonight, the increase in both diversity and volume of congregants was clear.

Oneg Shabbat provided a weekly cornerstone for many in the congregation. A chance to catch up with friends and begin unwinding after a long week. Ethan knew the seminar participants could have been anywhere at nine on Friday evening—bars or clubs or the beach—but they came to Beth Elohim. Hope sprouted in his chest at the sight.

"Ira, this is my friend Craig, one of the Modern Intimacy seminar participants," Ethan said by way of introduction. "Craig, I'd like you to meet Ira, one of our board members."

"Nice to meet you, young man. Glad you could join us for services. Is this your first time at Beth Elohim?"

Craig finished swallowing a big mouthful, gesturing in apology with a plate full of cookies.

Finally he came up for air. "Hi. Sorry. Yeah, this is my first time. I don't usually come to synagogue unless I'm, like, with my parents or something, but a bunch of us decided to show up after this week's lecture." He pointed to where a couple of his friends stood. "Pretty good time. Rabbi C, you're no slouch at singing, huh?"

Ethan laughed. "Lots of practice."

"Can I ask you," Ira started, "um, why you decided to come?"

Craig considered for a moment.

Ethan shifted his weight from one foot to the other.

"I guess I realized, going to the seminar series in the past few weeks, that I missed having a community. Feeling connected to my heritage or something. The people in our course, they're from all over L.A. Some of 'em are way older than me, and some might even be younger. We get all these different perspectives in one room, and suddenly you realize that people are going through the same stuff you are, even though we've all got our own stories. I like being connected, and I thought I'd find more of that here."

Ethan found himself grinning. Sure, Craig was only one person, and maybe he wouldn't become a full-time member anytime soon, but his answer proved Ethan's plan had worked. He'd created a new pathway to Beth Elohim.

"Hey, Ira, would you take a picture of us for me?" He reached into his pocket and pulled out his phone before throwing his arm around Craig.

"Updating your Jdate profile?" Ira teased.

Ethan waved him off. "I wanna show Naomi."

He shot her a quick text, adding *Progress!* as a simple caption to the image. *Hope your night is going well*, he typed, and then deleted it. He didn't want her thinking he was prying into her social life. He shoved the phone back in his pocket to avoid staring at it, waiting for her reply.

When he looked up, Craig had wandered off to join his friends.

"Ethan," Ira said, "there's something I want to tell you."

"Sure." He frowned at Ira's grave tone. "What's wrong?"

Ira took a long sip of the ice water he held. "Listen, you didn't hear it from me, but some of the board still have their reservations about Ms. Grant."

"What do you mean?" Ethan hadn't heard anything from the board since Jonathan had stopped by his office at the beginning of the month.

Across the room, Morey had pulled out a checkerboard.

"Oh, no." Ethan moved toward him, ready to intervene. He'd made Clarence cry the week before after a particularly heated match.

Ira hung on his heels.

"Shabbat shalom, Rabbi Cohen." Morey beamed up at him in greeting when they reached his table. With deft fingers, he arranged his pieces on the board.

"Shabbat shalom," Ethan returned. "What have we got going on here?"

"Just a little friendly game."

"Mo—"

Ira placed a hand on Ethan's arm, drawing his attention. "Ethan, Ms. Grant is very . . . attention grabbing. Some of the board members have questioned whether she brings the right kind of attention to B.E." He pulled out a handkerchief and wiped his brow.

Ethan sighed. This again? Didn't the turnout in front of them prove that Naomi made a measurable impact on their attendance goals?

"Morey, keep it clean. I've got my eye on you," he warned as he let Ira draw him away.

In a quieter corner, he turned to the older man. "Can I ask you something? In confidence?"

"'Course," Ira said.

Even when he'd been offered the position as rabbi, Ethan had known he didn't have unanimous support. "It's not just Naomi that the board has concerns about, is it?"

"No," Ira confirmed, wincing a little. "Their reservations aren't exclusive."

He patted Ira's shoulder. "I appreciate the confirmation."

"Wait just a minute." Clarence's voice rang across the hall.

"Now, if you'll excuse me, I can see that I'm going to need to stage a board game intervention. You better grab one of those sugar cookies before they're gone."

Ira hurried off without further prompting.

The news of the board's disquiet didn't surprise Ethan. He'd figured it was only a matter of time before concerns about Naomi and the seminar bled into concerns about him and his role within the synagogue. On the one hand, he should probably focus more attention on damage control, on keeping the peace, but on the other hand, he knew that through words, he'd never convince those with concerns that this new direction benefited the congregation. They needed to see the impact of the new initiatives for themselves. Tonight was a perfect example. Still, something sank in his gut. He couldn't shake the feeling that sooner or later, he'd have to choose between making everyone feel welcome and making certain people comfortable.

Chapter Sixteen

....

NAOMI HAD BEEN secretly attending services at Endmore Boulevard for a few weeks.

It was all very innocent, if incognito, at first. She'd run through her podcasts on Judaism quickly and wanted to learn more. Turning up for services or classes at Beth Elohim wasn't an option.

Not when it was all she could do to keep from grabbing Ethan and kissing him every time they got within ten feet of each other, not to mention that she didn't want him thinking her interest in religion had anything to do with interest in him, even if he had been the catalyst for her reeducation.

Endmore Boulevard was nice, friendly, and fancy, but not in an exclusionary way. She'd first visited because Cassidy was a member and had recommended it, but then she'd kept coming back.

Following her heart-to-heart with Ethan after this week's seminar, when she'd decided to pursue matchmaking for him in earnest even though it felt like sliding bamboo under her fingernails, it just made sense to scope out the female membership over here.

A quick glance at the upcoming events roster conveyed that her best chance of finding Ethan an eligible bachelorette from among the synagogue's congregants was either Shabbat meal prep or Israeli dance. Since dancing didn't lend itself to interrogation, she found herself in the synagogue kitchen after work on Friday, her hands covered in flour, trying to braid challah without looking completely incompetent.

She told herself it wasn't a betrayal. Not even a lie. It wasn't as if she told Ethan everywhere she went when they weren't together.

The air was hot and thick with the smell of roasting meats. Congregants, mostly women young and old, took their places at different stations, chopping, mixing, carving, cleaning—almost a dance in and of itself—all while maintaining a steady stream of gossip. Many removed their wedding rings to cook, placing them in a colorful ceramic plate by the door, making Naomi's scouting mission a little more challenging. She was going for incognito, though she might be the only one here who hadn't brought her own apron.

Despite Naomi's longstanding unease with her Jewish identity, she never felt more Jewish than when she was eating. She might not know all the prayers or remember every custom associated with some of the minor holidays, but she knew exactly how brisket melted across her tongue. Knew the way a good latke should be dark brown and crispy on the outside and soft, almost creamy, on the inside. She even loved gefilte fish. Unfortunately, eating and cooking were two very different activities.

"Your plaits are too loose," said a voice from behind her.

"I know. I think I'm ruining it." Naomi raised her dough-covered hands like a convict. "Is it supposed to be this sticky?"

She turned to find a familiar face. "Oh. Hey. You're Ethan's sister. I mean, Rabbi Cohen's sister." She corrected herself hastily when a pair of women a few feet over shot her an inquiring look.

No doubt the local, eligible rabbi was a frequent topic of conversation at these types of gatherings. Naomi needed to watch what she said or risk adding fire to the flames of speculation about his extracurricular activities by sounding overly familiar.

"Leah," the petite woman supplied. "And yeah, you probably shouldn't try to bake that. You've worked the dough to death."

Naomi frowned at her handiwork. "I don't really cook . . . or I guess technically this is baking, right? I thought challah would be easy, but I might be hopeless."

Leah gathered a handful of her ingredients and moved into the counter space on Naomi's left. "Don't worry, you're not the only one. Craft services have ruined me. The only reason I'm here is because my mother likes the apple cake." Leah leaned in and whispered conspiratorially, "She sent me to steal the recipe."

"Sounds like my kind of woman." It was easy enough to detect the inherent tension between Ethan's devout practice and the rest of his family's apparent religious ambivalence. Did that make him more or less likely to accept a romantic partner with a lot to learn?

"My mother's certainly lively." Leah paused in chopping a bunch of cucumbers to gesture with her knife at Naomi. "Are you here recruiting for the seminar series?"

"No . . ." Wow. Definitely should have come up with an alibi beforehand. But this was Ethan's sister. Maybe she could help. "I'm actually sort of casing the joint for single women to set up with your brother."

Leah put down her knife. "You're still playing matchmaker for Ethan?"

Only the sound of several oven timers going off at once saved them from the primed ears of their fellow cooks.

Still? Naomi slid closer to Leah, pretending to observe her knife skills. "You heard about my role as your brother's personal matchmaker?"

Leah wiped her hands on her apron. "Yeah, he, um, might have mentioned asking for your help."

"Oh," Naomi said. "Well, yes, I'm still helping, but you can't tell anyone." The rumors around the rabbi dating were already overwhelming their programming, and poor Ethan had looked ready to faint over his pack of admirers loitering at the JCC.

Leah seemed to pick up on the need for discretion and casually resumed her prep. "Are you sure this is what Ethan wants?"

"Of course." This was the last mission Naomi would ever undertake alone. "He asked me to. As a favor. I guess the seminar series or the singles mixers inspired him to get back into the dating game."

"Oh, I'm sure that's exactly where he found inspiration," Leah said with a disconcerting glower.

Siblings were always tricky. That unique combination of protective and perceptive. Naomi forced herself to remain relaxed. The last thing she wanted to do was appear covetous.

"So, do you know any of these women?" She peeked over her shoulder. "I'm trying to get a sense for their personalities, but it's difficult to distinguish anything over the noise in here."

Naomi let her gaze continue traveling across the room. There were over twenty women crowded around the counter space, but probably only eight or so, Naomi and Leah included, that fell into the appropriate age range for Ethan.

Leah slowly let her chin roll over her shoulder, surveying the space with more subtlety than Naomi had managed. "Tara Ginsburg over there with the kugel is a current admirer. She went to high school with us. I think she's an interior decorator now? Always wears lipstick to any bris or bar mitzvah so she can kiss Ethan's cheek and mark her territory."

"Seriously?" Naomi couldn't identify with that kind of possessive behavior. She usually selected romantic partners who she knew she wouldn't mind sharing. For years, both her profession and her proclivities had made monogamy less than ideal.

"Oh yeah. Women loved my brother when he was a Hollywood brat, running around on yachts with celebrity kids. They loved him more when he settled down and became a physics teacher. He really leaned into the whole elbow-patches-on-tweed-blazers thing. But now that he's the rabbi, he's a JAP wet dream. He's practically got *husband material* written across his forehead."

Naomi tracked Tara Ginsburg for a few minutes. Cute, but also a bit aggressively loud.

"She doesn't strike me as Ethan's type."

Leah seasoned some chickpeas before tossing them in a food processor.

"And what do you think his type is?"

Naomi had heard Ethan's perspective, but she knew from experience people often didn't actually know how to articulate what they wanted. "The kind of person who listens when he talks, even though his face is distracting."

Leah switched on the blender and then leaned across Naomi's mixing bowl to steal an olive off a serving tray. "Know anyone like that?"

Naomi started on a new batch of dough, pretending to hunt for flour to buy herself time. Leah didn't know her well enough to notice, but Naomi's plan to add distance between herself and Ethan through this matchmaking exercise wasn't working. The more she tried to think about the kind of person who might deserve him, the more she realized she was going to have to let go of wanting him for herself. And she had a really hard time letting go of things she wanted.

Pausing the blender, Leah tested her hummus mixture before adding more red pepper flakes and a splash of olive oil. "You know, I might actually have someone. But you wouldn't find her here."

Finding compatible candidates was her job, Naomi reminded herself, a sinking feeling in her stomach. "Oh yeah?"

"Her name's Amelia Greene. She was Ethan's camp girlfriend. Blond, nice teeth, perfect tan. She recently moved to Santa Monica from Atlanta. I heard she's playing first base for her synagogue's softball team, funny enough, and you're in luck, because word on the street is they're playing Beth Elohim in the Sunday synagogue league this week."

"Beth Elohim has a softball team?" For a place lacking in members, they certainly kept the ones they had busy.

"Oh yeah. Ethan pitches. Not 'cause he's particularly good, but he's one of the few members without arthritis." Leah gave her a once-over. "You look pretty athletic, and they always need more women for the team. Maybe you should sign up as a walk-on. It'll give you a better lay of the land than this situation. Softball's like fifty percent standing around."

Considering her total failure at cooking Shabbat dinner, a recreational sport sounded like a pleasant reprieve. Naomi had played varsity soccer in high school, and by the sounds of it, most of Ethan's softball teammates were senior citizens. How hard could it be?

Chapter Seventeen

NAOMI KNEW ABOUT baseball pants, in theory. Her high school soccer team had practiced a few fields over from the baseball players, and she'd seen a few glimpses of the catcher's well-muscled thighs. Since then, she'd caught a few games on television casually while at a bar and thought, *Wow, those are pretty damn tight.* Casual observation had not prepared her for the sight of Ethan Cohen's butt in a pair of snug white capris.

The vision took her so by surprise that she blurted out, "Holy shit. That ass is working overtime."

Thankfully, she was out of his earshot.

Leah's suggestion had seemed simple a few nights earlier, and Ethan had confirmed they needed more female players over text. Apparently, Mrs. Rubenstein's hip was bothering her, and they needed a right fielder.

Naomi had borrowed an old glove from Josh, who had smirked and told her she'd gone soft as he thrust the worn leather into her palm.

"Since when do you play organized sports? Actually, since when do you do anything organized?"

Naomi had told him to mind his own business.

The Beth Elohim softball team was painfully wholesome. According to Ethan, they met an hour before the game for warm-ups and "general camaraderie," whatever that meant. When she'd pulled up to the field, she'd seen one of the players unpacking orange slices—"for the seventh-inning stretch."

Ethan had seen her arrive and jogged in from the outfield to meet her. Up close, the bright white of the uniform contrasted sharply with his dark hair and beard, drawing her attention to his face.

"What's with the full getup?" The opposing team played in matching T-shirts and gym shorts.

"Oh." He pulled on the bottom of his shirt. "Morey ordered them. He said if we want to play like winners, we have to look like winners."

She eyed his uniform from top to bottom. "So, all the other teams make fun of you?"

"Oh, yeah." Ethan smiled as he bent down to retie his shoelace, blinking up at her against the sunshine. "Big-time."

"You get a lot of heckling from the crowd?"

Ethan followed her gaze to the mostly empty bleachers dotted with a few older women Naomi recognized from the synagogue, wearing giant straw hats and passing around cookies.

"You're about to find out." He handed her a soft pile of neatly folded clothes, her very own uniform. "You can get changed in the public restrooms over there."

She shook out the shirt and held it against her tank-top-covered chest. Not a bad fit. "How'd you know my size? You been checking me out?" Flirting with him was still fun, even if he couldn't really keep up.

"Wish I could take credit." Ethan adjusted the brim of his cap. "But I can assure you the uniforms are all Mo."

Naomi got a glimpse of Morey out in the field with a whistle between his teeth. He had everyone in a line, touching their toes in what must have been some sort of stretching routine. She shot him a little wave.

When she looked back, Ethan was staring at her borrowed glove. She'd pulled it out of her bag and tucked it under her arm on the way in.

His dark brows drew together. "Aren't you left-handed?"

"Yeah." Maybe Morey wasn't the only one checking her out after all.

"That's a right-handed glove." He reached out and took it from her, flipping it over so she could see the thumb.

"Oh. I didn't realize." She was going to maim Josh. "You definitely need a glove to play, right?"

Ethan squinted at her. "Wait a second, have you ever played softball?"

Naomi snatched the glove back. "Not exactly."

Leah had said she'd be fine. Besides, it didn't look all that athletic on TV.

Ethan's eyebrows climbed. "Have you ever held a bat?"

"Strictly speaking, no." She smirked. "But I am familiar with the relative shape of the instrument."

He closed his eyes and exhaled slowly through his nostrils.

"Is that gonna be a problem?" She figured a synagogue rec league populated by senior citizens would be grateful to have anyone under fifty join the team.

Naomi could tell Ethan was holding himself back from answering.

"Seriously, do you not want me to play?"

He could have told her before she'd driven all the way out here.

"I just . . . don't like to lose," he said quietly, not meeting her eyes.

A harsh burst of laughter punched its way out of her chest.

"You don't like to lose?" Never in a million years would she have pegged Millennial Moses as a poor sport. Metaphorical insects took up residence in her belly.

He took off his hat and ran his hands through his hair. It was growing past his ears—too long for a rabbi, probably, but just right for his face. "It's pretty embarrassing, actually. A family trait. Leah's almost as bad as I am. My mom refuses to play board games with us anymore. She literally burned our Uno deck after a particularly brutal game at brunch."

For someone who wanted to win, Ethan had a team that didn't exactly inspire confidence.

One of the players Morey was leading in the outfield was using a walker. Though she supposed he'd have time to adjust to that before the game started.

"I know they don't look like much," he said, following her gaze, "but we've been practicing for months, and they're surprisingly spry." He gave her a critical look. "We've got some extra gloves in the equipment shed. There might be a leftie. I suppose you can't do that much damage in the outfield."

"Hey." She thwacked him in the chest with Josh's glove. "I could be great. You don't know. I happen to have great hand-eye coordination."

"All right, then. Let's see what you've got." He pointed to a bunch of bats resting against the metal backstop.

Naomi dropped her uniform, glove, and purse on the bench and then grabbed a bat, surprised by how heavy the metal was in her hand. The ball was the size of a small grapefruit. Surely she could at least make contact.

"What if I hit someone?" The last thing she needed was to clock Morey in the head before the game even started.

Ethan brought two fingers to his mouth and whistled, gesturing for the team to clear the outfield. The sight of his parted lips made her shiver. *Down, girl.*

This whole picture—uniformed, competitive, bare-forearmed Ethan—was affecting her breathing. Maybe instead of hitting the ball, she could just run at him and throw her legs around his waist?

Taking his place on the pitcher's mound, Ethan demonstrated his windup so she could anticipate the motion. "Ready?"

Naomi bit her bottom lip and nodded. She traced the movement of his arm as he pulled back for an underhanded lob. The ball soared toward her, and she turned her whole body as fast as she could, spinning like a top while the ball crashed against the backstop.

Okay, so she wasn't a natural.

Ethan abandoned the mound and jogged toward her.

"Probably should have given you a demonstration first. Watch me." He picked up a bigger, longer bat and then moved to stand in front of her, and wow, did Naomi not have to be told twice.

Why wasn't he moving behind her and positioning her hips like they did in the movies? This really seemed like a perfect opportunity for her to press her ass back against his dick and—

"Hey," he said, noticing she was completely not listening. "Stay with me here. We don't have much time."

"Right." *Don't look at his dick. Don't look at his dick.* "Sorry."

"See how my knees are slightly bent and my back elbow is up?"

Okay, but did the pants have to be so tight? Surely that was restrictive rather than helpful? Did they wear cups in baseball?

She swallowed. "Yes."

"So, your front leg stays planted, and you just wanna pivot on the toes of your back feet." He swung a few times, slowing down so his body moved like he was slicing through water. If she didn't get to spank that ass at least once in her lifetime, it would be a crying shame.

Naomi attempted to mimic him, torn as to whether she should purposely mess up to get his arms around her. Just when she was ready to thrust her butt out in a way she knew was a fan-favorite position, he headed back to the mound.

"That's looking better." He put down his bat. "Let's try again."

This time when the ball reached her, Naomi made contact, sending it almost straight up into the air. Hey, it was an improvement, even if Ethan ducked under it and caught it easily.

"Okay, so," she called. "I'm probably never going to be an all-star, but I can run."

It was one of the perks of being, like, seventy percent legs.

He studied her form, his gaze heavy. "Let's try bunting."

Naomi had zero clue what that meant, but when he came and reached for her, his big warm hands wrapping around her wrists and positioning her arms, she decided she liked it.

"So when I give you the signal, you can square up just like this, and then all you have to do is tap the ball with the bat and try to get it to go between the pitcher and the catcher. That way they have to move, and you can hustle to first base. I'll put you in the top of the lineup."

"Got it." She tried to match his somber tone. "Don't worry. I'll bunt the shit out of it."

Finally, he smiled. "Hey, I'm glad you're here."

"Even though I might be terrible?" She tipped her head to the side.

Ethan nodded. "Even though you might be terrible."

"And even though I might embarrass you in front of your cool softball friends?"

"Even if you embarrass me in front of my 'cool'"—he looked at the rest of the team doubtfully—"softball friends."

She dropped her hand to her hip. "If we lose, are you gonna pout?"

"I don't pout," he said, indignant. Which meant yes.

Her heart did something dangerous in her chest. Was this . . . pining?

"Are you gonna stamp your foot? Maybe throw your hat in the dirt?"

He took a step into her personal space, so she could feel his breath against her neck. "You think you're cute, huh?"

Naomi's voice came out not much louder than a whisper. "I *know* I'm cute."

She stared at the rise and fall of his chest. Her fingers ached to grab the front of his uniform and close the final few inches between them.

"You better get dressed, Ms. Grant," Morey shouted from the sidelines. "You can't play without regulation uniform."

Ethan stepped away from her but lifted his hand and brushed it gently over her forearm. "Go ahead. I gotta rearrange the batting order anyway."

Naomi nodded, not trusting herself to say words at the moment.

"See you out there," he yelled, jogging backward to where a man in catcher's gear waited. "Don't let me down."

She waited until she'd turned the corner to let out the breath she was holding.

The bathrooms off the side of the field were surprisingly clean, and full of people who were obviously changing from workwear into sweats for their game or one of the others on the surrounding fields.

Naomi pulled on her own uniform, deciding to leave the shirt open to frame her tank top. She couldn't afford to completely surrender her identity in this quest to matchmake for Ethan. And if the idea of him admiring her cleavage when she bent over to bat flickered across her brain, well, it wasn't the worst thing she'd ever thought about doing to entice him.

Even though she'd confirmed that Amelia Greene's synagogue was playing Beth Elohim tonight, Naomi had expected to have to work harder to find her. When she practically ran into the blonde standing over the sink, she didn't have the wherewithal to control her reaction.

"Fuck. You're gorgeous." Way hotter than Google Images suggested.

The woman, who was definitely Ethan's camp girlfriend, blinked a few times. "Oh. Um . . . thanks?"

Amelia wore the kind of incredibly expensive workout gear *Sports Illustrated* swimsuit models favored in their fitness posts on Instagram. Even using L.A.'s high standards, her hair was the perfect beach blond and tousled in loose waves that definitely required multiple curling irons. All this for a rec league softball game?

"Are you Amelia Greene?" If so, her eyes were the same color as her last name.

"Yeah, I am." She shook her head and reached for a paper towel. "Sorry, have we met?"

Naomi was supposed to be smooth. Cold as ice. But she could not for the life of her think of a good excuse for recognizing this woman.

"Did you go to camp with Ethan Cohen? He was showing me old photos and I thought I recognized you." *Oh, nice. Real subtle.*

At least the familiar name did seem to relax Amelia. Her shoulders fell away from her ears.

"Yeah, I did. We used to date, actually," Amelia added with enough challenge in her voice that Naomi concluded Morey's baseball uniform had not successfully canceled out her hotness.

"You're a friend of his?"

"A business partner." In order for this plan to actually work, Naomi needed to put as much distance between her and Ethan as she could manage. The last thing she wanted was to get into some possessive staring contest with this woman. "We're running a seminar series for eligible Jews. Oh, and we've got singles mixers now too, I guess."

Molly, bless her heart, had taken over the event-planning portion of the mixers after Ethan's first clumsy attempt.

"Oh." Clearly not the answer Amelia had been expecting.

Naomi grabbed one of the flyers Clara had designed for them from her bag and handed it over as proof. "You should stop by one of the lectures. If you're interested, I mean."

Amelia studied the form. "Ethan will be there?"

"Definitely."

"I haven't seen him in years. I heard he's a rabbi now." The blonde smiled. The kind of secret smile that said she knew exactly how hot Ethan still was. Amelia leaned in conspiratorially. "I don't actually like softball, but I heard he pitches for Beth Elohim."

That explained the three hundred dollars' worth of spandex coating her lithe form. Fair play.

Naomi smoothed her hands down the front of her pants. "Right.

Well, you might not get much time to catch up tonight. What with all the balls. Flying." *Kill me. Just kill me.* "I'm sure he'd be glad to see you at one of our events."

Grabbing the reins on her composure, Naomi made her voice light and confident. "If you're interested in attending, just RSVP through the link on the flyer. We have a short screener for participants."

Or at least they would when Naomi went home tonight and made one. It wasn't that she was against the idea of Ethan and Amelia falling in love. There was no denying they'd make gorgeous Jewish babies together. But Ethan was so special, and he was so nervous about dating again. Naomi owed it to him to make sure that Amelia Green was as good as she looked on paper.

"Okay. Thanks," the blonde said. "Maybe I will. And hey, may the best team win tonight."

Naomi smiled. "You bet."

As soon as Amelia walked out onto the field and saw Ethan in his uniform, that *maybe* was gonna skyrocket to *definitely*. Which was fine. It was good, even.

Naomi didn't have a claim on Ethan. In fact, once he paired off neatly with this chick, she'd be able to go back to focusing on Shameless.

Work was simple, even when it was hard. Work reinforced the reality of who she was instead of making her feel like all the truths she'd built her life on were peeling back like cheap paint. Work didn't ask anything more of her than time and commitment.

"It was nice meeting you," she told Amelia, only sort of lying. "I'll see you on the field."

Amelia might be Ethan's future: the perfect Jewish wife for the perfect Jewish man. But that didn't mean that tonight, Naomi wasn't gonna bunt like her life depended on it.

He wasn't the only one who didn't like to lose.

Chapter Eighteen

ETHAN NEVER FELT less qualified to be a rabbi than at the bottom of the fifth inning.

It was always right around then when his arm started going rubbery and he'd managed to chew through his bottom lip. His defenses against uncharitable, unsportsmanlike thoughts fell with each passing pitch.

Winning was like a drug. As far back as he could remember, he'd let the heady perfume of victory go straight to his bloodstream until he could feel the power of it when he flexed his fingers. And like any drug, the lack of it kept him up at night.

If he were a better man, he'd have avoided the softball league altogether. It presented too much temptation for his competitive side on a good day, and that was before Naomi had shown up and turned a seemingly innocuous uniform incendiary.

He had been a good athlete through high school and college. Not that good, obviously. No one had tried to recruit him or anything. But he'd earned himself a bit of a reputation. Teams didn't like to see his name on the opposing side's roster. The Sunday synagogue league wasn't much, but there weren't that many sports where short Jews with bad knees thrived. Ethan took what he could get.

Former glory days aside, he didn't particularly want Naomi witnessing the sore-loser side of him. It was fine if the team saw him as a little hotheaded. Not great, but not lethal either. He never yelled or threw his glove or anything. The worst he did was go a little quiet when they lost in spectacular fashion.

It was undeniably embarrassing how much he cared. Rec softball was meant to be a respite from the hectic demands of capitalism. Or, in many of his teammates' cases, from the monotony of early retirement.

Thankfully, Ethan's congregants appreciated how hard he played and how many hours he put into strategizing and organizing practices around his other synagogue commitments. Morey said the team believed in Ethan because Ethan believed in the game.

There was no point denying that he'd be a lot happier if they weren't losing right now. It ate at his pride that he couldn't stop exposing his flaws in front of Naomi. He'd been trying to play it cool since their last seminar, but by the second time he walked a batter with a full count, it got a little bit harder.

The score was close enough that he couldn't let go of hope. Despite his flagging arm, they'd managed to close out the top of the inning without letting in any more runs. This next turn at bat was their best chance for a comeback.

They were back at the top of their order. If Beth Elohim could pick up three runs, they could tie the game, and Ethan could salvage what remained of his dignity.

Ethan pulverized a tacky stick of gum as he called out the lineup and tried not to let Naomi catch him scowling. She'd been quiet all game. He'd caught her staring at the opposing team's first baseman a handful of times before he realized he recognized the player.

Amelia Greene. Man, he hadn't seen her in forever. He'd had no idea she'd moved back to L.A. She'd sent him a really thoughtful card from Atlanta back when he was sitting shiva for his dad. It had been nice. *She* had been nice. Though Ethan couldn't look at her without thinking about the disastrous results of trying to French kiss while they'd both had braces.

First base made sense for her. Like Naomi, she was both tall and left-handed. Though judging by the way Naomi was currently sawing the sleeves off her uniform with a pocketknife while Morey looked on in horror, the similarities didn't extend to their dispositions.

Ethan shook his head and went to search for his batting gloves. He'd just managed to pull them out from under two heavy leather-bound books in his bag when Naomi stepped in front of him and put her hands on her hips.

"I wanna try that bunting thing."

Before the first inning, he'd told her to start out with a normal swing so he could get a sense for their pitcher and be strategic about when to deploy the bunt. She was 0 for 4 at bat and, judging by her scowl, wasn't having fun.

Ethan shook out the gloves before pulling them on. "It's a bad idea. Their pitcher's been cutting inside all night. It's not worth the risk of you getting hit."

"Come on." Naomi's raised voice attracted attention from the rest of their team. "If there's one thing I know how to do, it's handle balls," she said at the same volume, smirking at the disapproving titter of their elderly audience.

He'd never seen someone relish making other people uncomfortable as much as she did. It was pretty spectacular.

But there was still no way he was going to let her go out there and get hurt.

"No. I'm sorry. You might be an expert handler." His mouth twitched, despite his attempts to convey the seriousness of the situation. "But you're also stubborn, and I fully believe you'd take a line drive to the chest before you'd admit that you don't really know what you're doing out there."

Her eyes went dark enough that he half expected steam to start pouring out of her ears.

Whoops. Maybe telling Naomi she couldn't do something in front of the entire team wasn't such a great idea.

"Ms. Grant, you're up," Morey called from the other end of the dugout.

Naomi pivoted on her back foot so fast she threw dust.

"Wait a second." Ethan reached for her hand, but she was too fast. His fingers closed around air.

"Excuse me," she said, her voice dangerously light. "They're calling my name."

The way she swayed her hips as she grabbed her helmet and bat and walked to home plate was absolutely designed to punish him.

Ethan groaned. He had a feeling that no matter what the outcome of her at-bat was, somehow he was going to live to regret it.

Naomi stopped just shy of the batter's box to take a few warm-up swings. Ethan wiped sweat from his furrowed brow. That stance wasn't anything like what he'd shown her. She was wiggling way too much.

Unlike Ethan, who could feel a migraine starting behind his eye sockets, the pitcher on the opposing team didn't seem to mind Naomi's admittedly limber routine. His mouth was practically hanging open. It was a wonder the ball didn't roll out of his slack grip.

Instead of course-correcting when she finally stepped into the batter's box, Naomi adjusted her stance so it was even more outrageous. With her legs completely straight, she lowered her torso toward her knees, which had the effect of . . . Ethan swallowed. *Oh dear.*

"She looks like she's shooting a pinup calendar," Morey whispered to him, in half awe and half fear. "What's she playing at?"

If Ethan had the answer to that, he'd sleep a lot better at night.

The first pitch went wild, missing the strike zone by a solid three feet.

Naomi stepped out of the box again, this time to . . .

"Oh, you have gotta be kidding me," Ethan yelled, loud enough for her to hear.

She gave him a heart-stopping wink as she continued to roll her shirt up and tuck it to reveal her navel.

"Well," Morey reasoned, wiping his brow with a handkerchief, "you gotta admit that's a strategy we haven't tried before."

Ethan's desire to win wasn't strictly opposed to distraction techniques, and his body definitely wasn't opposed to seeing any part of Naomi's, but he still had a problem with her putting herself in danger by squaring up toward the mound. His every instinct told him that was what this whole performance was leading up to.

The opposing pitcher could barely take his eyes off the planes of her bare stomach. As for Ethan, well, he tried his best to control where his gaze landed.

Halfway through the windup, Naomi moved into the bunting position Ethan had shown her. Luckily, the pitcher was so bamboozled, there was barely any heat behind his throw. Naomi kissed the ball with the fat edge of the bat, and it fell in a perfectly executed bunt a few feet in front of her.

Both the pitcher and catcher froze at her unexpected show of technique following so many minutes of misdirection. By the time they got the throw off to Amelia, Naomi had already cleared first base and was now smiling at Ethan like he could very much go fuck himself.

Honestly, he wished he could. That entire display was one of the sexiest things he'd ever seen in his life. There might as well have been cartoon birds floating around his head as their next batter made his way to the plate.

Morey nudged Ethan with a sharp elbow. "Look alive. You're on deck."

He pulled his gloves out of his back pocket and grabbed a helmet while the batter managed a line drive. Ethan's desire to win cut through all his other emotions like a knife through butter. With runners on both first and second, he had a chance to tie the game in his next at-bat.

As he took his stance and checked the positions of the outfielders, Amelia gave him a friendly little wave from first base. He nodded in recognition and was taken even more aback when Amelia's smile bloomed wider. It was a bit more of a warm greeting than he'd expected, and his cheeks went warm.

Apparently, he wasn't the only one confused by her attention. Amelia's pitcher shot her a warning glare. He was sour after Naomi had so transparently played him, and had barely made anything within the strike zone during the last at-bat. Maybe Ethan could goad him? He certainly didn't have the same assets at his disposal as Naomi, but he could ham it up, Major League style.

Why not? The Sunday synagogue league had certainly never seen anything like today's Beth Elohim team before. Now that Naomi was safely on base, he didn't see anything wrong with putting on his own performance. With extreme bravado, he made a show of slowly pointing beyond the fence. His face as stoic as Babe Ruth himself.

The pitcher rolled his eyes and then checked the runners before entering into his windup. What Ethan had taken for a curve sank into a fastball just as he made contact, sending a pitch that might have only skimmed the fence into a straight shot headed directly at— Oh no. His heart hammered as the ball slammed into Naomi's shoulder.

Ethan raced toward her, even as the umpire called the ball fair.

"What the hell are you doing?" Naomi held her shoulder with the opposite arm as she raced away from him toward third base. "Go to first, you moron!"

He pivoted at the last second, too shocked to argue, but was still out by a mile.

Ethan got in the ump's face as soon as he got back to home plate. "Time out. My player's hurt. She needs to come out of the game."

"I do not," Naomi shouted from third base. "Ethan, sit down."

The ump gave him a *Better you than me, buddy* look.

It wasn't until Morey came and steered him toward the bench that Ethan closed his mouth.

He buried his face in his hands and tried to calm his racing pulse. He'd spent the entire game worried about her getting hit with a ball, and then to be the one to do it? There was a decent chance he might die of embarrassment.

He missed whatever play brought her home, had no idea if it was good or bad. The next thing he knew, Naomi was back in front of him.

"What is wrong with you?"

Ethan jumped to his feet. "I'm so sorry." He reminded himself it wasn't okay to hold her. "We've got ice in the first-aid kit—"

"We could have had that play if you'd just run to first like you were supposed to," she interrupted him. Her cheeks were flushed, and a few strands of damp hair fell out of her ponytail to curl against her neck. She looked like a vengeful queen. "I thought you were obsessed with winning!"

His blood felt too heavy for his body. He could barely think through his still abating panic.

She made him feel like he was unraveling.

"I am," he yelled back. "But I'm more obsessed with you." Everyone else on the field turned to stare at them.

"I mean," he said, looking around, his eyes catching on Amelia's calculating gaze. "The collective you, obviously. As in, the team. I don't want anyone getting hurt." His breath came out in harsh puffs.

Naomi's face was guarded.

Morey shuffled over with an ice pack, which she took with a small "Thanks." Her eyes flashed to the field, and Ethan followed her gaze to Amelia.

The rest of the game passed in a blur.

Ethan tried to focus on the team. On the score. On anything but the flash of surprise across Naomi's face when he'd admitted how much he cared about her. There was a slim chance she wouldn't recognize his confession as an outright declaration.

He barely even noticed when they lost.

"You all head out," he told the rest of the team. "I'll stay and lock up the equipment."

Morey tried to protest, but Ethan told him the deli on Fairfax was having a sale on pastrami, and he was gone in a flash.

It didn't take long to pack up the catcher's gear and the bases, but when he walked back from third, Naomi was waiting for him, ice wrapped to her shoulder with gauze.

His heart felt powerful enough to walk out of his body.

Without saying anything, she took the bases with her good arm, leaving him to haul the gear and bats to the storage shed on the edge of the field that they rented along with a bunch of other teams.

Neither of them said anything on the walk over. For his part, Ethan was trying to decide what to apologize for first. He locked up everything with sweaty hands. When he finally turned to her, Naomi stood very still.

"I, uh." He stared at the cobwebbed ceiling for a moment. "I guess you're probably wondering what that whole outburst was about?"

"Do you have feelings for me?" The words came out aggressive enough to match her foreboding posture.

His chest went a little tight, a familiar reaction to stress. He thought about lying, even though he never lied. But not wanting Naomi was like trying to pause a hurricane. She might as well know.

Ethan leaned back against the storage bin, balancing his weight on his hands pressed against the cold metal. He sighed. "Yes." The word stuck in his throat. "I'm sorry. I hope it doesn't make you uncomfortable. You've become an invaluable resource to the synagogue, and I don't want you to think that my feelings for you have any implications for the remaining seminars. I'll get over it. I've been trying to get over it, honestly. I'm sure this happens to you all the time, so you must know how hard—"

Naomi shook her head. "Shut up."

Ethan let his eyes close in shame. Of course she didn't want to hear any more about his unwelcome adoration.

He startled when something wrapped around the front of his uniform, yanking him into an upright position. When he opened his eyes, her face was a breath from his.

"Kiss me," she said, voice both soft and demanding.

Oh.

He brought his hands up slowly, in case she changed her mind, but she let him cradle her jaw in his hands. Let him brush his lips against the hard, mean line of her mouth until it melted into something lush and warm. Let him slide his thumb down the smooth column of her throat, tracing her pulse, until Naomi tipped her head back and parted her lips in a gasp.

Ethan didn't know how long this moment would last, so he took the opportunity to kiss the proud, precious crest of her cheekbone, the velvet-soft skin just under her ear, before returning to her mouth, finding it already open, waiting on a catch in her breath.

He kissed her harder this time, lips moving with the force of weeks' worth of wanting, until the hand she had fisted in his shirt released and moved to the back of his neck, threading through the hair at the base of his scalp and pulling until he shivered against her.

Naomi ran her nails down his spine and grabbed a handful of his ass.

Ethan's head was empty except for the word *please*. He moaned, desperate and delirious.

Suddenly she shoved away from him as someone rattled the handle on the door of the shed.

"You don't kiss like a rabbi," Naomi said, her voice full of furious accusation as she tugged him past the innocent bystander hunting for their lost keys.

Ethan focused on exhaling. "How many rabbis have you kissed?"

Naomi brought her fingers up to her swollen lips. "Evidently, not enough."

Chapter Nineteen

EVEN IN THE days before he was a rabbi, Ethan had never considered himself a master of seduction. Whether or not it was fair, in his twenties, he hadn't needed to work very hard to get women to fall, more or less, into his lap.

It wasn't something he was proud of. It was just a fact.

Now that he was a rabbi, women treated him more like a detour sign on a crowded street—they drove toward him, but eventually his occupation redirected them down alternative, less demanding roads.

No one had covered finding a wife at the rabbinate. Not explicitly, at least. There were plenty of perspectives on marriage in Judaism, and some of them had been a part of his study, but the old books didn't get into navigating modern courting rituals, or lack thereof.

Ethan knew he was on borrowed time with Naomi after he'd basically confessed his undying devotion on the softball field. He'd just expected her to let him down gently instead of kissing him and instructing him to drive them both to an undisclosed location.

Having her tongue in his mouth and her body pliant against his made him feel alarmingly alive.

It had taken him at least five minutes in the aftermath simply to gather his wits.

"So . . . can I ask where we're going?"

"The beach," Naomi said, pointing for him to merge.

"Oh. Okay. Is there, um, a particular reason?" Ethan's stomach was doing a lot of dangerous swooping.

"Because the sound of the waves is soothing."

Somehow the answer made him both more and less nervous, but, not for the first time, he decided to trust her.

When they arrived at the entrance of Hermosa Beach, they were unsurprisingly the only people in the little lot. They awkwardly toed off their shoes in silence. The April air was cool but without bite. Naomi walked toward the water, and Ethan followed her.

He stopped beside her, a foot from where the sea met the shore. She set her shoulders, defiant, battle-ready.

"Okay. Tell me the plan." Her words were loud enough to carry over the crash of waves.

As she hugged her elbows, Ethan was struck by the huge number of times in her life Naomi had had to be brave.

He wanted to show her that she didn't always have to be the strong one. That if she let him, he'd carry some of the weight. No matter the outcome of this discussion, Ethan wasn't ready to go back to his life before he'd met her, but something told him to wait out Naomi's reaction.

What if the trick to reaching her, one of them at least, was just patience? Standing still long enough that she would grow used to him. That she would let herself relax.

"A kiss doesn't have to mean anything. I'll give you a get-out-of-jail-free card if you've gotten cold feet." Her voice was softer this time, less sure, the statement almost a question.

She was offering them both an out, he supposed.

Ethan had no intention of taking it.

He moved so he was standing in front of her instead of beside her, so he could look her in the eye. The wet sand was cold under his feet, grounding him.

"Kissing you," he said, determined to be explicit about it, "meant something to me."

She sucked in a breath like the words had sharp edges. He could tell she wanted to move, to look away even, but she didn't. "Whatever it is, this thing between us, it won't be easy."

"Whatever it is, this thing between us," he repeated, "I want it."

A shiver broke out across her body, and she moved her gaze to the shoreline.

"Yeah, but with me?" She laughed. Higher than normal. Nervous.

Her vulnerability pulsed between them, breaking his heart. Putting it back together.

Ethan brought his hand to her chin and redirected it, slowly, gently, until her eyes met his again.

"Naomi," he said. It might as well have been a prayer.

There was a spectacular unspoken truth hanging between them.

That what they risked, their careers, their hearts—the ideas, so vastly different, that defined them—they risked for the potential of something it was too soon to call love.

"I feel like I'm falling," she told him, her eyes wild with an emotion that might have been fear. "Not like in a romantic, greeting-card way. I mean falling like the ground is disintegrating under my feet."

"It's scary," Ethan agreed. "But that doesn't mean it isn't right."

"I've never done something this complicated before." She let her head fall forward, against his shoulder. "I didn't really mean to do it now."

He kissed the top of her head, let his hands find their way to her neck, where her pulse hummed against his fingertips. "I'm not sure this is the kind of thing you get to plan."

He tipped her head back again; he couldn't help it. He didn't want her to hide.

Moonlight hit the hollows of her cheekbones, the divot of her upper lip, her stubborn jaw. If they weren't both barely breathing, he'd tell her how looking at her was sometimes so good that it hurt.

He knew in that moment that if they chased this connection, there would be no writing it off as casual. No "getting it out of their systems" or "seeing where things went." Ethan didn't know the right words to ask for what he wanted.

"I think I could be good at loving you," he said, "if you let me." Adrenaline raced under the surface of his skin, urgent and electric. "That's a lot. It's a big thing to say, and it's a bigger thing to deliver. I promise that I know that, but I still want you to give me a shot."

"Ethan." She leaned her cheek into his palm, kissed the thin skin of his wrist.

Was she telling him to stop? Telling him good-bye? Her lips were just as hard to diagnose as her words.

He took a step back toward the beach, reaching for her hand, wanting space to think, to get the words out, but needing to stay tethered to her at the same time.

"Say the word, and we can forget this ever happened. I'll pretend that I never thought about loving you." Ethan searched for the seam of the horizon. "I'll look at you less, and without so much longing." He took a deep breath. Giving speeches was part of his job, but no amount of reading Torah had prepared him for this.

"I won't forget that we kissed. Sorry"—Ethan tried to grin a little—"but you have to cut me some slack on that one. Because, I mean, come on, you're you."

She nodded, not guilty at all.

"But I promise not to think about it too much. I'll save it for those really dark moments, when I look at everything wrong with the world and I feel helpless. When every good thing I've ever done, ever seen or heard about, pales against the garish human capacity for hate and corruption."

He bent forward quickly and kissed her cheek, lingering more than he should but less than he wanted to before pulling back.

"I'll think about it then, if it's okay," he said gently, "just for a few seconds, so I can remember what it was like to feel transcendent."

Naomi blinked at him for what felt like a lifetime.

"Don't you want to marry Amelia and make Jewish babies?"

"What?" He stepped back. "Man, that speech was worse than I thought if somehow that was your takeaway."

She ran her thumb across his knuckles. "She was at that game for you. Perfect on paper. The woman I would have picked for you, if you'd let me."

"Naomi, look—yes, I do want to get married someday, and the Jewish babies, if I'm lucky, that would be nice, but the only reason I asked you to find me someone was because I assumed you'd never have me, and I didn't know how to get over it."

She stuck her tongue into her cheek and shook her head. "You're not exactly deescalating the intensity of this situation, you know."

"I'm not trying to." Ethan reached for her other hand, relieved when she let him have it.

"So you, what . . . want to date?" The wild emerald of her eyes matched the shifting waves.

"I want to date you, specifically." He began to brighten. Not taking it for granted that she was still here, still talking. "Look, I should have been honest with you before. Somewhere between watching you punch a guy in the teeth and watching you lay a perfect bunt, I realized you're ruining me for anyone else."

She searched the empty beach like it might have answers. "And you don't think us dating might be . . . I don't know, career suicide?"

Ethan winced. The board might not love it, but they'd come around eventually. Naomi had a powerful orbit. Sooner or later, she pulled everything in.

"I'm allowed to date," he said firmly.

"Yeah . . ." She kicked at the sand a little. "Nice girls."

He bent his knees to catch her eye. "You're nice."

She tilted her head and lowered her brows. "I'm not, and I've never wanted to be. Ethan, I need you to really think about this. I've never been ashamed that half the population of greater Los Angeles has seen my tits, and I'm never going to apologize for the fact that no matter how much time passes, how many suits I buy, I'll always have been a sex worker."

"I don't have a problem with any of your work, past or present," he assured her.

"I know that." She sighed. "But you're really taking it for granted that other people think the same way you do."

"You're right." The hope that had been building up in his body all night started to fade. He ran his hands over his face. "I understand what you're asking me and why. I just hate that you had to."

"Look," she said, "I'm not a stranger to being ostracized. As long as you understand the consequences of pairing up with me, I'm not going to tell you how to live your life."

There was still so much fight in her. So much resistance to the idea.

"I understand your reservations," he promised. "As much as I wish it weren't the case, I know there will be people, probably people in both of our lives, who won't want us to be together. But I'm a Jew, I've experienced discrimination before. It didn't change what I believed then and it's not going to change what I believe now."

"Let's say I agree. We do this. We date. How does that work exactly?"

Ethan couldn't tell if she was warming to the idea. If it was something she wanted, or if she was just taking the scenic route to talking him out of it.

"What do you mean?"

"I don't know how to date a rabbi. Honestly, I'm not sure I know how to date anyone. At least not seriously. And this"—she waved between them—"feels serious."

"Yeah." Ethan swallowed hard. "It does."

"Ugh." She pushed his shoulder. "Don't look at me like that."

"Like what?" he frowned.

"Like—where did you even get those eyelashes?"

He smiled. "If this look is working for you, can you do me a favor and describe it in more detail, 'cause I'm not sure I could re-create it intentionally?"

"No. I'm not making you more powerful." Naomi pushed him again, farther toward the water. The bottoms of his pants were wet, and he definitely didn't care.

"Hey, wait." Electricity ran through him the way it always did when he fell for an idea. "We could use the syllabus."

She raised her brows. "Excuse me?"

"You literally wrote step-by-step instructions for establishing modern intimacy." He was practically bouncing on his feet.

"I guess that's technically true." Naomi bit her lip.

"Well, it doesn't get more modern than this."

"At least if it doesn't work out, we could probably write an article and sell it to the *New York Times*," she conceded.

"Pragmatic, as ever." He brought his hand to her back and steered her toward the parking lot. Ethan was pretty sure it was going well at this point.

"Okay, yes." Naomi said finally.

Ethan held very still. "Yes to what?"

"Everything." She ducked her chin. "All of it. All of you."

She reached out and kissed him then—not his ear or his forehead, his lips. Naomi kissed him, and it was, impossibly, better than before.

He wrapped his arms around her waist and let his palms spread across her back. It was a kiss that felt like winning. Wine, red and warm, if he could paint it.

After a while, Naomi pulled back. "The syllabus gets us through seven weeks, if we're lucky. After that, we're on our own." She narrowed her eyes. "Why are you smiling again?"

He wasn't sure he'd ever be able to stop. "You said 'after that.'"

Naomi spoke into his shirt collar. The ocean crashed against the shore. "You do realize if this intimacy experiment doesn't work, it means we're failures both professionally and romantically?"

"No." He pulled her closer. "That's not how science works." Ethan reached around her to open the car door. "Even when they fail, experiments move us closer to the truth."

Chapter Twenty

....

NAOMI FOUND HERSELF welcoming the structure of using the syllabus as a road map for her controversial courtship with Ethan. Going on a first date after spending multiple nights a week together for almost two months was a recipe for awkwardness. In the midst of so much uncertainty, having any kind of reference material to cling to went a long way.

After minor debate the night before (interspersed with more heated kissing in the beach parking lot), she and Ethan had settled on dinner and a movie as their initial outing. Something about adopting such a traditional model for their untraditional pairing held irresistible appeal.

This morning, Naomi had texted Ethan three restaurant choices.

He had chosen her least favorite.

She hated trendy restaurants. The kind that spent more money on light fixtures and whiskey tumblers than they did on actually testing their menu or paying their staff a living wage. They'd only been here ten minutes, but already her ass was sore from the midcentury modern chair's flat wooden seat. She supposed it served her right for issuing a low-key compatibility test out of the gate, but old habits died hard.

Ethan lowered his menu and smiled at her from across the table, every inch of him wholesome, eager in a way most people learned to hide.

"Do you come here a lot?"

She tried to decide if the house salad was a safe bet, even though it came, inexplicably, covered in kelp.

"No. It's my first time."

So far, nothing about this date was her idea of normal. For one thing, Naomi had spent an inordinate amount of time getting ready. Usually, she didn't waste energy considering what to wear, especially for dates with men. She cared what women thought about her clothes. But in her experience, men usually unanimously agreed less was more. Of course, in this matter, like so many others, Ethan remained an outlier.

He barely seemed to notice her slinky silver dress. Thankfully, the long sleeves covered the grapefruit-sized bruise on her shoulder. Not that Ethan would know. His eyes hadn't slipped below her neck once. He was probably too busy thinking about world peace or the capacity for human suffering or something else equally righteous while she sat here shimmering like a horny disco ball.

Ethan, in all his dark-chinos-and-perfectly-pressed-dress-shirt-with-the-sleeves-rolled-up-to-reveal-his-taut-forearms glory, scanned the room and seemed to come to a conclusion.

"Did you offer to come to this restaurant as a trap?"

Naomi took a long sip of her water, trying to decide if it was unnerving how quickly he'd seen through her plan. "If only you'd figured that out before they brought the bread."

He closed his menu and leaned forward, keeping his voice low. "I picked this one because it's the closest to your house. The other options you gave me were all the way across town."

"Wait, you picked this place because you wanted to cut down my commute?"

Measuring the distance between the various restaurants she'd picked from their respective work neighborhoods hadn't occurred to her. She knew people like Clara, who consulted menus online before deciding where to go, but not Google Maps.

"Well, yeah." Ethan took a bite of the aforementioned bread and then very quickly put it down on his plate with a look of distaste. "Traffic on the 405 sucks, and there's construction again this week."

"That's really . . . sweet," she said, chewing on the foreign word.

"Not that sweet." Ethan fiddled with his napkin. "I figured you'd be in a better mood if you didn't have to battle rush hour. If I'd known that you would dock me points for picking the only restaurant on the list with four types of bone broth on the menu"—he shook his head, teasing—"I'd have let you hike out to Koreatown."

Ethan crumbled a corner of the weird bread between two fingers and lowered his voice even further. "I'm not sure anything here is actually edible."

Naomi frowned. Why was he worried about her mood? Sarcasm and snark were the calling cards of her hard-won persona. Had her surliness lost its charm already?

She had no desire to sit here and question her every move, but she also couldn't stop thinking about how high the stakes for tonight felt.

Even people who knew Naomi well occasionally accused her of being fearless. They didn't realize that her daring didn't come naturally, that she'd built a persona to protect a girl who'd had her plans for the future taken from her. The first time Naomi had stepped on set and shrugged out of her clothes, it had been a dive into the deep end.

People were always saying "Oh, I could never do that," when they found out she had performed. *Of course you couldn't*, she constantly wanted to answer, *you'd never have the guts*.

Dating Ethan also required bravery, but it didn't inspire the same swooping belly and trembling hands she'd felt all those years ago. Instead, sitting across from him required her to flirt with her own softness. To decide if she was willing to put down the armor she'd worn for years and risk finding, when this whole thing ended, that she'd lost the strength to pick it up again.

Ethan reached for her hand across the tabletop. "Naomi, you still with me?"

"Yeah—" she started to say—only then she wasn't.

Her ex-girlfriend Jocelyn, arm threaded through another woman's, ducked through the cheesy beaded curtain hanging in the entranceway. The hostess led them straight toward Naomi's table.

Joce quickly covered the little start of surprise that passed over her face when she saw Naomi, smoothing her brow and painting on a quick, if resigned, smile.

Naomi got to her feet, not thinking, and oh man, was that a mistake, because now it wasn't just Jocelyn looking at her, it was everyone in the restaurant, including Ethan and the woman on Joce's arm. Why on earth had she picked out such a stupid, shiny dress? She might as well have worn a neon sign around her neck inviting disaster.

"Hi," she said limply.

She hadn't seen her ex in five years, but not much had changed. Joce's beauty was still the arresting combination of sharp and delicate. The specter of their former relationship hung in the air between them, mocking Naomi with a failed future she'd never know.

Jocelyn hadn't looked tired when she'd walked in. She did now, as if simply coming into contact with Naomi were draining. If only someone in this restaurant would knock over a wineglass. Send it shattering against the wood floor in a hundred jagged pieces, creating a big enough distraction that Naomi could slip away and not have to face these two people, one past and one present, who wanted something from her she wasn't sure she could give.

"Hey. It's been forever." Joce threaded her fingers through her companion's, and Naomi caught the flash of a gold band even in the low light of the restaurant's Einstein bulbs. "This is my wife, Alice."

Naomi sucked in a sharp breath and tried to cover it with a cough. Ethan stood up and handed her a glass of water off the table.

"Nice to meet you," he said, offering his hand to first Jocelyn and then Alice, covering for the fact that Naomi was still swallowing. "I'm Ethan."

"Right." Naomi shook herself. Put the water down before she dropped it. "Ethan is my . . ." Rabbi? Friend? Shit, what was she supposed to call him?

"Date," he offered lightly.

"Nice to meet you." Jocelyn tucked her sleek black bob behind her ear. Was that sympathy in the look she shot Ethan, or something else?

Alice bumped her shoulder gently against her wife's. "How do you two know each other?"

"We used to date," Joce and Naomi said at the exact same time.

Ethan laughed, but Alice's brows drew together.

"You're not . . . wait . . . are you Hannah?" Something heavy pulled Alice's face taut.

Any traces of mirth soured in Naomi's mouth.

"Umm, yeah. Or I guess I was, back when . . . back then."

The waiter fidgeted with his pad.

"We should get going," Jocelyn said after a long, awkward pause. She reached for Naomi's wrist for a second, pulled her in just enough to whisper, "You look happy. I'm glad," before walking away.

After they left, Ethan didn't demand an immediate explanation for what had admittedly been a very odd encounter, but Naomi couldn't suffocate the urge to explain.

"I treated Joce like shit. That's why that was so weird." She ran her thumb through the condensation on her water glass for something to do. The truth had escaped before she'd thought to bury it. "We met shortly after I moved out here from Boston. She owns a flower shop a couple doors down from the place where I used to waitress. I'd give her free drinks, and Jocelyn would bring me all the errant blooms that wouldn't fit into her arrangements." Naomi still couldn't smell hyacinth without thinking of Joce's smile. "We dated for two years, and it was great. No big problems. Just . . . nice."

A frown painted Ethan's dark brow. "But something went wrong?"

Naomi nodded, needing the extra seconds to find the words. "She bought me a ring. It was gorgeous." Silver, not gold.

Ethan sat back in his chair, the firm set of his lips taking on a new air of gravity. "The idea of marriage scared you?"

"Not exactly." She'd loved Jocelyn and seen a future with her. It had been the inscription on the ring, of all things. *Yesterday. Today. Always.*

The last word, tiny and precise, had scoured Naomi's skin, echoing another promise from years earlier. One that still sent her bolting up in bed in the middle of the night sometimes, heart racing. *Come on, baby, just a few pictures. You can trust me. You know I love you. I'll always love you.*

Fuck. She still hadn't responded to that email invitation from her high school. Mostly because she hadn't decided how to best articulate her disdain, but also because she couldn't shake the hypocritical feeling of rejecting the exact kind of opportunity—one to change the conversation about sex ed and intimacy—she consistently fought to receive.

The waiter came and poured the red wine they'd ordered. Naomi took a big swallow, half the glass, before she continued.

"I have this thing where, when people promise too much, when something seems too good to be true . . . I don't like to wait around and see it break down."

She'd learned early the cruel fact of life that you could lose everything more than once.

"It's easier, at least it seemed easier then," Naomi said, "to cut and run."

"So you said no?" Ethan took a sip of his own wine instead of cutting his losses and whistling for the check. Naomi experienced an extra surge of warmth toward him for acting like this date was normal in spite of everything.

She wished she could write her cowardice off, attribute it to being young and stupid, but Naomi knew it was no excuse. "I didn't say no so much as I ran out of her house and never answered her calls again."

Joce had obviously moved on, married someone else, but Naomi knew more than anyone that good things happening for you didn't make the bad things fade any faster. Time might heal all wounds, but in Naomi's experience, never as fast as she needed.

"So, this is the first time you've seen each other since . . . Wow." Ethan's eyes had gone wide, the blue sharp and brighter than usual. "But . . . if everything else was good, if you'd worked through things before, why not work through that?"

The urge to change the subject pushed against her lips, but what had she told her students?

Sometimes first dates went deep, whether or not you felt ready. Did her and Ethan's rapid foray into old wounds tonight speak to compatibility or false intimacy, sure to crumble at the first sign of real strain?

"I would make a terrible wife," she said, voice matter-of-fact, stabbing for nonchalance.

"You don't really believe that, do you?"

"Why not?" She crushed her napkin in her fist. "I'm selfish and I'm mean. Most of the time, I'd rather be alone than spend time with other people, even people I love. I never pull my punches, even when I should."

"Naomi—"

But she wasn't done. Naming her flaws, showing them to him here in public, was like trial by fire, and more than part of her relished the burn.

"I'm messy. I can't cook. I never remember to call when I'm going to be home late." She took a deep breath. It was almost all out there. For him to weigh and measure. To decide if she was still worth the risk. "But mostly, I don't trust anyone. Especially not myself."

"I see." Ethan finished his own wine in a long swallow. "Let me ask you something. Why do you think I want to be with you?"

"Novelty?" There was still a hint of teasing in her voice, but not enough.

"Try again."

"Oat-sowing?" she offered, a little more cheerfully.

His mouth quirked up. "Hardly."

"Morbid curiosity?"

"Naomi," he said again.

She played with a curl by her temple. "Hm?"

Ethan cleared his throat. "I wanna talk about God for a second."

"Oh." She sighed, feigning annoyance. "Him."

He flipped his fork over a few times, breaking eye contact as if it cost him. "I promise not to do it too many times tonight. I'll be cool."

"I'd like to see you try."

That earned her a small smile.

"All right then, go on, Rabbi Cohen. Tell me something about God."

"Okay." He pushed his hair out of his eyes. "There's this Hebrew meditation I read about. It's called husa, and it means, roughly, 'compassion for something that is flawed.' Husa is acceptance, devoid of judgment. The kind of love an artist has for their creation, even as they recognize its imperfection. To practice the meditation, we ask God for husa in prayer." He lowered his voice as he recited, "'The soul is Yours, the body is Your creation, husa, have compassion for Your work.'"

Naomi sat back and tried to catch her breath. His words hammered against her heartstrings.

"What I'm trying to articulate, probably a little poorly, is that you're precious," Ethan said, "not in spite of, but because of all the ways you believe you're broken."

Naomi ducked her head, going so far as to chew the terrible bread to buy herself time to respond. "I've spent my entire adult life in therapy learning to love myself, because I believed that if I loved myself, I wouldn't need anyone else's love. But that's not really how it works, is it?"

"No, I don't think so," he said softly.

Naomi was so . . . gone over this man. No map, no compass. Gone.

"I'm starting to think all those years of emotional depravation just made me hungrier. So, sure, I guess I'll take God's love. If he's offering."

"He's offering," Ethan confirmed.

She resisted the urge to ask if God was the only one.

"Do I have to love all of my art? Because some of my early work is pretty bad."

"You have to love all of it," he said, "at least a little, because it's created by your hand."

"Oh, all right." She crossed her legs. "I'll love my garbage if you and God think it's so important. I'll be Oscar the fucking Grouch."

Ethan's eyes warmed. "Can I borrow that analogy for a sermon?"

"Okay," she said, leaning forward, tipping her head just slightly, asking without words to be kissed. "But I'll expect payment in lieu of attribution."

"I'm afraid we're low on funds at the moment," he said, gaze going from warm to hot and hungry. "You know, maybe we should just . . . go."

"I don't suppose you're going to take me home and let me have my wicked way with you?"

Ethan put a bunch of bills on the table before standing up and offering her his hand. "Only one way to find out."

Chapter Twenty-One

ETHAN HAD HOSTED women in his house before. *Before* being the operative word.

Before he was a rabbi. Before he'd met Naomi. Before he started craving a future that felt both like kismet and infinitely complicated.

His house, tucked away in the hills of Santa Monica, wasn't a typical bachelor pad. He didn't have a wet bar or a stereo system that cost more than his car. Books took up the majority of nonessential living space. In fact, his entire life seemed to revolve around words on the page. Textbooks from his teaching days, tractates of Mishnah and Torah interpretations, nonfiction guides for community organization, memoirs from people he admired, sci-fi novels that provided his favorite escape.

As Naomi wandered around his living room, taking in his couch and his coffee table, his lack of art that wasn't crayon masterpieces from last week's Sunday school class tacked to the hanging corkboard that he used to plan his sermons, he grew concerned his library would topple her in an avalanche.

"Would you like a glass of wine?"

"No, thanks." Naomi had perched herself on a stool that tucked under the island in his kitchen as if she were a judge on a cooking competition show preparing to watch contestants, or in this case Ethan, vie for her approval.

"I'll take a water, though," she said, moving to the cabinets and waiting for him to nod at the one that contained glasses. She did seem more relaxed now, her sway languid as she helped herself to water from his fridge.

Ethan wanted to ask her how she moved like that, every inch of her dripping seduction. Was it practiced or innate? Did everyone react this way, tongue too big for their mouth and hands sweating, or just him?

"This place looks like you," she said, eyes warm and sparkling as she took in his kitchen.

"Haphazard?"

"Satisfying," Naomi corrected, taking a sip of her drink.

Ethan made himself stop watching her throat work and opened the fridge under the premise of looking for something to prepare. Hopefully, the blast of cool air would stop the sweat forming at his temples. He lingered over the vegetable drawer.

What was sexy food? The shelves were full of Tupperware containers of kasha and bow ties and apple cake. Somehow, serving Naomi Grant the leftovers foisted on him when he'd performed a bris last week didn't seem very romantic.

The freezer was a last resort but also somehow his best option.

"How do you feel about Bagel Bites?" He didn't have a ton of time to cook and stocked the comfort food for emergencies.

She tipped her head back and laughed. "Good. I feel good about them."

What had his life come to that in his midthirties the best he could offer a date was frozen pizza . . . on a bagel? Maybe bringing her here hadn't been the best idea. After they'd run into her ex at the restaurant, his main priority had been making sure she wasn't so spooked by the encounter that she tried to bolt.

It had been a struggle not to smile as Naomi attempted to convince him she wasn't marriage material. As if a single one of the paltry flaws she'd presented could even hold a candle to how vibrant, how determined, she was. He never worried about her convincing him to beg off, but he had grown concerned, the longer they'd sat in that disastrous hipster haven, that she'd talk herself out of giving him a chance.

Ethan ripped open the cardboard box with a flourish. "This is all a part of my grand plan to seduce you."

"Is it?" She raised her eyebrows.

"Yep." He put on the checkered apron his mother had given him as a housewarming gift. "The beauty of the plan is how clumsy and deceptively mediocre it appears."

"I see." She stepped behind him to secure the strings, letting the backs of her fingers rest against the base of his spine for a moment before returning to her perch. "I'm looking forward to seeing how the rest of this plan plays out."

Ethan gulped. Like a true scientist, he wanted to regain control of the variables. To take her somewhere he knew the food was, if not good, then at least palatable. Where he could hopefully get her to relax without having to worry about anyone else. More than that, though, he wanted Naomi all to himself, even if he wasn't sure he could handle her now that she'd arrived.

So much of their time together was public, crowded, belonging to the people they served rather than to each other. Before they'd established this plan to date, he never would have dared try to monopolize her company like this. But since she'd agreed, since they'd both admitted that the feelings between them were serious enough to risk a potentially awkward disillusionment, he decided to indulge.

Naomi moved to preheat his oven, her shiny dress throwing light like confetti across his kitchen.

There was an urgency under his skin every time he spoke to her. Hell, every time he thought about her. She was the very definition of out of his league. It was like something in his biology sensed that her liking him back was too good to be true, and he needed to act fast. Beneath the frantic beating of his heart was also a quiet hum of comfort, a sensation that scared him even more.

"What are the chances that if I put on Miles Davis, some of his suave factor will rub off on me?"

Naomi gazed at him over her shoulder. "I think you've got a better chance of my suave factor rubbing off on you."

Those words in her lush voice made him fumble the pan he held, earning him one of her laughs.

Was there a German word for water rising over your head, but in a way where you wanted it?

Naomi asked him questions about his house while he made a mediocre Caesar salad out of items left in his fridge. None of his answers were particularly witty or charming. He was probably boring her. Pride blown to smithereens, Ethan tried to conjure up tips from the seminar series for navigating first dates, but they'd already gone so far off book.

According to Naomi's second lecture, they were supposed to be in a restaurant right now with other people and bad lighting, atmospheric elements that presented barriers to the kind of hungry intimacy that seemed to fill his kitchen and spill out into the living room.

He wasn't supposed to have her in his home this soon. Likely because now the evening kept presenting him with extremely inconvenient details. Like the fact that she was less than forty feet from his bed as they sat down at the kitchen table. Or the particular pink shade of her tongue as she licked sauce off her thumb while they ate.

"Do you want to watch a movie?" Ethan blurted out later as he cleared their plates. He didn't particularly want to watch a movie, but he definitely didn't want her to leave.

"Sure," Naomi said, lowering herself down onto his couch in a way that made her silver dress curl dangerously high around her thighs, the material moving like water against her skin.

Ethan told himself to calm down and hunted for the remote.

"What kind of films do you like?"

She let out a little low huff and then folded her palm across her mouth.

"What?"

She didn't remove her hand. "Nothing."

Ethan dropped onto the couch next to her, close enough to smell her perfume but not nearly as close as he wanted to be.

"Come on, tell me. You'll give me a complex. I thought that question was benign."

"I'm sorry." Finally, she let her hand fall into her lap, fingertips resting at the hem of her dress, toying with the fabric where it met her bare skin. "It was just the way you asked that question. I got this ridiculous idea."

"What kind of ridiculous idea?" Something told him he wasn't going to like her answer.

Naomi curled her lips together, obviously weighing her next words. He'd noticed she was careful around him in a way she wasn't with other people.

Which one of them did she think she was protecting?

"I almost made a joke about how the kind of films I like are ones with fucking in them."

He swallowed thickly. "Well, that's okay."

Naomi pulled her hair over her shoulder. "And then, because bad ideas are infectious, I started thinking about how wild it would be if we watched one of my performances," she said, but not like a dare or even a real suggestion.

She said it like, *Wouldn't that be silly*, high and light and like never in a million years would he agree.

Ethan had suspected before that she saw him as neutered somehow, and her answer now proved it. She painted him with an unnecessarily virtuous brush.

Annoyance flickered in his chest.

When he said "Good idea," it came out harder than any other words he'd ever spoken to her.

Naomi's reaction was immediate. The way her mouth opened as her breath caught. "Wait . . . you . . . want to?"

Which yes, of course he did, now that he had her permission. He knew she'd made a career performing, and the idea of watching one of her old videos had occurred to him pretty much an hour after they'd met. He'd immediately dismissed the idea, mainly because it was so clear that there was a difference between the way Naomi worked, sharp and shiny and untouchable, and the way she might be if he ever got to see her, to touch her, for real.

"Why wouldn't I?" They'd have to have this conversation sooner or later.

"Because you're religious," Naomi said, as if it were the most obvious thing in the world.

Ethan tightened his jaw. "What exactly do you think that means in this context?"

"I don't know"—she searched the living room as if looking for witnesses to back up her hypothesis—"but I figure if you can't have sex before marriage, then we probably shouldn't sit here and watch porn together."

"You think I won't have sex before marriage," he said slowly, because his brain was sort of collapsing.

"Right." She folded her legs beneath her. "I did some reading, and I know it's a sort of a gray area nowadays . . . I assumed that, as a rabbi, you'd want to err on the side of caution, and so we, you know, *wouldn't*."

"Naomi, I—"

"I still wanna do this," Naomi rushed to assure him. "Date you, I mean. I . . . like you. It's okay with me. I get it. I respect your values even though they're different than mine."

"I appreciate that, but, Naomi, I think your reading might have given you a bit of a false impression. I certainly take sex, and all intimacy, seriously, but I'm not sure I know any Reform rabbis who saved themselves for marriage. Honestly, lots of the people I knew in rabbinical school hooked up with each other."

"I'm sorry." She shook her head. "It sounded like you just said . . ." She trailed off, voice weak.

Ethan needed to make her understand. He took a long breath in and out through his nose. "Naomi."

"Yes?" Her eyes were wide, and at this range he could see flecks of gold among the green.

He reached for her hand and ran his thumb across her knuckles. "I want you to hear me when I say this."

"Okay," she said, tongue dipping out to trace her bottom lip.

"If we're going to date, I want you to know that I'm not immune to desire, and I'm very capable of acting on it."

"I'm gonna need you to say that again, and maybe use smaller words."

Ethan thought for a moment. "Okay. How about this? I'm a man," he said, each syllable calm and clearly articulated, "and I'm going to fuck you."

"Okay," Naomi said on an exhale. "That was good."

"Look," he sighed, "I'm not saying it's going to be tonight or even anytime soon. We can decide together when we're ready, but I want you." His voice came out a bit ragged. "Very much."

"I see." Naomi's breathing was strained. "Thank you. For telling me."

"Of course." He brought her hand to his lips and placed a ghost of a kiss against the inside of her wrist before releasing her. "Glad we cleared that up."

"You know, in that case"—she swallowed visibly—"there is this one video I like. It's not a full scene, but it's a self-pleasure tutorial we shot for Shameless a few years ago as part of a Getting to Know Your Erogenous Zones series."

There was vulnerability written across her face, but also something hopeful, something fragile. "It shows how I like to be touched. We could watch it together. If you want?"

"Is that a joke?" Ethan was already so turned on from this conversation and her proximity.

And that was how he found himself sitting with scant inches between himself and Naomi Grant during the single most erotic experience of his entire life. Once he'd handed over his laptop, it took her all of a minute to find the video she'd referenced. *Shameless must have a solid search feature*, he thought stupidly.

The video she pulled up was labeled "A Tutorial on Orbiting," a term he'd never heard applied to the female body until this moment. But before his brain could linger on possible definitions, he was greeted by the sight of a very naked Naomi Grant. Any blood previously powering his essential organs redirected between his legs.

"So that's what my tits look like." The fully dressed Naomi next to him gestured toward the screen, pushing her tongue against her cheek and fighting a laugh.

Ethan balled his hands into fists at his sides. She . . . there weren't words for how perfectly crafted she was, for how hot and wild looking at her made him feel.

His brain couldn't process the image on screen as a whole. It was too much. Too good. He took her performance in as pieces.

The artful curve of her wrist as her hand moved between her legs. The flush and sheen of her skin as she worked herself into a sweat. How she parted her lips on a tiny, gentle sigh as she set her tempo. The clench and release of her taut thighs as they trembled.

Lust rolled over him in waves. Crashing, again and again. Fantasy brushing the edge of reality and then carrying it away.

The way she brushed her thumb across her nipple. The arch of her back. Her gasps, high and needy.

Naomi shifted next to him on the couch, pressing her thighs together, rubbing a hand down her throat.

Why had he ever thought this was a good idea? What exactly did he mean to achieve by sitting here, in the dark, learning firsthand all the ways Naomi liked to be teased and stroked while she began to softly pant beside him?

"How much longer is this?" He forced the words out roughly. Any minute now, he was going to become so hot his body would turn to dust.

Observing the pressure and speed and depth she preferred as she tested herself with two and then three slick fingers. Watching her rake her nails across her inner thighs.

Ethan tried to focus on the pain of his dick pressed against his zipper. Tried to breathe through his nose. Tried not to make noises that made him sound like he was being murdered.

"Not very long. I'm close." Her words pressed against his skin like velvet. "On screen, I mean."

She was inches away when he turned to her on the couch. And the vision she presented here was almost alarmingly vivid in contrast to the one on screen. Pink cheeks. Wet lips. Nipples obscenely hard under the smooth material of her dress.

Ethan's mouth watered. "Fuck."

He had to call this off. Had to slam the computer shut and walk straight into a cold shower.

He couldn't do this, not in front of her, not when he wanted more than anything to touch her, or for her to touch him, or—he closed his eyes for a second before forcing them back open—to be able to touch himself.

It was like his heartbeat was everywhere at once.

Confession pushed against his lips. "Listen, I can't stand—"

"I'm about to come," she said, and then his speakers filled the room with her desperate mewls of pleasure, and Ethan threw his head back and groaned, not even watching the video anymore, because it was too much.

He was on fire. His sheer, undiluted wanting so strong that it eclipsed the painful way he was grinding his teeth. Any moment now he was going to pass out.

"Ethan?" Naomi leaned forward and shut the laptop, cutting off both the picture and sound from the video. Her voice was huskier than he'd ever heard it. He could feel her vowels against the nape of his neck.

Barely, he managed to sit up, to take in the splashes of crimson marking her cheekbones.

"I had a great time tonight," she said.

"Me too," he grunted after counting silently to three.

"Think you can walk me to the door?"

He assumed at that point that she was teasing him, which was honestly fair.

But when Ethan stood up, hissing at the pressure the new angle put on his hard-on, he saw that she wasn't being coy after all. Naomi's legs were trembling.

He offered her his hand to get to her feet, and through sheer force of will managed to escort her to the door.

Naomi lingered at the exit, staring at him like he was something feral. He must have looked like a complete mess. He felt like a complete mess.

Please strive for a sliver of normalcy.

"I'll see you tomorrow for coffee?" They had a standing date to review her seminar notes.

For a moment she just looked at him, the rise and fall of her chest dramatic.

"Yeah," Naomi said, and then gave him the filthiest kiss he'd ever received. Quite possibly, he corrected as her tongue pressed against his, the filthiest kiss anyone had ever received.

She pressed herself against him, and he rolled his hips helplessly in time with the greedy press of their mouths. It was all Ethan could do to keep from rubbing his dick, well, all over her, anywhere he could reach.

Naomi pulled his hair until he moaned against her mouth, out-of-his-mind wrecked, but then she stepped away so suddenly he actually stumbled forward. Barely keeping from breaking his nose by catching his arm on the door frame.

"I should go." Her lips were swollen and her hair was mussed. She looked like the first meteor shower he'd ever seen—impossible and brilliant, so far away but somehow also right inside his chest.

Ethan briefly considered dropping to his knees and begging her to stay.

Instead he said, "Of course."

"This was great. Again." She pressed the back of her hand to her cheek, eyes somewhat incredulous before smiling at him and reaching under her dress to slip off her panties and shove them into his hand. "Bye, see you tomorrow."

The door crashed closed before he had time to process his good fortune.

He slumped against it, jerked open his belt buckle, dragged down his zipper, and fisted his cock, pumping a handful of times against the slip of silk, warm from her body, until he came, shaking like a leaf.

If that was what a first date with Naomi Grant was like, how on earth was he supposed to survive the second one?

Chapter Twenty-Two

MODERN INTIMACY—LECTURE 4:

Friends don't let friends lie to themselves

NAOMI WAS A firm believer that if she told herself something wasn't a big deal, and then forced herself to behave in accordance with that version of reality, she could conquer just about any type of social anxiety. Unfortunately, ever since she'd started dating Ethan Cohen, that strategy had gone completely to shit.

For example, she currently stood behind a now-familiar lectern at the JCC, preaching about the modern dating milestone of introducing the object of your affection to your group of friends, while a drop of sweat snaked down the back of her top. Before she and Ethan had started actually following the steps she'd written for their experiment in love, she'd gotten into a groove with the syllabus. Each lecture flowed pretty seamlessly. Organic connections started forming in their conversation. Participants actually started to show up with positive anecdotes about people they interacted with, rather than the negative—albeit funnier—stories from the first few weeks. But now . . .

"If you're afraid to introduce the person you're seeing to your friends," she said, reinforcing the key theme of the evening's seminar as they hit the midway point in the session, "it's probably because you know they're not right for you."

Smile, your grimace is scaring the audience.

"So," she continued after a deep breath, reading directly from her notes, "quit kidding yourself and cut your losses, or prepare to face the truth you've buried about the inevitable failure of your relationship because you're afraid to die alone." Yikes. She'd written the outline for this module a few weeks ago. Now each easy proclamation fell from her lips like a personal sentencing.

"And with that"—she forced herself to release her death grip on the lectern—"let's break up into groups of three to five. I want you each to go around and share some commentary you received from your friends about your last significant other. See if there are any patterns that you've been ignoring."

Had her outlook on dating always been so bleak? She needed to find the thermostat and crank up the A/C.

Okay, yes, she was nervous about introducing Ethan to her friends. Not because they weren't wonderful. She loved them with her whole heart. But they were going to make fun of her mercilessly for throwing her well-loved independence manifesto out the window for a man with great hair and a decidedly squeaky-clean vocation.

She walked over and began to futz with the old-fashioned thermostat on the wall.

Ethan's friends were easy. He spent most of his time with Morey and the other members who made up the core of his congregation. The softball team seemed to like her well enough after her crowd-pleasing bunt. Maybe they could count that and move on to the next milestone?

Except their next lecture was on sex. Her brain practically hummed the word.

She glared at the thermostat. She had no idea how this dial worked, but at least while she stood over here facing it, she could avoid making eye contact with Ethan.

She considered herself exceptionally well-versed in the erotic arts for obvious reasons, but still, last night had been an outlier. Sitting close to

Ethan while he watched her perform, both of them fully clothed and not even touching on the couch, had given a whole new meaning to the word *foreplay*. It had been so perfectly Ethan—restrained and powerful and surprising and devastating in the best way.

Naomi wiped her palms on her pants and let her thumb brush just barely against her inner thigh.

Her first thought when she got home was *Holy shit, having sex with him might actually kill me*, and her second was *We have got to shoot a piece of content about filming yourself masturbating and then watching it with your partner, forcing yourselves not to act until you achieve climax on screen.*

Naomi finally gave up on adjusting the temperature and turned back to her class to see a hand up.

"Yes?"

"Ms. Grant," Molly said, "we were wondering if you're dating anyone?"

Naomi had told her a million times to quit calling her Ms. Grant.

A few nearby students stopped talking to listen. Ethan raised his head from his notebook as well.

Naomi chewed her bottom lip. She could hardly tell them to mind their own business. She and Ethan had built this seminar around the idea of radical transparency and a safe space for self-disclosure.

"Why do you ask?" When in doubt, answer a question with another question.

"Well, I guess we just wanted to know if you follow the course methodology yourself, or if it's based more on theoretical concepts."

Sheesh, what a question. Naomi supposed this was a common pitfall of academia. The gap between research and lived experience.

"I am dating someone, and we are currently employing several of the strategies and techniques developed for this seminar." There, that was honest but opaque.

Molly leaned forward in her chair. "Will you tell us about the person you're seeing?"

Naomi cleared her throat. "Excuse me?" She reached for her water bottle and took a long sip.

"I mean, if you're comfortable opening up about your relationship, it would mean a lot to us. You're so good at this stuff." Molly's dogged determination was another thing that reminded Naomi of her younger self.

"Are you dating someone famous?" Molly's neighbor had her thumbs poised over her cell phone, no doubt ready to tweet about Naomi's personal life.

"Uh . . ."

Jaime had their hand in the air now. "Is it someone we've heard of, at least?"

Naomi tried to make eye contact with Ethan, tried to say, without moving her mouth, *Help me! You're the one who thought this whole thing was a good idea.* His frown had slipped completely into his beard.

This was a test neither of them had anticipated facing, at least not so soon. It was one thing to decide to date when they were the only two people who knew about it. Announcing they were dating in front of a room full of people seemed like far higher stakes.

Like so many other times since she'd met Ethan, she was torn between a choice that made her comfortable and a choice she thought was right. She held Ethan's gaze for a long moment and then gave him a tiny, almost imperceptible nod.

"Actually," he said, loud enough to draw the attention of the room. "I'm the person Naomi's dating."

A pulsing silence filled the room as Naomi imagined the participants trying to figure out whether they'd been unknowingly cast in a televised social experiment.

They'd just entrusted a room full of people with a piece of information that could jeopardize Ethan's career, not to mention their fragile relationship. Naomi had rules about arming people with information they could use against her. She'd had a lot of rules before she met him.

"Yeah, right." Jaime waved them off.

"No. Seriously." She gave the classroom her scariest look, the one Josh had once sworn caused a street harasser's hairline to visibly recede. "Rabbi Cohen and I are dating."

One of the students in the front row shook his head back and forth. "But . . . how?"

"What do you mean, how?" Naomi snapped. This dude's tone implied that someone in this equation was out of the other's league, and in either scenario, she was offended.

"You can't date Rabbi Cohen, you're not Jewish," a girl toward the back said dismissively.

Naomi folded her arms across her chest, stung against her will. "Okay, let's cool it with the assumptions."

"Wait . . ." The first woman was looking back and forth between Naomi and Ethan like they were a tennis match. "Are you Jewish?"

Naomi had about ten retorts for that question on the tip of her tongue. "I'm—"

"Hey," Ethan stood up. "This is not a forum for you to interrogate your instructor on her personal life. Naomi and I have been generous enough to trust you with details about our relationship as an act of community in this space. I expect you all to honor the covenant you signed at the beginning of this course and treat the information we've shared with you in the same respectful manner with which you'd want sensitive information about your own romantic engagements protected."

A few eyes dropped sheepishly, and one or two groups resumed their conversations. Naomi thought the worst might be over, until another hand went up.

She sighed. "Go ahead, Craig."

"The only thing I want to know is whether Rabbi Cohen has met Josh Darling."

Ethan's blank stare told her he didn't recognize the name. Apparently, Craig came to the same conclusion.

"All I'm saying is"—Craig turned to address his rabbi—"I would be shaking in my boots knowing that the woman I was dating still worked with the man she'd labeled the best sex of her life in multiple major news outlets. I don't have the chutzpah to live up to that standard of screwing."

"The best sex with a man," Naomi muttered under her breath. "Okay, I think sharing time is over." She directed them back into the exercise, but she could tell by the way Ethan's eyebrows drew together thoughtfully that the damage was already done.

Inviting Ethan to Clara and Josh's engagement party this Saturday night had seemed like a good idea when she texted him about it this morning. She'd figured her friends couldn't share too many incriminating stories or ask Ethan too many inappropriate questions in a group that size. But if this lecture hall was anything to go by, she'd severely miscalculated. A significant amount of dread dropped into her stomach. If only she'd volunteered to go to bingo night at the synagogue instead.

Chapter Twenty-Three

BY ALL ACCOUNTS, out of the two of them, Ethan should have been the one more nervous about meeting Naomi's friends. After all, these people already knew and liked her. Ethan's expertise in winning over strangers, while an occupational requirement, mainly revolved around sharing various pieces of wisdom from other rabbis and/or artfully disseminating what could judiciously be termed "dad jokes."

So, yeah, he was at a disadvantage here.

But you'd never know it by the way Naomi kept tapping her fingers against the pad of her thumb in obvious agitation as they cruised down the freeway toward her friends' engagement party. It had been her idea to arrive together, and he was beginning to suspect it had something to do with controlling how much exposure he got to the people who knew her best.

"Hey." He raised his eyebrow at her from the driver's seat. "What's the worst that can happen?"

Naomi kept so much of herself in her head. Locked down. It might assuage her anxiety to call her fears out into the open.

"Maybe your friends won't love me, but I doubt I'm gonna walk away from tonight with any enemies." He reached up to touch the almost-gone bruise around his eye. "The likelihood that I get punched in the face for a second time this month seems slim."

"I'm not worried about what they'll think of you," Naomi said, a little impatiently. "I'm worried about what they're going to think of me."

Well, that was not at all what he'd anticipated.

"But they already know you."

"Yeah, and I have a very specific reputation to uphold."

"What kind of reputation exactly?" The question was out of his mouth before he could decide if it was a good idea.

Naomi shifted in her seat.

He tried to imagine what she might be thinking, but there were almost infinite possibilities.

"Okay," he said slowly, "you want me to guess?"

"You'll guess wrong." Naomi tugged on the neckline of her shirt, but instead of pulling it up the way Ethan assumed she might, she yanked it aggressively downward. What had previously been an illusion of cleavage became a declaration.

Damn. He supported whatever made her feel better. That said, he would need to figure out how to keep his eyes on the road for the duration of the trip.

"Ugh. Fine." She leaned forward and faced him. *Eyes on the road, Ethan.* "As far as my friends know, I'm dark and filthy and unwinnable."

"Oh," he said, for lack of anything better.

Naomi narrowed her eyes at him.

"That does sound very . . . specific," he offered.

"It is." She crossed her arms. "But now, they're gonna see that you make me . . ."

"Laugh?" He flexed his fingers around the steering wheel.

"Mushy," she conceded with a pout.

"Mushy?" He pulled a face. "That doesn't sound pleasant. No wonder you don't want your friends to find out."

"Was this conversation supposed to be reassuring?"

Oh, right. Ethan reached for Naomi's hand, wrapping his own fingers around her vent-chilled ones and squeezing. Just a little. Just for a moment. "Look, you're happy, right?"

"Yes," she said, not sounding very pleased at the moment.

"So I bet that's enough for your friends to overlook a little"—he smirked—"mushiness. And, if it makes you feel better, I'm pretty confident that there's no way your friends could possibly hold you to a higher standard than the one you set for yourself."

"That makes a certain kind of sense," she admitted with reluctance.

"Now, me on the other hand? I'm very aware of my own weakness. Despite the obvious honorific, I'm not always particularly good. And if these people are anything like you, they'll have a penchant for sniffing out bullshit."

Sometimes he had too many questions, too much desire to know, when he would be better served to accept the vastness of what he could never comprehend.

"I'm always striving to be better," he said sincerely, "but it's an everyday uphill battle."

Naomi scoffed.

"What?" He let a car in ahead of him. The GPS promised they'd almost reached the final turn toward their destination. "You got to exhume all your alleged flaws on our first date. Now it's my turn."

She shook her head. "It's that one up there."

Ethan pulled up at the end of a long line of cars.

"Besides," Naomi said as he parked, "you don't have flaws, at least none I've seen."

Ethan unclipped his seat belt. "Maybe you're not looking hard enough." He pressed his nose against her throat and inhaled, greedily, the scent of her skin. When she just barely gasped, the sound stifled by her lips at the last moment, Ethan opened his mouth over her pulse point, kissing her neck, soft and careful. Desire built in his body quicker than he'd anticipated at the taste of her, and suddenly a kiss he'd intended to be light, playful, wasn't.

Naomi threaded her fingertips through his hair, shifting his face so she could get at his mouth.

Too many logs had been left on the fire between them, left to cool, but with embers still dancing, red hot and wanting. The kiss turned frantic almost instantly. Naomi's mouth, her taste, made Ethan reckless in ways he didn't recognize, until their bodies pressed together over the gearshift, until they were both twisting against the angle, their frustration manifesting, licks turning into bites, the scrape of teeth ratcheting them higher, further from anything resembling Ethan's original, quieter intent.

A knock against the window, sharp and insistent, forced them apart.

"Thought you'd retired from performing, Grant?" The interruption was jovial, obviously a fellow partygoer, but Ethan and Naomi's ardor was doused anyway.

Naomi shielded her face with her hands, her cheeks uncharacteristically pink.

"Fuck off," she yelled back, reaching over and wiping her lipstick from Ethan's mouth. "Classic," she muttered under her breath, shaking her head. "Come on." She threw open her door and started for the entrance without another glance at him. "Let's get this over with."

After a last, quick check in the rearview mirror, he followed her into the house. Its decor was covered—per the theme, he assumed—in papier-mâché palm trees and cardboard pineapples.

Before he knew it, he was being handed a lei and ushered toward a tiki bar in the backyard, where a live band played island-inspired music and torches cast a golden glow on the makeshift dance floor.

Naomi was obviously popular; there was a playful scuffle over who would get to "lei her" that she defused by grabbing the flower garland and twisting it into a crown that she placed on her own head.

Ethan figured he'd make himself useful and ordered them two drinks from the shirtless bartender, each of which was presented in a fresh coconut with a charming mini umbrella. Armed with social lubricant, he made his way through the crowd to Naomi's side. She accepted her coconut with a grateful hand on his forearm, steadying amid the jovial cacophony around them.

"You made it." Naomi's friend Clara, one of the guests of honor, made her way toward them from the center of the dance floor, looking almost luminous with happiness.

"Thanks for inviting me," Ethan said, very pleased to see a familiar face.

Naomi and Clara embraced, and he could make out the way Clara's lips moved against Naomi's ear, the quick, sharp shake of his date's head in return.

"You have to meet Josh." Clara turned, clearly impervious to Naomi's warning, and waved over someone still on the dance floor.

Ethan didn't have time to react to the fact that he was about to meet another one of Naomi's exes. Almost immediately, a man with burnished-gold hair and a terrible Hawaiian shirt appeared behind Clara, wrapping his arms around her waist and placing his chin on top of her head. He seemed to be the icebreaker others were waiting for, because suddenly Ethan was surrounded by Naomi's friends. Hands and names shot toward him in rapid fire.

"It's so nice to meet you, man. I've heard a lot about you," Josh told him, causing Naomi to tense beside him and shoot daggers at Clara. She seemed to notice, because she extracted herself from her fiancé's hold, stood on her tiptoes to place a quick kiss on his jawline, and grabbed Naomi's hand, yanking her off toward the house. "We'll be right back. Just need Naomi to help in the kitchen for a moment."

"That's not even a good lie," Naomi protested, but she let herself be dragged away.

"So," Josh said, valiantly trying to fill the awkward silence that followed, "sorry, I don't know the proper etiquette, should we call you Rabbi Cohen or—"

"Ethan is fine," he said, taking a long swallow of his drink for courage. Josh had a good four inches on him, at least. "Congratulations on your engagement. Clara was kind enough to help Naomi and me with some publicity, and it's made a big difference at my synagogue. She's very talented."

Josh's face relaxed instantly. "Yeah, she's pretty fucking great." He gazed toward the house, either a little drunk, a lot in love, or both. "I still can't believe she agreed to marry me."

"She seems wild about you." That much was obvious to anyone within a five-hundred-foot radius.

"Well, love is madness." He raised his coconut to knock against Ethan's. "Someone said that, right?"

Ethan thought of Naomi, her throaty laugh and her long limbs and the way she'd sooner tear out her own heart than let someone else get at it.

"Shakespeare, I believe." He had to physically stop his feet from following her.

"I guess I'm supposed to say something macho, as Naomi's ex. Threaten to kill you if you hurt her, right?" For all his size and deep voice, Josh looked like he wouldn't hurt a fly.

"I'll consider myself appropriately warned," Ethan promised. "Though I have to say, I think if anyone's at risk of losing their heart in this gamble, it's me."

"Nah, see, if she's still got you thinking that, she's in trouble." Josh straightened up a bit and leaned toward him. "Naomi's got her tells just like anyone. She'll double down on a pair of twos, every time, just to prove she's not afraid. Thinks it makes her immune, building up a tolerance to losing. But I'm not sure she'd even know how to play it if life gave her a hand she actually wanted." Josh shook his head ruefully. "Sorry, I only ever speak in poker metaphors when I'm drunk. Clara keeps handing me piña coladas. You seem nice. And smart. I'm glad you came." Another guest grabbed Josh's attention, pulling him away, but he turned back at the last second. "Hey, Ethan?"

"Yeah?"

"Will you do me a favor?" Josh grabbed his shoulder, his grip loose and friendly. "Will you actually try not to hurt her? If you can? I know it's not always easy."

"Yeah. I'll do my best." Even that shallow promise felt hollow, but Josh looked relieved, and it was his party.

"Thanks." Someone yelled for Josh to get back on the dance floor, and he nodded. "She deserves someone who wants all of her," he said, quiet enough that the words barely carried over the music. "Especially the parts she's tried to banish."

Somewhere to their left, the band hit a crescendo, guests whooped and hollered, and applause filled Ethan's ears. It didn't matter that making Naomi happy gave him almost as much pleasure and purpose as his work.

At the end of the day, how much of him was left to offer her? Would she settle for sixty percent of a man? Thirty on hard days? Would she change not only her habits but her way of thinking, in order to honor a commitment he'd made long before he ever met her? Was he really ready to ask her to?

Josh grinned at him as he walked backward. "It only takes one."

One what? Ethan wanted to ask. One person? One time? One mistake?

Ethan's brain was in the habit of filling in blanks, testing variables, running running running, but Josh was already gone, apparently satisfied that his last words of wisdom—or warning—would be enough.

Ethan headed into the house to search for Naomi and found her climbing out of a pop-up photo booth, feather boa wrapped around her shoulders, a laugh breaking free of her lips as one of her friends helped her out. She met his eyes and smiled, warm and sweet, and then mouthed, *Get over here.*

As he walked toward her, skirting other guests, he wondered if the rapid beat of his heart was potentially fatal. If he'd sink to his knees at the halfway point. If she'd make up the rest of the distance.

In the end, he reached his destination and let her loop the feathers around his neck.

"What did Josh say?" Her eyes were guarded, and she'd folded her lips together while she waited for him to answer.

"He offered me some poker advice."

Relief washed over her face in a wave. "I don't know why. He's terrible. Should we try to dance?"

Ethan forced himself to relax too. Just because the stakes kept ratcheting higher didn't mean this relationship would end in disaster.

"It's a party. Dancing is practically mandatory," he said, taking her hand and leading her back outside. The music wasn't strictly slow enough for the way he tugged her against him, but she leaned into him anyway, her hair soft and floral under his nose as she let her cheek rest against his neck.

He didn't want to hurt her, but with his track record of neglecting the people he cared for most, the odds didn't look good.

Chapter Twenty-Four

ETHAN WAS SUPPOSED to drive Naomi home after the party. That had been the plan, anyway.

But then he'd been so good all night. So sweet and surprisingly funny with her friends. Smiling for goofy pictures. Bringing Naomi lemonade before she even knew she wanted lemonade.

Her coworker Lance, one of their male tutorialists for Shameless, had come up to her in the middle of the dance floor, beaming, to tell her Ethan had invited him to play bass at the reception after Shabbat services next week.

It almost wasn't weird. Having him blend into her comfort zone.

Naomi had forgotten the luxury of having a date at a party. The way you could roll your eyes at them when someone made an inane comment. The delight of finding them with your coat already slung over their arm when you were ready to leave. The closeness, gentle and fond, of having them hold it behind you, arms straight, while you slipped inside.

She'd lost him for a while during the end of the night, only to find him at the kitchen sink, up to his elbows in dishes.

"It always sucks waking up to a mess the next morning," he explained sheepishly. "Also, your friends kept trying to get me to play drinking games." He ducked his chin.

Naomi kissed him until someone walked in.

They made it as far as the exit before hers on the highway, but when Ethan flipped on his blinker, Naomi put her hand on his forearm.

He seemed to understand the question in it. The *Are we ready for this?* Naomi couldn't push past her lips.

"Yeah?" He glanced at her out of the corner of his eye.

Naomi swallowed. "Yeah."

On the way into his house, she touched the mezuzah by the door without thinking. Two fingers, pressed against the marble and then brought quickly to her lips before she pulled them away. As if he wouldn't notice if she managed to shove them back in her pocket fast enough. Not something she would have done a few months ago, but now she moved without thinking.

She liked his place, despite the old-money cues that didn't quite fit with the way she saw Ethan in her head. It wasn't that he didn't look good against all the dark cherry wood and granite countertops. He did. But there was something about the chandelier hanging over a dining room table big enough to seat eight that felt aggressively vacant, formal and expectant. As if at any moment it would ask her just what exactly she thought she was doing here.

The other rooms were better. Easier. Books filled almost every available surface and spilled out of places she didn't expect. Left open to specific passages or closed but sporting sticky notes like flags out the side. While he hung up their coats, she ran her fingertips across a heavy leather one left open beside the coffeemaker.

"You're like a dog who sheds pages," she told him when he came back.

He laughed in a way that made her think he enjoyed the characterization, head thrown back, eyes crinkled at the corners.

She had so many grand plans to ravish him.

"I'll be right back," she said, and escaped to the bathroom to run cold water on her wrists, trying to cool down. Her nerves multiplied when she reached for a hand towel and saw he had good ones. Thick and clean smelling. She'd never dated anyone with such nice accessories in their powder room.

Was it too much to wish for a little mess? A couple of loose ends to underscore his humanity?

Hands braced on either side of the sink, she stared down her reflection. Her makeup was smudged in the happy, post-party way that reflected a night spent sweating on the dance floor and leaving her lipstick on the rim of cocktail glasses and the collar of Ethan's shirt.

There were a lot of ways she could play this next part. She could strip off her clothes, piece by piece, leaving a trail on the way to his bedroom. She could turn on the shower, and when Ethan came to investigate, she could tug him under the spray, wait until the water plastered his shirt to his body, and then bite his collarbone until he whimpered.

She could drag him only as far as the hallway before dropping to her knees. The carpet was plush enough that she could spend hours edging him without inviting bruises.

But while each imagined scenario excited her, made her blood hum in her veins, something in her mind kept whispering, *Not now. Not yet.* Like her body wanted something else from tonight.

She tried to shake it off, to get her head in the game. She'd come home with him for sex, after all. Because she was tired of waiting. She'd known him for months now; if she put it off any longer, they'd never be able to bridge the gap between her imagination and reality.

Her friends had teased her from the doorway as they waved goodbye. "Have fun riding that beard!"

She'd had to duck her head so they wouldn't see her heated cheeks. How was it possible she hadn't even seen Ethan naked yet? Hadn't touched him anywhere below the waist? And while they'd watched her video and kissed enough to wipe out any expectations of virtuous intent, still she hesitated.

She didn't know why.

All these nerves, they couldn't belong to her. She never got like this. All giddy and vulnerable and . . . shy?

She knew it meant something, that she hadn't mounted him yet, and that was sort of terrifying.

The barrier wasn't Ethan. For all he loved God and wanted to get married . . . he wasn't the one pussyfooting around. It was Naomi who'd pulled away first when he kissed her good night after their last seminar. Who had shaken her head, just barely, when he'd tilted it in inquiry.

He wasn't pushing, not even close. But his eyes, when they caught hers and lingered, held a trace of invitation that Naomi had been diluting, dancing around.

It was embarrassing. She hadn't even had the good form to be smooth about it. The way she kept him at arm's length didn't hold any strategy. The difference between teasing and avoidance was intent.

This was ridiculous. Enough was enough.

She stormed out of the bathroom and grabbed his hand. Then, tucking her chin and batting her lashes, she did the voice, just a little. "Show me your bedroom."

"Okay," Ethan said, low and soft, and pushed against the door at the end of the hall with one hand, letting her lead the way.

Naomi swayed her hips, calculated, camera-worthy, an exaggerated one foot in front of the other right up to the foot of his massive, well-made bed. She picked up one of the two books resting on top of the comforter.

"Rilke, huh? This keeps you warm at night?"

He moved so he stood behind her, close enough to raise goose bumps on her arms even though he didn't touch her.

His arm snaked against her side as he reached around her and took the book. "This," he said, letting his breath hit her neck, his lips trace the shape of her ear, "is how I stop thinking about you long enough to fall asleep."

It was the perfect segue. All she had to do was pick up her cue.

Might need something stronger after tonight. The line practically wrote itself, but she saved her quip and turned to kiss him.

Ethan kept his arms at his sides for a moment. Maybe he was nervous or waiting for something. Or maybe, she realized when she ran her nails down the nape of his neck and he groaned, biting her lip hard enough that she clenched everything below the waist, he didn't trust himself not to push for more than she wanted to give.

Her head went fuzzy, lust and other emotions she didn't recognize and refused to examine fighting for purchase. Getting him naked seemed like the best antidote. Once she had him undone, then she'd know what to do, surely.

Naomi Grant's got a pleasure-seeking missile beneath her skirt. Some reporter from *GQ* had actually written that about her, once upon a time.

She sat on the bed, spreading her legs wide so Ethan stood between them, and started unbuttoning his shirt.

"Are you sure about this?" Ethan tried to make her look him in the eye.

Naomi didn't want to, for some reason. In fact, she suddenly decided that would be a terrible idea. So she pulled her top over her head, enjoying the few blissful seconds when she had an excuse not to make eye contact almost as much as the cool air pressing against her heated skin.

She was a professional, so she got almost all his buttons undone even as he twisted to drop to his knees in front of her. Bringing their faces level.

"Hey," he said, and it was the softest word she'd ever heard. Not in volume but in intent.

"Hi," she said back, because her brain wasn't working that well.

She tried to kiss him, to cut this conversation off so he wouldn't realize how off her game she was, but he pulled back, out of her reach again, concern drawing his brows together.

"Wait. What's going on? Talk to me for a second."

"Nothing. It's nothing." She reached for his wrists, trying to get his hands on her. Anywhere. If this was how it felt to be naked in a new way, there was no doubt in her mind about which one was more vulnerable.

"It's not nothing," Ethan said. "Naomi, hang on."

Her heart hammered against her ribs, dangerous, thunderous. She started taking her bra off before she could fall into the abyss of it. A missile indeed.

"Wait." Ethan's voice came out strangled as he took in her breasts, but he still shook his head. "Please."

The *please* almost killed her. How could she be this horny and this confused at the same time? It was ridiculous. Unacceptable. An unwelcome exception to her lauded experience.

"I just . . . need some water, I think. I'm thirsty." She did a little cough that was wafer thin and just as transparent.

"I'll get it for you." Ethan's unbuttoned shirt flew open as he stood. The moonlight coming in through his curtains cast his chest in shadows. He was beautiful. Defined but not overly muscled. His nipples flat and brown and begging for her teeth.

After all the people she'd fucked, this was the scenario where she couldn't land the plane?

She'd never considered herself wicked. In fact, Naomi thought of herself as a pretty good person at the end of the day. But tonight, this disconnect between her mind and her body felt like punishment, and frankly, she was pissed.

When Ethan came back, he had two waters, one with ice and one without, that he held out for her to pick from. She took the ice water and wrapped both hands around the smooth, cold glass. The ice cubes knocking against her teeth as she took a sip helped ground her, oddly enough.

How could she tell this man—who she was more attracted to than anyone she had ever met—that maybe she wanted something less than carnal tonight?

Naomi took a deep breath while Ethan stood there, accepting her empty glass once she'd drained it.

Okay, she needed to back up. What were the facts here?

She wanted to have sex with Ethan. To feel his body in and around hers. She wanted possession of his heat and his scent and the growl that came from low in his throat. But she'd never been nervous like this before.

Not the first time she'd fucked her high school boyfriend. Not her first day on set. Never.

Sex was easy. People made it complicated with their expectations and their insecurities. Naomi had never given sex that power. She'd mastered the movements like any other dance, and as for the accompanying chemical reactions?

Well, she'd never put that much stock in those feelings.

Even the best sex with Jocelyn and Josh had never been that complex. It was just fun and nice. An expression of how much she cared about them. Hell, sometimes it was just a way to blow off steam.

Naomi had devoted most of her waking hours and many of her sleeping hours to dirty dreams of Ethan. She had employed every ounce of filthy, sexual energy she had to the idea of working him over like he was some juicy Regency wallflower and she was a highwayman with the middle name *corruption*.

So now that he was laid out before her, she wasn't . . . scared. Because that would be ridiculous. It was just . . . she wanted . . .

It felt like holding on to the side of a cliff, hanging by her fingertips, and if she let go, she'd fall hard. Hard enough that she might lose herself and fly apart into a million pieces.

It was a good thing she was sitting down.

Ethan dropped to the bed beside her, leaning forward to rest his elbows on his knees.

"You're not ready," he said, gentle again, soft again, into the darkness.

Denial formed on her tongue, urgent and a little bit mean.

She was always ready. He wasn't special. He was just a man.

Except.

She wanted to kiss every sharp point on him, every curve. But something inside her had locked up, and okay, maybe it would be braver to examine it instead of trying to suffocate it with her bare hands.

"I'm maybe, inexplicably, not ready," she said, still a little mad, but also kind of in awe.

"You wanna talk about it?"

She shook her head. Emotion sat in her throat. A weird place for it, in her opinion.

Ethan leaned back, just a little, to look at her. Why was his face so . . . good? Why did his nose make her want to weep? Why did she want to find a color that matched his lips and use it to paint?

She closed her eyes against the onslaught. Breathed in and out and in again. Finally, asked her body what it wanted from her. The answer, like so much else this evening, caught her off guard.

"Can I just . . ." She moved so that she was above him, her knees hugging either side of his thighs, hovering, waiting for confirmation, because if she was confused, Ethan had to be completely thrown by this entire display.

"Of course." He pulled her down so she could sit in his lap, wrapped his arms low around her back until she was flush against him, his scent draping over her like a blanket. His warmth bleeding into her body.

After a few minutes, her heartbeat evened out and her breathing calmed. Part of her still wanted to fight. Didn't want to want this. But that part faded along with the tension from her limbs. Okay, so their pace was different than her usual speed. No one really talked about how so much of letting other people in involved listening to yourself.

Naomi didn't know how long they sat like that, not speaking, her face tucked against his neck. He smelled like summer, like more daylight and going outside to lie in the grass.

Ethan brought his hand up and combed through her hair after a while, the gentle tugging the most soothing sensation she could imagine.

Okay. So this . . . holding . . . wasn't better than sex, but it was maybe more than sex, for her at least, tonight.

She hardly ever let herself be still with anyone, too afraid that if she did, they might see the hungry gaping wound of her heart. How it wanted and wanted and wanted so much that she never fed it anymore for fear of it growing too powerful and consuming her.

Naomi knew it was okay to want closeness and comfort without sex, but asking for that still felt a little like surrender.

As it turned out, maybe this was modern intimacy.

The way Ethan breathed, even and easy, his body moving hers like gentle swells on the ocean. The way his shoulders held steady under her hands. The way he ran his fingertips like a whisper down her back. The way she could fall asleep like this, if she wanted. Safe and cared for.

Apparently, sometimes even teachers had a lot to learn.

Chapter Twenty-Five

A FEW DAYS after what she'd started thinking of as "the cuddling incident," Naomi wrapped her hands around her third cup of coffee and, with an aggressive shake of her head, brought her attention back to the Shameless status meeting. Between the extra hours she'd put in studying for her class and waking up early this morning to adjust her lecture series notes, her head weighed about fifty pounds at the moment.

"Filming last week went even better than we'd hoped," Cass said, filling the founders in on last week's shoot. "Josh and I reviewed the raw footage last night, and we think we can extend the series from three videos to five, easy."

"Oh, that's great." Clara moved to adjust the magnetic note cards they used to map their content calendar across a wall in the conference room. "Let's do that and plan to keep one video exclusive for platinum subscribers. Naomi, you've been working on a new tiered programming structure, right? Can we review that now?"

Naomi blinked. "Sorry, what?"

Next to her, Josh furrowed his dark brows. "Last week you said you'd review the subscriber analytics and make recommendations on which types of content we should put behind the higher paywall, re-member?"

Fuck. Her stomach twisted. Three sets of eyes rested on her rapidly heating face. "I completely forgot."

"You forgot?" There was no judgment in Clara's voice, just genuine incredulity. Her co-founder didn't know what it looked like when Naomi dropped the ball, because Naomi never let herself drop the ball.

"Sorry." She shoved her chair back from the table, sending ripples across the surface of her coffee. "Shit."

"Hey," Josh said gently, more to her than to the room. "It's fine. It's not a big deal."

"Of course it's a big deal." Her reply was practically spitting. Didn't he realize what this meant?

Cass and Clara exchanged a look that Naomi didn't like at all. Worry.

How could she have let this happen? This was how it all started. Something seemingly small, innocuous. But before you knew it, she'd be forgetting to pay vendors or missing a call that led to everyone's health insurance lapsing. How the hell had she let herself get sucked into someone else's life? Distracted from her responsibilities. People counted on her here. They trusted her to lead.

"Let's just plan to review it next week instead," Clara said, folding her hands in front of her, diplomatic.

Naomi got to her feet, picking up her mug as an afterthought, an excuse. "I need a refill."

The hallway was cooler than the conference room, at least. The hum of the A/C was stronger in her ears as she leaned against the wall, tipping her head back and taking a deep breath.

Josh followed her out, closing the door behind him with a soft click. "You—"

"Don't start." She tried to glare at him, but her aim must have been off, because he kept talking.

"You're allowed to make mistakes."

"Yeah? Says who?"

He raised his hands helplessly. "I don't know. The universe? I'm not personally trying to govern you. I don't have a death wish."

She holstered her lethal gaze, staring down at her shoes. "I can't believe I forgot."

Josh sighed. "Honestly," he said, "I can."

Naomi whipped her head toward him. "Excuse me?"

"You're fucking exhausted, Stu."

He was the only one who called her that goofy nickname. A play on her legal last name, Sturm. All the years they'd known each other hung in that word, all the times he'd asked and asked and asked her to tell him what was wrong—first as her co-star, then as her boyfriend, now as her business partner—and she never let him all the way in.

Naomi thought about protesting now, but he was right, she couldn't even muster up the energy to fight. "I didn't know it was so obvious."

"Well, it's kinda ridiculous that you thought you could add the lecture series and night classes"—he held up a hand, stalling, soothing—"yes, Clara told me, you can hiss at her later—to your already packed schedule, all while starting a new relationship. There aren't enough hours in the day. Anyone would be struggling to keep up."

"I don't wanna—"

"I know you don't wanna be just anyone," he finished, indulgent, "but too bad. You messed up, and you're gonna mess up again. We're gonna keep on forgiving you, so you might as well just get used to it. The business won't fold if you're not constantly circling it like a hawk. It's time for you to have a little faith in what we've built. And in your friends."

She studied a chip in the handle of her mug, pressed her thumb over the rough ridge of it for a long moment.

"I promised myself when this whole thing with Ethan started that

I wouldn't compromise. That I wouldn't succumb to the temptation to trade in Shameless for any other community."

Josh moved so his back was against the wall beside her, and then he slid down until his butt hit the ground, long legs splayed out in front of him. "Come down here."

Naomi scrunched her nose. She wasn't in the habit of sitting on floors. But Josh pointed his big dumb cow eyes at her—and whatever—she guessed a tiny part of her was still fond of him or something, because she sat, creasing her pencil skirt.

"It's not us versus them, you know. No one's asking you to choose," he said softly. "You've got every right to have a whole, messy life—with all the different parts of yourself spilling over each other."

She shook her head. "I'm supposed to be tough."

"You *are* tough." He brought a hand down to squeeze her knee. "You're the toughest person I know, but fuck anyone who tries to tell you that's all you're allowed to be. What a terrible, gross burden."

"Yeah," she agreed. A simple world acknowledging the countless hours she spent upholding the mantle of *bad bitch*. "It really fucking is."

"You know what you taught me?"

"That wrist flick thing for when you're—"

"Besides that," Josh said, cutting her off. "You taught me that the bravest, hardest work anyone can take on is facing their own shit. Challenging all the lies we tell ourselves. Admitting when we're wrong. Cleaning up our own mess. You're the queen of all that stuff."

"Yeah, but no one wants to see it. It's not glamorous." She blamed exhaustion for the way she let her head fall against Josh's shoulder.

"When have you ever given a single fuck what other people want?"

"Good point."

Maybe it was hypocritical to preach about balance after hours, to hound her employees about taking all their PTO, to demand transparency and trust from everyone else, and not live by her own rules.

"Go home. Get some sleep," Josh said. "I'm gonna talk to Clara.

She's been angling forever to get some of the administrative stuff off your plate. That's the whole point of having staff, of hiring people we know and trust. We would have delegated at least twenty percent of your workload a year ago if you'd let us."

Naomi's mind caught on a wisp of a lesson from her courses. A scholar from Jerusalem posited that two types of rest exist.

One is rest from weariness, respite when our bodies and minds are worn down. Tired. We rest only so we might wake up and continue working. This first rest—sleep—brings relief, but not joy.

The second type of rest, the one Naomi had never really considered, came only at the end of reaching a goal, never in the middle. This was the rest of release. Of knowing that one had done something or made something worthy of satisfaction. Menuhat margoa, rest in achievement. Rest that brings peace.

Naomi supposed she could bask. A little.

Eventually, Josh got to his feet, offering her a hand up.

She refused to recognize it as a metaphor and only accepted because her heels were slippery on the concrete floor.

"I'm sorry," she said, and they both knew she wasn't just talking about the work. They'd done a lot for each other over the years, and yeah, he definitely owed her for the whole falling-in-love-with-their-financier-after-promising-not-to thing, but he'd also always believed in her, even when she didn't return the favor.

What was more, Josh didn't just believe in her ability to conquer worlds, he'd always believed in her humanity. He'd never seen her mistakes as fatal—never seen them as more than glancing blows.

"Two apologies from Naomi Grant in one hour? Quit it before I get smug." Josh smiled at her, dimples and all. *Fucking show-off.*

He reached for the door handle, but she caught his wrist, using it to turn him toward her.

"What are you—"

And Naomi did something she should have done a long time ago.

She hugged him.

His arms came around her waist tentatively. "Is there something you're not telling me? Are you sick?"

"Shhh," she said, her chin on his shoulder. "I'm trying this new thing."

The door opened behind them.

"Oh," Clara said, obviously surprised to find her business partner and her fiancé embracing.

But the next thing Naomi knew, Clara had folded herself around Naomi's back, cheek pressing into her shoulder blades, completing the hug like they were cartoon kittens on some kind of deranged greeting card.

"It's about time," Clara said, sighing happily.

"You two really are the worst," Naomi muttered under her breath. But she didn't mean it.

Chapter Twenty-Six

MODERN INTIMACY—LECTURE 5:
Get more naked

NAOMI'S MUSCLES COMPLAINED as she pulled herself out of her car in the parking lot of the JCC on Tuesday night. She'd expected the discomfort, having finally made it to the gym that morning for the first time in a while. Her brain read the ache as achievement. As conquering herself. Bending her form to match her will. The sharp edge of each step reminded her of progress. As it turned out, the sensation of falling in love with Ethan Cohen was very similar.

Except, of course, that it was her mind changing. Her brain instead of her body working to transform. The promise in the sweet burn of this new kind of work was comforting in its familiarity and heady with potential. It was hard to explain. She just felt . . . full when she was with him, satisfied in a way she hadn't realized she'd been craving.

Naomi had lain in bed last night and given her ceiling all the sappy smiles she'd tried to hide during the day, asking herself what it was about him that made her softer and stronger at the same time.

The best articulation Naomi could come up with was that he made her tender. Which was . . . not a word that anyone had ever used to describe her.

Tender like petals pressed between pages of a book. Tender like a release of poison from her bloodstream. Tender, a cousin to weak, but with a quiet power she couldn't deny.

Naomi had built Shameless. She knew what it felt like to take a theory you held about what the world needed and make it real. For the entire duration of her twenties, she'd rioted in art and business both. But this lecture series with Ethan was different.

It still held notes of rebellion, of steering social change, but while Shameless had operated outside of established systems, in open defiance of them even, the Modern Intimacy series was designed to build a bridge between a synagogue that had existed for a hundred years and people searching for belonging in an increasingly distant culture. And it was Naomi's job to see them safely across.

She hoped she was up to the task.

Something about the parking lot was weird tonight. She shoved her keys in her bag. There were too many cars. Too many people lingering by the entrance, their voices kicking up as she passed.

"Is that her?"

"No way. That's not her."

Naomi ignored them and the warning crawling down her spine. She had somewhere to be. Her lecture started in ten minutes. Those people weren't her problem. She had a class waiting.

Except when she got to their usual room, it was empty. She pulled out her cell phone and saw two missed calls from Ethan and a string of text messages.

6:30 Have to move to auditorium C.

6:45 Some members of the press here. Did Clara invite them?

6:47 Looks like standing room only.

Naomi closed her eyes and tried to slow the beating of her heart. She inhaled deeply and let it out through her nose. Okay, so her audience had grown. That was fine. Still just another lecture. Another type of performance. This group of people would see exclusively and exactly what she wanted them to, just like everyone else.

According to a sign bearing city ordinance, auditorium C could safely seat 750 people. But when Naomi entered the room and skimmed the audience, attendees had spilled into the aisles, sitting on the steps or leaning against the back wall.

She took her place behind the podium. This one didn't have wheels. For some reason, she really didn't like that.

"I suppose you're all here tonight because you heard this was the lecture about sex, right? You wanna know what a self-declared pleasure professional is going to say about taking off your clothes." Her voice carried through the microphone, too loud and not languid enough by half.

The audience rippled, elbows pressed to desks as heads ducked forward, pens poised, fingers braced over keyboards.

Naomi found Ethan in the back row, like always, and straightened her shoulders.

"Well, I don't know if you've all noticed, but in our formerly puritanical and currently patriarchal society, sex makes some people nervous," she said, this time at the right volume. "Sometimes, even me."

The click-clack of someone typing with enthusiasm rang out across the auditorium. Naomi straightened her shoulders.

"I've spent a lot of hours having sex. A few of you know that better than others." She nodded at a male reporter in the front, earning her a few laughs.

"It's always been a bit untenable. There's no way, really, to predict how sex will be with a new person. All the theories about the way they kiss or the size of their instep are nothing but grasping at straws. I've had ugly sex with gorgeous people. Sex that's not worth remembering. Sex that made me forget my own name. Sometimes it's bad. Sometimes it's funny. Occasionally, it's funny how bad it is."

Naomi focused on her students, the ones that kept coming back week after week. She'd come to talk to them, not the press. "Listen, I want you each to have exactly as much sex as you'd like. Maybe that's no sex. Maybe it's tons. Probably it's somewhere in the middle."

"I'd prefer tons," Craig shouted out, cupping his hands around his mouth so it carried.

"I know you would, bud. Hang in there." She gave him a conciliatory nod before continuing. "I can't tell you the right way to have sex. I'm pretty sure there is no right way. I'm also definitely not going to tell you what not to do. Own your own boundaries."

Someone snapped a photo with a flash. Naomi blinked. *It's okay. You're okay.*

"All I can tell you is that for the last decade of my life, I've mostly treated sex as a litmus test. My partners passing and failing to varying degrees." She paused to tuck her hair behind her ear, staring out at a guy clearly filming on his cell. "I wanna be clear that performing in adult films didn't make me like that."

Naomi would throw herself down a flight of stairs before she'd let another journalist write a think piece about how sex workers couldn't emotionally connect.

"I considered myself discerning. But really, I was just young and arrogant. I thought I knew where sex maxed out. Where it peaked, no pun intended. I used to think—and to be fair, I thought this was extremely profound at the time—that if you made someone come in the right way, you could get them to reveal things to you that they kept hidden from the rest of the world. Sounds powerful, right?"

"Sounds like some potent pussy, Ms. G."

Naomi shook her head, recognizing another familiar voice. "Thanks, Dan. I try."

Ethan shot him an intense *Watch it* look that made her laugh.

"Potency aside, I recently realized that sometimes it's better to ask yourself not just what do you want, but what are you willing to give?"

Tender like a fading bruise. Tender like a slow dance. Tender like a beating heart.

"After all, a trade that only goes one way is actually called stealing, and after a while, even the most callous hearts grow guilty."

When Naomi was young, she'd thought hardening herself to vulnerability was radical. Now, she knew it was both foolish and impossible.

"Access to your body is one thing. To let someone see your feverish wants. To let them hear the noises you make as you surrender. When you think about it a lot, having sex is kind of . . . insane."

More laughs. Naomi took them in, let them keep her warm.

She found Ethan again. He wasn't taking notes like usual. His eyes held hers. *Hey*, he mouthed.

Hi.

Naomi walked away from the mic; she was loud enough on her own.

"Sometimes sex can mean giving someone access to the parts of yourself that you spend a lot of time and energy covering up. And I know what you're all thinking. Isn't that hard enough?"

Tender like a promise. Tender like a sunrise. Tender like your key in the front door at midnight, letting you in, welcoming you home.

"And here I am, asking you to give away more."

Naomi let her hands fall open at her sides.

"I guess what I'm saying is, try to figure out, ideally before you get naked, if the person you're with wants you. Not anyone. Not a fantasy. Or a pedestal-poised ideal. Not the *you* they wish you were. You as you are. Full stop. No modifier."

This time when she looked for him, Ethan wasn't in his seat. But that was okay.

"I'm talking about the type of intimacy that happens when someone's looking right at you, and most of all—this is the important part—when you let them."

A commotion in the hallway caught her attention. Raised voices. She shook her head to refocus.

"Listen, for all my experience, I'm not an expert. What I'm telling you isn't a rule or a secret ingredient. It's a theory, like anything else you've heard in this class. You can have great sex with someone you just met. You can have terrible sex with someone you love. It's all okay. I can't stress enough that there's no shame in fucking without feelings."

Someone to her left clapped.

"You decide what makes sex exciting. What makes it special for you. When you're ready."

A sea of faces stared back at her. Some nervous. Some mildly scandalized. A few thoughtful.

The hallway altercation grew louder. Footsteps over shouting. Naomi fought to hold the audience's attention, to keep them focused through her gaze and the volume of her voice.

"Sex doesn't have to be a big deal to be worthwhile. But sometimes it *is* a big deal, and that's okay too."

The restless room grew quieter.

"Maybe this is the kind of dare that only appeals to me, but what if your next great sex doesn't come from a position or a technique or a toy? What if it comes from you, letting go of whatever it is you thought you were supposed to be?"

A hand went up, an older woman she'd never seen before. "It sounds like you're saying that if we try hard enough, any of us can have great sex?"

"Yes," Naomi said, catching a flash of dimples in reply. "Absolutely. I'm not gonna lie, sometimes you have to work for it. But you can have great sex even if it takes you hours to come. If you cry afterward, or hell, in the middle of it. Believe it or not, I have it on good authority that you can have great sex even after accidentally giving someone a bloody nose."

An unfortunate accident.

"There are a lot of ways to be intimate with someone. And what you need will change over time. One of the things that makes sex worth having is the ways in which it can surprise you."

Something hit the door of the auditorium hard. Heavy, like a person's entire weight pushed against the wood.

"What the hell?"

Naomi was up the aisle before anyone else could react, pushing open the door to see what in the world was going on. Her breath caught in the base of her throat, and she fell back a step.

Oh no. Not again.

....

SHAME STARTED AS a hot breath against her neck. The scene in the hallway hit Naomi by degrees. First, the posters with images frozen from her films, screamingly vivid. Then the flyers, scattered across the ground like broken glass, corners torn like they'd been ripped from someone's hand. She had to bend her knees and tilt her head to make out the photos of Ethan's face Photoshopped over Josh's to create a warped version of Frankenstein's monster. She closed her eyes. Took a step back until her heels hit the wall.

Faces turned toward her, twisted in anger, mouths open, yelling, lashing pink tongues.

Their words crashed together, slamming against her temples. As ruthless as any hit she'd ever taken at the gym.

When Naomi had first decided to star in adult films, she'd conducted an exercise alone in her room. She'd written down every word she could think of that disparaged women and sex workers, her hand shaking as she formed the letters, carefully, one after the other, on scraps of paper until they covered her carpet. When she was done, there were close to a hundred of them. Each sharper than the last.

Words meant to leave shrapnel in their victims. Words with teeth. She made herself look until her vision blurred. If she couldn't take them alone in her room, she'd never survive. Naomi read the slander, the curses, the labels, one after the other. She let them sink beneath her skin, testing their weight. It got easier after she started imagining herself as a master of poisons, building up a tolerance by letting the insults pollute her body, her mind, until she built up a resilience. Her plan to reclaim her identity required that sort of immunity.

It had taken a week for her to be able to say some of them out loud without growing nauseous. The first two nights, she'd actually thrown up. Not from the definitions, but from the memories they evoked.

A different hallway, the mass of people younger then, and with less to lose. The startling knowledge that life as she'd known it was over, wiped clean, or rather dirty, by a single night. A single boy.

Slut had been the clear favorite back then. She'd wondered once, years later, half laughing, if it was because of the hard *T* at the end. The satisfying way teeth came together at the back of the word. She'd considered, briefly, getting it tattooed somewhere on her body. So that the next time someone called her a slut, she could flash them her wrist or her shoulder and answer, "Damn straight."

The thing that had stopped her in the end was an old rule. Leviticus. She couldn't be buried with her Jewish family if she bore the ink. Enough doors had slammed in her face by that point; she wasn't going to invite another one just to prove a point.

What a fool she'd been to think she and Ethan could get away with just deciding to date. She'd let herself grow complacent, confident from the lectures, the casual acceptance of the younger community members, their eagerness and excitement.

"You should be ashamed of yourself," an older man said to her now, pushing himself forward so he could get right in her face.

A moment later, Ethan was in front of her, stepping between her and the crowd that had gathered outside the classroom, creating a barrier with his body. Enough that she could finally process what was happening. Protesters. News crews. Anxious JCC members, brought out of their Zumba classes and bocce ball games to investigate.

THE INTIMACY EXPERIMENT • 235

"How dare you talk about shame," Ethan said, rage rolling off him in waves. "In a world that knows so much injustice, so much suffering, you've come here to scream at people you don't know about practices that are none of your business, feet from where children play."

"I'm sorry, Rabbi Cohen." A short woman with gray curls was touching his arm. "I tried to keep them outside, but they wouldn't listen." The director of the JCC, Naomi realized. "I've called security. They'll be here any moment."

Ethan turned so his whole body faced Naomi. "I want to get you out of here," he said, leaning in to speak against her ear. He pulled back to look at her, his jaw strained, changing the planes of his face into something hard and unyielding as stone. "What do you want?"

What did she want? She wanted to sit down with her back against the cold concrete wall. She wanted to wrap her arms around her knees and lower her head until she couldn't see any of this, could pretend it was a nightmare. Forceful but fleeting. She'd had plenty of them over the last decade, similar enough in pitch that the idea wasn't a stretch. But she didn't say any of that.

"I want to finish my seminar." She brought her mouth to his, quick but soft, a reminder that what they had was sweet enough to challenge the vitriol in this hallway. Maybe even the vitriol that lay outside too. Anti-Semitism was the reason this JCC and every other had security guards at all hours. "I trust you to take care of this."

He nodded, worry so harsh across his face that she wanted to smooth it with her fingertips.

But she never left an audience waiting. Naomi pushed her way back to the door, moved to the lectern, and adjusted the volume on the microphone. "Sorry about that."

The auditorium was out of sorts, people halfway out of their seats, eyes anxious and unsure.

A hand went up: Molly, of course. "Ms. Grant, are you sure you're okay?"

Behind the door, new voices joined the throng, louder, calling for order and meeting resistance.

Craig and Dan got up silently and stood on either side of the doorway, facing in, arms crossed and eyes fierce, nodding at her from adopted sentry positions.

Naomi's heart clenched. Tears welled in her eyes. She'd known censure and scorn before, but this part was different. The part where there were people on her side, taking up her defense. The part where she had more to lose than her dignity. The part where she was fighting not out of spite, but because she believed that one day her rebellion might make it easier for someone else to know peace.

She nodded back.

"I know I'm supposed to keep talking about sex, and I promise I have a lot more to say on the subject. But before I do," Naomi said, "I want to acknowledge something about modern intimacy that falls outside the original bounds of the syllabus."

Tender like the ocean returning to shore, no matter how many times it's sent away.

"This world is full of people who would rather hate you than examine the pain in their own hearts. They will try to limit who you can love, who you can spend time with, who you can fuck. Some of these people will act like their condemnation is in your best interest. Like one day you'll thank them for showing you the error of your ways. Some of them feel better about their own lives when they can deny the validity of yours."

The voices in the hallway were fading, footfalls carrying them away like dust on the wind. She released a breath and then another, rolled her shoulders back, offered her skittish audience her best attempt at a smile.

"I've been a social pariah for many years now, and I can tell you that it's worth it to not spend a second of your precious time on earth worrying about what other people believe you should do, believe you should be. Your body is a gift. Your life is yours alone."

This time when her eyes shot to the door, it was because Ethan was standing there, arms crossed over his chest, color high in his cheeks, the curls on his head in disarray. His mouth made a now familiar shape. *Hey* like 'you're safe.'

She wrapped her hand around her opposite wrist, held on tight.

"Sometimes love is your own quiet rebellion." Her words were almost a whisper, but the microphone carried them to their intended destination.

Chapter Twenty-Seven

THE MOOD IN Ethan's living room later that night was tense, to say the least.

Naomi put on a pot of tea, because that seemed to help soothe people in movies and because he had an electric kettle that made the process foolproof.

"Thanks," he said when she handed him a steaming mug, and then immediately placed it on the coffee table.

So much for that idea.

His guilt practically radiated off him.

"It wasn't your fault," she said gently.

He paced in front of his bookshelves, hands flexing in and out of fists. "I hate that you had to experience that. I hate that I didn't see it coming. That I didn't do something to prevent it." He lowered his voice. "To protect you."

Naomi walked over and took his hand, making him stop. Making him look at her.

"That is a beautiful impulse and I appreciate it, but those types of reactions are a sort of inevitable, unpleasant reality. The world we live in doesn't exactly welcome our relationship for all sorts of reasons. But I'm not interested in their approval. I've already won."

His mouth stayed in an obstinate frown. "How's that?"

Naomi tried to think of a way to explain.

"You know how when you give a sermon, sometimes you use a story as an allegory?"

"Yes."

"I'm gonna try to do that."

His cheek twitched. "Okay."

"Once upon a time—"

"Hmm." He frowned. "Not my usual opening . . ."

"Hush." She kissed him quickly, because he was being annoying but also because he was very cute.

"Once upon a time," she repeated, "there was this cat, and she grew up in a nice cat home and had everything a cat could want, but then one day she met a boy, and this boy was very mean to her. And she figured that all boys, all people, were probably mean as well. So she decided to get tough, grew out her claws, learned to fight. She let herself become mean too."

Ethan rubbed his thumb against her jawline. "Poor cat."

"Don't feel sorry for her. She was very successful. For a long time, she kept everyone away, hissing and scratching and biting, and she liked it like that. But then when she got older, she met a new boy, and he was the softest boy in the whole world."

He groaned, "I am not."

"He pretended he wasn't that soft," Naomi continued, talking over him, "but the cat knew better. Because he let her hiss at him on occasion, and he kept saying things like 'I think you're a great cat. Maybe the best cat. I haven't met them all, but I have this hunch.'"

Ethan shook his head. "You didn't say this story was going to be embarrassing for me."

"I figured that was a given."

He opened his mouth to protest.

"I'm almost done," she promised. "The cat liked this soft boy. So when he tried to hold her and be kind to her, she wanted to let him. At first, she didn't always know how. She'd spent so many years fighting. But he was patient, and he showed her he wouldn't hurt her, even when she was cruel to him. So she grew a little softer herself."

Naomi's insides felt warm and gooey. It was almost intolerable. But she kept talking anyway. "But sometimes the cat would still get scared. Even though she knew the boy would never intentionally hurt her, she would bite him just to see if he'd still be kind. If he'd stay."

"I'm not going anywhere," Ethan said quietly, holding her gaze.

"And so he did, and the cat tried to bite him less, which was a work in progress, but alas, aren't we all."

"Very true," he agreed.

"What did you think of the story?"

"Well, I gotta say"—Ethan wrapped his hands around her waist and pulled her against him—"I prefer the version where we're both human."

She wrapped her arms around his neck. "That's fair."

"But"—he kissed her, soft at first and then deeper—"I appreciate the message."

Naomi relished the heady press of his perfect mouth. "I guess I should tell stories more often."

Holding her gaze, Ethan lowered himself to his knees in front of her.

Naomi caught her bottom lip between her teeth as her heartbeat kicked up. He was just that beautiful. Looking at him made her feel lucky. Made her want to paint, despite having never painted a day in her life. It felt like the least she could do. To capture this moment somehow, so that other people could know half the pleasure of it.

He'd been so sure in his movement, the downward trajectory, but she could read the hesitation in him now—the way he tapped his fingers against his palm and shook his head a little.

"Can I . . . um . . . would you mind if I . . ." For a moment she didn't know what he wanted, truly couldn't figure it out because her brain had emulsified into lust lava, but then Ethan traced his bottom lip, the soft, too-pink-for-its-own-good bottom lip with his tongue, leaving his whole mouth wet and shiny, and he tipped his chin toward her and grunted.

"You're asking if I want you to go down on me?" she said, genuinely surprised. The idea of it, the anticipation of his beard against her tender skin, getting his face all messy . . . oh man. "I definitely want you to go down on me."

The confirmation seemed to set something loose in him. He brought his hands to the back of her calves, running them slowly up her legs.

"The cat story really did it for ya, huh?" Naomi said, mostly to cover for the fact that she was terribly close to trembling.

"Please shut up," he told her pleasantly. His fingers met the hem of her skirt, his thumbs flirting with the material.

She hadn't been ready before, but now she was nothing but shivery desire, aching, arching.

He pushed her skirt up around her waist, leaning forward to kiss her through her underwear.

"Okay, but I think you should acknowledge the tremendous restraint I'm showing," she said, breath catching, "in not making a pussy joke right now."

"Noted." The wet heat of his breath against her core made her groan.

She loved the tension in his back. The reverence of his grip, fingertips pressed to the fullest part of her ass. The messy eagerness of his mouth as he licked her, once, through the damp fabric.

Naomi threaded her fingers through his silky hair, tugging, directing his movement, urging him on. She'd waited so long that everything about this felt like life or death. It wasn't about wanting him to touch her, to make her come. It was need.

Ethan turned his head against her grip, nipping at the tender skin of her inner thighs. Her golden boy.

She bucked her hips, trying to get his mouth back on her clit. "Just a friendly heads-up that there's no foreplay needed at this time. Thanks."

In response, Ethan tightened his grip on her thighs.

"Yeah, well," he said, voice rough. "I've got plans."

Normally, Naomi would scoff at that. Would take charge. Claim her pleasure. But he'd made her soft, and she found she couldn't deny him even this. For once, she tried to listen. Tried to stay standing on trembling legs.

"I thought you were gonna be nice to me." She pouted.

He hooked his thumbs in her underwear and yanked them down to her knees, grinning up at her. "I am."

The rough scrape of his beard against her bare, wet skin made her gasp as he licked a broad stroke across her slit.

With shaking hands, she reached for the bottom of her top, wrenching the silk open so she could get at her tits, pushing down the cups of her bra. A porcelain button pinged off the hardwood floor.

Ethan groaned, looking up at her with wild need. He sat back on his heels for a moment. "Did you just rip open your own top? How are you so . . ." He closed his eyes. "So . . ."

She loved the crease of his forehead. He looked moments from shattering, and she hadn't even touched him yet.

"Impatient?" Naomi tugged at her nipples, hissing at the way the ministrations made her clench between her legs.

He laughed against her belly. "That too."

Naomi dug her nails into his scalp. "Nice," she reminded him.

He brought his thumb to tease her entrance.

She thrust herself forward, seeking.

Pumping shallowly inside her, just enough to drive her nuts, Ethan traced teasing circles around her clit. "How nice?"

Wrapping one hand around his wrist, she held him steady while she fucked herself on his hand. "Nicer than that."

He let her ride his fingers for a while, using his mouth on her clit. When she started whimpering, so close she could taste it, he knocked her hand aside and pulled her toward his face, kissing her pussy so well that her thighs shook and her knees locked. She couldn't believe she'd ever thought he was safe.

Naomi came when he slid two fingers inside her, his thumb whispering across her back entrance, because wow, the shock of that, the barest suggestion that someday, he might want to . . . yeah, she fucking came.

After, he got to his feet, looking positively pleased as punch. She would have smacked him on the arm if her entire body hadn't been made of Jell-O at the moment. He grabbed a towel from the bathroom, wiping his hands and his chin and his . . . good lord . . . his neck. She was going to ruin this man's sheets.

"Bedroom?" he offered.

"Too far." She yanked off her half-removed clothes.

He laughed and followed her lead, stripping in his living room. His hands fell to his belt. It was nice, thick brown leather. She wanted him to wrap it around his fist, just so she could catalog that visual. She also wanted him to slap it against his thigh.

Oh God, now she was looking at his thighs and the muscles there, and where the hell had those come from, anyway? Was he riding horses in his spare time or something?

He'd stripped down to his boxers. Green and white checkers.

She felt like it was her birthday. Like this moment, so bright with promise and possibility, could only come around once a year. Because the other 364 days were meant for longing, for closing her eyes, touching herself, and whining for the way Ethan looked right now. Eager and open and shy. His eyes soft but his cock decidedly not.

It had been a while since she'd seen a dick outside of a professional context, and it was frankly alarming that her mouth filled immediately with saliva.

All of a sudden, Ethan was extremely naked, and honestly, she could come like this. She could come looking at his fucking gorgeous dick and his stupid face that she was so fond of that right now she kind of wanted to punch him in it.

She was ready to write poems about his footlong eyelashes and the texture of his beard and the way his chest was covered in dark hair that made her want to whimper, physically whimper, at the sight of it, at the contrast of the color against his skin.

"Please tell me you have condoms?"

He moved to grab some from the other room and returned still smiling, following orders and showing off his ass, which, yeah, someone was getting spanked later, because fuck. What on earth?! The amount of squats required—

She pushed him into his leather armchair and then straddled his lap.

He leaned forward, capturing her lips again and kissing her, fast and filthy. Naomi gasped, grinding against his thigh. He smelled so good, like old books and strong coffee, and she was probably losing her mind, honestly, but she really cared about him.

The actual alignment was rushed, clumsy, both of them too eager, but in the end he slid in smooth as silk, and slow, as if savoring the entire trajectory of the push.

"Fuck," he said when he was fully seated inside her, and she couldn't help it, she giggled. She loved the very idea of him coming undone. With her. Because of her.

She looked at his face, which was very dear to her now, and not hated, in this moment. His eyes were so, so blue.

"This is the best sex I've ever had," she said, and meant it even though no one was moving yet and it hadn't even been a minute.

He huffed in answer, warm breath hitting her shoulder, like maybe he thought she was mocking him. But she wasn't, so she pushed his damp hair off his forehead and kissed his mouth, still tasting traces of herself on his lips.

She braced her arms on the back of the chair and started moving, setting a languid pace. He used his free hand to rub her clit without her even asking. Someone had taken notes from the tutorial they'd watched together. Her dashing scholar.

Naomi could fuck like this for hours, honestly. Each thrust reminded her that she loved sex, that she was good at it, that her body was built for the Olympics of orgasms.

She was making, she realized, an extraordinary amount of noise. Whining and gasping, babbling about how good it felt, how much she loved his dick, how she never ever wanted him to stop.

She slammed her molars together, absolutely terrified he was going to think she was faking it, because of course he was going to think she was faking it, she was a performer complimenting his cock.

Ethan noticed the tension in her limbs and stopped her movements with his hands on her hips.

"You okay? Need a minute?" He placed kisses behind her ear that were soft as fucking butterfly wings.

Naomi thought about lying. Lying was a thing she could do. But also, she didn't want to lie. Didn't want to taint this experience in any way.

"I wasn't exaggerating," she said, quietly, into the crook of his neck.

"I didn't think you were." He sounded a little guarded.

Oh great, Naomi. Look what you've done now.

Shit. Her eyes stung a little, but no chance in hell would she cry right now.

"Hey." He kissed her and started moving his own hips, building back their rhythm. "I know what good sex is too, you know," he said into her hair. "I can feel you squeezing my dick. Can feel the way you've soaked your thighs. I know I earned those whimpers, Naomi Grant."

The sound of their bodies meeting was harsher now as he increased his pace.

"Ethan, fuck." She drew out the *K*.

Everything in her body had gone hot and tight.

"Just so we're clear," he said against her ear as he pinched her clit between his thumb and forefinger, just the right side of brutal. "When you come on my cock, we're both gonna know why." Her second orgasm struck deep in her core, pulsing, and as promised, she clenched around him in a way that was so obviously organic, the alternative ceased to exist.

Instead of robbing her of her strength, this orgasm gave her something to prove, so she repositioned herself so she was facing away from him, making sure he had a perfect view of her award-winning ass, and moved her hips in a way that she had specifically designed to ruin men's lives. She called it that. The move. The life-ruiner.

She was extremely powerful.

The grunt her pace punched out of him was so rewarding, she could have lived on it for years.

"Shit," he said, fucking up and into her helplessly, his thumbs pressing bruises where her back met her ass.

She looked over her shoulder and blew him a kiss. Ethan swore again as he spilled his pleasure, arching his back so far she almost lost her seat.

"Do you think the sex is better because we know we're pissing people off?" she asked him later, when they were eating ice cream out of the carton over the sink, ravenous.

He swiped chocolate off her lip and sucked his thumb into his mouth. "Probably."

Chapter Twenty-Eight

....

FOR BETTER OR worse, Ethan and Naomi were all-or-nothing kind of people. Neither of them really understood the concept of doing something halfheartedly.

Their professional lives weren't average, so why should their dating be?

Ethan knew he sounded defensive, even in his own head.

Naomi had awakened this . . . wanting in him. Not just physical sensation. Although it had been only a few days since they'd slept together, and he did already feel like she'd rewired his nervous system into something powered by pleasure. But no, the wanting was for everything. Her brain, and her smart mouth, the way she made him feel important and like something worth having.

Naomi. Just thinking her name made Ethan sit up straighter at his desk. Made him grin, goofy and distracted, at the paperwork piling up around him to dangerous heights.

The synagogue was flourishing; attendance was up ten percent in the last four weeks already. And yeah, he had to work longer hours, barely managed to sleep between serving the needs of his expanding congregation and spending time with her, but that was fine.

He hardly even noticed. Only yawned twice during evening prayers. His hand closed around his third—no, fourth cup of coffee.

Everything was fine. No. Everything was great.

He wasn't sure he'd ever been happier, and that was sort of terrifying if he looked straight at it.

He'd started studying again last week, without really thinking about it. At first, he'd thought he was looking for things to spice up his sermons. To expand the aperture of his philosophy and help find fresh connections and ideas to appeal to the new members brought in by the potent combination of Clara's PR and the rising popularity of their seminars.

But then this morning he'd found himself lingering over passages about love. And then reaching for cross-reference texts. Calling Mira, who recommended books by mystics Ethan had never heard of, heavy ones that weighted down his bag and spilled off his desk. At least he was learning. He wasn't exactly trying to predict the pattern of his feelings for Naomi. To give them a name. Ethan wasn't afraid of love. The problem was that love didn't seem big enough, wide enough, for the way he felt about her.

He started in his chair when she showed up at his office door. Like he'd dreamed her up. She wore loose pants and a T-shirt, her hair pulled up and away from her face. She looked softer, the apples of her cheeks almost impossibly round.

Ethan's heart shot into his throat. He had to cut himself off from staring at her when he started admiring the tiny curl of her ears. That was a new low, even for him.

"Just when you thought dating me couldn't get any better," she smirked, and Ethan wished he could capture that irresistible quirk of her lips and keep it in his pocket to run his fingers over when he felt nervous, "I come bearing Chinese food." She raised the take-out bag like a trophy over her head.

"I'm already batting way out of my league." Ethan went to smile at her only to realize he was already grinning, that he had been since she'd walked into the room. He got to his feet and tried to clear off a space for her to put down the parcels. "Quit showing off."

"What can I say?" Naomi leaned across the desk and captured his mouth for a quick kiss that still shot all the way down to his toes. "I'm trying to keep you eager to please."

"Trust me," he said, making himself pull back, voice a little rough, "you've got nothing to worry about in that regard."

Her gaze snagged on his mouth, and he had to remind himself to cool it. He was in shul, for crying out loud. "I thought you had that Shameless screening tonight downtown?"

"Oh yeah. Josh and Clara said they could cover." She handed him a take-out container before removing one for herself.

A double dose of guilt slid down his spine. Her commitment to him, both personal and professional, was definitely to blame for tearing her away from the things she cared about, from the life and business she'd worked so hard to build.

It was one thing for him to run himself ragged, but he didn't want to inconvenience Naomi. He definitely didn't want her to come to resent all the time she spent with him, in his spaces, more than half of it working at a job that didn't pay her enough to cover gas. She shouldn't be bringing him dinner. Ethan should be cooking for her. He winced. Something better than Bagel Bites.

He had flourished since he'd met her, but could she say the same?

She tore the plastic wrapper off a fork with her teeth. "Oh, I saw Morey on my way in. Gave him your spring roll—sorry. Did you know he has a new lady friend?"

Ethan reached for a handful of napkins from the bag. "What?"

"Yeah." She stabbed a piece of broccoli. "Met her at Molly's last mixer. Apparently those things took off without us, by the way. She might be better at matchmaking than I am." Naomi tilted her head, considering. "Certainly better than you. Anyway, Morey showed me a picture. Dashing dame in her late sixties. Lives over in Venice. Beach-front."

"Wow." He blinked slowly, taking it all in. "Good for Mo." Opening a new container released fried-onion-scented steam. Naomi ordered as well as she did everything else.

"I didn't even know he was serious about dating again." Guilt climbed up his throat. Apparently, Ethan's new schedule also meant missing major milestones in his friends' lives.

"Me neither." She helped herself to a bite of his vegetable lo mein. "I mean, obviously he was married to Gertie for fifty years, so he probably didn't get to do much exploring, you know?"

"Right." Ethan poked at his scallion pancake with a chopstick to have something to do with his hands. Taking a step back from work or Naomi, just when things seemed on an upward trajectory, when he was so happy and fulfilled . . . he wasn't sure he even could.

"Hey, can we stay at your place tonight?" Naomi pulled out the flask she kept her water in and took a swig. "I wanna finish reading your copy of *The Puttermesser Papers*."

"I'm actually staying here overnight, but I can get it for you tomorrow." He finally popped some food in his mouth, the aroma getting to him. The flavors burst on his tongue, salty and rich—perfect.

"You're sleeping here?" Naomi frowned and lowered her fork.

"Yeah," he said once he'd finished chewing. "Sorry, I should have told you sooner."

He was so bad at texting. Had stopped taking his phone out of his bag back when the bubbes had turned it into a dating hotline.

Come to think of it, the solicitations for dinner and drinks had actually slowed to a crawl. Word about him dating Naomi must have spread since their last seminar. "Sometimes the homeless shelters get full when the weather's bad. We turn the rec room into a place for people to sleep overnight," he explained. "It was the congregants' idea, actually. They do all the work. Organize the volunteers who take shifts making sure everyone's safe and as comfortable as possible. I don't have to be here, and I can't always make it"—he ran his thumb across his eyebrow, hoping she didn't think he was posturing at nobility or something like that—"but I try to, just in case they need anything."

"You've got yourself some good congregants." Naomi folded her legs into a crisscross position on her chair. "I forget sometimes," she said, "how many people you have to think about besides yourself."

More guilt. Thick and sour in his stomach. "You have a lot of other people to think about as well."

She made a little dismissive noise. "I have employees. It's not the same. I help people because they serve my company and my interests. You just help people, full stop. Because you like them. Or no." She pointed her fork at him. "You don't even have to like them, do you? You just help them because you can."

Sure, he helped strangers and his community, but what about the people closest to him? Who took care of them when he couldn't? He hadn't called his mom this week. Hadn't asked Leah when she'd leave to start filming for the upcoming season. They never complained, and maybe Naomi never would either, but . . .

His dad would never have let his loved ones come second, not if he could help it.

"Naomi." He wasn't entirely sure he could get the words out. "Do you wish . . . do you wish I did something else? Had another job, I mean?" Ethan didn't see himself ever giving up his calling, but he still had to know.

She put down the container of rice she'd been hunting through. "That's like asking me, do I wish you were a different person."

He recognized the truth. Being a rabbi wasn't an expendable part of his identity. Emotion sat thick in his throat, crawling up his vocal cords no matter how many times he tried to swallow it down. He'd made his choice after his dad had died, and he didn't regret embracing

Judaism, choosing a life of service. But running to something good was still running away.

"Do you?" He'd thought about asking his family the same question a million times. Knew they'd never answer honestly. But Naomi wouldn't lie to him.

And she didn't.

She got up out of her chair and crouched down next to his, reaching for his hand and placing his palm flat against her chest, above her breast, where he could feel her heart, steady and sure. It was the oddest, singularly most comforting thing anyone had ever done for him.

"No, Ethan," she said, slow and clear. "I don't wish you were different. No more. No less."

With her steady heartbeat under his fingertips, her eyes devoid of pity but colored with compassion, Ethan knew what he'd been looking for in all those books. He placed his hand on the nape of her neck and brought her mouth to his, said thank you in his kiss.

The milestones in the Modern Intimacy curriculum were supposed to be spread out over weeks, or even months. But they kept diving into them headfirst, one after the other. A crash course instead of a seminar.

What if it was all too fast? If in their haste to get to their destination, they were burning all the rubber off their tires?

Ethan didn't feel less selfish when he kissed her. Or even less afraid that he'd always hurt the people he cared about by not giving as much as he took.

But he did feel achingly present in that perfect, fleeting moment.

And for now, it was enough. Or something like it.

Chapter Twenty-Nine

ETHAN STILL GOT surprised when he saw Naomi at his own synagogue, so he was completely shocked to find her coming out of Endmore Boulevard the next afternoon.

She sat on the steps of the shul, book open in her lap. Hair up and away from her face again, forehead crinkled in concentration. She didn't notice him until he got within a foot of her, his shadow falling across her page. When she did tip her head back to take him in, shielding her eyes from the sun with a hand, her lips fell open. "Ethan? What are you doing here?"

He shifted his weight from one foot to the other. It seemed asinine to repeat her question back at her. "I'm meeting Rabbi Rosen for coffee."

"Ah. That makes sense." She closed her book. "I guess you're probably wondering the same thing about me, huh?"

"I think that's fair to say." He dropped down to sit beside her, nudging her leg with his.

Naomi took a deep breath. "So, I've kind of been attending classes here."

"What kind of classes?" He would have been less surprised if she'd said she came here to wash windows.

She flipped her book over so he could see the title. *To Be a Jew* by Hayim Halevy Donin. "An eight-week series on reconnecting with faith."

"Oh. Wow." He shifted his bag off his shoulder and placed it between his knees. "Okay. And uh . . . what week is this?"

Of course he supported her pursuing religious study. The idea of her with a pen between her lips, poring over ancient texts, actually made him kind of hot. But the fact that she'd kept this obviously relevant detail about her life from him still sat squirming in his gut.

Naomi bit her lip. "Three."

So that was . . . the entire time they'd been dating. Most of the time she'd been running the seminar. "Right. Okay," he said again. He guessed he couldn't really blame her. Endmore Boulevard was great. He'd grown up coming here. The staff, congregation, all of it was topnotch, thriving. Shiny and well-funded. Practically dripping in respect. Not that Ethan was envious or anything.

"I'm sorry I didn't tell you. I actually signed up under my given name." Naomi pushed her hair off her face, sending it cascading in a wave of shiny red silk. "It made things easier. Let me blend in. No baggage."

"That makes sense." He tried to process this new info, but his brain struggled to keep up.

"At first I didn't want you to think I was doing it to impress you, and then I just got into it, I guess. I liked having this part of my life to myself. Growing up, my parents weren't super religious, and so I never really got the chance to figure out my relationship to faith. My mom is actually—"

"I get it," Ethan assured her. He'd had a similar experience, after all. Faith was so personal. Sometimes sharing that part of yourself felt like exposing something fragile to the windstorm of the world.

"Hey, if you were gonna cheat on me with another rabbi, you couldn't find a better one than Sarah." In addition to being beloved, she'd built her own organization dedicated to advancing access to sustainable energy solutions. He couldn't begrudge another religious scientist, even if he wanted to.

Naomi wrapped her hand around his arm and pulled him in so she could lean her chin on his shoulder. "You're still my favorite."

Ethan kissed the top of her head, breathing in the lavender scent of her shampoo. "Yeah, but for how long? Her singing voice is way better than mine."

"Oh, well, yeah," Naomi teased. "I assume I'll have to leave you when I'm ready to start a band, but we can have fun until then."

"In that case, I'll see you at softball practice on Sunday?" Ethan got to his feet reluctantly, already late.

"You know I'd never miss a chance to admire your butt in those pants," Naomi shouted at his retreating form.

He gave her a dorky wave, cheeks hot.

Are you sure we can still have fun? he wanted to ask her.

After three nights ago, when she'd walked out of their auditorium and into a snake pit? When Ethan hadn't been able to protect her from people condemning her, condemning them?

She'd come home with him after the seminar. Let him make her tea and fuss over her for a while until she told him she had better ideas for how he could use his mouth than wasting it on apologizing for things he couldn't control.

He hadn't gotten a chance to talk to her about what she'd said—he swallowed tightly—about love. Tuesday night had been so overwhelming in every sense of the word, and she'd said it from across a huge auditorium. Through a microphone. Knowing he couldn't answer. Did that mean something? Ethan wanted her love without question, but the more she cared about him, the more power she gave him to let her down. To take from her. Naomi had just said how much it meant to her to have this independent relationship with faith, but if they kept dating, wouldn't he want her to belong to Beth Elohim? To come to his services? To be able to share that part of her?

He pushed down a wave of unease as he walked toward Sarah's office, nodding to a few people he knew from the community on the way. Naomi wasn't the only one who hadn't been completely forthcoming. He'd asked Sarah to get coffee today because he wanted her advice on how to handle moving forward with the seminar series after the incident at the JCC.

He'd gone through deescalation training with his local precinct several times as part of his responsibilities at Beth Elohim. Had spoken at length in the past with fellow rabbis and religious leaders from other faiths about how to respond to hate speech or violence. But nothing had prepared him for how rabid and helpless he felt in the moment when Naomi stepped out of their lecture Tuesday night to those protesters.

Obviously, he wasn't taking the matter lightly. They would probably have to increase security and maybe even move the remaining seminars to a more controlled location. Ethan probably should have seen something like this coming, but he'd been so blinded by his own happiness. Drunk on dreaming about what he and Naomi could accomplish together.

They board had backed off a little as enrollment steadily climbed over the last month, but would the increased costs of maintaining the Modern Intimacy series change their minds? Convince them the investment outweighed any potential benefit to the shul?

He didn't know how to make them see all the intangible gains. Like the way the audience had rallied around Naomi. So many of them had volunteered to walk her to her car that she'd ended up fenced in like a pop star. Or how week after week her vulnerability made them brave enough to reach out for connection themselves. He had at least five new members a week coming to his office, saying things like, "I didn't think shul was a place for me, but if this synagogue is open enough to host a seminar like that, I guess I was wrong."

But . . . for how long could Ethan keep putting her in difficult situations? She'd said she used her given name here because it made things easier. Well, she deserved easier. Deserved the chance to walk around unguarded for once. Secure in the knowledge she was welcome.

As long as she continued to date him, both the people who respected their relationship and the ones who resented it would want a piece of her. Would demand attention and access.

There are certain expectations of a rabbi, Mira had told him when he first confessed to his mentor that he'd enrolled at the rabbinate. *It's hard, and even though people tell you, you won't believe them. The hours are impossible. You'll never feel like you're doing enough. You sign up, and your life is no longer just yours. Your first duty becomes service. Half the time you're acting on behalf of people who don't even want to be helped, and that's not even the hardest part. The hardest part is, you can't simply make the people you love okay with the life you've chosen. Either they're along for the ride, or you have to let them go.*

Ethan's insides twisted, his body rejecting even the idea of losing Naomi. But there was one truth he couldn't deny: no matter how much he wanted to, an easier life wasn't something he could offer her.

Chapter Thirty

RUNNING OUT OF road was the latest problem Naomi had discovered with using the Modern Intimacy syllabus as an outline for her relationship with Ethan. Tonight would be their penultimate lecture. The milestone was how to talk about having a future together, which was apt, to say the least.

"Where do you keep your spices?"

Ethan had offered to make her scrambled eggs before work—had gone out to the corner deli this morning while she stayed in bed, even—but at twenty to seven, various bangs and curses said he was finding the task more difficult to accomplish than anticipated.

"I don't have spices," she called from down the hall. She was trying to do a smoky eye, but the bathroom was still hot and humid from her shower, and the shadow kept sliding down her eyelid.

He popped into the doorway, his gaze following the way she bent over the sink, trying to get close enough to make use of the still-foggy mirror. "You don't have salt?"

She wiggled her ass at him, for fun, until he stepped behind her and put both hands on her hips, bending to kiss her neck, light and maddening.

"I might have, like, a packet from a take-out order lying around in a drawer somewhere?" She hunted through her makeup bag. Where the hell was her eyeliner? "If it's part of the recipe or whatever, why didn't you pick it up at the store?"

"Why didn't I pick up salt?" He stood up and made a face at her in the mirror. "Because salt is a standby. It never crossed my mind that you might not own such an incredibly"—he bit her shoulder a little—"basic ingredient."

Naomi turned and looped her arms around his neck, leaning back to better admire the way the humidity had curled his hair against his cheeks. "I have hot sauce."

"Not a valid substitution." The words fell against her lips, chased by his mouth. "How do you cook anything?"

"I'll let you in on a little secret." She loved the minty toothpaste morningness of his breath, how it led to the kind of kiss you could only get from waking up in the same place as someone else. "I don't."

Ethan pulled back. "Wait, ever?"

She tilted her head, considering. "I order takeout or I make a salad or cereal or something. Maybe a sandwich. I have cold cuts, I think." Ethan didn't need to know that they'd probably passed their expiration date a while ago.

He wrinkled his nose.

"What? It's fine. Usually we're at your house, and you put on that cute little apron"—she threaded her fingers through the belt loops of his jeans, pulling his hips toward hers—"and I get to watch your hands move while you chop things." They probably didn't have time for sex before work, but maybe she could get him to—

"I'm buying you salt," he said, extracting himself from her grip with surprising stealth and walking backward out of the bathroom.

She batted her eyelashes at him. "Are you sure it isn't too soon for a grand gesture like that?"

"And pepper," he shouted from somewhere down the hall.

"Stop." Naomi picked up her mascara, noticed her reflection was grinning, and didn't mind so much. "You'll spoil me."

When she'd gotten her makeup to behave, she headed to the kitchen.

"Can we run though the plan for tonight's seminar?" She grabbed her cell phone and thumbed to her notes app.

Ethan worked a fork in sharp circles around a mixing bowl Naomi couldn't remember ever purchasing. "Yeah, of course."

He didn't turn to look at her, even when she leaned far enough over the counter that she knew her cleavage was stunning.

"Okay, so," she said, ignoring a petulant little sting. "My opening is about how talking about having a future with—or even thinking about a future that depends on—someone else can be really scary." She let her voice go up a little on the end, a question waiting for confirmation. Also waiting for Ethan to pick up on her casual lead-in to discussing their own trajectory.

He set a pan on the stove and turned on the burner, watching while it click-click-clicked and then ignited. "Mm-hm."

Apparently subtlety wasn't gonna cut it here. She stood up, pushed her shoulders back, straightened her top. This conversation wasn't something to make herself sick over. Not with Ethan. He'd mentioned his desire for marriage and kids—not explicitly *with* her but not *not* with her—before their first date. Commitment didn't scare him. Responsibility didn't make him want to run.

She scrolled further down, reading the bullet points she'd put together, hanging on to them like rope. "But I'm gonna recommend just going for it. Just saying what you want and seeing if the other person wants the same thing."

Ethan opened her fridge. "Do you have any butter?"

Naomi lowered her phone. "Probably not," she said tightly.

He made a dissatisfied noise between his teeth and settled for olive oil. Adding a splash to the pan. His shoulders stretched the seams of his button-down.

Naomi cleared her throat. He wasn't ignoring her. He was just cooking. For her. It was fine. It was nice. She decided to try another approach.

"You know, I've been thinking. We're almost at the end of the seminar series. We should probably talk about what the next iteration looks like. Might make sense to hand out a preview of a part two syllabus during the final session next week?"

Ethan added the eggs to the pan, their sharp sizzle filling the silence where his answer should have been.

"Ethan?"

Now that the eggs were in the freaking pan, he didn't have any more excuses not to meet her eyes. He rolled his sleeves higher up on his forearms. "I hadn't really thought about evolving the program."

"Oh." Naomi snuffed a flicker of disappointment. "Well, I thought we could invite guest lecturers. Get some different perspectives. My friend Cass would be great."

There was something so tight across his face, his jaw stiff. "I'm not sure now is the right time." He reached for a spatula and poked at their breakfast.

"What do you mean?" Not the right time? But they'd made so much progress . . . and it was working. The seminars were feeding the synagogue, broadening the community, making it richer and more diverse. Sure, they'd had the protesters last week, but so what? Anyone who'd ever stood up for social change met resistance.

They just needed to get more milestones laid out. For . . . for the sake of the class, obviously. Not because she didn't know how to—for the class. There had to be hundreds of other ports of intimacy to navigate. First holidays. First time one of you got sick. First stretch of long distance.

Just tell me where you wanna go. I'll go anywhere with you.

Ethan turned down the burner, shook the pan in a way that didn't look like it did anything. "Well, you know, you might not want to keep doing it. You might be busy with work and the gym and stuff at End-more Boulevard."

Naomi reeled back. Was that what this was about? Her going to another synagogue? But he'd been fine with it. Hadn't she explained why she wanted to keep that part of her life separate for a while? And it wasn't as if she wasn't at Beth Elohim all the time. She went to stand next to the stovetop so he couldn't keep turning his back on her. On this conversation.

"Ethan, have you thought about what you want? In terms of our relationship?"

She shouldn't have said it like that. A non sequitur. Charged. It was stupid to try to have this conversation right now. When they didn't really have time before work, and besides, they hadn't even been dating that long, and everything was going so well. Better than well. The sex was amazing. She got a little dizzy thinking about it.

He didn't answer while he took down two plates from her cabinets. Didn't answer while he divided the eggs and transferred them from the pan. Handed her the one that held slightly more. "I . . . I have thought about that, yes."

They didn't have forks. Naomi pulled out the silverware drawer, handed him one, and waited.

She didn't want to say, "Well . . ." or "And . . ." but she could tell her body language did it anyway.

Ethan put down his plate. He crossed his arms. "You make me so happy." His smile came out all wrong.

"You make me so happy too," she said quietly, stabbing her eggs in a way that meant they could let the conversation die there. Since he obviously didn't want to keep talking about this right now. Maybe didn't want to talk about it in general.

Naomi swallowed her first bite. The eggs were good. Surprisingly light and fluffy.

They needed salt.

For some ridiculous reason she felt like crying.

It didn't make sense, she thought as Ethan poured them both coffee. When Jocelyn, who was just as sweet, just as good as Ethan, who Naomi had loved in so many similar ways, had offered her *always*, Naomi had run.

She'd run from the promise of a future laid out before her, open arms, certainty. She'd known then that love didn't last. That it ebbed and faded with age, with self-interest. That people grew apart or revealed all the rotten parts of themselves they'd hidden from you.

And now, Ethan wasn't saying *always*. He wasn't saying anything beyond that he liked what they had. But this time, the lack of *always* struck her as sure as any arrow. As sharp and deadly as Joce's inscription. Because—well, before, he'd wanted—hadn't he said he wanted—? Back before, when she hadn't known yet what she could handle?

Didn't he realize that now she wanted his plans? Couldn't he see, as he ate his eggs across from her at her shitty IKEA kitchen table, that they needed more highway? To keep driving?

Couldn't he tell that now that they'd started, she didn't know how to stop?

Chapter Thirty-One

ETHAN DEFINITELY WANTED a future with Naomi. He wanted vacations, and anniversaries, and mail with both of their names on it. He was even looking forward to their first big fight. Okay, not the fight itself so much as the possibility of makeup sex.

And sure, he was a bit tortured over wanting those things, knowing that she could pick a thousand people less high maintenance than him to share them with. But he'd started trying to make peace with it. Because hiding how he felt from her—not telling her this morning that ideally he wanted to fill multiple scrapbooks with memories spanning the rest of their lives together—had given him a stomachache. Seriously, it was four p.m. and he was sitting at his desk eating saltines.

He should just tell her he was all in. There was no use trying to fight it. He knew he couldn't make decisions for her, even ones that might, in theory, make her life less stressful. And anyway, she'd never do something unless it was exactly what she wanted, what she believed to be right. She didn't get scared, not in the way that he did, of asking too much of other people. She knew exactly how much she deserved.

He reached for his cell, but then thought better of it and reached for his Dodgers mug instead. This wasn't the kind of thing you sent via text, he decided, taking a sip of lukewarm tea. He'd tell her after the seminar tonight.

Which—he glanced at his watch—he needed to leave for soon if he didn't want to get absolutely annihilated by traffic. He wanted to get there early, with plenty of time to check in with the new security guard, to run through all the updated safety procedures with her and Naomi. Having a trained professional guard the door to their auditorium wasn't ideal, but it was responsible and necessary.

Ethan wanted to protect their vision—this modern intimacy course that gave people an open forum to talk about the evolution of relationships. But as much as he wanted to preserve the cozy, unconventional sense of community they'd developed, he also wanted everyone to feel safe.

He crunched on another saltine, the cracker drying his mouth out like the desert. Yeesh. Under a pile of paperwork, his phone vibrated.

A text from Jonathan: Emergency board meeting. Need you in my office ASAP

Ethan sighed and sent back the hand making an "okay" sign emoji. Emergency board meetings were not that irregular at Beth Elohim. They had a run-down synagogue on the brink of closing. They'd had an emergency meeting last week when the pipes in the basement had burst, for example.

Ethan stopped to grab some water on his way to the meeting room, shooting Naomi a message to say he might be a little late to the JCC but that Julia (the guard) should know to ask for her at the front desk.

She sent back: sounds good. see ya soon. thinking about your 🍑

He grinned down at his phone and thought about her lying tangled in her sheets this morning. When he'd gotten up to say his prayers, she'd sighed like it was fabulous that he was leaving and stretched out like a starfish. But then just when he'd gotten to the door, she had whimpered a little, eyes closed, until he'd come back and kissed her for a minute. After that she'd smiled, cat-with-the-cream, eyes still closed, and gone back to sleep.

Jonathan's office smelled musty, like the old radiator in the corner had been working overtime, even though it was spring in L.A. and the thing definitely hadn't been turned on in the last five years. Ethan thought about moving to open a window, but figured he should wait until things got going and it was less conspicuous. There weren't enough chairs in here for everyone crowded inside, so Ethan leaned against the back wall.

He knew he'd lost a lot of the goodwill of the board. In hindsight, he could see that when they'd hired him and said they wanted results, what they meant was they wanted results accomplished in ways they were accustomed to.

In the early days, they'd smiled down on him, doting and indulgent, but with each new idea he brought, each change he proposed, each convention he broke, their smiles got a little tighter, until they'd stopped smiling at all. He'd received a few concerned calls over the last few months, in addition to Ira's careful warning. His inbox held a few chiding, carefully worded emails. Occasionally he caught a pointed look from the pews during services. But he'd let it all roll off his back.

It just didn't make sense to him, how anyone could see Naomi and not recognize her as a blessing.

The board couldn't deny that Ethan's updated programming and partnerships had gotten results. Attendance had hit a three-year high last Friday night. They'd had enough in the bank to call a real plumber last week, instead of Mrs. Glaser's son, who mostly watched tutorials on YouTube. Not to mention the fact that thanks to Clara, Beth Elohim had gotten more press in the last few months than in the shul's hundred-year history.

No one liked change. Ethan understood that, but surely they'd see soon that this new direction was for the best.

Except . . .

"Ethan, we're getting threats," Jonathan said from behind his desk, without any attempt at his usual preamble. Every head in the room turned to stare at Ethan, who stopped leaning immediately.

"I'm aware," he said carefully, hand tightening around his water glass.

"We're getting threats," Jonathan said again, this time hitting all the *T*s extra hard, "specifically related to your personal relationship with Naomi Grant."

Ethan knew that too.

"We manage any threat against the synagogue through our security team." According to his records, the synagogue had seen a four percent uptick in hate mail in the last five weeks. Some of it did call out his private life, though more of it objected to the seminar in concept, and neither of those kinds made up the majority of the correspondence that contained the same censure and objection that any synagogue in the country received on a day-to-day basis, unfortunately.

Jonathan and Ira exchanged a long look. "We believe these specific objections are not wholly unfounded, and they're not just coming from outside the shul. We've received significant complaints from members."

"Excuse me?" Ethan's mouth went dry in a way that had nothing to do with the crackers he'd eaten earlier.

Jonathan gave him a look—a *Don't make this harder than it already is* look. "It's not suitable, Ethan. You're meant to set a model of Jewish values, and you're out here in tabloids with a woman who doesn't even attend services, not to mention her background is . . . shall we say . . . less than ideal."

There was so much wrong with that last sentence. Ethan put down the water glass he'd brought on the windowsill, because his hands had started to shake. "If you'd like me to continue to sit in this room, you'll refrain from veiled maligning of the woman I love."

He said it without thinking. Without considering that probably he should have told Naomi how he felt about her before he told this man trying to condemn her—but, well, he'd never had great timing, as it turned out.

"Love?" Ira covered his mouth with his hand. "Ethan, you love this woman?"

He nodded because his throat was too tight to speak, but it wasn't enough. "Yes," he managed, and then "yes," again, but louder. At some point Ethan had put his hands behind him and started gripping the windowsill. He noticed because flecks of paint were coming off against his palms.

Ira shook his head, making his wrinkles stand out sharply in the topography of his face. "Jonathan, who are we to stand in the way of love?"

Jonathan's mouth remained a thin line. "She's not Jewish."

Ethan laughed because it was ridiculous. "Of course she is."

Why were these people all looking at him with a terrible combination of pity and anger?

Ethan hated it. He wanted to start yelling. He never yelled.

"Her mother is a gentile," Jonathan said, his voice a bit lower now, perhaps in sympathy. "Cynthia Palmer. A Quaker from Woburn, Massachusetts."

Ethan shook his head. "What are you talking about?" Naomi had never commented on her religious background specifically. She hardly talked about her parents, and he . . . he hadn't really asked. "What did you do, get a background check on her?"

Jonathan's silence was his answer.

"That's so completely out of line." An emergency meeting. He'd planned this, to catch Ethan unawares, to present evidence of what he saw as Naomi's betrayal.

The calculation of it all made another wave of nausea wash over him.

"Was that the best you could do? Her mother's not Jewish?" He raked his gaze over the board director like coals. "We're a Reform synagogue, in case you've forgotten. If her father is Jewish and she identifies as a Jew, then she is."

Jonathan pursed his lips like he'd swallowed a spider. "No one here is sure she does identify as a Jew."

"I can't believe this." Ethan began to pace. "Did you ask her?"

"It's too late," Jonathan said. "The board has voted six to five that you must terminate any shul-affiliated programming associated with Ms. Grant. And, privately, I think you ought to seriously consider your personal relationship with her as well."

"The board has no authority over my personal life." Was it possible to clench your jaw so hard you dislocated it?

Jonathan was standing now, with his desk still between them like a barrier. "The board has the right to ensure that your behavior is ethical and moral and sets a good example for the congregation. If you don't agree to end your attachment with Ms. Grant, we'll need to discuss whether you're still fit to hold your position as rabbi of Beth Elohim."

A dangerous silence followed. Ethan's own breathing was so loud in his ears.

Jonathan reached for his arm, and he was too numb to pull away. "Ethan, surely this dalliance isn't worth the dark shadow it's casting over your career?"

A sinking started in Ethan's chest and pulled through his whole body, until he realized he might have to bend over just to stay standing.

This was wrong. That much was so, so clear to him. Like a bell tolling. Wrong. Wrong. Wrong.

But the fight was draining out of him through all the invisible fissures their words had carved across the surface of his skin. Naive questions pressed against his lips. *What do you hope this will accomplish? What about everything we've built? Where would you tell me to go, if not here?*

He was too young for this, and also somehow too old.

Ethan didn't consider himself a huge worrier. Because it was always the stuff you couldn't predict that took you out at the knees anyway.

He'd been sitting in his car in the parking lot of the grocery store when his phone had started ringing. It could have been any other afternoon. The sun had been hot on his face through the window, a Beach Boys song playing on the radio. His mom's number had flashed across the screen, but then when he'd answered, it hadn't been his mom.

"Ethan, Dad's sick."

No, she hadn't said *Dad*. She'd said—he swallowed hard—"Daddy's sick."

Daddy, like Leah hadn't said since she was a little kid.

"Ethan?" Ira had tears in the corners of his eyes.

He felt like lying down on the ground. Like telling them that if they wanted him to leave, they'd have to forcibly remove him.

Moses and Abraham had been turned away too. Blasphemed. At least he was in good company.

He'd never thought about failing when he took this job, even though most people probably expected him to end up here or somewhere like it.

Ethan closed his eyes, because he couldn't look at them a second longer. "I've heard enough."

"We can give you a week to wrap up your affairs with the woman," Jonathan was saying, but his voice was far away. "We don't want to cause either party any more pain than necessary."

Ethan opened his eyes. "I don't need a week."

Some of the board members settled back in their chairs, slightly more at ease.

He headed for the door, was almost all the way into the hall when he remembered he had to tell them. He put his hand against the wood frame, trying to get the words out.

"I quit."

Chapter Thirty-Two

MODERN INTIMACY—LECTURE 6:
A ship with no oars

A QUIET THREAD of discomfort unspooled in Naomi's chest the first time Ethan didn't show up in a place she expected to find him. She kept glancing at his usual seat in the lecture hall and losing her train of thought. From the first day, he'd always directed the spotlight of the seminar series at her, but his impact left fingerprints across each session, and now she shivered from the lack of them.

She wasn't the only one. The whole room shifted in his absence, losing some of its form. Ethan subtly guided the heartbeat of these conversations, keeping them focused with little interjections or reminders. Without him, the whole class grew itchy, frustrated that they couldn't quite descend to their usual depths of discussion. They needed Ethan to broaden their perspective, tying modern experiences to age-old stories, holding up a mirror between the past and the present.

Naomi looked at her notes more than usual. Drank two glasses of water instead of one.

She wasn't the kind of woman who needed a man. Except. What if she was?

What if she needed someone? Would that be so bad?

She rolled her shoulders. Then her neck.

She didn't, and resented the entire suggestion.

What would needing someone even look like, anyway?

Naomi didn't have time to think about that right now. Ethan wasn't here, and Molly had broken up with her lumberjack, and she just—she didn't have time. It was fine for other people to need someone, but for the record, she didn't like the implications. You could love someone and not need them. That was fine.

The lecture ended without incident. No more protests, even though they had their new security guard standing sentry in the corner. Nothing out of the ordinary.

She checked her phone after everyone left, but there was nothing beyond her last message to Ethan, so she drove to his house.

And if she drove a little faster than normal? If her hands were a little clammy on the steering wheel? Well, no one was there to see.

She felt jittery. Like she'd done something wrong. Even though she hadn't. She knew she hadn't. Tonight's seminar had been fine. Not her best, maybe, but still interesting, engaging enough.

Ethan trusted Naomi. Not with stipulations or reservations. Not after she'd proved herself. He'd always trusted her to represent him and the synagogue, to do right by their participants, to serve his community alongside him. That trust made her open in ways she'd never considered before, and she couldn't just go closing back up because he'd missed one night.

He was a rabbi. He was busy.

She found him bent over his telescope on the back porch. Ethan straightened up when she opened the door.

"Hey," he said, letting it float on the breeze, but he didn't move to her the way he normally did. The absence of affection was palpable. One of the first shifts she'd noticed when they'd started dating was the way he reached for her. Ethan was a hugger. It shouldn't have been surprising, given his general demeanor.

Basically the second she'd given him permission to put his hands on her—"You can," hot and harsh in his ear, "I want you to"—he'd lit up like the skyline and started holding her. In fact, since then, he'd never really stopped.

Until now.

She gripped the door handle a few extra seconds, for something to hold on to. She didn't know why.

Maybe he wanted her to come to him? To prove that she would. Fine. She wasn't afraid. Her legs ate the distance between them in six strides. *See*, she wanted to say as their bodies met, *I can be the one who opens my arms first.*

"What's wrong?"

"I'm no longer a rabbi at Beth Elohim," he said, stiff in her arms, each word careful, as if he wanted to test their weight in the open air. It was such a heavy sentence, and yet it floated like any other.

Naomi pulled back, and then stepped back, to look at him. "What did you say?"

That wasn't true. That wasn't right. Naomi knew, the way she knew she could crush a man's nose with the heel of her hand.

"I don't understand." She didn't want to. For a terrifying moment, her body begged her to run. Muscles tensing. Ears ringing. *Go. Go. Go.*

"There isn't . . ." He looked at the dark sky. Black with a beating heart. "The board had some concerns and I couldn't . . ." Ethan swallowed and shook his head.

Oh. Calm descended over her. A padlock, clicking closed. She'd known somewhere, in her bones maybe, that this day was coming.

"It's me." Of course. "They fired you because of me."

Ethan shoved his hands in his pockets. "Not exactly."

Not exactly? Then that meant . . . "You quit?"

"I guess." He scrubbed a hand across the back of his neck. "Yeah, I did."

That was better. Less messy in a lot of ways. And it had only been a few hours, probably. So word might not have traveled far. The board might even still be in session, trying to figure out what to do. How to play this.

"Okay. Good."

"Did you just say 'Good'?" Ethan looked like he'd taken a softball to the chin.

It wasn't exactly something they could play off as a misunderstanding, but between the board and maybe Clara, they'd think of something to make it right.

"I just mean it's easier."

Ethan flinched. "Is it?"

"Yes," she said simply. Didn't he get it? All that mattered was the board still wanted him. They just wanted him without Naomi. She could fix it this way. "You'll just have to break up with me. That's what they want, right?"

Ethan's eyes went hard. "I don't care what they want. I'm not going to break up with you. I love you."

It was stunning, the way everything in her was dying, and that sentence still seeped into the dusty soil of her heart and gave it life.

"You love me?" Fuck. "Okay." Breathe. Keep breathing. "Okay. You're right." It wasn't really fair to ask him. Not after that. "I'll have to do it."

His backyard was so quiet. No sounds from the road. Just wind through the trees. Just her own frantic heartbeat in her ears. Ethan's sharp inhale.

"Naomi."

A sick sense of triumph pumped through her like adrenaline. Making her jittery, a twisted euphoria. She knew what to do. If she could just hold on to it. Seeing it through, righting this wrong, that would be enough. It had to be enough.

"I'm sorry," she said, voice cracking against her will. *Stop it. Stop.* "We came close, didn't we?" She needed to hear him say yes. That their love counted for something.

"We're not—I'm not going back there," he said. "It's done."

Naomi shook her head, indulged the impulse to kiss his frowning mouth and tasted salt. "No, sweetheart. It's not."

Ethan reached for her hand. "I need you."

What dangerous words, and oh, how she wanted to keep them.

Naomi closed her eyes. She couldn't look at him and keep going.

What was the name of that guy, the one who'd gotten stuck on a mountain with his arm trapped under a boulder? He'd had to saw through his own muscle, his own bone, with a pocketknife or something, to get free. To survive.

The human body must send something, some chemical, up to the brain, dulling the pain, the horror. And later, that same adrenaline cocktail must dissolve the memory too. Take care of making it hazy and dull. So people could forget, at least for a few moments, at least years later, that they'd ever had to swallow so much pain. Naomi was grateful for her body in a new way tonight. Grateful that after all this, she could surrender and let it carry her, all on its own.

She could do this. Could face the perfect temptation of having him join her as an outlier. Of them building a life together that made everyone else furious. She could deny the dream of that. The way it reinforced every truth she'd used to build her life.

This must be growth, right? Putting the community's interests over her own. Letting him love thousands of people instead of just her.

This was the right thing to do, wasn't it? This was their only option.

If she could just keep saying that. Keep believing it. She could walk out of here on the strength of her own two legs. The edges of her vision darkened a little.

Shouldn't there be some freedom in this ending? Shouldn't she get to relish regaining her independence? Cutting all the new ties that had bound her to organized religion and ordinary people?

There wasn't.

She didn't.

"You will always be the best thing that ever happened to me," she told him, hands chasing every part of his face, his arms, his chest, trying to commit them to memory, trying to force herself to say good-bye.

She felt like she'd been poisoned and had to spit the antidote back in the grass.

"No," Ethan said again, but there wasn't as much behind it this time. His whole body shook. "Don't do this. Please."

Naomi might love him until the day she died.

Wouldn't that be an exquisite tragedy? She had to douse a hysterical laugh.

She held Ethan tighter and wished she could pour herself into him, abandon the pain flowing through her own body.

Even though she was still standing there. Still holding him. She was already gone.

I am a stick of dynamite.

It was no great tragedy when dynamite destroyed itself, not when that was exactly what it was designed to do.

Chapter Thirty-Three

ETHAN OPENED HIS door the next morning to find Leah holding a bottle of whiskey in one hand and a carton of chocolate milk in the other. She pushed them toward him, one after the other.

"Which one do you want?"

He took the chocolate milk and walked back inside. It took a lot of restraint not to open it and chug. Also to avoid pressing the cold, sweating carton against the side of his face, puffy as it was from lack of sleep. Everything ached. That premonition kind of sick when you could feel illness on the horizon, waiting to descend. Sore throat. Limbs that weighed twice what they ought to. A weariness that went deeper than his bones. It was like his immune system had heard about last night and given up the ghost.

"Are you gonna tell me what happened?" Leah helped herself to one of his glasses and poured in a few splashes of whiskey. "You don't look like you got in another fistfight."

Oh. Right. He'd texted her one word, hours after Naomi had left, somewhere around sunrise. *Ow.*

He'd felt like he should tell someone. You were supposed to call for help while drowning.

Ethan opened the cabinet. Sighed. Of course he was out of clean glasses. Lifting down a mug instead felt like a Herculean effort.

"I've recently become unemployed." The chocolate milk sloshed out of the carton, making a satisfying *glug-glug* noise as he filled the mug to the rim. It didn't hurt as much—the second time he said the words out loud—but the difference was negligible. For the first time in his life, he felt like he understood why dogs howled at the moon.

"What?" Leah lowered her whiskey, slamming the glass down hard enough that amber liquid splashed up and onto his counter.

"And single," he said, because why not get it all out at once? The chocolate milk was good, smooth and rich on his tongue, conjuring comforting memories chock-full of nostalgia. It was fine that he was thirty-two, without prospects for either employment or matrimony, and drinking chocolate milk. F-I-N-E.

Leah walked around the kitchen island to smack him on the arm. "Are you serious?"

"Afraid so." He swiped at the chocolate milk running down his chin. He'd been midsip when she'd hit him.

"What in the . . . why would . . ." She huffed indignantly several times. "What the fuck did you do?"

That was the problem. Or one of them, at least. He hadn't done anything. He'd let the board push him out of the synagogue. Let Naomi push him away. He'd run, again, because it was easier than staying and cleaning up the mess of his loss.

"The board accused me of improper contact." Ethan had questioned for the first time last night, deep into the evening when it seemed like his limbs had melted and become one with the sofa, whether he could see their point. Had he acted outside the bounds of his position? Jeopardized the synagogue's chances at rehabilitation? But he kept coming to the same conclusion. His religion didn't stand in opposition to his love.

Leah rescued what remained of her whiskey and drained the glass.

"Is that code for dating someone way hotter than you?" She proceeded to drag him by the sleeve to the kitchen table and push him into a chair, bringing the bottle with her.

"Among other things."

Ethan wanted to tell her that every room in this house was haunted. Full of memories and plans he'd had of and for Naomi. He wanted to tell her he couldn't stay here. Couldn't sleep or eat or pray in these rooms that reeked of her.

"I can't believe you dumped Naomi Grant because she made you look bad." The judgment in Leah's voice was hot enough to sear.

"What? I didn't break up with her." He reeled back, indignant. "You really think I'm that dumb?"

Leah relaxed her shoulders. "Just making sure."

"Naomi ended things." Bitterness spilled out of him and practically dripped on the countertop. "She basically told me to beg on my belly for my job back."

". . . Are you gonna?"

Ethan sighed. "I don't know yet." He was still in shock. On the one hand, shouldn't he try to cut his losses? Try to keep fighting for Beth Elohim? If he couldn't have love, he could at least retain his sense of purpose.

But how could he go back and try to work with a board who didn't trust him? Leah traced circles on the table with her finger. "What would Naomi do?"

"Not ask forgiveness, that's for sure." She'd never give someone who rejected her a second chance. Would probably stop saying their name. Refuse to even think about them. Ethan wasn't like her in that respect. He'd thought about her so much since she'd left, it didn't even feel like thinking anymore. His imagination had grown so vivid, so visceral, she might as well have been sitting at the table with them.

"I can't believe it's over," Leah said, shaking her head like when she tried to solve the Sunday crossword.

Ethan couldn't exactly say the same thing. He'd imagined Naomi dumping him a few times, sharp and brief, but it was never under the guise of self-sacrifice. Never for his own good.

"I mean, it's really shocking." Leah drilled her fingers against the table in agitation.

"I guess." Adding whiskey directly to chocolate milk was probably gross, right? What did they put in White Russians?

Leah took a long swig directly from the bottle, wiping her mouth and wincing from the burn. "It makes more sense that you messed up."

He raised his head to glower at her. "Me? What did I do?"

Ethan wasn't desperate to play the victim or anything, but any way he sliced the events of the last twenty-four hours, they still felt like something inflicted upon him.

His sister shrugged. "You let her leave."

"This is Naomi we're talking about." Ethan reached for the whiskey bottle but ended up just holding it. "No one has ever 'let her' do anything."

Leah issued an extremely put-upon sigh. "Ethan, you're smart, but you're also Big Dumb."

"I thought you came over here to make me feel better," he said, wounded.

"Well"—she waved her hand for him to give back the bottle—"maybe this will finally teach you to stop jumping to conclusions."

"So you're just gonna drink whiskey and insult me?" Were all little sisters like this? Forever?

Leah checked her watch. "For at least the next ten minutes probably, yeah."

Ethan groaned. "She didn't want a life with me, Leah. Not really. The second that one was laid out in front of her, she threw me back like an undersized fish."

"That is a vivid metaphor." She wrinkled her nose. "But also, no, that's not what happened."

"Can I at least set a timer for this attack?" Wasn't there a saying, *Bad things come in threes*? So at least this should be the last of his excruciating punishments.

"No. You have to listen." As a tiny mercy, Leah gave him back the whiskey bottle.

Ethan took a sip, letting the burn wake him up. He preferred the chocolate milk.

"I know you thought you were being cute," Leah said, slow and calm, like he was the one being difficult. "Using that syllabus as guidelines for falling in love or whatever. But"—she threw her arms up—"sometimes there is no map. No plan. And just standing still, staying, is the bravest thing you can do."

"She didn't want to stay, Leah, I told you."

Naomi's eyes had been bright, almost feverish, as she'd seized on the demise of their relationship like it was the simplest, easiest solution.

"She was so quick to cut everything off."

Leah's voice was lower when she said, "She thought she was saving you."

"What?" The single sip of whiskey had gone straight to his head.

"Ethan, anyone who loves you knows how much Beth Elohim means to you and would want you to keep your position—would probably do whatever they could to make sure you had the opportunity to help as many people as possible." Leah dropped her gaze to her lap. "Even if it meant losing some of your love."

He swallowed, throat tight. They weren't just talking about Naomi anymore. "Leah, I never meant to—"

"I know," she said, quick to cut him off. "We all know." She gave him half a smile. "You're insufferably noble in that way."

Confirmation of his fears washed over him, but instead of burning like acid the way he'd always expected, it fell like rainwater—surprisingly clear and clean. Acceptance had a funny effect on weakness.

"Mom and I, we're so proud of you, E. Even when we don't always get what you're doing or why. We love you for believing in something bigger than yourself. For wanting to make the world better. For caring so much it's actually kind of painful to watch sometimes." She reached across the table and squeezed his hand. "And I'm sure Naomi does too. I'm sure she did what she did out of love, like a fool, and I know that's why, like a fool, you let her."

"I let her." Realization came slowly and then all of a sudden. He'd let his own fears of demanding too much from her muddy his conviction.

"You've always struggled to accept that sacrifice is an inherent part of love. That it's inevitably going to hurt sometimes if you care enough." Leah took a deep breath. "Think of this experience through the lens of your syllabus. Love, like faith, asks us to be less selfish. Less greedy. It asks us to trust. To sit with our doubts. To keep coming back and proving our commitment."

"When did you get wise?"

"Look, no one could work in reality TV for as long as I have and not become an expert at observing and orchestrating the human condition."

Ethan got to his feet so fast he sent his chair rocking back on its legs. "Leah, I have to go."

"Yeah. You do," she said, folding her arms behind her head. "The smart one rests her case."

Chapter Thirty-Four

NAOMI HAD BROKEN up with people before.

Usually, the dissolution of a romantic attachment made her hungry in every sense of the word. Made her seek out activities that caused her hair to whip across her face. Sent her in search of loud bars and spicy food. People who would bite her neck and press her against door frames. Experiences that hurt, but in a good way.

Not this time.

Ending things with Ethan had made her numb. Turned her heart into a fail-safe. Nothing in. Nothing out.

Evidently, some people had noticed.

"I've got a plan," Clara announced, storming into her office like a pint-sized cyclone the day after the breakup.

Naomi paused the footage she was reviewing and took off her head-phones.

"No."

Plans meant action, and Naomi mostly wanted to stay as still as possible. Everything hurt when she moved.

"Yes." Clara waved a notebook at her. "I've made a list of things you can do to feel better, with various action items on a sliding scale of intensity."

Naomi wiped a hand across her face. "I don't need your list, Connecticut. I need a nap."

Sleep had become an intangible concept last night. Something so foreign and inaccessible, it felt like the kind of thing she'd read about in a book once but couldn't quite imagine experiencing.

Every time she closed her eyes, she saw Ethan's face. Saw the destruction she'd wrought over someone she held so dear. Her actions had held so much purpose in that moment, but now she struggled to remember why she'd felt so certain that parting was the only path available to them. Naomi didn't let herself linger on dangerous thoughts like that.

She focused on her work. Something she knew she was good at. Something she'd never had the impulse to ruin.

"I'm worried about you," Clara said, voice wavering as she took up residence in her usual seat.

Naomi could imagine her heart—clanging against the cage that had descended to protect it.

"Don't be," she suggested.

Clara had enough on her plate. Even Naomi couldn't stomach spoiling her wedding plans with borrowed tragedy.

"I'll be okay." And who knew, maybe she would. Someday.

Her business partner chewed her bottom lip, eyes lowered to the notebook clutched in her hands.

When had Naomi grown so, so soft?

She sighed. "Fine. Read me the first few items on the list. Quickly." No one found as much comfort in organization as Clara Wheaton.

As evidenced by the grateful smile that graced her face. "Okay. I really think these could help. You're a woman of action. You respond best to challenge and—"

"Clara," Naomi cut in.

"Right. Sorry. Reading." She ran a finger down the paper, obviously searching for her most persuasive pitch. "Well, you're maybe not going to love this one, but I've got sub-bullets detailing an affirmative argument for why this is the right thing to do."

Naomi placed her chin in her palm. "Can't wait."

"Actually," Clara hedged, "before I get into the specifics, could you promise not to yell in response?"

"I don't yell," Naomi said loudly.

Clara raised her eyebrows.

"Much."

"Mm-hm." Clara straightened her skirt.

"You have my commitment to reply at a low to average volume." She picked up her pen dejectedly, for something to do.

"Right. So, a few weeks ago the office got a call from a Ms. Michelle Router."

The name sounded vaguely familiar, but Naomi was in no mood to hunt for the connection. "Uh-huh."

"And she happens to be the new principal at your old high school in Boston." Clara raised her eyes to the ceiling, acting innocent. "Ms. Router said she'd tried to reach you a few times via email and found our office number online."

Naomi gritted her teeth. "Tell me you didn't." She indulged a certain volume of Clara's meddling, chalking it up to misplaced affection, but this really took the cake.

"She said she'd invited you to present a seminar on the future of sex education but hadn't heard back," Clara continued, seemingly undeterred. "But I assured her that you'd love to come speak to her seniors at the first available opportunity."

"Clara Annabelle Wheaton." Naomi got to her feet. "You have got to be kidding me."

"Holy shit," Clara blanched. "I didn't know you knew my middle name."

As if Naomi hadn't done her research before they went into business together years ago.

"You are the most meddling, devious—"

Clara pulled an envelope out of her notebook and passed it across the desk. "They're expecting you on Friday."

"I'm not going," Naomi said, even as she opened the envelope and pulled out the plane ticket inside. Begrudgingly, she found herself slightly mollified that Clara had sprung for first class on the cross-country journey.

"Yes. You are. Because I know you. I know you want those kids to be more prepared than you were for the realities of lust, love, and everything in between." Clara pressed both palms to the desk. "I know you care about that even more than you care about the satisfaction of abandoning the institution that abandoned you over a decade ago."

Clara leveled a steel gaze. "And look, we can sit here and go back and forth about it for an hour until I wear you down—and I will wear you down because I'm better rested and more hydrated than you are right now—or you can just agree up front and save us both the trouble."

A thousand denials pressed against Naomi's lips. Reasons she didn't owe anyone anything. Ever. Promises she'd made to herself about erasing parts of her past, robbing her memories of any power they tried to wield over her.

Maybe it was the exhaustion. Or the heartache. Maybe she'd depleted all her reserves of strength walking away from Ethan. Maybe this was giving up. Or growing up. Moving on. Evolution. Whether she wanted it or not.

In any case, she found herself saying, "Fine."

If she could save one person in the ways she wished she could save herself, she reasoned, that could be worth it.

"What the hell else did you put on that list?" Naomi said later, after she'd let Clara buy her fish tacos and two jalapeño margaritas. She couldn't imagine how outrageous Clara's fallbacks must have been, given her plan A.

Clara shook her head, looking guilty. "Trust me, you really don't wanna know."

Chapter Thirty-Five

WALKING THROUGH THE halls of her old high school reminded Naomi of trespassing in a graveyard. It sent the same chill down her spine, the one that warned of hovering too close to the line between things living and dead. It made her pay too much attention, in the same way, to her own footsteps. Each landing of her heels smacked sharp against the linoleum. The same sense of borrowed grief hovered across her shoulders.

The administration might have turned over, but the silver-haired receptionist currently leading Naomi toward the auditorium hadn't changed much at all.

She squinted behind her glasses. Someone trying to place an actor in an infomercial. "You were a student here?"

"Yeah," Naomi said, voice flat and tired. "My boyfriend leaked nude photos of me when I was a senior." They'd changed the paint color on the walls. It looked even more like undigested oatmeal now. "It was a big, messy scandal. I came into the office while you were on the phone discussing how I was a slut who deserved it."

The receptionist blanched.

"You probably don't recognize me," Naomi said, walking ahead. "I used to be blond," she tossed over her shoulder. "And less of a bitch."

Inside, the rows of the auditorium held restless seniors. In contrast to her usual audiences, they didn't make any effort to hide their nervous giggles when she walked into the room.

Whispers sparked and spread, but for Naomi, they barely penetrated. After months of dreading coming back here and returning to the scene of her trauma, she now stood back and observed it as if through an old, frosted window. Detached. Disinterested.

"Ms. Grant?" A woman who bore a passing resemblance to the new principal's online photo stood before her. "Are you ready to begin?" She gestured toward the microphone stand in the middle of the stage. It was the same one they'd used for the production of *Hello, Dolly!* the year Naomi had graduated. Schools really needed better funding for the arts.

"Yeah, I'm ready." She'd prepared her presentation on the plane. "Sex Should Be Shameless." Half of it came straight from the slides they used for sales meetings. The usual stats about how recent studies showed that nearly thirty percent of college women could not identify the proper location of the clitoris, and only eleven percent of women experienced climax the first time with a new heterosexual partner.

She'd added some context around her own path to studying intimacy, starting to unpack the stigma against sex work for them, along with a discussion of different resources available to help supplement the Greater Boston Area School District's sad offering. Not that she'd ever admit as much to Clara, but the plan did help a little.

Naomi took the stage. It was easily ten degrees warmer under the old-school spotlight.

"Hey," she said into the mic. The room settled surprisingly quickly. She wondered why for a moment before remembering she was both hot and famous.

"I'm . . ." Hundreds of faces stared back at her. Younger and softer than the ones she'd grown used to. Wanting in every sense of the word rolled off these seniors in waves. She couldn't decide if they were more open or more closed than her Modern Intimacy participants.

"I'm . . . well, you might know me by my stage name, Naomi Grant." She rotated her ring around her index finger. "That's how most people know me. It's the name on the poster outside. But, honestly, it feels weird to step back into the footprints of my old life and not acknowledge them. So, yeah. I guess I'll add that my given name is Hannah Sturm, and I graduated from this high school in 2008."

"Whoa, dude. That's, like, so long ago," a guy in the front row said to his neighbor, who nodded.

Naomi laughed. "You know, in Hebrew, my birth name means *grace*. I'm not sure I'll ever go back to being Hannah on a regular basis, or if I even want to, but I'm okay with making room for a little more grace in my life."

She breathed in a sense of release. Was this what veterinarians experienced when they caught and healed a wounded animal and then eventually got the chance to release it, healed, back into the wild?

Over her shoulder, she saw her slides projected on a big screen someone had wheeled in. The title bold and big. A merry declaration. She gestured at it. "Actually, I don't think I'm gonna use those today."

It wasn't as if she was ever getting invited back here. She might as well discuss what she wanted to.

"None of you know this. But I actually started teaching in live environments for the first time this year. I know it sounds wild, but someone actually let me teach a seminar about modern intimacy." Someone— because she couldn't say his name. "I was asked here to speak about the future of sex education, but in putting together that course, I committed to the idea that intimacy is so much more than sex. And I'm more than sex. I planned out a syllabus across seven weeks, and I didn't get to finish the last one." She smiled a little. "It's actually pretty rich in karmic hilarity. You'll understand why in a minute, I promise."

A group of teachers had clustered, hands up over their mouths as they whispered to each other. Naomi wasn't worried. Most of them had been cowards then. They were likely cowards now.

"Anyway." She took a deep breath. "The last lecture I was supposed to deliver was about how to break up with someone, and I think I'm just gonna talk about that now, if it's okay with you?"

No one answered. She hadn't expected them to. Naomi nodded back at the projector. "I'll put the sex ed slides up on the Internet or something. You can look at them later if you want."

The seminar was canceled, but the course she'd started with Ethan didn't feel complete. As if, like their relationship, it had ended on an inhale. She desperately wanted to see it to the finish line. Enough that she'd stand up here and keep talking until they physically carted her away.

"No one ever teaches you how to end a relationship. You go through a breakup, and it doesn't matter if you were blindsided or if you were planning it for months. It fucking— Can I say *fucking*? Probably not, huh?" She blinked into the crowd. "Oh well, sorry."

She gave a little wave to the teachers, who seemed to be debating who would have to storm the stage. Good thing she was terrifying. "As I was saying, it fucking sucks. And I just . . . I want you to survive it." She stared down at her hands wrapped around the mic. "I want to survive it too."

The students must have sensed the recklessness of what she was doing, going off book when she already had *liability* stamped across her forehead. They ate it up like bees to honey, buzzing in their seats.

"I'm not saying all relationships are doomed. Relax. I'm a grown-up who can handle the demolition of the most important and valuable relationship of my life." *Try to sound a little less bitter.*

"But I am saying, endings happen all the time. Sometimes for reasons you'll never know or understand. Other times prompted by logic. Occasionally fueled by rage and resentment. But almost always, at the root of these partings, there's pain."

Naomi closed her eyes for a second. Was she really doing this? Really going there? What did it say about her personal brand that she was suddenly maudlin and poorly lit, publicly lamenting the loss of love in front of a bunch of high schoolers?

She didn't have time to examine her downfall.

Naomi opened her eyes.

"Depending on where you carry your hurt, it might manifest as an ache between your ribs, a crick in your neck. Maybe your jaw is sore, your stomach sour and unsettled. I carry my heartache in my throat. In a tightness that makes it hard to speak. That no amount of tea or honey can soothe. My voice is getting raspier by the day. This isn't like a sex-kitten effect I'm putting on. I sound like this because everything in me is grieving."

Her heartbeat slammed, angry, against her chest.

"I don't know if any of you are Jewish . . ."

A little holler went up in the back.

"Oh, yay." She smiled and raised her arms. "Go Jews!"

Someone coughed.

"Uh . . . anyway, there are a lot of Jewish mourning rituals. We say the Kaddish. We cover our mirrors. We don't have sex for seven days. There's comfort in tradition. So I thought I'd write a breakup ritual. It's not sacred or anything, and probably this is exactly the reason the board of Beth Elohim doesn't want me hanging around, but maybe it'll help someone. It's been helping me a little. And let's be honest with our-selves, in times like this, it can't hurt any worse, right?"

No one laughed. Okay . . .

"Hang on a sec." She pulled her phone out of her pocket. "I wrote it down."

Naomi licked her lips, tried not to let her mouth go completely dry. Probably half these people were wishing she'd hurry up and get off the stage, or at least take out her tits or something.

"Before I start, I just wanna say that you don't owe anything to the person who broke up with you. You don't owe them your ear to listen to their rationale. You don't owe them forgiveness for any grievances, real or imagined, they may have committed against you. You don't owe them a response when they text you at three a.m., drunk and lonely. If you see them across the street ten years from now, you don't have to wave."

Naomi pushed her dirty hair out of her eyes. She was talking to Ethan, even though she knew he couldn't hear her.

She didn't expect him to wait for her to come to her senses and beg for him to take her back. Didn't expect a cordial card on her birthday. If he wanted to hate her—she really hoped he didn't hate her, but if he did—she'd allow it. If he'd broken up with her, she'd never have forgiven him. She was a hypocrite like that.

"Okay, here's the breakup ritual." She scanned the note. "I've been doing it for about a week now." Naomi took the mic off the stand and started pacing a little. It was harder to hit a moving target, right?

"That's the thing. About ritual or religion. Sometimes just going through the motions, even when you're struggling to believe in them, sometimes that's enough. To keep you going. Keep you sane. Keep you tethered to the disastrous fireball spinning toward destruction that we call earth."

She cleared her throat. "Right. Here we go. 'Wake up,'" she read, "'wash your face, and brush your teeth, even if you don't want to, even if it seems like it doesn't matter. Like nothing has ever mattered or will again.'"

Reading was a little easier than just talking off the cuff. "'Drink two glasses of water. Make it a challenge. Make it a race.'" She made eye contact with a guy in the first row. "You like to win, don't you?"

Don't think about Ethan.

"'Light a candle and let it burn as long as you like. Down to its wick, even.' I'm always saving candles for special occasions, hoarding them like I can't buy ten more on sale at TJ Maxx." She found another face in the audience, a student with tears tracking down their cheeks. "You're the special occasion, baby, take what you need."

Her voice got a little steadier as she kept reading, a little louder.

"'Boil hot water and add your favorite aromatics, handfuls of fresh mint or curls of ginger and lime.' I like cinnamon and cloves, with a pinch of cayenne. 'This is not for drinking. Put your head over the pot. Breathe in the steam. Try to wake up your senses.' I promise you won't be numb forever."

Students were reaching into their backpacks, pulling out pens and notebooks like this mattered. Like it made sense and they wanted to remember it. Some cell phones came out, held up and steady, probably recording.

Naomi kept going.

"'Wash your sheets. Masturbate, but only if you can do it without thinking about your ex.'"

Hey, they'd asked for sex ed.

"'Put a pair of socks in the dryer for ten minutes, take them out, and put them on.'" She didn't know why literal cold feet were a physical symptom of sadness, only that they were.

"'Find a book you loved in your childhood.'" Naomi pictured her dog-eared copy of *Anne of Green Gables*. "'Read it. Let it soothe the parts of you that were broken before you found the person who's no longer yours. Let it touch the hurts they couldn't fix. No one else can ever save you. It's okay. You don't need saving.'"

She was talking to Hannah now, to her younger self, as much as these students.

"'Follow your feet until you find nature. Mountains or a body of water or a field of wildflowers. Lie down on the ground. Let the earth carry your weight for a while. Let your tears mix with the soil. Lie there until you feel lighter or until the sun sets, whichever comes first.'" Naomi didn't mind crying when no one could see her.

"'Then go home. Make or buy some soup'"—obviously she bought hers—"'and a loaf of fresh bread. Eat it.' I don't know why soup is so soothing, but it is."

Her fridge at home was full of them right now: noodle soups, curries, stews of all shapes and sizes.

"'Find a piece of paper and a pen. Write the person you broke up with a thank-you note. Even if you hate them.'"

She lowered her phone. "Now, we don't send this note, so if you want to write, 'Thanks, Jeff, for making it easy to leave your tiny dick,' I'm not gonna stop you."

That earned a brief round of applause.

Naomi scrolled again. Ran her fingertip across words so painful they pierced several vital organs.

"'Pour everything into the note. All your dead dreams of a future together.'" She swallowed a few times before she could keep going. "'Every tiny moment that you've been saving in the safe of your mind, collaging for children you thought—just maybe—you might someday make.'"

The first time we met, he said my name like he'd known me his whole life.

"'Thank them for the way they made you feel.'"

Like I was the dawn, driving the light, inviting a new day.

"'For the way they let you love them.'"

Wild and eager. Ravenous. Rapturous.

"'Thank them for waking up dead parts of your soul. Tell them how lucky you feel that even for a moment, even if it was only for one brilliant second, you got to have them, you got to breathe the word *mine* against their skin. Got to climb into bed with someone who somehow made your heart beat a bright, brilliant gold.'"

She took a deep breath.

"'Thank them for making it so hard to leave. So hard to say goodbye that you thought, well, if this doesn't kill me, nothing will.'"

After all of this, after everything, she'd do it again. For Ethan, she'd do anything.

"'Fold up the letter, tuck it away somewhere. All that pain, that longing, that anger. The fear that leaving was the worst mistake you ever made. That you'll never recover as long as you live. That you'll spend a century looking over your shoulder for the life you let slip through your fingers.' Well"—she tried to shrug—"that's the universe's problem now."

She sat on the lip of the stage. Wanting to be closer to these students, these people on the cusp of adulthood, their whole lives ahead of them, waiting to be written.

"I promise that one day you'll wake up and your hands will feel like they belong to you again. Some morning, you'll look in the mirror and you won't have to whisper, 'You're still alive. You're still alive. You're still alive.'"

Naomi wanted every good thing in the world for these people. Every happiness, every rush of daring, every surprise.

"I know you don't know me. And you probably think I'm unstable at this point, but just in case you need to hear it, I think you're bursting with potential. Even the rusty, bleeding pieces of you. So hang in there for me, okay? Eyes on the horizon."

Sometimes you had to go back to go forward. Sometimes you had to wrap your arms around something in order to let it go.

"Remember, each new day is another chance to heal your sorry, broken heart."

For so long, Naomi had carried it as a point of pride that she could wreck herself. That she could survive the fallout of abandoning love.

She didn't need anyone, she'd said. She was independent.

How long had she believed that pain made her sharp? That enduring it made her strong?

Society wanted her to beg for approval, and she'd spit in its face.

Except. This time it was less clear who she was fighting. Less clear who was winning and why.

There was no glory in a soldier who kept fighting when the war was over. No honor in championing a cause that carried no one.

Coming back here, all the way to her high school, showed her how much she'd grown. Institutions, she realized, drew their power from the people inside them. This building couldn't hurt her anymore. She'd let herself back in.

And maybe if she could do that after all these years, she could let herself back into other spaces too.

Naomi had found her footing in synagogues, after all.

Maybe—she took a deep breath—it wasn't only physical locations once closed to her that she could revisit. She'd found a home in Ethan. Naomi needed to know if he'd let her in again if she knocked.

Her phone buzzed in her hand, and Naomi glanced down at an email. Her heart turned over like a pancake.

"And you never know," she told the auditorium, getting to her feet, searching for the exit, her mind already three thousand miles away, "maybe one day you'll find out the end wasn't really the end."

Chapter Thirty-Six

....

MODERN INTIMACY—LECTURE 7:
As you can see, I'm not Naomi Grant

ETHAN REALLY HOPED this would work, because he was already sweaty—emotionally and physically.

The bar he'd rented out, the same one where they'd held their first mixer, had quickly turned standing room only. The bartenders removed all the tables, pushing them out onto the patio in an effort to accommodate the crowd.

He supposed it was reassuring to know that so many people made sure that the Modern Intimacy email discussion list didn't go to their spam folders.

Leah had made him wear a microphone. One of the little lapel ones he'd bought for outdoor events. The pack sat heavy in his pocket as Ethan stared back at his expectant observers. He reached down and switched it on.

"Hey, everyone." The sound of his own voice echoed back in his ears. "Thanks for coming to the final lecture of our Modern Intimacy seminar series."

He forced himself to plant his feet, despite the impulse to pace.

"I know you're used to a different instructor. I'm sure you're wondering why I've asked you here for our last session."

The path of Modern Intimacy never did run smooth.

"I didn't think it was right to use the JCC anymore, because, well, we can't really have any affiliation with the original synagogue-sponsored series." He swallowed against the tight knot in his throat. "Now that they no longer endorse this program and I no longer work there."

Those words still didn't feel real. Didn't feel true.

"What are you talking about?" someone shouted from the back.

A plethora of emotions played across the faces of those gathered. Confusion and doubt chief among them.

"Rabbi Cohen." Molly made her way to the front. "What's going on?"

"I'm sorry." It was the only answer he could offer. "We won't be able to continue on in the same capacity," he clarified, voice tight. "But I thought you deserved a full course, regardless of the circumstances. I wanted to do right by you, to the best of my ability."

And to do right by Naomi, in finishing this wild endeavor he'd invited her to undertake.

"The last dating milestone we set out to cover in our syllabus was 'how to break up,' and normally I'd say I'm no expert in that subject, but I've recently gone through two simultaneous breakups. One with a job I thought I'd have for the rest of my career, and one with the woman I'd hoped to be with for the rest of my life. So, yeah"—he smiled a little—"I've got a lot of stuff to talk about, at least."

The crowd broke into panicked whispers and heated gasps, the combined news of his departure from Beth Elohim and now his split with Naomi striking them all at once.

"You'd think my work as a rabbi would have prepared me for this kind of conversation." Ethan kept going, because he knew if he stopped, he'd never finish. "Both types of oration are about tackling these huge, universally variable themes, trying to provide tangible advice on how to navigate them, in ways that don't merely fall back on platitudes. It's not easy. There are so many pieces of the human experience that can't be explained, that fall outside the scope of our comprehension."

Ethan had spent the past few days in reflection and meditation, trying to sort through his tangle of emotions.

He missed the synagogue every day. Missed his congregants, even the ones who didn't understand or agree with the choices he made. They were trying to protect their beliefs, the same way he was. Even the members of the board who had voted to end the seminar series—even Jonathan, whose personal censure Ethan could still feel like a thumbprint on his heart—he could see how they had tried to navigate their uncertainty in ways they felt honored their community. They weren't bad people. They just weren't interested in the evolution—the intersections—of faith in the same way.

Choosing between the people he served at Beth Elohim and his relationship with Naomi felt like cleaving his soul in half, but no part of him could let her walk out of his life again.

"I don't want to give the impression that any kind of ending—any breakup—is easy. You're still losing something that matters to you. Still failing when you wanted to succeed. And it's awful."

It would take time for Ethan to process the loss of the work and the community he loved so much. Each morning he woke up and experienced the rejection, the shame of finding that he'd been naive in his optimism, all over again.

"A breakup is a crumbling of something you believed in. There's always going to be collateral damage. Time and energy, sometimes years of your life, that you'll never get back. And you deserve to mourn in whatever way makes sense to you."

Perhaps someday he would find work at another synagogue, but right now he couldn't imagine himself in a leadership position anywhere else.

Focus on these people. He could serve them in other ways. Helping them, even if it fell outside the bounds of the synagogue.

Focus on Naomi. On being the man she sees when she looks at you.

"Sometimes people break up, and afterward, they realize they made a mistake. And that can be terrifying too, in a different way."

He scanned the mass of people in the bar, the mix of familiar faces and some he didn't recognize, searching for red hair. Ethan had hoped that sending out an email announcing a last lecture might catch Naomi's attention. Might show her that for him, what they'd started wasn't over. But so far he saw no sign of her.

He wiped a hand across his forehead.

"If you're anything like me, realizing your breakup was a mistake will probably terrify you, because things ended for a reason, and most likely the doubts and fears that pulled you apart are still there in some capacity. Often it seems easier to look for a clean slate, but sometimes the decision comes down to the simple fact that you look at your life and it's just immediately so much worse than before—"

He stopped, emotion climbing out of his belly and into his windpipe, choking him. He missed Naomi so much his teeth hurt. Ethan didn't know how to undo the events of the past few weeks; he only knew he had to find a way.

Leah nodded at him from beside the bar. Apparently she'd managed to make fast friends with the bartenders, which wasn't surprising. Her nod said *You can do this.*

Ethan took a deep breath and pushed forward.

"The advice I can offer on breakups is limited. But one thing I have learned recently is that you can't run from the life that's meant for you. Don't get me wrong. Plans fall through, even when you hold tightly to them. People change and relationships surely end, but humans find ways to fight for what they need. And it's not always because suddenly they know how to overcome disagreements or set aside past hurts. The path forward isn't always clear, even when it's inevitable."

From the back of the bar, Morey hollered, "Get out the way, you schmucks," and the crowd started to part.

Ethan frowned, trying to clock the disturbance.

And then Naomi was standing in front of him, and a heady combination of joy and nerves hit him like sickness. He swayed a little on his feet.

She had on a mint green dress, her hair flowing loose around her shoulders.

If he never saw another lovely thing in his life, he'd be okay. Naomi was filling up his quota. Infinitely beautiful.

"Hey," he said, mostly breath.

"Hey," she repeated, smiling, and then there was a long moment in which they gazed at each other, goofy. "Aren't you in the middle of something?"

"Oh." Ethan shook his head while people in the audience laughed and wolf-whistled. "Yeah."

"Something about how your life is worse without me," Naomi supplied gently.

"Right." He wanted to drink her in. Every inch, every detail. Ethan wanted to get drunk on her.

"You can't end a lecture in the middle. Not on my watch." She pushed him back with a light hand, letting herself fade back into the first row of the audience. "I'm not going anywhere."

"I hope you find the courage to start again when you need it," he told the seminar participants. "Whether it's with someone new or the one who got away. It's always going to be easier to stand still than to move forward. An object at rest and all that. If you decide to go back to something you've lost, you may have to humble yourself—in a dive bar, perhaps." He grinned ruefully. "You might have to admit that you wish you'd fought harder. You'll have to prove that you're ready to fight now."

A grin split across Naomi's face.

"One of the best things about love, real love, is that it doesn't demand perfection. It simply invites us to live up to our potential."

Ethan took in the crowd again, their expectant eyes and the energy of the moment they shared.

"I'm a mess right now," he told them, trusting them to share in this truth. "I'm afraid of not being worthy of what I want. I don't . . . I don't know how to be this happy and also devastated at the same time. I don't think it's really hit me yet that I'm not going back to Beth Elohim."

Naomi's grin faded. "Wait a minute, yes you are."

He cleared his throat and tried to ignore the fact that the entire room hung on their every word.

"I'm not"—he placed his hand over the lapel mic—"I want to build a life with you, and I'm not looking for anyone's opinion on the matter except yours."

Naomi shook her head and then stepped forward, reaching into his pocket and switching the mic off entirely. With a hand on his forearm, she steered him back into a corner, blocking the crowd with her body.

Their spectators booed accordingly until Morey climbed on a chair and told them that in his day, all good shows came with an intermission, and if they didn't like it, they could go home and miss the finale.

With surprisingly minimal groans, they settled—looking at their phones or lining up for the bathroom.

"I owe you an apology," Naomi said to Ethan, voice lowered but still firm. "I was selfish. When you told me you left the synagogue, I knew that you wouldn't be able to stay away. Not for long. I wanted to be the one who ended things. Wanted to leave you before you left me for your congregation. But I've been thinking about it, and loving me and loving Beth Elohim aren't mutually exclusive values." Something soft lit her dark eyes. "What if we could convince the board to change their minds?"

But Ethan had seen the anger, the fear in Jonathan during that last meeting.

"The board made it clear they don't want me there. Not in any way that I can abide."

Naomi arched a brow. "Look, I'm the queen of not asking for approval. I could write a book about carving out a home for yourself outside the norm. But even on the outskirts, there's community. There's accountability. And there's trust. I don't know if you heard that whole speech you just gave—not bad, by the way, for a first time—but if you thought you were just talking about our breakup, you're out of your mind. I'm great, don't get me wrong. But ours is not the only relationship in your life worth fighting for."

He should have known Naomi wouldn't be easily deterred.

"You really think I should go back?"

Naomi had her hands on her hips, full warrior pose. "The real question is, do you want to?"

"I . . . I don't know. I'm still hurt. Aren't you?"

"Yeah," she conceded. "I am. But I've realized that life allows for those multitudes. Our actions, the future we choose—more often than not, it all comes down to one simple question. What are you gonna let win—your love or your pain?"

Like so much else, Naomi made something so complicated, so fraught, effortlessly clear.

Ethan nodded. Whatever it took, he would find a way to convince the board to trust him again.

"That's what I thought." Naomi wound her arms around his waist, bringing their bodies together. Her smell, warm and lush, surrounded him—soothed him.

She spoke quietly in his ear. "No less. No more."

He brushed her hair back from her face. Ethan would have given her anything in that moment.

"Okay," he said, voice artificially amplified, as Naomi stepped back and ushered him toward the crowd. She'd switched his mic on again. Minx.

The bar's occupants graciously returned their attention, eager for Morey's promised conclusion.

"I'm sure most of you had a lot of questions the first time you heard about a Modern Intimacy lecture series sponsored by a synagogue. Maybe it didn't make sense to you—the overlap between ancient practice and contemporary courtship. Honestly, maybe even after seven lectures it still doesn't make sense to you. But for me, the connection has always been clear: I wanted us to learn, together, how to be good to one another. The course isn't called Modern Love or Modern Sex, though I know some of you—Craig—occasionally forget that."

Craig waved away a burst of whooping at his expense.

"Judaism's enduring theme is the pursuit of a good life. 'To do that which is right in the sight of man, and good in the sight of God.' And you know, before this seminar series started, we talked about the love of God every day at Beth Elohim, but we weren't reaching enough people. We weren't reaching all of you."

He wouldn't exchange his ragtag, sometimes smart-mouthed new congregants—new friends—for anything.

"It's easier to share behavioral ideals, to have them take root—especially in people who haven't grown up with a firm commitment to practicing Judaism—through concrete, everyday examples. In other words, it was my hope that in helping you find connection with each other, I might introduce you into the wider community of our synagogue. That love of man might beget love for God."

Ethan had always known that he wouldn't succeed in winning over everyone who came to Naomi's lectures. He'd considered it, like so much in his life, a great experiment, another chance to learn and grow, not only for the participants but for himself.

"I would like to say to all those members of Beth Elohim who didn't join our course—for whom, perhaps, my ways of living and working and loving seem strange and unfamiliar—I hope that you will find comfort in the assurance that our course was built on the same foundation as the synagogue you hold dear, and my commitment to our shul and our congregation remains—whether I am your rabbi or not."

There was no obvious cue for applause. So Ethan offered a lame "That's all I wanted to say. Thanks for listening, and uh . . . Jimmy"—he waved at the bartender—"I'd like to buy everyone a round."

At that, there was a clear cheer as everyone turned away from Ethan at once.

He gave Naomi a shrug. He'd done his best off the cuff.

She raised her chin at something over his shoulder.

"Ira," Ethan said, shocked to find the board member making his way through the throng toward him. "What . . . what are you doing here?"

Naomi answered, "I might have added the board members to the Modern Intimacy email list. I figured we ought to give them the opportunity to experience the lecture series for themselves, since they were so up in arms over it."

"But . . ." Ethan sputtered. "How did you know anyone would come? After everything, it was such a shot in the dark."

"Yeah, well, that's why Judaism complements reason with faith, right? So that they might compensate for one another's limitations."

Naomi pushed his slightly gaping mouth closed with two fingers on his chin.

"Ethan," Ira said, finally having broken free of the thirsty patrons. "That was quite the speech—almost a sermon, one might say."

"Thank you, Ira." Shock had stolen most of Ethan's vocabulary.

"May I take that little declaration at the end to mean you've changed your mind about resigning? We haven't had a chance to fill your position just yet."

Ethan's heartbeat kicked into overdrive, but he needed to make something clear. To Ira and Naomi both.

"The seminar series may be over for now, but I'm not going to stop trying to bring people to Beth Elohim in nontraditional ways, not least because we know it works."

Ira nodded. "I understand. I wish I could tell you that the board has reversed their vote on the Modern Intimacy series, but I can't."

Ethan lowered his eyes. He hadn't really expected to hear differently, but the news still hurt.

"The reason I can't," Ira said carefully, "is that Jonathan resigned from his position in protest when I proposed we reexamine the issue. We couldn't vote without a full board."

"Jonathan resigned?" After almost thirty years as a member of the shul and fifteen on the board?

"Yes," Ira confirmed, looking grave.

"I'm sorry to hear that," Ethan said honestly. For all they didn't see eye to eye, Jonathan had contributed a lot to Beth Elohim over the years.

"We won't be able to reinstate you until we appoint a new board member. But Ethan—"

"Yes?"

"We want you back. And not just the remaining board members. The congregation started a petition calling for your return. It's got over two thousand signatures." Ira smiled. "Before we hired you, we didn't even have that many members."

Ethan let out a surprised burst of laughter—of joy. "I'd be honored to return as your rabbi."

"Good. Good." Ira patted his arm. "I'm glad. You know, I kind of like the idea of us being the wacky, nontraditional Reform shul. It's certainly better than being the shul no one goes to."

"Yeah," Ethan answered. "It certainly is."

Ira bid them good-bye, promising to call with more news on the board appointment before shuffling off to get his own drink.

Ethan turned to Naomi. "Well, what about you? Still committed to sticking around, even if I go back to working eighty-hour weeks for a synagogue that tried to censure us?"

"Are you kidding? I told you, proving people wrong is my favorite pastime. Besides, I've got a lot of new ideas for recruitment."

Ethan tilted his head. "What kind of ideas?"

He had a feeling he should sit down, but Naomi grabbed his hand and led him toward where Morey and Leah stood waving glasses of what he was sure was the bar's most expensive champagne.

Naomi shot him a wink, and he went up in smoke.

"You'll see."

Chapter Thirty-Seven

NINE MONTHS LATER . . .

NAOMI GRANT HATED weddings. She had long believed things worked out better for everyone involved if she simply sent a big fat check along with well-wishes in her stead. But this was Clara and Josh's wedding, she reasoned as Ethan pulled up in front of their Sonoma Airbnb. These were her best friends, and over the years they'd supported her through a lot worse than exchanging vows.

The little house off the vineyard was surprisingly lovely—even when taking the hefty price tag into consideration—with a balcony off the bedroom. She rested her elbows atop the wrought-iron railing and let the wind blow her hair off her face. The setting sun bathed the groves in embers of orange.

After a while, she wandered back inside, leaving the door open, inviting in the heady scent of grapes a breath from ripeness. A bit more investigating around the space revealed a claw-foot tub big enough for two.

Downstairs in the living room, she found Ethan puttering around, working to build a fire in the stone fireplace—more for ambiance, she assumed, than warmth. She poured them both big glasses of Cabernet—

a thoughtful gift from their hosts—and reclined on the sofa to work on her maid of honor speech.

Okay, so she was mostly admiring Ethan while thinking vaguely about writing her speech—but to be fair, that was not an unusual part of her process.

She let the dry black cherry and cedar flavor flow across her tongue, watching Ethan's forearms flex as he worked. As he bent over to stack some logs, she crossed her legs and took another deep sip, admiring the way his jeans cupped his ass. It had been a while since she'd gotten in some quality, uninterrupted ogling time.

They were both usually so busy. Him managing the steady influx of congregants and renovation at Beth Elohim, and her with packaging their seminar series for a national tour while keeping Shameless growing. Luckily, they didn't have to be at the rehearsal dinner for a few hours.

Ethan started crawling backward on his knees to retrieve a new log from the pile beside the grate.

With an ass like that, he could have been a terrible person and she still would have fallen for him. It was really lucky that he was such a sweetheart so she could go to sleep at night, well-laid and guilt-free.

But all of Ethan's goodness aside, Naomi was not buying for a second the doe-eyed innocent look he was putting on right now. He knew exactly how horny he made her.

In all fairness, he probably didn't know that she'd spent most of the six-hour car ride from L.A. thinking about his tongue. But honestly, they'd been together long enough at this point that he probably should have been able to guess.

She had a very active imagination. He leaned forward again to place some kindling, and Naomi indulged in a little moan.

"Everything okay over there?" Ethan got to his feet, his beard masking half a frown.

"Did you know," she said, putting her wineglass down on the coffee table and padding across the hardwood floor to join him in front of the fireplace, "that you are supremely fuckable?"

Ethan's ears went a delicate shade of pink. She loved that she could still make him blush.

He ducked his head and laughed a little, eyes crinkling at the corners. "You know someone trying to fuck me?"

It was a real battle royale in Naomi's brain, trying to decide if she had the patience to wait until after he actually got a blaze going before she took all his clothes off and straddled him.

On the one hand, a fire would be nice. The crackling wood would underscore those soft throaty groans he made when she wrapped her lips around his dick and ran her nails down the inside of his thighs.

On the other hand, the wine weaving through her veins was making her feel deliciously predatory. The urge to sink her teeth into his neck, to drag them across the soft skin covered by his happy trail until he whimpered, was vivid and visceral. Naomi wanted to mark every vulnerable place on his body until she left him rumpled, satisfied, and sleepy.

She nodded toward his careful arrangement of lumber. "How much longer does that take?"

He rubbed his thumb across his upper lip. One of her favorite tells. He was thinking about kissing her. "Fifteen minutes?"

Heat pumped through her body in time with her heartbeat.

"No, thank you." Naomi carefully removed the log he was holding, tossed it somewhere in the vicinity of the others he'd arranged, and pushed him onto his back. His shoulder blades hit the carpet followed by a soft *oof.*

She had one leg over him and both hands on the hem of her silk dress when he gripped her wrists.

"What if," he said, voice promisingly low, "I make it worth your wait?"

She flipped her gaze between the stack of wood and his face.

"Yeah, no. I wanted that nose pressed against my pussy, like, yesterday."

Naomi attempted to scoot forward on his chest, but his hold was firmer than she'd thought. She raised an eyebrow at him in question.

Ethan gave the sauciest grin she'd ever seen.

"If you let me finish this fire, I will let you do that bedroom thing you've been trying to talk me into."

Naomi practically squealed. "Really?"

He released her wrists and shrugged. "Yeah. I trust you."

She clapped her hands together. "If we weren't already engaged, I'd totally ask you to marry me."

Ethan rolled his eyes, but the color high on his cheeks gave him away.

"Hey"—she leaned forward—"you know all kinds of ancient Jewish wisdom, right?"

"Sure," he agreed, preoccupied with running his hands back and forth from her hips to her thighs.

"Wanna help me with this speech? I keep coming up with ribald jokes that Clara's already vetoed. She won't even let me mention the time I walked in on them dry-humping, even though I've told her a million times it was the most romantic dry-humping I've ever seen."

Ethan kissed her behind her ear. "I can see why she might not want that particular anecdote shared with her relatives."

"Well, that makes one of us," Naomi grumbled.

He let his hands ghost across her rib cage, teasing the sides of her breasts. "You already know my favorite scholarly Jewish position regarding maintaining healthy relationships," he said, voice just a little rough. "'Do not hurry in arousing passion. Prolong till she is ready and in a passionate mood. Approach her lovingly and passionately, so that she reaches her orgasm first.'"

Naomi grinned down at him. "I love it when you talk dirty to me."

Okay, so maybe weddings weren't so bad after all.

Acknowledgments

....

Writing this book might be the scariest thing I've ever done. It is certainly one of the most rewarding. I could not have pulled it off without the support of the following people and so many others whose words of encouragement, advice, and empathy have kept me going over the last year. I will strive for brevity below, but please know I am full of love and gratitude for you all in ways I cannot adequately express.

Jessica Watterson. Thank you for always making time to listen, even when I'm talking about the same thing I've been stressed about for months. Having you in my corner has made me believe in myself—not just as a writer but as a professional in this industry. I'm eternally grateful for your cheerleading, hand-holding, and artfully deployed emails.

Kristine Swartz. Despite my insecurities and reservations, you've encouraged this big, bold idea since day one. Thank you for helping me bring this story to readers.

Jessica Mangicaro, Jessica Brock, and the entire crew at Berkley. Has anyone ever had such a fun, creative, hardworking team? I think not! Thank you for bringing so much energy and enthusiasm to your work. I feel lucky every time I get an email from any of you.

Vasya Kolotusha. Thank you for the beautiful cover art. You've brought these characters I love so fiercely to life.

My Slack found family. When they talk about the power of a writing community, they're talking about you. Every day you inspire me, you delight me, you surprise me, and you move me. Finding and keeping you has been the greatest gift.

Karen Averill. For so many reasons, I could not have done this without you. You showed up for me again and again over the course of development for this project. Your knowledge and passion have made these pages more honest and more powerful. I hope reading this makes you at least a little bit proud.

Heather Moran. One of the most brilliant (and busiest) people I know. I'm incredibly grateful that you found time to read this story early and provide invaluable feedback. I have always looked up to you, and it is an honor to have your influence touch this story.

Rachel Lynn Solomon. You changed my entire relationship to this book with your reading and response. I don't think I can ever convey what that meant to me. You're so special. Thank you for being my friend.

Felicia Grossman. Your early support and incisive close reading of this work helped me draw out important nuance. Your passion for Jewish stories not only helped encourage me to write this book but also helps push the entire romance genre toward more inclusivity.

Sonia Hartel. You GOT *The Intimacy Experiment* in ways I had previously only dreamed it could connect with an audience. I'm so glad we made that deal to forever exchange work. I love laughing with and learning from you.

Lyssa Smith. My alpha reader. You looked at that first messy draft and said *Keep going. You've got this*, and even though I wasn't convinced, as usual, it turns out you were right.

Denise Williams. The dictionary defines friendship . . . No, but really, you are just the best. Smart, kind, compassionate, and SO

FREAKIN' FUNNY. You have hyped me up and talked me off the ledge. I'm amazed by you—by what you accomplish, by your Goodness, by your effort. I'm grateful for you on good days and bad days and every day in between.

Ruby Barrett and Meryl Wilsner. I could write a lot about how you believe in me. How it keeps me going. How it lets me strive and fail and flourish. But for today, I will write about how you believed in Naomi. How you pushed me to give her the story she deserves. How you never doubted she would find her readers. How you have yelled—with and at me—about your love for her in ways that make her feel larger than these pages. This is her story and my story and our story. It is a privilege to create at your side.

My family. Moments collected from a lifetime of our discussions around faith, heritage, and history have found their way into this work. The exploration of these themes through art has challenged me and given me so much catharsis and joy and hope. Thank you for raising me to question and to analyze and to believe.

Micah Benson. It's hard to find the words (yes, I realize the words are my job). I know the universe is indifferent, but our love makes me feel like it isn't.

THE

Intimacy

EXPERIMENT

ROSIE DANAN

Questions for Discussion

1. A core theme of *The Intimacy Experiment* is the concept of personal identity and how we reconcile who we have been, who we are, and who we would like to become. Do you feel you have or have had multiple identities over the course of your lifetime? If so, how do those roles intersect and/or challenge one another?

2. Naomi has made herself hard in response to the reception she's received from the world. Over the course of her relationship with Ethan, she works to make herself softer and more open. How does she go about this, and what obstacles does she encounter? What benefits come from this exercise?

3. In his role as a rabbi, Ethan sets out to make ancient ideals accessible to modern audiences. What are some of the ways he goes about this? Did his reasoning and approach make sense to you?

4. Connecting with her Jewish heritage does not come easily to Naomi. Have you ever struggled with any kind of faith? Do you believe this is a worthy endeavor? Why or why not?

5. Naomi writes the syllabus for Modern Intimacy, but when she and Ethan try to test her hypotheses, they run into challenges. What did you observe from the ways their relationship went off track from the seminar's structure?

6. There are many different communities represented in this story: the inclusive sex education community built around Shameless, the Jewish community both at large and specifically at the two synagogues, the community of Naomi's former high school, and more microcommunities such as Naomi and Ethan's friends and family circles. How do these spaces facilitate different kinds of belonging and acceptance for the characters in the novel?

7. From the way they dress to their personalities, Ethan and Naomi are opposites. How do their different worldviews lead to each of their growth? And what do you think their best qualities are? Have you ever dated someone who was your opposite?

8. Naomi and Ethan are both venturing into new professional territory with their Modern Intimacy seminars. When was the last time you had to go outside your comfort zone, and how did it help you grow professionally or personally?

9. Naomi's main takeaway from her lecture on breaking up is to practice self-care. What are your favorite things to do to practice self-care? Are any of her suggestions something you'd like to try?

10. Throughout the book, Naomi teaches a seminar on modern intimacy for Ethan's shul. Did her lectures make you realize anything new about your own ideas on modern intimacy? What do you wish more people knew about dating in today's world?

ROSIE DANAN writes steamy, bighearted books about the trials and triumphs of modern love. When not writing, she enjoys jogging slowly to fast music, petting other people's dogs, and competing against herself in rounds of *Chopped* using the miscellaneous ingredients occupying her fridge. As an American expat living in London, Rosie regularly finds herself borrowing slang that doesn't belong to her.

CONNECT ONLINE

RosieDanan.com

🐦 📌 RosieDanan

Ready to find
your next great read?

Let us help.

Visit prh.com/nextread